Australian author **Ally**  strong coffee, porch sw beautiful notebooks an inquisitive, rumbustious, spectacular children are her exquisite delight, and she adores writing love stories so much she'd write them even if nobody read them. No wonder, then, having sold over four million copies of her romance novels worldwide, Ally is living her bliss. Find out more about Ally's books at allyblake.com.

Rachael Stewart adores conjuring up stories, from heartwarmingly romantic to wildly erotic. She's been writing since she could put pen to paper—as the stacks of scrawled-on pages in her loft will attest to. A Welsh lass at heart, she now lives in Yorkshire, with her very own hero and three awesome kids—and if she's not tapping out a story she's wrapped up in one or enjoying the great outdoors. Reach her on Facebook, Twitter @rach_b52, or at rachaelstewartauthor.com.

SECRETLY MARRIED
TO A PRINCE

ALLY BLAKE

RELUCTANT BRIDE'S
BABY BOMBSHELL

RACHAEL STEWART

MILLS & BOON

First published in Great Britain 2024
by Mills & Boon, an imprint of HarperCollins*Publishers* Ltd,
1 London Bridge Street, London, SE1 9GF

www.harpercollins.co.uk

HarperCollins*Publishers*, Macken House, 39/40 Mayor Street Upper, Dublin 1, D01 C9W8, Ireland

Secretly Married to a Prince © 2024 Ally Blake

Reluctant Bride's Baby Bombshell © 2024 Rachael Stewart

ISBN: 978-0-263-32128-9

04/24

SECRETLY MARRIED
TO A PRINCE

ALLY BLAKE

MILLS & BOON

This book is not only dedicated to the wondrous Rachael Stewart, Michelle Douglas and Kandy Shepherd—with whom this book and this series were so lovingly crafted—but to the intricate back stories, and the heartbreakingly deleted scenes, and the deeply curated tales of the Waverly sisters and the Waverly women before them that simply could not make it into the *One Year to Wed* books if we hoped anyone might be able to physically lift the things.

PROLOGUE

Garrison Downs,
June

IT WAS THE first day of winter.

Yet that was not the reason behind the unnatural chill that had settled over the Garrison Downs cattle station. The reading of Holt Waverly's last will and testament was underway.

Matilda Waverly sat curled up on the velvet couch in the centre of her father's large office. The bright cushion she hugged tight to her chest and the fluffy pink jumper she wore over her denim overalls the only bursts of colour amongst all the dark, custom-built wood and masculine brown leather.

She fussed with the ring on her right hand, distracting herself from the strangers milling round the room. Lawyer, accountants, who knew? She wished they'd all sod off, but Rose, Matilda's oldest sister, must have allowed it. For while this day was painfully personal, Garrison Downs was a community, an industry, an economy unto itself, and what happened in this room and how that news was shaped would affect more than just their family.

Rose sat stiff-backed in the guest chair closest to their father's desk. Eyes front, light brown hair pulled back into a ponytail, dust motes floating about her head, as she'd come straight in from checking fences over by Devil's Bend.

Eve, their middle sister, was there in spirit. Or, to be precise, video conferencing from the PR office in which she worked in Central London. Matilda wished she could see *her* face, but since that first minute before proceedings, Eve had been on the screen on the wall behind her.

Hugging the cushion tighter as George Harrington, the family lawyer, droned on about investments, stocks, equipment, trust funds, and the robustness of the station's financial standing, Matilda noted how swamped the older man appeared, sitting behind her father's iconic desk.

Famously featured in most news stories in which her father appeared, the bold antique desk had fit Holt Waverly perfectly. Tough, savvy, immensely respected countrywide, Holt had been a mythical character in modern Australian folklore. An icon.

Dad. *Gone.* Their new reality coming at them in increments. From the accident that had felled him, the outpouring of sentiment from all over the world. The honour—and weight—associated with a state funeral. Only after which had they been able to bury him in the family plot under the shade of a flame tree atop Prospect Hill. Next to their mother, the love of his life.

Matilda blinked to find Harrington had moved on to the gem at the centre of her father's estate. Garrison Downs. One and a half million hectares of red dirt, hills, and vales. Verdant river to the east, ancient craggy outcrops and shadowy canyons to the north. There was the Homestead itself—or "the New House" as those within the family called it—a colossal home built by her parents when Matilda was a toddler, the Old House her father had grown up in, and the Settler's Cottage, a place full of ghosts and snakes and other dangers, which had made it as tempting as it was terrifying when they were kids.

Add a dozen outbuildings, seasonal staff lodgings, machinery, maintenance equipment, feed barns, ghostly gum trees, kookaburras, kangaroos, and sweeping planes of prime cattle grazing land…and it was just home.

Needing something to hug, Matilda clicked her fingers for River, their old lilac border collie—once a working dog, now happier sticking close to home—to come keep her company.

When River didn't instantly appear, Matilda glanced over her shoulder to find the dog sitting in the back corner of the room by a young, dark-haired woman, who was playing with his ear. The woman sat in the chair by the telescope, the chair with the view down the long front driveway. Her mother's favourite chair.

She seemed a little young to be one of the lawyers, and not so slick. She was familiar somehow. Matilda's mouth lifted in a quick smile, her conciliatory nature winning out, even under the circumstances.

The young woman startled as she caught Matilda's eye, before leaning down and saying something to River that had the old dog padding over to Matilda and jumping up onto the couch beside her, panting happily.

Matilda turned to sink her face into River's familiar fur, looking up only when the old lawyer cleared his throat.

"Now to the nitty-gritty," said Harrington, his old voice a mite shaky. "To my daughters, I leave all of the above and all my worldly possessions not listed hereupon, including, but not limited to, the entirety of Garrison Downs."

There, thought Matilda, breathing out. *That's that then. All as it should be.*

Harrington went on, "Let it be known that it is my wish that my eldest daughter, Rose Lavigne Waverly, take full control of the management of Garrison Downs. If that is *her* wish. If not, I bow to her choice."

Rose flinched, then briskly retied her ponytail: a classic stress move. The passing of the torch no doubt made it all feel absolutely, terribly, irrevocably real. That she was on her own now.

Not on her own, Matilda upbraided, threading her fingers into River's soft fur.

For she'd be there, sprinkling enthusiasm, keeping spirits up. Not because farming was her bliss, but because she knew how it felt to *not* be there when it mattered most. Knew the guilt, the soul-deep bruise it left on a person, and never wanted to feel that way ever again.

"Ah," said the lawyer, glancing over the top of his reading glasses, his gaze settling on some spot over Matilda's left shoulder for a beat, then back to the papers on the desk. "At this point, could we please clear the room of everyone bar family."

A collective wish to stay and not miss a juicy detail pulsed off the walls before the room emptied.

"Now," said Harrington, taking a moment to gift the sisters with a kindly smile. "That was quite the ask, I know. But necessary to cover all the intricacies of your father's will with those who will best help you manage the ongoing running and reputation of the station. There is just one more thing—"

Harrington stopped. Then rubbed his hand across his forehead.

Rose leaned forward; always sensitive to changes in atmosphere. Only Matilda felt it too, enough that she pulled River a little closer.

"There is a condition placed over the bequest. One that has been attached to the property since its transfer to your family years ago." Harrington took off his glasses and set them atop the papers. "As I'm sure you know, the history of Garrison Downs is complicated, what with your great-great-grandmother having won the land from the Garrison family in a poker game in 1904."

The poker game was legendary in the region. And there was no love lost between the Waverlys and the Garrisons, who still ran another cattle station to the south, though not nearly as big, well-known or prosperous as Garrison Downs.

"Anytime the land has been passed down since, certain conditions had to be met." His hands shook, just a little, as he put on his glasses and read directly from the will. "Any male Waverly heir, currently living, naturally inherits the estate."

"Naturally," Rose murmured.

"But," said Harrington, lifting a finger, "if the situation arises where there is no direct male heir, any and all female daughters, of marrying age, must be wed, within a year of the reading of the will, in order to inherit as a whole."

A sound crackled through Matilda's ears. The past catching up with her? No, Eve was laughing, humourlessly, as if this was somehow no surprise to her.

Some back and forth took place, questions as to what it meant, but Matilda, the history buff of the family, who in her studies had gleefully read about all kinds of mind-boggling hereditary conditions in the lineages of European royal houses, understood all too well.

"The land," Matilda said, her words cutting through the heavy air, "is entailed to sons. If there is no son, the Waverly women *can* inherit—you, Eve, and I—but only if all of us are married."

Protests rose from both of her sisters then, while Matilda's mind stuttered, *married, married, married*, like an old record stuck on a groove.

"It is…arcane," Harrington agreed. "But it has been a part of the lore of this land for several generations. So far as I see it, and so far as your father must have wanted, it stands."

Rose, now up and pacing, shook her head. "How has this never come up before?"

"Sons," said Matilda. "Dad was an only child. Pop only

had brothers, though one died of measles and the other drowned, meaning the farm passed straight to him. Waverlys have always been most excellent at having at least one strapping farm-loving son. Until us."

Rose looked to Matilda. Made full eye contact for the first time since the reading had begun. It seemed to shake something loose in her. A flash of real fear, before Rose was back to being Rose. Strong, steady, honourable.

"And what happens if we refuse to…marry?" Rose asked.

As far as Matilda knew, Rose had never had a boyfriend much less a marriage prospect. As for Eve? Who knew what her love life was like—so far away, so busy, so hard to pin down. While Matilda—

Matilda stopped fidgeting with the ring on her right hand and, surreptitiously, sat on the thing.

"If the condition is not met," said Harrington, "the land goes back to the current head of the Garrison family. Clay Garrison."

Rose lost it then. For she had plenty to say about old Clay, and even more about his son, Lincoln.

"Don't waste your time worrying about it, Rose, because that's not going to happen," Eve said, sounding sure. "Not now. Not ever."

Though how any of them could feel sure of anything anymore, Matilda had no clue.

Harrington cleared his throat. "As it stands, unless all four of Holt Waverly's natural daughters are married within twelve months of the reading of this document—"

"Twelve months?" Rose shot back, clearly only *just* having picked up on that bit. "But I can't… I'm not… I mean *none* of us are even *seeing* anyone right now. Eve? Tilly?"

Matilda shook her head. Slowly. For she wasn't *currently* seeing anyone.

"Wait," said Matilda, stilling a moment, before her socked

feet uncurled from beside her to drop to the floor. "You said *four* daughters. There are only three of us."

River jumped to the floor, nudging her knee, whimpering. And the pity in the lawyer's gaze made her sway.

Then, feeling as if someone had taken her by the chin, Matilda turned and looked over her left shoulder to find the dark-haired young woman from earlier, the one who'd been sitting in her mother's favourite chair was still in the room.

"Who *are* you?" Matilda asked, not unkindly.

"Ana," the stranger said, standing and wringing her hands. Her voice was lilting, as if in question.

Eve, now visible to Matilda on the larger-than-life screen, shifted in her seat. "Who are you talking to, Tilly? I can't see."

The chair behind the desk squeaked as Harrington pressed it back and stood. Then he was out from behind the desk, his arm outstretched. "Come forward, girl."

The stranger came forward. A small, hesitant step.

"Anastasia," said Harrington, "this is Matilda Waverly. That there is Rose. And up on the screen there is Evelyn. Girls, this is Anastasia Horvath."

Ana lifted her hand in a small wave and said, "Hi."

Matilda waved back because…habit. Good breeding. Pathological Pollyanna Syndrome. A deep-seated loathing of all things confrontational. When she glanced back to Rose, it was to find her staring at Ana as if she'd seen a ghost.

"Ana, here," said Harrington, "is your father's daughter. Your half-sister. And therefore, according to your father's will, due an equal share in the estate. And equally beholden to the condition."

The silence that descended over the room in that moment was suffocating. Because… *No.* How?

A half-sister meant… Meant their father had had an *affair*? The very thought was ridiculous. He'd *adored* their mother. Famously. Their partnership as legendary as the land they ran.

Then there was the way they had met—a whirlwind, love at first sight, holiday romance between big, gruff, cattle baron Holt and brilliant, elegant, titled socialite Rosamund, after which he swept her home and they'd lived happily ever after. Until Rosamund's sudden death several years before.

That story was foundational. The keystone to their family.

And he'd had an *affair*?

"Impossible," Matilda whispered, only realising she'd said it out loud when Ana flinched.

While her heart shook, rejecting the very thought, Matilda looked harder. Ana appeared younger than her by a smidge. Her hair was dark and straight, compared to the shades of light brown to blond shared by Rose, Eve, and Matilda. But her eyes—that vibrant piercing blue—they were their father's eyes.

Matilda's hand, the one that had waved, dropped to her side, feeling as heavy as lead.

"Rose, Eve, and Matilda, you still have the trusts your mother left for you," said Harrington, dropping to sit on the arm of Matilda's couch.

Her eyes moved to him, the easier target. He looked tired. As if the past few weeks, leading up to this day, this bombshell, must have been hard on him too.

"They exist outside of the scope of the conditions. So don't fret on that. But the land itself, the Garrison Downs station and all of its holdings, will belong to the Garrison family unless you, Rose, Evelyn, Matilda, *and* Anastasia, are all married within the next twelve months."

This was real. *Really* real. Meaning they had to get on the same page, and fast.

Which was where Matilda usually came into her own. As the youngest, it had fallen to her to find some creative way to lighten the mood. But all she could think was that she had information that might bring a modicum of relief.

"Rose?"

"Hang on. Evie, did you *know*? Is this why—"

"I have to go," said Eve, looking as pale as the white walls surrounding her. Before the TV turned to black.

"Ah, Rose—"

Rose threw out her arms and stormed toward the office door. "I can't—I don't have time for this. I have a station to run." At the door she stopped, turned, pointed at Ana and barked, "Stay!" And then she was gone.

Matilda knew Rose didn't mean to sound so autocratic, that she was used to having to deal with brash young station hands testing her authority on the daily, but the situation meant everyone was tense.

Including Matilda, who swallowed the words she'd been readying to spill, a secret she herself had been keeping for several years, with a discomfiting level of relief.

From somewhere inside the house they all heard Rose holler, "Lindy! Can you see that the yellow guest suite is made up for Anastasia please. She'll be staying with us for a bit."

She would? Matilda thought. Then, *Yes, she would.*

For Anastasia was clearly as crushed by the whole situation as the rest of them. And she was here, on her own.

This was their father's fault. Every last drop.

He'd *left* them, not only when Rose, Eve, and she were so young, to have an affair with some other woman, but he'd left them again, with this 'condition' hanging over them like an anvil about to drop on their heads.

He'd left them with nowhere to put their shock, their anger, their hurt. No one to ask why.

As rage, and fear, and panic rose inside of her, Matilda too would have loved to have flicked a switch and shut it off.

Or walked out of that now claustrophobic damn room, and outside, where she might scream at the wide blue winter sky.

But the clock had already started ticking.

One year.

One year to wed or lose the land that had been their life-blood, their safe space, their connector since birth.

Rose, for whom Garrison Downs was the love of her life.

Eve, who was not exactly known for toeing the family line.

And Ana...

From the corner of her eye, Matilda glanced at the girl, only to see that she was shaking like a leaf, her bright blue eyes glassy, as Harrington gently tried to talk her out of leaving.

Dad, Matilda thought, a ball of fury clenching in her belly. *How could you? Why would you? Did Mum know? Oh, poor Mum. How dare you do that to her? How dare you do this to us?*

Then again, she thought, her thumb once again playing with the ring on her right hand, when it came to family secrets, who was she to protest?

Matilda closed her eyes. Trying to find a kernel of anything in her life that she could trust anymore.

Rose. Eve. *That* she could trust. Her sisters.

Matilda turned to face Ana. For she was in this now too.

Fortifying herself with a big breath, Matilda offered up a smile. Gave her a nod. Letting her know it would all be okay.

Matilda would make sure of it.

And the clock was ticking.

CHAPTER ONE

Chaleur,
one month later...

MATILDA WAVED TO the taxi driver.

"Bonne chance!" he called, waving back happily as he drove away. His grin was no doubt due to the generous tip she'd added on top of the fee for the trip from Nice Côte d'Azur Airport to Côte de Lapis, a coastal town in the picturesque principality of Chaleur.

Or it could be the fact she was no longer in the car, talking his ear off.

"What's in Côte de Lapis?" he had asked as he'd angled his way out of the airport queue. "We have lovely beaches here in France."

"I'm not after a beach," Matilda had said. "I'm looking for a man."

"We have those in France too," said the driver, eyebrows waggling at her in the rearview mirror.

"A specific man," she'd said, smiling. Then frowning. Because it wasn't a laughing matter at all. In fact, in the space of a couple of months, life for the Waverly sisters had become a big old mess.

Rose was still deeply mourning their dad—his physical loss *and* the loss of the man they'd thought him to be—while also frantically trying to fill his shoes.

Eve, still resolutely sticking it out in London, was proving even more bull-headed than usual—flat out denying the condition of bequeathment in their father's will was valid. While acting as if Ana didn't exist at all.

As for Ana, in the short time they'd had together before she'd gone home to her family, it had been clear how overwhelmed she was feeling. Navigating a life with sisters she'd never known, all of whom looked at her and saw their father's betrayal, was hard enough without the pressure of the will.

Then, there was Harrington, the lawyer, still insisting the will was as their father must have wanted.

Add the need to keep the will condition under wraps, so that the vultures didn't start circling, and to keep Ana's existence private for as long as possible, and it was near impossible to call on outside help with any assurance it wouldn't blow up in their faces.

Meaning, as far as Matilda saw it, it was up to her to figure out a plan.

"Ahh," the taxi driver had said, "is this a dating app scenario? Or you are a woman scorned?" He sounded intrigued more than accusatory.

"No! No, nothing like that. It's a man I… I *knew* some time ago. A man I very much need to track down again."

Though after two solid weeks of searching, she was fast losing hope of finding Henry at all.

Henry. Her not so little secret that had finally come home to roost.

She'd been nineteen when they'd met, having skipped off overseas midterm in the final year of her history degree in search of an infamous, missing, handwritten love letter her favourite professor had been wanting to authenticate for years. Keen to follow in his footsteps and become a renowned graphologist and authenticator of celebrated letters herself, she'd flown to Vienna with the intention of making his dream come true.

But the truth of it was she'd been looking for an excuse to do something wild and wondrous for years, having been told tale after tale of exotic adventure by her well-travelled mother in lieu of bedtime stories since she was a little girl.

What she hadn't counted on was meeting a boy. A boy named Henry.

When she'd caught his eye across that crowded bar in Vienna, *phew*, that had been a moment. The way his thick dark hair swept across his forehead, somehow immaculate and unkempt all at once. The pale hazel of his bedroom eyes. The most perfectly carved lips. Pale skin that flushed pink in the cold. Then there were squiggly horizontal lines furrowed permanently into his brow, making him appear deeply thoughtful, über-masculine, and tragically Byronic all at once.

Like lines of verse, Matilda used to think.

The kind he was always reading her from that beaten up, blue, leather-bound book of letters and poetry she had bought him from a second-hand bookstore in Paris.

All of it had been made even more enticing by the fact he was one of a crew of bright young things who knew nothing about one another bar their names.

That had been the deal. Something she'd discovered when Andre, Henry's cousin, had swooped on her at the bar in Vienna after having seen the way she and Henry had been swooning over one another, laying out "The Rules".

They were a wandering band of merry travellers having what he called a Summer of Freedom.

Their intent: suck the marrow out of life before responsibility and consequence sucked the life out of them.

Their terms: names only, no talk of home or family. No selfies or group photos.

Anyone found to breach the rules was out. Cut off. Left behind.

From the outside it had had all the hallmarks of a cult, but she'd known their ilk in boarding school. Bored, cloistered rich kids desperate to break free.

Besides, she'd helped her dad break horses and birth calves, told off grizzled stockmen for swearing in front of her gran. She could take any one of them without breaking a sweat.

Yes, she probably ought to have thought through the logistics, and the why, but it had been so thrilling, and a million miles from where she'd grown up. She had, with intent, put herself in adventure's path and adventure had *found* her. And the lure of anonymity, of adventure, had been too strong.

As had the lure of Henry. Enough that one night, off the coast of Gibraltar, by the power vested in the yacht 'captain' who'd sailed them there, she had vowed to love him through all her forevers.

A whirlwind wedding, a fairy-tale romance—it had mirrored the way her parents had met so beautifully it had felt meant to be.

Only later that same week, as if her karma had swung so far past the edges of exhilaration her life had overcorrected, she'd learned that her mother was dying.

By the time she'd made it home, it had been too late. The household in disarray, her father crushed, Rose a shadow of herself, there had been no time to tell them her 'good news'. It had felt cruel to have been that happy at the same time her mother had been so unwell.

There was the fact that Henry hadn't followed, hadn't even been in touch, even after she'd broken the rules and left a note telling him how. With no way to contact him, no information bar his name, she'd never seen him again.

After such severe romantic whiplash, she'd hunkered in,

put her head down, burned through her studies, put all her love into the family she had left, and lived as if none of it had been real.

Until George damn Harrington had read out the conditions of her father's damn will.

The taxi driver had sighed, a gloriously Gallic sound. "I know that look in your eyes all too well. This man, he is the one that got away."

"Mmm…" she'd said, noncommittally, while shifting uncomfortably on the car seat. "The thing is, I've been looking for a couple of weeks now. Hitting places we'd been together. But staff have moved on, places have closed down. The trail is getting cooler and I'm running out of options."

"Can you not call him? Knock on his door?"

"All I have is his name. It was a thing."

The driver had cocked his head, as if he had misjudged and ought not to be encouraging her on what seemed a fool's mission. But whatever he saw in her face, her ragged last vestiges of hope, had him shaking his head in a fatherly manner and saying, "Have you tried stalking him? On the… *comment dit-on*? On the socials?"

She had. With no luck.

"Mmm," the driver had said, "let me think on it."

Leaving Matilda to slump back in her seat and worry that, while thinking his name still brought on warm swoopy feelings inside her, echoes of the way he'd made her feel all those years before, he might not remember her at all.

What if he was some weirdo who collected wives then let them go with nary a word? What if he wasn't a weirdo, but had changed? Irrevocably? What if he wasn't exactly as she remembered him? What if he *was*?

What if he was *with* someone? What if he had married again, and she was about to open a massive can of worms?

What if she never found him at all? Or never found proof

that they'd said *I do*? Did that mean the condition would be impossible to fulfil right from the start, and it was all her fault?

"What is his name?" the driver had piped up. "This man of yours?"

"Henry," she'd said, a hopeful lilt at the edge of the word. "Henry Gallo."

The driver had looked front, his expression thoughtful. Then he said, "I thought it rang a bell, but I have nothing."

Now, standing on the beach path, one hand waving as the taxi driver edged his way through the lethargic traffic, the other resting on the handle of her small suitcase, Matilda took a deep affirming breath and checked out Côte de Lapis.

Bougainvillea cascaded down the pastel-stuccoed facades of centuries-old buildings tucked up together on the other side of the curving coastal road. Tables and chairs, and pots of brightly coloured flowers took up every spare inch of footpath, with café after café taking advantage of the view of striped umbrellas lining the craggy beach behind her, and beyond that the glinting Mediterranean.

It was exquisite. And dripping with history. But no matter the urge to soak herself in it till her fingertips turned pruney, she wasn't there to sightsee.

She was there to find Henry.

To convince him to stay married to her for one more year, on paper at least, in order to fulfil the provisions of her father's will, after which they could shake hands and move on with their lives.

And then—if they couldn't find some other way out— her sisters might magically meet wonderful men to love and marry and it would all work out. It had to. The alternative was unthinkable.

As if on cue, her phone rang.

"Rose!" she answered. "Everything okay?"

"Just checking in," said Rose, her voice overloud as if she was outside. "Still in Paris?"

"Nope. I just arrived in Chaleur."

"Oh." Then, "And where is that exactly?"

"Tiny principality in a crook of the south of France." Matilda laughed. "Let me guess… If it doesn't import Waverly beef, it might as well not exist?"

"True that."

"Now, Tilly, remember," said Rose, her tone dropping into serious big sister mode, "while you will undoubtedly become best friends with every person you happen upon, use discretion. If news gets out—about the will, or Ana—"

"So the T-shirt I had made, the one that says Marry Me or I Lose the Farm, you want me to take it off?"

"I'd appreciate it," Rose deadpanned. Then, "Now go poke an old building, look at mouldy statues, sniff a tulip. Whatever people do over there."

"All those things," Matilda assured her. "Now you remember, Boss, since I'm not there to remind you every minute of every day, you could run that place with one hand tied behind your back, and you'd still do so with grace and aplomb."

A pause. "I'm currently knee-deep in bore water and smell like cow dung."

"And yet, I bet," said Matilda, "glorious with it."

With that, the sisters hung up.

Reinvigorated in her quest, Matilda tipped up onto her toes and peered over the top of the traffic, checking the faded names on the café awnings. Searching for one name in particular.

Though they'd not visited Chaleur, Andre, Henry's cousin, had mentioned a café in Côte de Lapis more than once. Either his family owned it, or they had the best coffee in Europe. She couldn't quite remember, but there was some connection.

There. Beneath the yellow and white awning, café tables,

small dogs loosely tied up to wrought iron chair legs, friends meeting, cheeks bussing, a cacophony of style and colour and life, just as Andre had described it. Café du Couronne.

Her stomach swooped again, for it was a real place, and still standing. Or maybe that was hunger. Now she thought about it, she was starving.

She looked both ways, found a path through the slow-moving cars ignoring the lane markings entirely, and made her way to the other side of the road.

Where she would find a waiter, say, "Hey! I'm looking for an old friend. Henry Gallo? Wondering if you might know him."

But first, coffee.

Henri rested his elbow on the rim of the convertible car window and listened with half an ear as the news journalist on the car radio showed mild hope over the improved state of the economy, then moved on to the lack of royal family attendance at the Summer Festival celebrations.

When there was no hint of a clandestine meeting between the Sovereign Prince of Chaleur and a handpicked gathering of sympathetic members of both sides of parliament, the subject of which would have generations of royal ancestors turning in their graves, Henri switched the radio to silent.

His gaze skimmed over the traffic ahead. Cars had slowed to a crawl or a stop both ways, as drivers and passengers alike gawked at the view.

Boris and Lars, the security detail in the car behind, would not be impressed with the crowd or the delay. But impressing them was not on his top ten list of things he had to do that day.

Finding himself with a rare moment of nothing to do, Henri tipped back his head and breathed in the sea air. Côte de Lapis in summertime with its quaintly colourful architecture, plethora of shops and cafés, creamy sands dotted with striped umbrellas, and water the colour of sapphires, was a local jewel.

In fact… Henri sat taller, looking over the top of the cars to the string of cafés across the road.

And there, beneath the yellow and white awning, was Andre's old place. Café du Couronne. The Crown Café. Not the most subtle man on the planet, his cousin. Why he'd given the place up, Henri could not remember.

Though it was around *that* summer. The Summer of Freedom, as Andre had labelled it, once again lacking finesse. It had been a hell of a time, either way. The only time in Henri's life he'd been able to relax, dispute, go anywhere, make questionable choices, make love, and just disappear, all without needing to consider anyone but himself.

It was the summer that everything changed.

The car beside his moved a few inches, giving him a direct view to the café. To a table where a woman sat, alone.

Messy blond waves tumbled down her straight back, her shoes were tipped up onto their toes, and her finger trailed up and down the handle of her coffee glass.

And Henri was hit with a wave of déjà vu, of *longing*, so strong it slammed him back in his seat.

Hands gripping the steering wheel, tight enough the leather groaned, he forced himself to face front. For it wasn't *her*. It couldn't be. It was his mind playing tricks, having harked back to 'that summer'.

And yet… He turned and squinted the woman's way, as if it might encourage her to turn. Just a little. Just enough so that he could be sure.

A waiter stopped by the woman's table, leaning a hip against it as if settling in. He tipped his chin, asked her a question, then laughed, head tipping back as he guffawed. Which did nothing to assuage Henri. For that had been *her*

way. Pure energy, like summer sunshine, collecting hearts
indiscriminately.

And then the woman turned, ever so slightly, tucking her
hair behind one ear in a move that made Henri's chest ache.
The feeling was akin to stepping into an ice bath, for it had
been some time since he'd allowed himself to feel much of
anything at all.

Look over, he begged silently. *Look this way.*

A gust of warm wind carrying the scent of brine from the
Mediterranean washed past him before lifting leaves from
the road, shaking the yellow and white awning.

Then the woman stilled. And slowly, as if time was playing games with him, she began to turn his way.

A car behind him hit its horn, and Henri, caught halfway between the past and this moment, took his foot off
the brake, only to hit the back of the car in front. A tap. The
slightest nudge. But enough for the driver's arm to fly out
the window, a string of curse words in vibrant French following, before the driver's door whipped open and he got
out of his car.

Henri switched off the engine and dropped his head.
Then, as he alighted from the car, Boris was there, flanking
him, while Lars moved quickly to placate the other driver,
who was now gesticulating as if it was the end of the world.

Yes, he was wearing sunglasses. Yes, to the untrained
eye, he was just another man in a suit. And he lived in such
a way that he was not nearly as recognisable as his father
and his uncle before him. Yet when the other driver saw
Henri, he paled.

He then gesticulated to the gods in apology, before he
began bowing and apologising profusely. Creating enough
of a scene to draw the attention of those in cars nearby.

"Sir," Boris intoned, as he too could feel the shift in the
atmosphere.

"Yes, I'm aware." Henri made to slip back behind the wheel only to find people were now holding up their phones. Whispers spinning out into the crowd. Tourists, walking the beach path with their zinc noses and Turkish towels, slowed and pointed.

Across the road, café chairs squeaked, and patrons turned, shielding their eyes to the glint off the water to see what was going on. Including, Henri noted, the blonde in blue.

Then her eyes found his.

Time seemed to stop, then swell and contract, as the world around Henri blurred, leaving only those big blue eyes and that lovely, achingly familiar face.

Matilda, he thought, as she pressed to standing so quickly her chair rocked. Then lifting to her toes, she raised her hand in a frantic wave.

What could Henri do but lift a hand and wave back.

Which only led to a rousing cheer from the gathering crowd, as if that one small move had given them all permission to engage.

"Henri! Henri, over here!"

"Where 'ave you *been*?"

"*Je t'adore*, Henri!"

"Henri! Marry *me*!"

For generations the more extended sections of family had lived openly, gone to local schools, worked regular jobs, moving in society in such a way that they were treated with respect but not shock and awe.

Only, since taking on his current role, Henri had not. Nor had he leaned into the more ceremonial parts of the job. Choosing, instead, to spend his time doing work that made a real difference.

In that moment his chickens came home to roost.

"Boris," said Henri.

The large man moved in. "Sir. We can get you out of here. Just say the word."

"Not quite yet," said Henri, lifting the edges of his mouth and waving at the crowd, who all cheered as one. "I need you to do something for me. The blonde woman on her own in the Café du Couronne. Bright blue eyes. Australian accent. If she is amenable, can you find a way to bring her to me?"

"Sir?" Boris blinked, nonplussed, then glanced across the way. For Henri had never asked Boris to bring him a girl before.

"Ce n'est pas comme ça," Henri insisted. "Her name is Matilda. She is an...old friend. Of Andre's."

Which was true. Just not the whole truth, which sat uneasily on Henri's shoulders. Was this how it had started for his uncle? His father? A small secret here, a bigger lie there? In for a penny, in for a pound?

But considering the subject of the meeting he had *just* left, the last thing he needed was the slightest whiff of scandal. And this moment had all the ingredients of a perfect storm.

"Boris," he said, angling his head toward the other side of the road.

"Yes, sir." Boris whistled to catch Lars's attention, twirled his hand in some bodyguard signal that meant *Finish up with the other driver and cover Henri as I have to go see about a girl.*

Once Lars was at his side, his general air of *I will bite off your head if you come too close* keeping the crowd at bay, Henri caught the eye of a woman nearby. Then an older man. Then another.

Not a crowd. People. *His people.* Their interest his interests, their concerns his concern. Everything he did, and was putting in place, was for them.

Despite his lack of match fitness in such public situations, and Lars's panicked gaze, Henri reached out to shake a few hands and answered any questions of those brave enough to ask. Most of which seemed to hinge on asking how *he* was.

"Sir?"

Henri turned to find Boris had returned. And with him…

Matilda, he thought, his throat constricting. For the last time he had seen her, she had been fast asleep, her lashes dark against her cheeks, while he'd felt full from the promise of all the days that lay ahead.

It had become habit for him to let her sleep, as the nights had been spent doing anything but. He'd kissed her forehead, taken the speedboat to the mainland so as to get in a run, grab coffee and supplies. When he'd returned, all that remained of her was an indent on her pillow, her scent on the sheets, and a note.

"Henry?" she said, snapping him from his fugue. And thank goodness. For he was surrounded by a hundred of his subjects, many now bearing mobile phones.

"Matilda," he said, the rough catch in his voice unavoidable.

Then she smiled, and laughed, her eyes bright, as if this was all so lovely and unexpected, and years' worth of attrition didn't loom between them like an unassailable gulf.

Then she tilted her head toward Boris. "Either Andre has had quite the makeover or this is a new, rather assertive, friend you've made."

"That would be Boris," said Henri.

"Hey, Boris," she said, hitching the strap of a bag, and readjusting her grip on a suitcase, a flutter of blue ribbons drooping from the handle. "Nice to meet you."

Henri shot Boris a look, after which the big guy turned away to join Lars in keeping the crowd at bay.

And when Henri's gaze once again met Matilda's, it was her giving him a lazy once-over. As if she too was swimming against a tide of memories. And he felt a flicker in-

side of him—a rebound of the instant spark that had drawn
them together all those years ago.

When someone called his name, and others took up the
cry, Matilda looked up and around, understandably bemused
to find herself in the middle of the street surrounded by
beeping cars and strangers pointing phones their way.

Remembering himself, Henri drew on the diplomatic
skills drummed into him from birth, and asked, "Do you
have somewhere to be?"

"No, no plans."

"Might I suggest somewhere not quite so crowded?" He
motioned to the gridlock. "So that we might catch up?"

"Yes!" she said, nodding vigorously. "That would be great."

Henri turned to Boris, who had not moved far, and beneath his breath said, "Time to go."

Boris nodded. Another whistle, and he and Lars had the
crowd moving back, cars shifting, making space.

Henri looked to her bags. "Is there anything else we need
to collect. A car perhaps?"

"It's just me. I came straight from the airport to head
to that café over the road, as Andre had mentioned it was
a favourite. I was literally just about to ask a waiter if he
knew you and there you were—as if I'd conjured you out
of thin air."

She smiled again, that bright wide sunshiny smile that
had, once upon a time, dazzled him. Meaning it took a moment for her words to sink in.

She was here looking for him?

Henri caught Lars's eye, motioning to Matilda's bags.
Time to go.

Lars swept in, took Matilda's luggage, and hoisted it into
the back seat of the convertible. Then, not wishing to appear completely inept, Henri moved around the car to open
the passenger side door.

He watched Matilda move with as cool a level of disinterest as he could manage—that bounce in her step, the swish of her hair, the way her eyes were constantly on the move, cataloguing every sight, every sound, every detail, as if the world had been drawn for her benefit. Then he made the mistake of breathing in as she swept past him. Apple-scented shampoo and warm feminine skin.

A quick glance out to sea, then up into the sky—calling on any gods who might be listening, asking them to gift him forbearance—he jogged back to the driver's side and leaped into the seat and turned the key.

As ever, the grunt of the engine spurting to life called to something inside of him—for it was the sound of freedom. Something he'd had very little of in his life.

Having been let off the leash, Boris and Lars worked their magic and miraculously cleared a path. Encouraging cars to angle away, others to nudge up onto the beach path, so that their prince could pass.

CHAPTER TWO

MATILDA TWIRLED HER hair into a low bun, stray strands whipping across her face as Henry drove them up, up, up into the craggy seaside cliff face looking down over Côte de Lapis.

The view was breathtaking. The deep azure of the water, the sun shining softly on the tightly packed dwellings dotting the cliffside. It was so wildly different from the red dirt and wide-open vistas back home, she barely let herself blink lest she miss a single thing.

The engine purred as Henry took the car down a gear, hugging a sharp curve in the cliff and yanking her back into the sharper reality.

Henry. She was in a car with *Henry.*

The suit and tie were new, as was the cool in his eyes. This Henry was stiff-backed as opposed to laid-back. But the bolt of awareness that had corkscrewed through her the moment their eyes had met was exactly the same.

Not that that would be a problem. For not only did the truth of her parents' fractured marriage have a tight grip on her heart, the stakes were just too high. There was also the fact that Henry hadn't exactly seemed *delighted* to see her.

Though he had suggested finding some place "not quite so busy" so that they might "catch up," which had to be a positive, right?

Where had all those people come from? Some sort of parade, or protest? It had come out of nowhere.

But in the end, all that mattered was that she'd found him. She'd found *Henry*.

Matilda turned to face him, slowly, aiming for subtle as she made to check him out.

He rested his elbow on the windowsill, the hand on the wheel loose and relaxed. He'd loved driving back then, a little fast but fully in control. Now his face told a different story. The furrows in his brow seemed deeper. Behind his sunglasses his eyes flickered as if he was chasing a flurry of troubling thoughts. Her showing up most likely one of them.

His hair was still matinee-idol dark, though he'd tempered the natural tousled wave. She used to play with it, curling her fingers against the back of his neck when he drove. The memory of him relaxing into her touch, one hand on the wheel, the other moving to her knee, his thumb stroking her thigh, was so strong she had to curl her fingernails into her palms.

She must have made a sound—probably a lusty sigh—as he turned to face her, his eyes hidden behind his sunglasses, before his gaze went back to the sharply curving road.

The moment was brief, and yet her insides twisted, roiling with echoes of how they had been. Followed by the thud of how easily it had all come undone.

Thankfully the air cooled as they left the cliff face and drove up into the hills, past beautiful old homes with mossy stone walls, plots of pretty farmland, before cutting through ancient forests of dark green pines casting cool shadows over the curving road.

Matilda sat up, the seat belt cutting into her shoulder as a castle came into view. Sandstone warmed by the soft Chaleurian sun, medieval windows, fairy-tale turrets and spires, built into a rocky outcrop in the foothills of the distant mountains.

"What is that place?" she said, her voice catching on the wind.

Henry's finger swiped across his mouth before it moved back to the wheel. "Le Château de Chaleur."

"Le Château de Chaleur," she repeated. How many generations of letter writers might have scribbled their fears, their regrets, their hopes, love won and lost onto the page in such a place? "Is it abandoned?"

"It is not," Henry confirmed. "It is home to the royal family of Chaleur."

"How charming."

Matilda knew little about Chaleur. Small in area and population, it was overshadowed by its bigger, flashier neighbours. Though, so far, it was exactly the kind of place her mother would have loved; secluded, unexpected, and breathlessly beautiful.

Soon the trees gave way to a long tall wall, built of the same sandstone as the castle they'd seen in the distance. Wild red rosebushes lined its length while ivy gripped its heights, giving the place serious *Beauty and the Beast* vibes. Which were only heightened when the car slowed, turned, and pulled up to a set of gates; two stories high, made of thick wrought iron twisted into sharp thorny shapes.

Then the gates began to open, slowly, groaning like some ancient slumberous giant, and Henry's convertible hugged the long, neat, curving gravel drive until they pulled up beneath the portico of le Château de Chaleur.

Matilda's hair settled about her shoulders as the car came to a stop. The wind now gone, her ears rang with the silence.

She screamed, then swore rather loudly, as something opened her door, only to find Henry's friend Boris standing there. Not her finest moment.

She uncurled herself from the car to find the other big guy, the one who'd swiped her luggage, standing by another car. A hulking great black beast with dark windows.

"Do you *work* for Henry?" she asked, when what she really meant was *Why are you following us and what am I missing?*

"Hen-ri?" Boris asked, an eyebrow scooting north, his pronunciation more *On-ree* than regular old Henry.

Though Matilda was soon distracted by the sight of the man himself prowling around the front of the car. All slow purposeful strides, furrowed brow, cool gaze, and sharp angles.

The Henry she'd known had been a romantic, a seeker, this *On-ree* had an edge of otherness, of disconnection that sent a chill down her spine.

Which was probably a good thing. A clear separation of then and now.

Hand on the open car door, she said, "It was lovely of you to stop here—you know I love a castle—but I'd love to have that catch-up you mentioned. I can find my way back here, another time."

Suddenly a team of what could only be servants spilled from the front doors of the castle, speaking fast French, then hauling Matilda's bag and luggage away.

"Wait! What? Sorry, can you bring that back, *s'il vous plaît*?"

"Why don't you come inside?"

She glanced up to find Henri beside her. His hand on the car door beside hers. His nearness made her sway. *Actually sway.* Her hand jerked, brushing his, sparks shooting up her arm. She tugged her hand free. As did he, his thumb running down his palm as if her touch had burned.

"Freshen up, after your flight. Then we can talk," he said,

his voice lower, more intimate. He lifted an arm, ushering her toward the front door.

Come in, he said. Not *go* in.

"Who *are* you?" she asked.

His gaze remained cool. As it had in the middle of the street, surrounded by the crowd, but not a part of it.

But if he thought he could out-stubborn a Waverly, he was about to learn a hard lesson. Matilda crossed her arms, her eyebrows lifting in question.

"Let's assume the statute of limitations on Andre's Privacy Pact has long since passed." She held out her hand, deep inside Henry's personal space, and out of the corner of her eye saw Boris take a step their way.

"Hi," she said, "I'm Matilda Waverly. I was born and bred in Garrison Downs, a cattle station in South Australia. I am an authenticator of old letters, by trade. I have two—" *Dammit.* "Three sisters. An aversion to any food that wobbles. What else? My favourite colour is blue—"

"Matilda," Henry said, his voice chastising but also, somehow, indulgent. As if he was enjoying her riposte, despite himself.

"Who. Are. You?"

She watched as a dozen thoughts tangled behind those pale hazel eyes, before he said, "I am Prince Henri Gaultier Raphael-Rossetti."

He pronounced his name *On-ree*.

A burr of pain settled behind her ribs. For while she'd known next to nothing about him, she'd thought at least he'd given her his true name.

Then her brain stuttered and she backtracked a smidge. "I'm sorry, did you say *Prince*?"

He nodded. Though it was more of a gentle bow. Elegant, practiced, princely.

Matilda blinked. "Since *when*?"

"Since birth," he said, a flicker at the edge of his mouth that might have been a smile. Or a grimace. "Though I have been Sovereign Prince of Chaleur for the past two years."

Matilda looked at the ancient sandstone structure, the burly bouncers hovering nearby, Henri's gorgeous car, and the beast parked in behind it. She remembered the crowd in the street, surrounding him, calling his name.

Then she looked back at *him*. The way he held himself, the way he dressed, the way he spoke. How educated and hungry for knowledge he had been back then. That *je ne sais quoi* that had drawn her in from the very first moment.

"Are you freaking kidding me?" she asked.

"I am not. Freaking or otherwise." Again with the flicker at the corner of his mouth. This time it came with a slight thawing in his gaze.

The requirement of anonymity, the money, the access, the way they had breezed through Europe with absolute entitlement. It all made sense now. It hadn't been a weird hazing thing, or bored rich kid thing. It had been about protecting Henry.

A *prince*.

A prince that she had fallen for. Had married. Which made her...

No. Nope. Nopetty no. There was no point getting ahead of herself. Not until she had legal paperwork before her own eyes. Legal enough to satisfy George Damn Harrington.

As to the rest? Part of her wanted to kick him, right in the shins, for keeping such a thing from her. Then again, she had vowed to love him for a lifetime, before bolting to the other side of the world. Maybe they were even.

Finding it within herself to choose amity, for she needed him onside, she said, "Well, it's nice to finally meet you, *On-ree*." Then, "But if you think I'm going to curtsy, you have another think coming."

At that, the flicker of warmth looked like it might actually become a smile. And as they stood there, just looking at one another, his gaze heated a good several degrees, before he cleared his throat and looked away.

Pull yourself together, Tilly, she said, choosing Eve's most unyielding big sisterly tone. *Ignore the flickers and the furrows and the warm tingles, as they mean exactly nothing.*

For if she'd stayed, those feelings would have faded over time. Surely. Or worse, fractured and turned to hurt. Perhaps they had been lucky, not to have had to go through that, not to have lived in her parents' footsteps after all.

"Shall we?" he said, motioning to the front doors of the château. *His* château.

"I guess so," she said.

Yes, she had come to help her sisters. But perhaps this trip would work twofold. Having met a handsome prince, she might finally face reality and let the fairy tale go.

Matilda got as far as the entrance hall before her feet stopped working. For there were châteaux and then there were *châteaux*. And the Château de Chaleur earned all its capitals.

From the pale mosaic floors to an elegantly curving three-story staircase, to the soaring ceilings bright with beautifully preserved frescoes and doors leading to rooms that hinted at more quiet luxury, it looked like something out of a Merchant Ivory film and smelled like history.

"You *live* here," she said, her voice sounding far, far away.

"This is my family home."

Turned out trying not to imagine what being married to the man might mean…was not as easy as she'd hoped.

Matilda reached out for a nearby chair, some gilded curlicued antique that had likely been in Henri's family for generations, and sat just before her knees gave way. Then she leaned over, slowly, till her head was between her knees.

"Lars," Henry—no, *Henri*—commanded, and Matilda saw a pair of very large black shoes lumber into her sight line. Though, next to Henri's sharp brown Oxfords they weren't much bigger at all. Okay, so if she was in the frame of mind to compare men's shoe sizes, then she was okay. "Have Celeste come down, *s'il vous plaît*," Henri murmured, his accent thickening. "Ms. Matilda is not well."

"I'm fine!" Matilda said, slowly sitting up and pushing her hair from her face. "It's probably delayed jet lag. And hunger. Where I'm from, we require more than a single *petit four* in our bellies before finding out our old..." She paused. "Old *friends* have their own castles."

She smiled up at Lurch—no, *Lars*—to prove that she was not falling apart. Though he looked as if he was far more comfortable dealing with über-cool princes than swooning farm girls.

"Sir?" Lars asked, looking to Henri, who was now frowning as if his brow furrows alone might save the planet.

"Lars," Boris chastised from his position watching Henri. *"Va trouver Celeste."*

"Ah, oui," said Lars before lumbering off.

While Matilda watched Henri watch her. His gaze had settled on her hair, making her wonder how crazy it looked. Or if it was some royal peccadillo. The royals she'd researched when first learning how to trace provenance of old letters, had certainly had some weird predilections. All that inbreeding.

"How were your parents related?" she asked.

Boris cleared his throat, bringing his fist to his mouth as if covering a cough.

While Henri's eyes narrowed, turning all bedroomy and beautiful and lit with mild outrage. "They were *not*. My father was a Raphael-Rossetti, born second in line to the throne of Chaleur. My mother was Italian, the granddaughter of a count."

"Cool," she said, thinking how *"the throne of Chaleur"* tripped off Henri's tongue like it was all so normal. Then she queried, "Was?"

Understanding her, Henri said, "They are both gone."

"Oh." So, he was an orphan. Just like her. "Mine too. My parents. My father only recently. My mother...several years ago."

She watched him, waiting for a flare of recognition, or discomfort at how he'd behaved, but he turned away.

"Boris," he said, "can you please check to see how Lars is getting on in finding Celeste?"

Boris nodded, turned on his heel, and left.

When Matilda placed her hands on her knees and pressed herself to standing, Henri moved in, his hand hovering below her elbow, in case she was still off-kilter. And when her gaze lifted to his, they were close. And alone. No wind and car noise, no curious gazes, no listening ears.

Was now the time to lay out her request? Find legal confirmation that their marriage was valid and hope he'd be amenable to keeping it that way for the next twelve months?

Perhaps. But instead, she found herself caught by that compelling, soulful, heart-achingly beautiful face.

"You've changed," she said, before she even felt the words coming. Her hand lifted, as if readying to trace her thumb along the deeper creases in his forehead.

"Matilda," he said, his jaw hard, his voice low, raw—

"Doth my eye deceive me?" a voice called from the top of the stairs.

Matilda flinched, and Henri's eyes drifted closed, before they both turned to find Andre, Henri's cousin, the enforcer of the cabbalistic rules of their Summer of Freedom, jogging down the staircase.

"Matilda?" he said, grinning as he reached the foyer floor.

"Hey, Andre."

He moved in, kissed her on both cheeks, then said, "If this was not so far beyond the realms of probability, I'd have thought my cousin tracked you down and brought you here to distract me from asking how his meeting with parliament went."

"Andre," Henri murmured, his voice deep with warning.

Andre's gaze sharpened as he took in Henri's hand, still hovering under Matilda's elbow. "She's not running away just yet. Are you?"

Ouch, thought Matilda.

Henri's hand dropped away and he took a step back.

"How on earth did you *finally* find us again," Andre asked.

"We found one another," she said, looking around him to catch Henri's eye. "On the street in Côte de Lapis."

"How lucky for us all." Andre's gaze swept to his cousin, the men sending coded messages with their eyes. Matilda knew because she and her sisters did it all the time.

A woman around Matilda's age, wearing a neat cream suit, elegant heels, blond hair pulled into a sleek low bun appeared silently a few feet behind the cousins. "Your Highness?"

"Celeste," said Henri, "this is Matilda. An old friend of Andre's."

Andre's expression turned incredulous.

"Oh," said Celeste, blinking at Andre, before fixating on Matilda. Then, "Welcome to le Château de Chaleur."

And Matilda found herself curtsying.

Andre burst into laughter. "Wrong one, darling."

Henri gave Andre one final dark look, said, *"Excusez-moi,"* then took Celeste to one side and spoke quietly while she listened intently.

Andre moved in beside Matilda. "So that's how we're going to play it."

"Play?"

"You're *my* friend, not his. For the best, I suppose. The last thing Henri needs right now is news of an old flame turning up on his doorstep. The royalists will be calling for babies, while the antimonarchists would have a field day."

She turned to him. "Antimonarchists?"

Babies?

Andre brushed it aside, his gaze hard on Henri and Celeste, as if trying to read their lips. Then he looked deep into her eyes, as if trying to ascertain her devious plans. "Why are you here, Matilda? Why now?"

She said nothing for it was Henri's business, not his, though Andre had always found it hard to separate the two.

"Are you are sticking with the *I didn't know who he really was* line?"

"Nobody knew anything," Matilda reminded him. "Thanks to you."

Andre blinked. "It was rather ingenious of me, though I still can't believe we pulled it off." He turned to face her. "What about since?"

"What about it?"

"Prince Augustus, our fiscally imbecilic brute of an uncle, abdicated not long after you disappeared into the ether. After which Henri's screwball father, Prince Marcel, took over. Far less subtle about the millions he stole from the realm. Still nothing?"

Matilda shook her head, while carefully storing away the precious morsels of Henri's life that she'd never known.

"Prince Marcel, Henri's father, died two years ago. Car accident. Drove off a cliff taking Henri's older brother, the heir, Pascal, with him. Our Henri has been Sovereign Prince ever since."

Matilda turned back to Henri, noting again the stiff shoulders, the perfect suit, the neat hair, the otherness that hovered around him like a cloud. With all that to contend with, no wonder he'd changed. No wonder he seemed so aloof.

"You ladies usually lap that stuff up," said Andre.

Matilda coughed out a laugh. "We ladies?"

Andre's gaze made it clear he was pushing buttons, looking to trip her up somehow.

Matilda crossed her arms. "Do you know where *I* live?"

His gaze flickered. "Australia, clearly, by the accent. Somewhere near Sydney?"

Matilda pulled out her phone, looked up a map app and found Garrison Downs. Then she pulled back, and back and back.

"That's Sydney," she said pointing at the east coast city. "And that," she said, dragging her finger dramatically, across thousands of miles of hostile land before poking a finger in the middle of South Australia, "is home."

Andre squinted. "Do you even have internet?"

"Of course, we have internet," she said.

And Andre shot her a victorious smile.

"Though it's unpredictable," she allowed. "Even then the news of the day revolves around stock prices, El Niño, broken fences, the new teacher in town. Not the ins and outs of teeny-tiny *lesser-known* European principalities."

Andre's eyes widened at her rebuff, clearly enjoying the fight. "Weren't you some kind of history buff?"

"My PhD would attest to that fact."

A flare of the nostrils, then a small tilt of the head in appreciation from Andre.

"Though my bent is handwritten letters. Collections thereof. Shove something of that ilk under my nose and my heart will go pitter-pat. Show me a gossip site starring young, hot, Euro royalty and I remain unmoved."

Andre shot a single eyebrow northward. "Unmoved? And

yet your gaze keeps tracking a certain real live young, hot Euro royal even as we speak."

Matilda felt a flush of heat rush into her cheeks. Then she realised Henri was approaching, close enough to have heard Andre's attestation. Which had, no doubt, been Andre's intention.

"Is my cousin playing nice?" Henri asked, unable to mask the edge to his voice.

Matilda felt it scrape over her skin like a touch. "Why you need security when you have your cousin around, I'm not sure."

Henri's smile was quick, then it was gone. "He's much improved since you last met. And far too busy acting as my closest advisor to commit to permanent guard dog duties."

"Woof," Andre shot back. Then, sauntering away, lobbed a final velvet-wrapped grenade, "I hope to see you again, Matilda. Before you leave."

With the tip of his chin, Henri beckoned Matilda to follow him toward the stairs, and Matilda followed. On hollow legs. For it had been a lot.

"Celeste will show you to your room. Then find you something to eat. Multiple *petit fours*, if you desire. Whatever you need, we are at your disposal."

Desire. Petit fours. Whatever you need.

That burr in his voice. It muddled her a moment before she realised his intent.

"My *room*? No, no, I can book into a hotel." She looked around to find Celeste following at safe minimum distance. *"Un hotel...?"*

Celeste looked to Henri for instruction.

"Matilda," said Henri, his voice low, engaging, as he waited for her gaze to settle back on his.

And settle it did. Till she felt warm and loose under the focus of that pale hazel gaze.

"We have room here," said Henri. "Many rooms in fact. Most of which could do with company to fill them. We have...things to discuss."

The guy had no idea.

"Allow me to indulge you in the hospitality my home was built for."

"Mademoiselle?" Celeste encouraged.

As Matilda followed Celeste toward the stairs, she saw Henri's mouth open a fraction before he snapped it shut. About to suggest Matilda was a married *madame*?

But then he said, "Celeste, one more thing. Matilda has an aversion to food that wobbles."

Matilda laughed, delighting in the fact he'd picked up on her sassy little comment from earlier and held on to it. A frisson of warmth came over her at the possibility that beneath the cool, her Henry was in there somewhere still.

Not that she wanted that. Or needed it. Or found it in any way helpful.

While Celeste, clearly used to the vagaries of a royal household merely said, *"D'accord,"* and led the way.

Henri watched Matilda head up the stairs, stopping every step or two to ask Celeste a question about a painting, or a carving, or a fresco. While Celeste answered, in her usual efficient way.

"So," said Andre, sidling up to Henri, "the prodigal wife has returned."

"Must you?" Henri growled, glancing around to make sure they were still alone. For the château staff's job was to be loyal to Chaleur, not to him.

Andre grinned. "I must. After this turn of events, am I to assume this morning's meeting did not go ahead?"

Henri breathed out hard. "It did."

Andre sighed. "And how did our parliamentary friends

take it when their prince told them that he would like them to consider undoing centuries' worth of governance by abolishing royal rule?"

"They were…surprised." Even while his predecessors had given them every reason to question the moral authority of the Raphael-Rossetti line, it was what they were used to.

"No," Andre deadpanned. "Really?"

"But they did listen." Henri faced his cousin. Needing him on board. "And they trusted my sincerity. They have agreed to put a poll into the field, couched language, careful. Gain some insight into how a referendum would pan out."

Andre shook his head. In dissent, or awe? Likely a mix of both. For while Andre took great pleasure in the trappings of their lifestyle, he had witnessed Henri's life up close. The scandal, the sorrow, a childhood spent at the mercy of their brutish uncle.

"On that," said Henri, "I was seen today, on the Côte de Lapis. A crowd gathered. You will be thrilled to know I engaged. Boris and Lars had to be talked down from karate chopping a dozen people."

"That is good news. And how did you cope?"

"Gingerly."

Andre laughed.

"There were questions. An undercurrent of concern. Are there rumours that I am unwell?"

Andre reached out and squeezed his shoulder. "You are their prince. They do not get to see as much of you as they would like. It worries them."

Henri shifted on his feet.

"Now, since one live grenade is not enough for you, *how is* she *here*?"

The timing of Matilda's arrival could not be more complicated. "She was sitting in Café du Couronne. Apparently, because *you* had mentioned, more than once, that we had spent a lot of time there."

"Ah," said Andre, running a hand up the back of his neck.

"Indeed. I brought her here, to keep her out of the public eye. At which point I blithely informed her who I am, waited for her to finish hyperventilating, then sent her upstairs. Now you're all caught up."

Andre glanced back up the stairs, where Matilda was now spinning slowly on the spot and looking at the fresco on the ceiling. "What happens now?"

What now, indeed?

When he and Matilda had met, he'd been a young man without a plan bar which book to read, which restaurant to eat clean, which town to hit next. Now, he spent his days reading parliamentary papers, speaking with industry experts, liaising with heads of state the world over, while also digging through piles of metaphorical rubble in the hopes of undoing the heinous mistakes of his forebears.

Matilda, on the other hand, looked fresh and vital and brimming with energy. As if she'd walked out of his life, then walked right back in.

At the top of the stairs Matilda looked back, saw him watching, and gave him a lift of her shoulders that said *How can any of this be real?*, then disappeared from view.

Henri breathed out hard.

"Wait," said Andre, "are those…? Yes, they are actual puppy dog eyes."

"Don't start."

"*I'm* not doing anything. You're the one who's going all gooey over the woman. Again. It must be pathological, considering how dark things went last time. If dear old Uncle Augustus hadn't abdicated in such a timely manner, thus dragging us both back to this godforsaken paradise, I fear what might have become of you."

While Andre's words were deliberately provocative, his gaze was concerned. For Andre had been there, keeping him from doing anything reckless, as he'd tried to understand where it had gone wrong.

"You are mistaken," said Henri. "Going 'gooey' is not my style."

"You honestly think that, don't you. Oh, cousin, you are so screwed."

Henri was concerned Andre might be right. But for a different reason entirely. For if anyone found out who she was and what had been, it could muddy the waters, making a true, people-led referendum moot.

He slapped Andre hard enough on the back to earn an *oof*. "Fun's over, we have work to do."

"Mademoiselle," Celeste said, "your room."

Matilda thought the guest rooms in the Homestead were over-the-top, but this was something else.

A duck egg blue velvet lounge suite, white fur rug, a fireplace as big as a bull. A series of French windows, draped in pale blue curtains, shed slivers of soft buttery light over the huge bed residing on a raised platform. Two sets of double doors she imagined led to walk-in wardrobes and an *en suite*. Though, considering her day thus far, they might just as well lead to Narnia, or outer space. Her suitcase with its cacophony of blue ribbons on the handle leaned in a corner of the room. Her handbag sat neatly on a stool, her laptop on a desk, charging.

"We hope this will suffice," Celeste said, deadpan.

"Suffice? I feel like I've walked into *The Princess Diaries*."

"I found the second movie superior," Celeste insisted as she drew the curtains open, letting in great shafts of sunshine and a view over the mountains beyond that took Matilda's breath away.

Which was probably a good thing, as declaring herself a princess clearly contravened the promise she'd made to Rose to stay under the radar.

"Shall I have the kitchen send up...non-wobbly food?" Celeste asked.

Matilda shook her head. Then yawned the yawn of a person who'd been up for much of the past twenty-four hours, driving to and from airports, dragging luggage from one plane to another, while quietly panicking about the state of affairs she and her sisters were in.

"I think I'll just chill for a bit, if that's okay?"

Celeste nodded. "My personal number is on a card I've left on the desk. Dialling eleven on the phone by the bed will get you through to the kitchen. Dinner is at seven. If you head down the way you came up, someone will show you the way."

Once Celeste left, Matilda climbed onto the platform, lifted her tired arms to the side and let herself fall, landing on the bed with a bounce. The soft, sweetly scented blankets enveloped her in their cloudlike embrace.

A minute, she said to herself, yawning anew. *I'll just shut my eyes for a minute.*

CHAPTER THREE

HENRI SAT AT the head of the long dining table, cradling a fresh espresso, and attempting to read over a speech Andre wanted him to give to close off the Summer Festival celebrations. He'd talked his way out of the event the year before, but this year his excuses were falling on deaf ears.

He wasn't sure that the unexpected arrival of a surprise wife would cut it.

He put his phone face down. Impossible to concentrate when he'd spent much of the night wondering why she was there.

The possible reasons were many. His family history was rife with so many stories of secret babies and communicable diseases, even he could not remember them all, and he had been schooled in Chaleurian history till his fingers had bled. Literally.

The likeliest reason was that she had met someone and was there to ask him for a divorce.

Henri sipped his espresso without thinking, wincing at the heat of it. Then, after a beat, downed the lot in one hit.

"Carefully, carefully, amore mio..." his mother's soft voice, a voice he'd not heard in over two decades, whispered into his ear. A voice that could not have been more different from the voice that had fostered his education after she'd died.

His uncle, Prince Augustus, a hand tight at his neck, eyes boring into Henri's as he commanded, "With strength and power, always."

"Hey."

Henri flinched at the sound, abhorring the fact that memories of his uncle could mess with his equilibrium still.

He looked up to find Matilda standing in the doorway, her hair loose and a little wild, her eyes crystal bright, her face soft with sleep. And despite the fact he'd spent much of the past several hours thinking of little but her, and how disruptive her arrival might yet be, there was no denying the slide of heat passing through him.

He brought a linen napkin to his mouth and pushed back his chair. "Good morning, Matilda."

"Sit, sit," she said, flapping a hand his way.

Unused to being given commands these days, he paused, then did as asked. "Join me."

"Are you sure?" She waved a hand over high-waisted jeans and a cropped T-shirt the same forget-me-not-blue of her eyes. "Most of my clothes are in dire need of a wash, and even then I didn't exactly pack for dining with royalty."

"I'm sure I could rustle up a spare tiara if that would make you more comfortable."

"So much more comfortable," she said with a smile.

After which they simply looked at one another, for far too long. Before Matilda bit her bottom lip and looked away. "On that, if someone could point the way to the laundry…"

"Let Celeste know. She'll get it sorted for you."

Matilda pointed one way, then another. "Do you not know where it is?"

Henri stalled. He was not entirely sure.

She reached out to grab the back of the chair at the far end of the table. "Do you remember, when we stayed in Sorrento, I had to teach you how to use a washer and dryer?"

He remembered watching her take charge, explaining the steps to him with exaggerated simplicity. No one had ever treated him with such a lack of deference. It had been a revelation.

"I assumed you were spoiled," Matilda went on. "Not, you know, a prince."

"One often comes with the other."

Matilda rocked the chair on its back legs. "I've seen enough movies to know that if I sit here, we'll come unstuck when one of us needs the other to pass the salt."

It was also, according to custom, where his wife would sit.

He motioned to the chair perpendicular to his. "Excellent salt-passing distance."

She moved down the length of the table, her hand running over the top of each chair, her gaze wandering about the room. "Anyone else joining us?"

Henri shook his head.

At one point in his childhood, the château had been filled with family. Noise. Life. For Prince Augustus and his wife, upon discovering they could not have children of their own, had opened the palace to Henri's family, and Andre's, and a dozen more distant cousins. Bar Andre, the rest were now gone—having moved as far away from Augustus and his pedagogy as possible.

Now it was a far quieter place.

Matilda sat, her knees lifting as her feet balanced on her toes. Then she asked, "So is it Henry or *Henri*?"

Her question appeared innocuous, but he saw the wound in her eyes. As if all that they had done in the name of being young and free had bruised them both in the end.

"I have gone by both. Henry, mostly, while studying."

"Where did you study?" she asked, her voice lilting, as if hungry to know more.

"Political science at the Sorbonne. MBA via the London School of Economics."

"That tracks. And *Henri*?"

"My birth name."

"Gallo?"

"My mother's maiden name. By Chaleurian law, while it appears on my birth certificate it is not an official part of my title."

She absorbed the information like a sponge. Then smiled. The clouds clearing. And he felt the same within his chest. An easing. A lifting. A lightness he'd not felt in quite some time.

Carefully, carefully.

She nodded. "Well, your place is pretty nice, *Henri*."

Henri felt his mouth tug at the corner. "We like it."

"And that bed of yours was amazing. I mean *my* bed. The one you put me in—*Celeste* put me in. The *sheets* are top-notch. And the blankets are so fluffy. And…" She stopped, took a breath.

"The pillows?" he asked, helpfully.

Her eyes found his, sparkled. "Meh."

He laughed. Loudly. Enough that he surprised even himself.

And Matilda's face altered in the most stunning way, her cheeks pinking, her eyes softening, as if his laughter was already her very favourite part of the day.

"So how does it work?" she asked, leaning her elbow on the table and looking up at him from beneath what seemed like a thousand eyelashes. "Your princeliness?"

"Do you mean politically?" he asked. "Or do I brush my hair a hundred times before bed?"

Her bark of laughter was infectious. "The former. For starters."

"We are a monarchical sovereign state, which means, as Sovereign Prince, I am head of state."

"Go, you."

"Mmm, but it's not because I have the best ideas, or the brightest mind, or the most empathetic nature, but because of who my father was, and his father before him."

"Mmm," she parroted. "So its actual work, then. Not just ribbon-cutting ceremonies, and smashing bottles of bubbly on the sides of ships?"

"I leave that to Andre."

That earned him another laugh. All husky and rich and true. Only the moment the sound hit him, he knew it had been a mistake. Encouraging it. Encouraging her.

For while much had happened since they'd last seen one another, to hone him, to inure him to outside forces, this woman had once upon a time proven she had the power to cut him to shreds.

"Are you hungry?" Henri asked, refocusing. One of the waitstaff waiting in the wing stepped off his mark in preparation.

"Nope. Eaten already." She mimed dialling a phone. "Someone brought me French toast, berries, yoghurt, fresh squeezed orange juice. No Vegemite, alas, but I can forgive that." Then, "I wasn't aware that this was an option."

"This?"

"Eating here," she said simply, "with you."

He felt a tingle in the back of his head, more in the tips of his fingers, as if his blood momentarily forgot where it was meant to be. Then a waiter cleared his throat. Henri had completely forgotten the man was there.

Which was when he saw it. Not on her left hand, where he had placed it that long-ago night, but on her right. His mother's ring. She had brought it with her. Along with a plan to give it back? Surely she'd not worn it all these years. Both thoughts turned his insides to knots. Meaning the sooner he got to the bottom of why she was there, the better.

"How are you on the water?" he asked, as he pressed back his chair.

"I'm Australian, Henri. We are two-thirds water."

Halfway to standing, Henri found himself coughing out another laugh. The feeling was both strange and addictive. "Matilda, we are all two-thirds water."

"Well, what do you know?" she said, halfway to standing herself. "I'm more similar to royalty than I ever knew."

"Henry!" Matilda laughed as his yacht tore across the crystalline surface of Lac d'Hiver, the private, near perfect circle of mountain water at the rear of the château. "This is spectacular!"

She glanced back at him, her cheeks pink from the sun and wind, her eyes bluer, if possible, than the famously blue water below.

"Sorry, *Henri*," she said, mirroring his accent, and adding a little flair just to rub it in. "Or should I call you 'Your Highness'?"

"Henri is fine."

When she had first called him Henry, over Henri, he'd not corrected her. But it hadn't been long before he'd longed to hear her call him by his proper name. For her to know him for who he truly was. It was Andre who had convinced him to stick to their rules. Insisted, in fact, reminding him the rules that had been put into place to protect *him*. To give him the freedom he'd so craved.

But that was all so long ago.

Henri eased back on the throttle, hand resting loosely on the wheel. "Matilda," he said.

Finger trailing through the water as they drifted, she looked up.

"Perhaps now is a good time to tell me why you are here."

"Of course," she said. Her cropped T-shirt lifted to flash a swathe of tanned skin as she settled back in her seat, and the chipped bronze polish on her bare foot poked out the bottom of her too-long jeans.

Then she closed her eyes, held out both hands as if steadying herself, and said, "I know you're busy, but I hope you can indulge me while I give you some background. Some context to what I'm about to ask."

Her eyes lifted to his. The words *for despite who we once were, we know nothing about one another, not really* remained unsaid.

She started with her sisters, Rose and Evelyn. Growing up together on a cattle station in the middle of the Outback. She spoke of her mother, Rosamund. How close they had been, how her mother was the reason why she'd travelled. How deeply the shock of her mother's death had affected them all.

She paused a moment then, as if waiting for him to say something.

But then she moved on to her father. "A little under two months ago, he was hit by a widow-maker—the falling branch from a gum tree—while mustering. He seemed okay afterwards. Bumps and bruises, aches and pains, but he was tough. Unstoppable. Until he wasn't. He collapsed one day, in the kitchen. Rose was out, so it fell on me. We were in the helicopter, heading to the local hospital, when he…" She swallowed. "Internal bleeding. A lacerated spleen. There was nothing they could do."

She stopped, then sat forward, her head in her hands.

And something shifted inside of Henri. Like a landslide, shearing away some great layer of self-protection. He reached for her, his fingers hovering midair. But no.

The best he could do was sympathise. "I'm so sorry that you went through that."

"It's fine," she said, sitting up, breathing through her nose, shaking her head. "It's okay. I'm okay."

And he saw her tuck her sorrow away, call up a smile, and present as if all *was* fine. A move that came too easily, as if pretending, for someone else's sake, was a cloak she had donned many times.

His uncle's words, *"Never show weakness. Never show pain,"* reverberated in his head, and he bucked against it so hard he pulled a muscle in his chest.

"I understand the impulse," he said, his voice overloud to drown out his uncle's voice, "to want to appear as if everything is fine. But you do not have to pretend with me."

Her surprised gaze found his. Then in the next moment she seemed to crumble, becoming untethered, as if she'd been holding so much in for so long.

"I…" She licked her lips. "It's been weeks now, but I still keep expecting to hear the thwack of the back door, his three-toned whistle, the scrape of his boots on the polished wood floors. And—even though she's been gone several years now—I find myself expecting my mother's voice too, telling Dad to take off his shoes before she takes them off for him."

She took a deep breath, then thumped a fist against her chest. "I had no idea that was sitting, right here." Then, "Likely because there's so much more taking up space right now. All of which started upon the reading of his will."

After that, she told him the rest of her story in one free-wheeling gulp.

The revelation of an affair. A secret sister. A century-old poker game. A neighbourly feud. And a wildly problematic stipulation as to the legitimacy of any female inheritance that did its best to out-dismay the stranger restrictions found in the Chaleurian rules of succession.

"My sister," she said, "Rose, has clammed up. Eve is furious, and thoroughly disconnected. Ana is like a deer in the headlights. While I'm… I'm mostly confused. Knowing him, and my mum, and how they were together—they were so tight. So loving. If they, who appeared to have the best marriage, nearly imploded, and so spectacularly, what hope is there for the rest of us?"

Her gaze connected with his then. Swirling with pain and shock and longing. Meaning it took a moment to sift through her story to find the point that truly affected him.

"You and your sisters, must be married, by…"

"The end of May, next year."

"Or your lands will be given back to the family who owned them generations ago."

"Correct. I have been trying to find a legal loophole that makes it redundant, while also being quiet about the whole thing, as the less people know the better. But we aren't having much luck. Meaning we have to start looking at Plan B."

Henri's throat was as dry as an autumn leaf, his voice crackling, as he clarified, "You wish to know whether we are, in fact, married."

"I do," she blurted. Then seemed to realise the words she'd chosen, and a pulse began beating in her neck.

He felt it too, a rise in temperature, a siren call back to those golden days and decadent nights. "And if we are legally married, you would ask that we remain that way, until such a date that your portion of the condition is satisfied."

She breathed out a *Yes*.

His response ought to have been an instant *No*.

If word got out that he, a prince in want of an heir, had married in secret years ago, royal detractors would have a field day. If word got out that he was engaged in a *fake* marriage, it would have the same outcome. It would weaken his position, or in the very least make it appear as if he put his own needs above the needs of the country. Which could not be further from the truth.

Though, instead of saying any of that, Henri watched Matilda's thumb twirl the ring on her right hand, his mother's ring, around and around, as if she was *used* to it being there.

And found himself saying, "What do your sisters think of your plan?"

"They don't know."

"That you are here?"

"They don't know about you."

His gaze whipped back to hers.

He had thought himself inured to the cut of a savage truth, his uncle having burnished his heirs with such methods until they shone. It seemed that this woman had power over him still.

Henri placed a hand on the throttle, turned the yacht and started the journey back to shore.

"I couldn't tell them," Matilda said, carefully manoeuvring her way up the boat till she took the seat next to his. "When I got home, Mum was in a coma, and she never came out. Our family was in disarray. Then it only became harder and harder to bring it up. Until it was just easier to forget it ever happened."

Henri pressed the throttle harder.

"Tell me it hasn't been the same for you," she said, her voice lifting to combat the roar of the engine.

Henri's jaw tightened. For she was right. The weeks and months right after were a daze to him now. But time healed. Patched over old wounds until they became no more than a scar.

"It seems a lot to ask of you all," he said, changing tack. "To make that kind of sacrifice for the sake of a plot of land. Would it not be easier to refuse. To start afresh?"

Matilda reared back. "How would you feel if you were

told that you were to lose the château? Off you go, find a new job, somewhere else to sleep. Thanks for nothing."

Matilda had no idea how close she was to touching on what had once upon a time been his dream. That the summer they'd met he had put it behind him, wanting a different life. Only to be pulled back in.

"Do you believe that we are married?"

"I would err on the side of yes. But in actuality, I do not know for sure."

She nodded. "No matter what happens next, can you agree that we *need* to find out for sure?"

She was right. Their marriage was out there, an anvil over his head. The truth *would* out, and while he would not lie, if there was some way that he could control the messaging, it might not upend everything he was trying to achieve.

"I have one condition," he said.

Matilda's eyes widened. Before she collected herself. Then, to cut the tension, she shivered and said, "That word."

And Henri's smile came from nowhere. It was a magic trick, her ability to pull that out of him when he least expected it.

"A consideration, then. While your situation is time sensitive, mine is sensitive in other ways."

"The prince thing."

"The prince thing."

How to put this?

"I have worked hard to let my people know that I can be trusted to put their interests ahead of my own. If news that I had been keeping a royal bride from them were to get out, it would be difficult to roll back."

The press, parliament, the people would all rightly be wondering. Was subterfuge simply in the Raphael-Rossetti blood? The fact that he was entertaining this at all sat ill within him. But what was he to do? Especially when discretion was important to her too.

"Whatever you need from me," said Matilda, "I will do."

Henri's eyebrow lifted of its own volition.

While Matilda blushed to her roots. "And by *that*, I mean, what steps do you believe we should take next?"

The dock grew larger as they approached. Henri slowed the boat right down, giving him a moment to collate his thoughts. "Allow me to find a way to *quietly* find the legal documents we require. Until then, no promises, no plans."

Matilda nodded. "Totally fair. And what shall I do until then?"

"That's entirely up to you. That said, you have arrived here at rather a pivotal moment, politically. So having you out of the public eye would be my preference."

"Henri," she said, leaning in to nudge her shoulder against his. "Are you asking me to stay?"

"Yes, Matilda, I am asking you to stay. So that you might stay under the radar."

"First Rose, then you. Why do people think I'm going to go about the place announcing myself. Hi! I'm Matilda! Secretly married to your prince!"

Henri glanced toward the deck where Boris and Lars were walking down the stone steps, readying to collect him. And only just out of hearing range. This was going to be a hardship on many levels.

"Will you stay?"

She looked over his shoulder toward the château, the morning sun picking up hints of peach in the stone, making it appear as if it glowed, and she, with an long-suffering sigh, said, "If I must."

"Then it's settled."

"It's settled." Matilda said, smiling at him as if they were now in this thing together.

While Henri focused on getting the boat away without a scratch, rather than the ripples of warmth spreading through him at the knowledge she wasn't leaving.

Not yet.

Carefully, carefully.

CHAPTER FOUR

IT WAS LATE the next afternoon before Henri was able to even think about how he might go about unearthing the validity of a marriage in a manner that could keep the search quiet.

He'd spent the hours in between as per usual, strapped to his office chair. On the phone to the Minister for Agriculture, who was concerned about predictions of a colder than normal winter. Then the chair of the Royal Opera, for which he was patron, wondering when he might actually attend an event. After which he'd taken part in an online video chat with a classroom of second graders from the local Chaleurian Charter School and had stumbled over the question, "What do you love most about being a prince?"

This, right on the heels of Minister of State letting him know, in sombre tones, that an anonymous poll had been put into the field; testing the waters as to which way a referendum regarding the future of the royal house of Chaleur might sway.

Stretching out tight shoulders, he moved to the window of his first-floor office to find Matilda sitting at a table in the rose garden below.

Snacks and coffee within reach, it was a miracle she didn't fall off the chair, the way she sat with one foot on the seat, arm wrapped about her knee, as she tapped away at her laptop.

He lifted a hand to his chest when he felt a strange tightness take hold.

"Why so glum?"

Henri looked to his side to find his cousin had finally deigned to join him, after being summoned a good half hour earlier.

When he realised Andre was mimicking his stance—all stiff shoulders and pinched face—Henri let his hands unclasp. "I am glum due to the fact I need at least forty-eight hours in every day if I have any hope of restoring order to this house."

"That all?" Andre asked after a long beat.

For his simple question had apparently unlocked a wave of frustration in Henri. Matilda, now walking barefoot through the grass, and collecting fallen rose petals, had no doubt loosened the lid.

"I cannot remember the last time I read for pleasure, enjoyed a leisurely glass of wine, took a drive for no reason other than wishing it." The boat ride the day before had come close, after which he'd been playing catch-up all day.

"You are aware," said Andre, giving him a side-eye, "that the only one putting such pressure on yourself is you? If you really wanted to find time to do those things, you would. Or you could halve your workload by nabbing yourself a princess. Oh, wait!"

Henri did not dignify that with a response.

"On that note, I see *she's* still here."

"*She* is staying for a short while."

"How long?"

"No end date has been determined."

"Not that that's stopped her before."

Henri's eye twitched. "Tell me again why I allow you to walk about the place, unfettered? As prince I could, by law, have you beheaded."

"You indulge me because I am endearing as hell. And since I too was raised under the regime of Prince Augustus the Beloved Brute, I alone understand your occasional twitches are psychosomatic and not reason to call the royal doctor."

"There is that."

The cousins stood silent for a few moments, watching Matilda, who was now on her phone—her movements animated, her smile wide.

"Look at her out there," Andre mused, "pacing a route. Like a caged cat."

Henri flinched at Andre's choice of words, then turned away from the view. "I called you here as I need you to do something for me."

"I will not write down the Netflix password again. Put a note in your phone like a normal person."

"I need you to find official record of my marriage to Matilda."

Andre's nostrils flared, but other than that, he did not react at all. He had been there that night. The lone witness to the event bar the yacht captain who, from memory, had limited English. And in the weeks and months after. When Henri had feared for her, longed for her, and cursed her very existence.

"You understand why I am asking this of you, and you alone. Why it needs to be done with subtlety and finesse. Whatever information you find must be unimpeachable. Can you do that for me?"

Andre waited a beat, then nodded. And that was that. For all that his cousin appeared the definition of imperious indolence, Henri knew why. To combat the darker parts of their childhood, Henri had shuttered himself behind physical and metaphorical walls. Andre had chosen snark.

"May I ask why now?"

"You may ask, but I cannot say." It was Matilda's story to share, not his. Even with Andre.

"Should I worry?"

"You will, even if I command you not to."

Andre's gaze flickered, as if surprised Henri had realised that about him.

"Make it a priority," Henri said, with gentle command.

Andre nodded, knocked twice on the doorframe, then left.

Henri turned back to the window to find Matilda looking up, her phone cradled in her hand. She blinked when they made eye contact and looked away, before looking back, as if she'd been caught watching him.

He lifted his hand in a wave. She waved back, before pointing up, asking if she might join him.

And while the backlog of work beckoned from his desk, he nodded.

The twist in his chest loosened when she smiled broadly, jogged to the table to collect her things, then disappeared inside.

Henri found himself glad Andre had already left the room.

Matilda—still getting used to the servants who seemed to lurk in doorways in this place, like security in a museum—muffled a scream when Celeste appeared from nowhere.

"May I help you, Ms. Matilda?"

"Ah, well I'm just heading up to see Henri. Prince Henri. His Royal…you know. He invited me up."

Good grief. Could she be any more obvious? Or less sophisticated?

Funny how she'd forgotten that side of things in the intervening years—the times she'd wondered how she, a bumptious farm girl with a penchant for gum boots and denim overalls, had ended up in their glittering circle.

Then she'd catch Henri's eye and she'd know exactly why she was there.

"He's in the room just above?" she said, twirling a finger above her head, then spinning a half turn.

"*Oui*, His Highness is in his office," said Celeste. "I can show you the way."

At which point a maid appeared, again from nowhere, asking if she could take the coffee and plate Matilda was juggling. Matilda handed them off gratefully, no clue as to whether they were family heirlooms or from some IKEA collection the kitchen used for non-royal guests.

If only they knew, a cheeky voice popped up in the back of her head. Before a shiver of discomfort wobbled through her, and she told the voice to shush.

Following Celeste, Matilda used one hand to send a quick message to Eve. Giving her an update on her phone call she'd just had with Rose. Not that Eve would respond, but at least she might feel part of things still. While frustrating, Matilda understood. It was hard on all of them.

Which was why she had to make this work.

Rose had to know something was up, for Matilda had not been able to stop peppering her with questions about home and telling Rose how amazing she was.

It was either that, or tell her about the rose garden, a near twin to their mother's, or the fairy-tale castle she had promised not to leave. Or Henri. Standing in the window above, like something out of one of the romance novels Eve used to read. All broad and distinguished and broody and gorgeous. The beautiful boy now honed, sharpened, perfected over time.

But there was still no point in getting Rose excited—or, more likely, furious—that she had gone rogue, until she had answers. Much like prepping a research paper for peer review, she needed to be fully equipped to stand by her premise. Whatever that turned out to be.

Laptop under her arm, she jogged up the stairs after Celeste.

That was one positive of the day. She'd woken with an idea for a chapter in the book she was working on. And outside in that beautiful soft sunlight, in the forest-fresh air, she'd drafted the first chapter.

Celeste glanced back to make sure she was keeping up.

"Sorry, daydreaming."

Celeste nodded, while looking as if she'd never daydreamed in her life.

Matilda wondered what Celeste thought of her—"Andre's friend," who had spent no time with Andre at all.

Unless that was some kind of code. Did Henri often have women come to stay? It would be more of a shock if he did not. For if he was not atop some list of eligible royals, she'd eat her skirt.

She had zero excuse for the thought to curdle inside of her, considering how things had ended between them. But the idea of him looking longingly into someone's eyes, reading them poetry, or…

Nope. Not going there. Draw a line under it and move on.

Anyway, it just didn't feel as if guests were commonplace. The château felt quiet. The ivy climbing the long stone wall leading to the big creaky gate, the surfaces clean as a whistle but with a ghostly sense of unstirred dust. As if it had once been a bustling home but was currently in an era of repose.

Celeste stopped outside an imposing double door, knocked three times, waited a beat, then opened the door.

Matilda poked her head in to find Henri sitting behind a large desk, on the phone. He held up a staying hand, indicating he'd just be a minute.

She nodded, put her phone and laptop on a coffee table near a comfortable-looking couch, then went stickybeaking, taking in the artwork, the books on the shelves, the detritus. For *this* room was lived in.

Is this the real him? she wondered, picking up a throw cushion that had fallen to the floor and tossing it onto a leather couch.

The Henri beneath the impossibly perfect exterior. A man who worked hard, took on too much, and thought little of the visuals.

"Matilda?"

She looked up to find Henri moving from behind his desk in his usual perfectly cut suit pants clinging to strong thighs, top button of his shirt undone, shirtsleeves rolled up to his elbows, veins roping down his beautiful forearms.

Her heart leaped as he neared, then panted like a happy puppy. She told it to sit. Stay. Leave.

Henri said, "Apologies if I've been unavailable."

She waved a hand his way. "I get it. You did mention that you have a country to run, and that you are all-powerful."

A beat slunk by. "I'm not sure those were the exact words I used."

"No?"

He slid hands into the pockets of his suit pants then, and she did not look down. Knowing what she was missing, she honestly deserved a medal.

"I trust Celeste has given you ideas of places you can visit within the grounds."

"Conservatory, orangery, rose garden, chapel. This place is like something out of a really well-funded historical TV drama."

"You've seen it all?" he asked, eyebrows lifting.

She had. Sitting still for long was not her thing. "I even found the laundry. I can show you where it is?"

She pointed to the door, but instead he leaned back against his desk, crossed his feet at the ankle, and basically looked ready for GQ to step in and start snapping cover photos.

"What were you working on?" He motioned his chin to her discarded laptop.

She opened her mouth to mention the book, but found she wasn't yet ready to talk about it. It was at that tenuous it-might-all-dissolve-away-if-she-described-it-wrong point. And besides the subject matter was a little too close to home.

So she sidestepped to work she'd done the night before. "A letter. Possibly quite important, historically."

His brow furrowed and she had to reach out a hand in case her knees went out from under her.

"You were *writing* a letter?"

"Authenticating." She sat on the arm of the couch, just in case his brow furrowed again. "I have a PhD in art history. Authenticating handwritten letters is my niche."

"Fascinating."

She smiled, remembering he was a history buff too. The way he'd speak about painters and architects and political figures, the way he'd never rush through a museum, absorbing every display, his arm around her shoulder, hers wrapped around his waist, his voice rumbling from his chest to hers as he read every plaque, had been like catnip.

Now, looking around this place, she understood why.

"What kind of letter?" he asked, and the burr in his voice made her wonder if he was remembering the same.

She paused a moment before saying, "Well, it's a love letter, actually. For that is my *niche* niche."

"Of course, it is," he murmured.

Or maybe she'd imagined it. For the way his eyes remained on hers had her blood rushing behind her ears. Had her remembering lying with her head on his chest as he'd read to her from the book she'd bought him in Paris, her fingers trailing over the hard ridges of his torso, his trailing down her spine, lower.

And the longer his gaze hooked hers, the more she felt it. The undercurrent of heat. Of attraction. Still bubbling away between them. Which was something she honestly hadn't expected.

Yes, they had once upon a time been everything to one another. But she'd been so young, so green, and the way things had ended between them had hurt, deeply. Add her dad's affair to the mix and the very last thing she could put her faith in was *feelings*.

But there it was. That pulsing magnetic pull. And she knew it was tugging both ways.

Matilda pushed off the chair and moved around the other side of his desk and pretended to look out the window. "Any news on the...thing we are trying to find news on?"

"Sorry," he said, moving to stand near her, but far enough away she was sure he was also keen on keeping minimum safe distance.

He ran a hand up the back of his neck, a classic stressed Henri move. "I know you must want answers as fast as possible so that you can...do whatever else you might wish to do while here."

"I have nowhere else I need to be." She made the mistake of looking at him as she said it and felt a kick of heat hit so hard she rocked on her feet.

"But you're right," she said, "the sooner it's all sorted, the better. I just spoke to Rose and she had a meeting with the family lawyer. Stubborn old goat is not being the slightest bit helpful."

"Time for a new family lawyer?"

"I did suggest that. Rose shot me down. She can wrangle a brumby and fly a helicopter, but she is too nice for her own good."

"Unlike you?" he asked, and when she looked to him again, it was clear he was baiting her. That whatever was humming between them he was leaning into, not away from.

"Are you kidding?" she said, "I'm a total dream."

"That so?"

So much for trying to cool things down. "Yep. My role is the family conciliator. I am in charge of general harmony. I am sunshine and light."

"Why is that?"

She readied for a comeback but nothing came to her. For while she wasn't a big fan of confrontation, and she honestly wanted everyone to be happy, the why of it was unclear.

Henri threw her a bone. "Everyone called my older brother, Pascal, a chip off the old block, but where my father was a loose cannon, Pascal was, at heart, shy."

His brow furrowed, but not in a seductive way so much as a thoughtful way. Not that her libido was all that adept at differentiating.

"I wonder," said Henri, "if he too believed that he was fulfilling a role. Only it was the one written for him by our father, rather than the one he might have wanted for himself." When he ran a hand up the back of his neck that time, he left it there, gripping hard.

Family, she thought. *Can't live with them but love them to death.*

"And you?" she asked. When he didn't answer, she extrapolated. "If you say he lived down to people's expectations, did that mean you were expected to make up for him?"

His gaze slid back to hers, cynicism warring with scepticism behind his pale hazel eyes. And it hit her that she'd found out more about his childhood, his life, about what made him *him* in a five-minute conversation than she had the entire time they'd been together.

"We each of us contain multitudes," she said, paraphrasing Whitman, one of Henri's favourites, back in the day.

"It seems that we do," he said, his voice rough as their eyes caught and held.

Again. It had become a bit of a habit. One she could not deny felt wonderful. Invigorating. Empowering. And terrifying. For she'd never felt with another man the way she felt when she was with him.

Right when she was about to source a bucket of cold water in which to dunk her head, Henri stepped back. Turned away. And the spell splintered.

Though the aftereffect remained, like fireflies just under her skin.

"Hungry?" he asked.

"Famished," she admitted.

He picked up the phone, politely asked for a selection of sandwiches, cheeses, and petit fours to be delivered to his office.

"Nothing that wobbles," he noted.

And Matilda's heart took a big tumble. Which was a very foolish thing for it to do. For she had been there once before, deeply, forever his. And when she'd been swept up in the most terrible moment of her life, he'd not followed. Not checked on her. He'd simply cut her loose.

So yes, protecting her heart was a fantastic idea. As the time would soon come when they would have to say goodbye, only this time it would be forever.

Henri's phone beeped as he was washing shaving foam from his cheeks the next morning. Then it beeped again. And again.

He ignored it. Needing to finish at least one job semi-well, even if it was only shaving his face.

There was also the fact that he was hoping to make it to

breakfast, as Matilda had asked, in her roundabout way, what time he normally ate, as it might be nice to cross paths.

Having company—bar Andre and Celeste or Boris and Lars hovering on the periphery—was something he had wilfully not sought out for some time. His role too important to allow for distractions. Having Matilda nearby hadn't been as disquieting as he'd thought it would be. In fact, there had been a kind of emphatic energy coursing through him the rest of the afternoon.

He'd also picked up on the fact that Matilda was used to having people around. Her sister, station hands, stable masters, seasonal staff, their housekeeper, Lindy. And her dad, not long lost. He wanted her to feel comfortable while there. Not, how had Andre put it? Like a caged cat.

His phone beeped again, three times in quick succession.

He checked quickly, his throat closing up when he saw Andre had sent a number of links to local news articles. Had someone read between the lines of the tele poll? Had news of a possible referendum been uncovered? Or had Matilda's arrival on the street the day before found traction?

As it turned out, it was none of the above. The overarching headline—Will Prince Henri Show His Face at the Summer Festival?

Henri's thumb hovered over the phone, a scathing response at the ready, but he called his cousin instead.

"Are you serious?" he growled.

"Thought you'd like to know your people miss you."

"I thought I made it clear what your priority needed to be." His marriage and its validity.

"That you did, cousin," said Andre. "And yet…the Summer Festival calls."

Henri thought back to the kindly response of the people on the street in Côte de Lapis. In his effort to not appear a show pony like his father, or remind them of the pain his uncle had caused, was it *possible* he'd gone too far the other way?

Then he remembered the piles of work on his desk, some of which he'd left half done while falling asleep late the night before. The referendum, which he might be pulling on them any day now. And wondered how on earth he could fit in an appearance for appearance's sake.

Matilda would enjoy it, he thought.

"Take Matilda," Andre said, reading his damn mind. "She's a venturesome sort. She'd love it."

"I can't *take* her."

"Too late for that."

Henri's unimpressed pause was answer enough.

"Look," said Andre, his tone placating, "you just…you need to get out of your own head. And if that means *getting out*, in general, then I, as your closest adviser and most stylish friend, encourage you to consider it."

Henri took a deep breath and thought back to the festivals of his youth. A welcome address. Judging a contest of some sort. Answering questions no more pressing than *"What do you enjoy most about being a prince?"*

But if he did let Matilda tag along, would their attraction be as blindingly obvious as it had felt in his office the day before? Like an arc of electricity connecting them. Making it impossible for him to keep his gaze from her.

He put the phone on speaker and dropped his hands to the sink. "This is not the time for parties and fun, Andre. This is my opportunity to make a difference. To fix mistakes. To give the people a real say in their futures."

"Henri," Andre said, sounding exasperated, "I have never heard someone say anything that made me more sure *they* were in need of parties and fun. Or perhaps some snuggle time with someone they found appealing."

"Moving on."

"As you wish."

"Do you have news? Regards—"

"Operation Is Henri Married?"

"Perhaps something with a little more tact."

"Noted. Nothing as yet, but I am on the case. Fingers in pies. Ears to the ground."

"And you are being careful."

"I was considering buying a trench coat."

Sighing, then patting his face with a towel, Henri said, "Just do what you need to do. Only quicker." With that he hung up.

Catching his own gaze in the mirror, he allowed himself a moment to wonder what *she* saw. *"You have changed,"* she'd said. And he had. In many ways.

In others, particularly those pertaining to her, it seemed he had not. For the more time he spent with her, the more he recognised the discomfort within him as a deep, primal longing. As if they were drawn to one another like twin storms, their edges bussing and bumping, waiting for the moment they hit at just the right angle and—

Henri closed his eyes against the image that came next.

Once he'd collected himself, he wiped his jaw, threw the towel to the sink and strode into his bedroom, where he dressed himself before heading straight to his office.

She could breakfast without him. For hiding the way they sparked off of one another from the staff would only become harder the more time they spent together. And it was not his job to make her feel at home.

For this was not her home. Oftentimes, he struggled to feel as if it was his. And they had agreed to a holding pattern.

No promises, no plans.

CHAPTER FIVE

"WHAT'S ON THE calendar for tomorrow?" Matilda asked that evening, while curled up on a chair in Henri's office.

Henri looked at her in the gilt mirror that had been brought in as his tailor fussed with the collar of a new suit.

Despite having avoided her at breakfast, she had found him once again at lunchtime. Knocking three times on his office, opening the door, then padding inside, the kitchen staff following, bringing a variation on the food they'd eaten together the day before.

Only this time, once they'd eaten and had fallen into a conversation about their respective school days—hers at a local country primary school with thirty children and two teachers, and his homeschooled by a retired professor with the personality of a taxidermised bug—she'd curled up on a couch in the corner with her laptop, humming under her breath as she continued working on her "letters and other things" while he worked at his desk.

Anytime he'd looked up from his work to find Matilda there, watching him, before shooting him a quick smile and going back to her work, his lack of progress felt less like he was drowning.

In the reflection in the mirror he watched her curious eyes follow as the tailor measured his inseam, tracing the run of the tape down his leg and back up again. Stopping to stare at his backside.

"Calendar?" he repeated. And when her eyes snapped to his, she had the grace to blush.

"Well," said Matilda, "I was thinking you must be dying to get out of here. And you shouldn't have to stay in on my account."

"There are options, certainly," said Celeste, who was standing to one side, overseeing the tailor's work. "If His Highness wishes to undertake them."

His Highness did not. Which Celeste knew all too well. He shot her a glance but she did not meet his eye, making him wonder how much time Andre had spent in her ear, rather than doing what needed to be done to find his damn marriage license.

"Ooh," said Matilda. "Options sound exciting. Maybe I could come along. I'd stay out of the way, of course. Shadow Celeste, as she shadows you. See a true day in the life of Prince Henri Gaultier Raphael-Rossetti. Assuming, that is," said Matilda, moving on the chair so that her legs swung from one side to the other, a move so sinuous, Henri had to grit his teeth and think of England, "that you do more than frown at paperwork, sign off on laws that change people's lives, and charm the masses in accidental beachside parades."

Henri lifted an eyebrow at her take on his position.

While he chose not to be the kind of royal to cut the ribbon on any new luxury car superstore, unlike his father, for Matilda, being stuck in a castle was clearly constrictive.

Henri, now duly triggered, took the foot off his own back. And looked to Celeste. "Options, you say?"

Celeste blinked, experienced what looked to be a moment of catatonia, then pulled up her phone and began flicking madly through the thing.

"Invitations that have been vetted by Boris include…a children's hospital visit. A science lab which has just had a breakthrough in dementia treatment. It's National Tree Planting Week—"

As Celeste went through the surprisingly long list of groups who had invited him to visit, Henri heard Andre's voice in the back of his head saying, *"The only one putting such pressure on yourself is you. You could halve your workload by nabbing yourself a princess."*

His gaze shifted back to Matilda, as it was wont to do, to find her smiling at Celeste. And he let himself wonder.

For *no promises, no plans* did not mean Henri was not constantly contemplating what might come next. If the marriage was valid, Matilda could have her marriage certificate, and his country could have its princess.

But then there was the referendum to consider. If it went ahead, and the people chose to move forward in a new way, it would take time, years perhaps, before the dismantlement of generations of royal rule was complete.

Only then would his life be his own. Not for a summer, but forevermore.

Henri felt the tug of the tailor's hand against his calf. Once again he'd forgotten he had company, Matilda's presence was so thick in the air.

"That will do, for now, thank you," he said, after which the tailor bowed, gathered his tools, and swept from the room.

Celeste, understanding a royal request for privacy when she heard one, quickly followed and shut the door.

Matilda, naturally, had no clue what had just happened. Or didn't imagine his dismissal included her.

He watched in the reflection as she hopped off the chair and padded his way. Her feet bare, as usual, her eyes warm as she slipped in behind him and brought her hands to the collar of his shirt, uncurling it and laying it flat. Only rather than the deft movements of the tailor, hers were slow, soothing, as she smoothed out the creases.

"That's been driving me crazy this whole time."

"Has it now," he asked.

Gaze captured by the slow movements of her fingers in the mirror, he lifted his eyes to hers. The hold of her gaze jerking something loose inside him, prying open some ancient lockbox that had been holding the gentler, softer, warmer feelings that she alone had on a string.

But then her hands slipped away, and she moved to lean against the edge of the mirror. "I think we should do this."

He raised an eyebrow.

And she laughed, not pretending to misunderstand.

"Do something useful, *tomorrow.* I could be in charge of passing you important papers. Or hold your crown when it gets too heavy."

"I was thinking of leaving the crown behind," he said, "what with a possible visit to a fishery, or the government subcommittee on road upgrades, but after your fine offer, I might reconsider."

She grinned and the lockbox inside of him flew open with a flourish, and feelings whipped about inside of him too quickly to catch.

He waited for the *carefully, carefully* to whisper inside his head, but he got nothing.

"Is that a yes?" she asked.

"It's a yes."

She leaped in the air, air punch and all, before telling a story about the one time she'd had a dress tailor-made, for some racing event her parents hosted each year.

And Henri let her voice wash over him as he imagined Andre in the corner, laughing at how quickly he'd capitulated.

Matilda stood by Celeste's side, mirroring her low-key movements as they followed Henri down a reception line of nurses and staff at a local children's hospital.

Celeste, taking the "shadow Celeste" mission literally, had had a half dozen skirt suits and low heels similar to her own sent to Matilda's room that morning. After which, Matilda had decided she might as well go full method—wrangling her hair into a slick low bun and practicing her "capable" face.

She'd been wondering if this was how a princess of Chaleur might be expected to dress—neat, inoffensive, inert—when Henri had jogged down the front steps toward the waiting car, looking strained and tunnel-visioned. Then, having spotted her beside Celeste, he'd done the most delicious double take.

"Matilda?" he'd said. "You look…"

She held out her arms and twirled a little. "Told you I could hide in plain sight."

Henri shook his head and muttered something in French. She wasn't sure if it was a good mutter, or if he was regretting his decision. For he was in supreme prince mode; fast-moving, fast talking, no smiles, dead serious, the way he'd been on the street that first day.

Making her wonder if his disinclination in regard to public appearances had less to do with time management than he claimed, and more to do with an actual disinclination toward public events.

But then Boris ushered Celeste and Matilda into the back seat of his car, while Henri went with Lars. After which a cavalcade of cars filled with extra security followed, careening down the mountain into town. Everyone a little giddy, as if they had all been hankering for such a day to arrive.

By the time they hit their third event of the day—the visit to a children's hospital—Matilda's feet were starting to pinch, and she could see the curls that had sprung from her bun. Working the land was physically demanding, but the smiling, listening, asking pertinent questions, keeping track of the logistics of cars and staff, names, all while trying to appear as fresh as a daisy was draining in a whole other way.

Not that you'd know it, watching Henri. For whatever stress he'd brought with him into the car that morning, he'd left there.

Around the people, *his* people, he was attentive and generous. They glowed under his gentle charisma, gushed as he shook hands, cooed as he crouched down to chat with kids in wheelchairs and listened to stories the nurses told.

When she'd passed a group of said nurses earlier, they'd pulled her aside, asking what he was like in "real life." She'd paused barely a second before leaning in, telling them how hard he worked, how much he cared for the country, till they looked at him like he was Superman in a suit.

And what had started out as a chance to see more of his country, ended up bittersweet. For it only nailed down how suited he was to the role. If he'd followed her, as she'd begged in the note she'd left him, he'd have missed this chance, and these people would have missed out on him.

Then Celeste cleared her throat to signal to all that it was time to move on, and Henri waved down the line to those he'd not been able to meet, had a quick chat to the administrator and then they were back in the car, on their way home.

No, not *home*. Prince Henri's *château*.

They'd fallen into whichever cars had come first—Celeste in the front seat, beside Boris, who was driving, Matilda in the back with Henri, who filled the space with his long legs, and some unexpectedly dark energy, considering how wonderful he'd been all day.

When he ran a hand over his face, leaving his matinee idol hair slightly mussed, the furrows in his brow etched in place, she knew something wasn't right.

"Well," she said brightly, the need to play happy-maker surging inside of her. "That last one was my favourite."

His hand dropped to the seat between them as he turned her way. His gaze hard. Apparently broody was a serious kink of hers, as she felt instantly twitchy all over.

"No?" she checked. "Not yours?"

His voice a little raw, as he'd been talking all day, Henri said, "The administrator asserts their funding is about to be cut. Budget constraints put in place by the previous reign."

"The previous reign being your father?"

A muscle ticked in his jaw.

Celeste shifted in the front seat, and a moment later a soundproof barrier slowly lifted into place, cutting the front from the back.

Their body warmth soon intermingled in the tight space. And when Matilda turned on the seat to face Henri, her knee knocked against his, the slide of bare skin against the wool of his pants sending shards of static up and down her body.

"Is it something you can change?" she asked. "Is that something you are able to do?"

He lifted a hand to the back of his neck and gripped it hard, and for a moment she thought he might not answer. That he might be so used to having to shoulder the load alone that he wouldn't let her in.

Till he rumbled, "Budgets are like big ships, slow and cumbersome to turn around."

"But you will try." It was a statement, not a question.

His gaze shifted to hers, his mouth quirking even as his eyes remained dark. "I have pushed parliament's patience rather a lot, especially the past few weeks. But yes, I will try."

"Then I have every faith you'll make it happen."

"I wish I had your belief."

Was it possible Henri did not see himself as the born leader that he so clearly was? She leaned in, her hand landing on his knee. Partly to get his attention and partly to stop her shoulder from bumping the seat in front.

"Henri, did you not see the faces of those you've spent time with today. They adore you. More than that, they trust you."

"They adored my uncle, but they did not know him."

A glimmer of an old conversation came back to her. "Andre said something similar to me once—that your uncle had been beloved by everyone outside of the castle walls. Meaning he hadn't been within?"

The darkness in his eyes only deepened. "He was a proud man who did not take failure well. Leading to a grave mismanagement of resources." Henri's gaze, usually so rich and warm, seemed to recede until he might as well have been behind a pane of glass. "After he was gone, the people then mistook my father's relative charm for a breath of fresh air, rather than seeing him as the crook that he was. Their continued faith in the royal house is not well-placed."

Oh, Henri. Matilda wasn't sure what to say—if she kept gushing, it might come across as insincere. Or worse, look like she was fast developing a crush on her ex-lover-slash-possible-husband who had once let her down so badly she wasn't sure she'd ever quite recovered.

Lucky for her, Henri got in first.

"Which brings me to something that has been weighing on me."

"Okay. Bring it."

"I know we said no promises, no plans—"

"You said that," Matilda reminded him gently. "I'd already planned out at least a dozen different eventualities long before I arrived here."

"Fair," he said, the darkness easing, thank goodness. "Now that I've had time to adjust, there is something that needs to be made clear. If news comes through that the marriage is valid, I will not lie to my people. And I will not put them through the farce of a royal marriage only for it to 'fall apart' a year later. You have enough insight now, I gather, into my family so that you might understand why."

She had some, but she had the feeling it was only the tip of the iceberg.

"So, what you are saying is, if Andre suddenly appears waving a marriage license, we stay the course?"

"Or," Henri offered softly, "we begin divorce proceedings immediately."

Matilda swallowed against the sudden lump in her throat. "Won't *that* be scandalous?"

"Perhaps. But it would be the truth."

For all that every eventuality felt fraught, some now more than others, Matilda's hand squeezed his knee. In support. And to show him that she understood, that she was on his side. Because she had the feeling, that, though he was a fundamentally amazing human, he'd had little of that in his life.

His gaze dropped to her touch. Staying for a few long hot beats, before his hand lifted to cover hers. His fingers curled around her fingers, tangling them. He breathed out hard, as if holding her allowed him to let something go.

"Matilda?" Henri asked, as she must have made some kind of noise. A purr. Or a moan. Good gods, did she have no survival instincts at all?

She gathered herself quick smart and changed the subject, "Do you think we got away with it? Did anyone notice the highly adequate new assistant in your midst?"

Henri's gaze roved over her face, her hair with its fuzzy curls, then kept on moving, all the way down to her feet, now bare, as she'd nudged off her shoes the moment she'd had the chance.

When his gaze swept back to hers, right as his thumb ran over the back of her hand, finding a magical pressure point, she sucked in a breath.

"If they did not notice you, Matilda, they were looking the wrong way."

At which point he lifted their joined hands to his mouth, placing a kiss to her knuckles, before letting their joined hands drop back to his knee.

And they sat that way for the rest of the drive to Chaleur Castle. Henri now far more at ease.

Meanwhile, Matilda's heart bucked with every bump in the road, her mind busy spinning castles in the sky.

"I hear the hospital visit was a big success," said Andre as he moseyed into Henri's office late that night.

Henri tossed a folder to his desk and ran both hands over his eyes. "That so?"

"Celeste wrote a gushing report." Andre waved his phone. "The press had nothing but good to say. The patients. The staff. All enamoured."

"The funding—"

"I know. I heard. The fact that you were there, on the ground, to hear about it means you can do something about it."

Henri had no comeback there.

"So what's next? I'd suggest a casual stop by the local farmers' market, a night at the National Opera, check in with Summer Festival—"

"I have too much to catch up on here."

"You'll always have too much to catch up on here, unless you learn to delegate. Celeste and I can help you source excellent people to help us bear the brunt of your martyrdom."

It was nothing he hadn't heard before, only he'd made the choice to do the work himself so that there was no chance of misdeed, or misappropriation. Only now Henri actually considered it.

For the venture had been a success, on multiple levels.

Then there were the moments Matilda had broken out of "shadow mode." Chatting and laughing with a couple of nurses, about him he had been sure. Playing one-handed patty-cake with kids in casts in the orthopaedic wing.

While he felt like a spotlight was burning down on him anytime he had to play Prince Henri in public, Matilda was a natural.

"Matilda enjoyed it too."

Andre's expression was neutral, which for Andre said everything.

"Am I being too careful? Keeping her locked up here feels beastly. As if soon townsfolk with pitchforks might come at me."

"Not if the townsfolk know you better." The man was a dog with a bone. "Look, if you are concerned that someone might notice you are spending time with someone of the female persuasion, who freaking cares."

"I do."

Andre bowed. "Then might I suggest you try to rein in your sparkle when she is near."

"My what?"

"Your *sparkle*." Andre batted his lashes. "It's really quite adorable."

Henri swore beneath his breath, before coughing out a laugh. "You've been watching too much *Twilight*."

Andre gasped. "There is no such thing as too much *Twilight*."

And somehow, after that, Henri agreed to trial more public outings. For no matter how the future unfurled, right now he had a job to do. And being around the people was the best way for him to get to know them. What they wanted, what they needed, not what he assumed would make their lives easier.

"We need more people in your retinue," said Andre, seeing his chance to bolster their staff, "who can sweep in and take notes and talk to people and gather the information in your wake."

Henri didn't demur, as the more people in the entourage the less likely Matilda's continued presence would stand out.

One afternoon was spent perusing sweet shops in a local village, famous for their hard candies. Another was spent donating books to a local library. A third was spent in a private viewing with a local glassblower, who gifted Matilda a glossy green horse that fit into her palm.

"I shall name him Peridot!" she had declared, as apparently all the horses back at Garrison Downs were named after gemstones. The details of her life building a rich picture of who she was and where she'd come from. Every addition sliding beneath his skin, like an itch, a glimmer in his veins.

Not a *sparkle*, as Andre had so delightfully put it.

But close.

Matilda woke up feeling frisky.

The little trips they had been taking in the townships near the château had been delightful. She'd picked up gifts—the glass horse from a local glassblower would go to Rose, a small painting of the château to Eve in the hopes it might call to the sweet romantic side she'd harboured as a kid, and she'd found some charms for Ana who, in the days after the will reading, had quietly admitted that she'd love to one day give up accountancy to concentrate on her fledgling jewellery design business.

And in her downtime she'd drafted three more chapters of her book and begun work on a backlog of letters her old professor had asked her to take a first sweep on authenticating when she had the time.

I could get used to this, she'd thought, and then something had clutched at her chest. *No promises, no plans.*

Heading down to breakfast, she found the dining room empty, a jar of Vegemite now on the breakfast buffet.

Henri, she thought, a fresh wave of warmth swarming through her, making her feel as if fireflies fluttered under her skin. And while she usually waited till lunchtime to give in to the urge to see him, her feet took her to his office. Promising herself she'd thank him for the Vegemite, then leave him be.

She found him there, in the dark, the curtains still closed up from the night before. He sat not behind his desk but in a chair, finger running over his mouth, forehead creases creasing like never before.

And he stared hard at an envelope he held in his hand.

She'd seen enough fancy letters in her time to pick up on its import—heavy, expensive paper, several pages thick, official looking, with a thick red wax seal.

"Henri?" she said, taking a step or two his way.

He looked up, his gaze unreachable. Impenetrable. *Regal.* As if with a wave of his hand he might banish her.

But the moment he saw her, his gaze cleared. And it was really hard not to read things into that. Not to let it slide beneath her skin and stay there.

"What you got there?" she asked, motioning to the envelope.

Henri's gaze returned to the envelope, and the storm clouds were back.

Having grown up surrounded by strong silent men, she was not fazed. Moving around his chair, she leaned down to ask. "Is it…an electricity bill? A place this size, it must be exorbitant."

Henri huffed out a deep breath. "Electricity, water, they are all state owned. Free for all citizens."

"Well, that's nice." She folded her arms along the back of the chair. "So, if it's not a bill, I'm thinking…jury duty?"

"I am exempt."

"Oh, to be a prince! If it's not a bill, and it's not jury duty—"

"Parliament have been polling the constituency as to the viability of holding a referendum as to whether or not the royal house of Raphael-Rossetti remains a valid means to oversee the political state of Chaleur."

Matilda's hands lifted off the back of the chair as if burned. She moved to stand in front of Henri, arms crossed. "Have they not *met* you? Have they not seen how hard you work? Have they not seen how the people react when you spend time with them? How deeply you listen and care?"

Henri's gaze had lifted to hers, his eyes moving over her face as she ranted. Which only made her rant more.

"How could they do such a thing—"

"Because I asked them to."

"What?" she whispered. Then, "You want to dismantle the monarchy from within?"

He looked to the envelope again, before tossing it to the lamp table at his side. Then he sat forward, elbows on knees, and ran his hands over his face.

Matilda found the nearest empty chair and dragged it so that she was sitting in front of him. Close enough their knees nearly touched. Close enough he'd have to climb over her to escape.

"Talk to me."

She thought he might brush her off. Go all stoic and strong. But when his gaze landed on hers, he told her his story.

"When it became clear that my uncle, Prince Augustus, was unable to have an heir, he made it his mission to groom the next generation of Raphael-Rossettis into an army of impeccable princes and princesses. We were indoctrinated in diplomacy, behaviour, proper language. Drilled in the fact that we were different, better, and must hold ourselves apart. Forced to repeat affirmations as to our God-given right to rule, hundreds of times, every day. For years. And it was made clear that our thoughts, our lives, our futures were not our own. That they belonged to Chaleur."

Matilda's hand was at her mouth, pressed to her lips as she tried to imagine the childhood Henri was describing.

"There were dozens of us, Andre included, though the numbers dissipated when it became clear how obsessed he had become. Until it was just me."

"Your parents?" she asked.

"My mother was long gone, my father happy to have me out of his hair. That summer—*our* summer—I had negotiated three months away, a final burst of freedom before returning to the fold. But I had no intention of returning. Especially after Vienna."

His gaze found hers. And their entire relationship existed in that look.

Their connection instant. Their relationship, hot and fast and fierce. Her naivete trusted life could be that way forever. While he'd been trying to live a lifetime in a single summer.

"My uncle abdicated the day summer ended. Fleeing to Brazil, having made horrifically damaging financial and political decisions, only to die there months later. And so I returned, as he'd known I would. Waiting in the wings until my turn came."

Oh, Henri.

"I wouldn't wish that on anyone, much less a child. But I'm not sure that burning down his house will fix anything."

She'd had that urge herself in the days after her father's will reading as she'd flipped from sorrow, to fear, to anger. Screw him and the fortune he'd built. Let it fall apart. Only time, and love for her sisters, had eased it to a dull pain.

Henri looked away from her then, out the window or into

the past, she couldn't be sure. "It's not that. Or not only that. In centuries past, it made sense to have the protection of a royal family who represented a country's history, its interests, its cultural identity. But now? It's too much power, and too much responsibility for one man."

All that frisky energy from earlier compacted into something sharper, more focused. Matilda shuffled to perch on the edge of her chair, then reached out and took Henri's hand.

His gaze dropped to the contact. Staring at their joined hands as he slipped his more fully into hers.

"Henri, what's in the envelope?"

"I imagine it will be the results of the poll."

"You haven't looked?"

He shook his head.

"Would you like me to do the honours? I promise, if the results are dim, I won't like you any less."

Henri laughed, though it was more of a moan. Used to the low light now, she saw, when his gaze lifted to hers, a question shift mercurially across his eyes.

How much do you like me now?

But then he reached for the envelope and handed it to her.

She took back her hand and ran her fingers over the paper. She usually saw such beautiful workmanship decades, or even centuries, after its import had faded. This was living history.

Yet, she wished she had a fire going nearby so she could toss it in the flames. If a single person had made a snide comment about this man, she'd wish boils upon their nether regions.

"Before what a bunch of strangers have to say becomes a part of how you see yourself forevermore, I need you to hear me." She looked up to find Henri looking deep into her eyes. "I think you might be a masochist."

At that he laughed, then leaned back into the chair. "How do you come to that conclusion?"

She waved a hand at him. "You are determined to make up for the mistakes of your uncle, your father, your brother, and probably another dozen ancestors who committed absolute horrors in the name of God and country. When all you have to do to improve this place is be you. The fact that you worry that you can't do the job justice is *exactly* why you will." Then, "And lastly, while I don't know all that many princes, I'd bet everything I have that you are top-tier."

"Is that so?"

Henri's gaze swept over her then, his nostrils flaring, his eyes hot. As if... Well, as if he'd like nothing more than to drag her onto his lap and kiss her. And she knew in that moment that if he did so, she'd let him.

But this had to come first.

Praying that the people of Chaleur had the slightest clue how lucky they were, she tore open the envelope without ceremony and speed-read pages of statistics, pie graphs, and explanatory prose.

It didn't take long to note that the patterns were clear.

"I knew I liked this country of yours, Henri." Her smile was so wide her cheeks ached. "Turns out they are *overwhelmingly* in favour of things remaining just as they are. And don't go thinking its due to some rose-coloured vision of the past or misplaced respect for your forebears. It's all you."

She handed over the papers.

Watching impatiently for Henri to say *huzzah*, as he read over the poll data, instead she watched as he read, and read, and read. Appearing to be completely and utterly in shock.

After a good while, he let the papers drop and lifted his eyes back to hers. "Thank you."

"For what? Anyone can open an envelope."

"Not with quite as much panache." One corner of his mouth hooked into a half smile and she was glad to be sitting down. For she felt like a champagne bottle uncorked, the fizz no longer in her control.

Matilda swallowed, some latent thread of self-protection warning her that the longer she remained, the more these feelings would wind about her heart like the ivy covering the walls of his castle.

"Do you have a minute?" he asked, breaking into her mild but important panic.

"I have all the minutes," she said, grinning like a fool.

"I'd like to show you something."

"Great!" she said, while frantically wondering how one might best hack metaphorical ivy clear. Before it was too late.

CHAPTER SIX

HENRI STOOD IN the doorway to his family's famous library—two stories high, gloriously appointed, filled with books that had been lost to other countries in coups and revolutions, kept safe here due to the longevity his family had ensured—and watched as Matilda made her way around the room.

Despite knowing how much she would love it, he'd avoided bringing her here, as this was the room in which his uncle's "lessons" had taken place.

He waited for the ghosts of his uncle's voice, the snap of leather across his knuckles. Only when he focused on Matilda, humming happily as her fingers trailed over spines of books, as she stopped and looked at framed family letters, copies of important speeches, the original plans for the château, he managed to keep the rest at bay.

There would be no referendum.

Meaning that this was where he would remain. Through all his days. Serving the people of Chaleur. When he'd imagined this possible outcome, he was certain he'd feel bereft. Lost to history before he'd even lived it. But for some reason that feeling had yet to eventuate.

Matilda, he thought. It was entirely due to Matilda. Not only her impassioned speech before she'd opened the envelope but the way she'd nudged him back out into the world again. As if she'd been sent to him, at the exact right moment he'd needed her obstreperous positivity most.

"Henri," she said, as she turned to him, her expression saying *I can't believe you were hiding this from me.*

"I had a feeling you'd like this room."

"I feel like Elizabeth Bennett when she first saw Pemberley." Then, "Do you remember the book of letters and poetry I bought you, the one with the blue cover?"

Of course he remembered.

"Is it here somewhere?"

"It's…it's been a while since I've seen it." He moved into the room. "As I remember it, you particularly liked the Emerson."

Liked him reading it to her in bed, her limbs twisted about his, her head on his chest.

She watched him as he neared, her gaze glinting, as if he knew *exactly* what she was remembering. *"'Thou art to me a delicious torment,'"* she quoted. "Heady stuff."

While the next line echoed in Henri's head: *Thine ever, or never.*

"Come here," he said, moving to the bookshelves in the corner.

And watched as she swallowed. Her cheeks warming. Her breaths coming a little harder and faster.

He ran his finger under a particular shelf. Felt the slight nub, pressed it, and a secret door popped free.

Matilda let out a delighted laugh, which was swallowed by a soft gasp when she entered the hidden room—temperature controlled with a soft light around the edges of the floor that warmed to a soft glow as they entered.

In the centre of the tight space stood a glass stand containing a single piece of paper.

"That," said Henri, his voice low, reverent, "is the letter assuring recognition of our independent sovereignty from

France by Louis XIII in 1642. Bar a short stretch in the early eighteen hundreds, during the French Revolution, Chaleur has been under the protection of the Raphael-Rossetti family ever since."

And it looked as if it would remain that way at least a while longer.

Matilda leaned closer, eyes drinking in the curve of the paper, the sweep of the signature with its slight splatter of ink at the end, the royal seal. "Henri," she whispered. "This is the real deal."

"Are you a letter *writer* still?" She'd written every night when he'd known her. Pages of descriptive joyful prose.

She lifted her eyes to his. They were dark in the low light. Gleaming. "It's been a while."

"Why?" he asked, moving around the case to look over her shoulder at the document. And so he could be closer to her. For while he'd been fighting it this entire time, and now a great weight had lifted off his shoulders, he couldn't remember why.

"No one to write letters to, I guess."

Her shoulders hitched, and he caught a waft of her scent. Sweet green apple, summer sunshine, and something earthier that further loosened the knots inside of him.

"You were writing to your mother," he said, the memory coming full circle.

Her eyes closed a moment before she blinked them open. "It was kind of our thing."

"How so?"

"It started when I went to boarding school—common for kids from farming families. Rose hated it and lasted a year before convincing our parents to let her head home and finish via correspondence. I'm not sure it was right for Eve either. She was such a sweetie, kind of shy, romantic, but she changed during those years. While I was so excited to *be* somewhere new. Every week my mother would send me a new book—history or travel or biography—with a hand-written letter tucked into the first page, telling a tale of how it had moved her."

She let her finger touch the corner of the glass, as if the tactile connection made it more real. "Letters became a fascination. Letters between soldiers at war and their sweethearts. Between authors and their siblings. Between poets and their muses. The intimate stories behind the public facade."

She took a breath and turned to face him. Close enough that even in the low light he could clock the myriad blues in her bright eyes.

"I'd been chasing such a letter when I was in Vienna. I so wanted to tell you all about it that night, but with Andre's rules stuck in my head I was terrified I'd lose access to…well, to you."

The room seemed to shrink around him. Then her mouth kicked up at one corner and the urge to touch the spot with his thumb, to tug at her bottom lip, to kiss her there, to know if she tasted as she once had, was like a whirlpool dragging him under.

"Tell me now," he said.

"Well, the owner of the letter was an old lady who spoke very little English. I had to drink copious amounts of very strange tea to earn her trust. Then I had to convince her to send her most treasured possession to the other side of the world for authentication."

"Did you, convince her?"

"I did. People find it very hard to say no to me."

Henri smiled. And time seemed to beat between them then, or perhaps that was just him. The whump of his blood as it rocketed around his body. Reaching places he'd long since believe atrophied. Lost when he'd lost her.

"I've missed this," Henri whispered, the words falling from his mouth, before he even felt the words coming. "I've missed the way I am with you."

Matilda blinked in surprise. Of course she did. For he no longer had the right to say such things. To assume—

"I've missed you too," she said, her voice breaking.

And there it was. The great, churning truth they had been politely dancing around for days. Despite past hurts, despite the fact that they were different people now, the connection they had once shared had been meaningful and bigger than both of them.

Matilda leaned into him then, her fingers lifting to curl into his shirt, her forehead landing against his chest.

And while he felt sure that giving in to the feelings swarming through him was a dangerous game, a beginning with an end built in, it was a battle already lost.

Henri slid his arms around her back, slowly, relearning the shape of her. Her softness and her strength. When she curved her body into his, he hauled her close and held her there.

"I'm sorry we didn't break the rules sooner," she said. "Didn't tell one another everything. It feels like so much wasted time."

His hand moved to her chin, lifted it gently, held it so that she could not look away. "You have nothing to apologise for. Even if you had told me everything, back then I didn't wish to be known."

Her body trembled against his. Or perhaps it was him, vibrating with the need to touch her, all of her. When her tongue darted out to wet her lips, the urge to chase it with his own was nearly his undoing.

Instead his thumb traced her cheekbone. His fingers moving into her hair. The thick waves spilling over his wrist like warm silk.

Rather than their twin storms colliding, as they once had,

the air around them seemed to settle on a whisper of a sigh, as Matilda's hand gripped his shirt tighter and she lifted onto her toes.

As if it was the most natural thing in the world, Henri met her halfway.

When his lips found hers, he felt as if he'd been marking time. Waiting for this moment his entire life. The touch of her mouth tentative yet familiar. The taste sweet and fresh and completely her.

Soft, learning sips soon grew into something slick and loose and achingly lovely. And when her hands crept up his chest, around his neck, so that she could press herself harder against him, a small moan of pleasure rose in the back of her throat.

And it became a slow burn of moving hands, shifting bodies. Slanting mouths and the world beneath him tipping and swaying.

When Matilda's leg wrapped around his, as if she wanted to climb onto him, *into* him, he lifted her into his arms. Carried her till her back hit the wall. His mouth tracing her jaw, her throat. Drinking in her scent—

Then came a whistle and footsteps, then the squeak of shoes on polished wood floor, followed by a familiar voice, saying, "Cousin? Ah."

Andre appeared in the doorway, his expression comically surprised as he said, *"Merde. Je suis désolé,"* before disappearing back into the library proper.

And like a bucket of cold water had been tossed over them both, Henri slowly came back into his own body. To find he had a hand up the back of Matilda's T-shirt, while hers was inside the collar of his, the hem of which had been pulled free of his suit pants.

Her spare hand went to her mouth, whether to hold back a groan or a laugh, he could not be sure.

Slowly they disentangled themselves from one another. Her hands moving to do up a slipped button of his shirt, his smoothing the back of her top.

"You okay?" he asked.

"Depends what you mean by okay."

Henri moved so he could see her face. The wild wide eyes, the plump moisture of her lips. "We need to go back out there, eventually," he said.

"Or," she said with the insouciant lift of a shoulder, "you could order your cousin to go away. Surely being a sovereign prince has some advantages."

Henri laughed. Then allowed himself a few last moments to imprint how she looked on his memory before he took her by the hand, led her out of the hidden room, and gently shut the door.

Andre was leaning against the back of a couch, his gaze on where their hands were joined. "I'm sorry, am I interrupting something?"

"Not at all," lied Henri.

"It's just… I heard a letter was delivered. With the parliamentary seal."

Matilda, behind him, leaned her forehead against his back a moment before she moved away. "I'll leave you guys to it. Thank you," she said turning to walk backward, facing Henri, "for showing me your special room."

"Is that what they call it these days?" Andre asked.

She shot Andre a look, crossed her eyes at him, then waltzed out the library door.

"The envelope?" Andre reminded him. And Henri, who had tucked it onto his pocket for safekeeping, passed it over.

And while Andre poured over the data, Henri was left to wonder how far things might have gone if Andre had not found them when he had.

When the referendum was still a possibility, there was a

chance he might yet be able to make choices that affected only him. But now that hope was gone.

Everything he did from now on had to be about the crown.

Whether that included Matilda, or excluded her, was still to be seen.

Hours later, having heard nothing from Henri since she'd left the library, Matilda paced her suite, the phone ringing and ringing and ringing as per usual when she tried to call Eve.

Because she *really* needed to talk to someone who was Team Matilda. A big sister who had been obsessed with romance novels growing up seemed just the ticket.

Which was why, rather than hanging up, as she usually did, she left a sassy message. "Hey, Evie, this is Matilda. Your sister. Remember me? Just calling to let you know I just kissed a prince. Who might be my husband. And, since that's just the kind of thing you'd once upon a time have eaten up with a spoon, I thought maybe you could talk me down from the ledge I'm currently dancing on."

She pressed finger and thumb to her temples.

"Or not. Whatever. Anyway, if you actually listen to this message, don't tell Rose. And get off your high horse and call Ana. She's sweet and none of this is her fault. And—"

The phone beeped when she ran out of time. She tossed her phone on the bed, then followed, landing on her front like a starfish.

What had she been thinking?

Things had been going nicely with Henri. They'd been learning about one another, communicating well, being supportive. Keeping things cool and measured—the opposite of whirlwind.

Then she'd grabbed him by the shirt and kissed him.

But, oh, what a kiss. Like the reins had snapped, and all

the feelings and memories and longing they'd been holding back had been set free.

Yes, they'd kissed before. A lot. But they'd been so young then, swept up in the drama and responsibility-free disconnect of a holiday romance.

Now, with context and experience and maturity at their backs, *new* feelings were at play. Respect and fascination, comfort and a sense of safe harbor. Feelings that ran wide and deep.

Which might have been a nice thing, a lovely thing, if there wasn't so much at stake.

She shimmied up the bed, found her phone and texted Rose. Needing a solid reminder of just what that thing was.

Rose: Hey! What's up?

Matilda: What's up with you?

Rose: Johnno had a fall, broke his wrist. Sally stood on a rusty nail so had to head into the Marni clinic for a tetanus booster. River went missing for half a day before we found him locked in the coat closet.

Matilda: So, nothing out of the ordinary.

Matilda rolled onto her back, holding her phone above her, feeling a comforting stab of guilt at not being there. Not that she'd ever been much good at mustering, or patching up busted staff, or remembering to shut gates. But she was a queen when it came to keeping up morale.

Matilda: Need me to come home?

Coward.

Rose: We are fine here without you!

Matilda: Well, that's nice to hear.

Rose: We miss you terribly, of course. River especially.

Matilda: He would.

Matilda: He's a good dog.

Matilda: Unlike the rest of you.

Rode: *laughing emoji*

Rose: Stop fretting. This is my vision board, not yours.

Matilda's face felt unusually warm as she typed.

Matilda: Meaning?

Rose: Helping to run a cattle station isn't what you really want to do with your life.

Matilda: Says who.

Rose: Anyone who's ever met you.

Rose: Gotta go. Talk soon. xxx

Matilda stared at the messages, reading over them again. Then she sat up, feeling as if she'd been smacked across the back of the head. Twice.

Sure, she'd stayed home not because being a farmer was her dream and not because she wanted to be there more than anywhere else, and… What was the point she was trying to make again?

Feeling tetchier now than she had *before* she'd contacted her sisters, Matilda pushed herself off the bed and went to her desk. Tried to write, but couldn't see the words on the screen. Tried to check her emails, but couldn't concentrate.

And in the end found herself back outside Henri's office.

Pacing to the door, then walking away. Then pacing back to the door again, where she rapped three times and entered.

He sat behind his desk, looking harried. His gaze was on his monitor as he typed something, his brow furrows deep and ingrained.

"Sit," he said, "I'll be a minute."

Matilda perched on the chair across from his desk feeling like she was back in the principal's office—having to explain herself inciting a strike unless an excursion to a museum she wanted to visit was included in the curriculum. Generally causing havoc in the name of trying to get whatever it was she wanted.

Rose's words came back to her: *Helping run a cattle station isn't what you want to do with your life.*

Henri chose *that* moment to stop stewing and sit back and say, "Matilda—"

This time she got in first. "We kissed," she blurted.

A beat slunk by before he sat forward, steepling his hands on his desk. "I noticed."

Matilda curled her feet up onto the chair in the hopes of holding in the sensations rocketing through her. "Kissing wasn't part of the deal."

"As far as I remember we had no deal bar—"

"No promises, no plans." *Right.* "So kissing is okay then?"

Something in the set of his shoulders, the directness of his gaze, made her sure he was about to enact a royal decree, negating all chance of further action between them. Until he breathed, deeply, his nostrils flaring as if he'd caught her scent on the air. And she wondered if he was only just holding himself together too.

"I think creating a set of rules that we must arbitrarily follow has not worked out so well for us in the past. Trusting that as adults we can communicate, consider, and make decisions on the fly seems sensible."

"Sensible," she repeated.

When all she could think was that it hadn't only been her mother's passing that had kept her at Garrison Downs. The ease with which Henri had cut her off had meant she no longer trusted her gut instinct. Which until then had been her superpower. Her driving force.

"If you agree," she said, choosing her words carefully, "that following a set of arbitrary rules has not worked out so well for us in the past, why was I the one who was punished for breaking them?"

Henri baulked. "I'm not sure what you mean."

"My note, of course."

She was doing this now? Yes, yes, she was. For it was all tangled up in the moment in her life where everything had shifted. The spanner jarred in the mechanism of her life, all her dreams coming to a grinding halt. Where she'd lost more than her mother—she'd lost herself.

Henri's jaw ticked. "I'm not sure how that relates—"

"The rules, Andre's rules. We stuck to them, faithfully, the entire time. Until I wrote that note. And then..." She swallowed, unprepared for the emotions it would reignite. "Then nothing. Silence. As if we had never been."

Henri blinked. And blinked again. "You were the one who left, Matilda."

"But the note!"

Henri ran his hands over his face, then looked at her as if she'd started speaking another language. "I did what I had done each day that week. Woke early, kissed your sleeping forehead. Made my side of the bed, even while knowing yours would stay rumpled. Took the speedboat into town to go for a run, pick up coffee, breakfast, the paper, provisions. I came back just before lunch to find a torn-off scrap of paper on my pillow stating you were sorry and you had to leave. And I never heard from you again."

Matilda opened her mouth to argue, before she realised there was a huge disconnect. "I couldn't contact you, Henri. I had no way. Which is why I left all my details. On the note."

Something in the way Henri stilled, his aura cooling before fading away entirely, had Matilda's instincts crackling. Like they were finally, *finally* sputtering back to life.

"Matilda," Henri said, his words slow and careful. "There were no details on the note. All it said was *I am sorry. I had to go.*"

She waited for the rest. But it was clear he was done.

"I… Yes, that's how it began. Followed by the news that Rose had called, and my mother was in a coma. I scrawled down my phone number, my address, my email." She swallowed. "And I asked if you would follow me, when you could. I knew I'd need you during what was to come."

Henri sat back, his hand tight on the back of his neck. "There was only one note."

"Only one."

"The one I found on your pillow."

"I never put it on my pillow…"

The trauma of that event meant Matilda remembered only patches of that morning, but those she did she remembered with aching clarity.

Her phone buzzing and buzzing, waking her from a dream. Rousing her far earlier than she preferred, and finding a dozen messages from Rose.

"Henry?" she'd called. "Henry!" Then, realising Henry

would have only just headed off, she'd gone looking for Andre and found him sitting on the bow, reading a book.

Andre had looked up. Stood up. "Matilda, what is wrong? Are you hurt?"

"It's my mother. I have to get home."

"Of course." Andre had pulled out a phone and begun speaking in fast French. She'd recognised some of it—plane, Australia, and her name. He rang off with a clipped *"Merci."* Then said, "My agent is organising a flight now."

"Thank you. But what about Henry—"

"You need to go, correct?"

She'd nodded.

"You pack. I will organise transport to get you to the airport. Diplomatic channels will get you on a plane within the hour." Hand to his heart, he'd said, "I will look after Henry."

And so, in a tunnel of panic and fear, she'd tossed her gear into her suitcase. Made sure she had her phone, passport etc. Then she'd ripped a page of notepaper from a notepad with the name of the charter company atop, and written:

I'm so sorry. I have to go. My sister messaged. My mum is really sick.

After an infinitesimal pause, she'd written her name, address, email, and phone number. Signing off with *Please come, if you can. I love you. M*

Back in Henri's office, her blood rushed fast behind her ears.

"I didn't leave the note on the pillow, Henri. I gave it to Andre."

Henri found Andre in the billiard room, lining up a small six. "I need to talk to you. Now."

"I have no news as yet," said Andre, rolling his shoulder and hunching over the cue. "Though I am on it. Every breath I take."

Henry leaned over and picked up the six. "I just spoke with Matilda. About the note she left me the day she left."

Andre let the cue slacken, then stood tall. "You read it. Several thousand times over the next weeks."

"She claims it was longer. Conveying how I might get in touch with her. And that she gave it to you." Henri looked to his cousin. Searching for tells.

There, the quick sniff that showed he was damn well lying.

He tossed the ball back onto the table and turned away, his hand tight to the back of his neck.

A few breaths later Andre spoke again. "I did what I felt I had to do."

Years spent learning how to curb his emotions was the only thing keeping Henri from grabbing the cue and snapping it in half.

"Why?" he gritted out, his voice raw.

"You think Boris and Lars are your only bodyguards, cousin? I've been doing the job since I was eight years old."

"What does that even *mean*?" Henri threw both arms to the side, then paced down the opposite length of the table. Better that than expel the energy coursing through him by decking the man.

"Augustus was not the only one who saw your potential. Who hoped that you might one day make it to the throne."

Henri ran a hand over his face and stared at his cousin. Feeling as if he was seeing him for the first time.

Andre took a step his way, before something in Henri's bearing pulled him up short. He held out placating hands instead. "When you were determined to make that trip, to have your... Summer of Freedom, I left a very cushy gig running my nice café slash bar, right on the beach, so that I might stick to you like glue. I created the Privacy Pact, acting like a goddamn Doberman, curating our group with people I hoped I could trust not to give you away. People on whom I had enough dirt it was worth their while to stay quiet."

"Why?" Henri asked. Which felt like the least of all the questions building inside of him.

Andre threw his arms in the air. "In case you did something stupid, something self-destructive that might follow you forever and make it impossible for you to trust that you could do this job." Andre stared at Henri. Waiting for the penny to drop.

"Say it," Henri growled.

"You did it anyway. You married Matilda."

"She was not some mode of self-destruction. She was—"

"What?" Andre asked, his voice careful, his tone patient. As if now that he'd admitted to what he'd done, putting their long, trusted relationship at risk, he had no qualms in saying his piece if it knocked something loose inside Henri.

But Henri did not wish to be knocked. Did not wish to feel loose. Or out of control. It was enough for the red mist to begin to clear.

"So you are admitting you read the note, altered it, and knew how to get in contact with her, all these years."

Andre's hands lifted to his hips and he shook his head. "I'm telling you, cousin, I knew who she was within an hour of you first meeting her."

Henri took a step back, wasted years roiling like a stormy sea inside of him. "You knew who she was, and you never told me."

"You never asked."

Henri looked to Andre in disbelief. "Are you kidding me, right now?"

But Andre was not to be cowed. "You were a prince of Chaleur. You had access to all the same contacts I did. And you were the favourite of Augustus, a man who clearly believed the world owed him whatever he desired. If you wanted to find her, you only had to ask."

It wasn't true. He was so smitten with her, he'd have followed her to the ends of the earth, if he'd had the slightest chance. Wouldn't he?

"Just as you could also have found out if the marriage was valid, years ago. Hell, you could have had it annulled."

"No," said Henri, remembering the wedding night, and the days after, in such detail it made his body temperature kick up a notch. "I could not."

Andre crossed his arms. "Never thought I'd see the day I know more about Chaleurian law than you. Turns out, unsurprisingly, a particularly randy forebear created a law allowing for royalty to have a marriage annulled anytime it suited. If you wish it, it can be done."

Henri ran a hand over his face and laughed. There was no humour in it. In fact, he rather felt like kicking something. Andre would do nicely.

Until Andre said, "You can't do it though, can you. And you know why? You are a romantic, cousin. And a martyr. A doomed love affair has suited you and the image you have of yourself far more than a holiday fling ever could. And she was nineteen, Henri, you not much older. The lives of thousands of people were about to turn on what you did next. *My* people."

Andre's words hit like a sling of arrows. Every one of them uncomfortable, painful even. Possibly because they were true. If he'd followed, if he'd been with Matilda when Augustus had abdicated, would he have stayed? Or would he be exactly where he was now?

It did not make Andre's unilateral decision to take it out of his hands forgivable.

"Henri," said Andre, begging him to see sense, "If my

choice was so very wrong, and you still want to be with her, marry her. Now. For real."

Henri shook his head. "It's not that simple."

For they'd only just begun to know one another again. And even if their attraction was still there, a living breathing thing, asking her to take on a role he'd fought against his whole life would be the single most selfish thing he could ever do.

But if the decision was out of his hands...

Hands clasped tight behind his back, Henri tilted his chin toward the door. "Go," he said. "Right now. And find me that marriage license."

Andre nodded, with ever so slightly exaggerated deference. And then he was gone.

Henri strode through the château in search of Matilda.

As if he was back then, on that yacht, he spotted reminders of her everywhere. A pair of sandals by the front door. A coffee cup left on a hall table. She could just as easily be walking a barefoot circle in the rose garden or hanging in the kitchen eating croissant scraps with the cook.

In the end he found her sitting by a window in the downstairs sitting room, her feet curled up onto a chair, a book face down on her knees as she looked pensively down the front drive. Wistfully. Wanting out? Or wanting home?

"Matilda."

She flinched and turned, her expression miserable. As if she too had been contemplating what might have been if Andre had let things run their course.

"Are you okay?" she asked, uncurling from the chair. "You took off like a bat out of hell."

"I'm fine," he said.

She glanced at the hand he held out, swallowed, then padded the final few feet to take it in hers.

Better than fine, he thought, tugging her a little closer. For his focus was sharp, his way clear. "Do you want to get out of here."

"Always," she said with a laugh. He felt like a beast for having kept her cooped up as much as he had. "Is this a Celeste suit-type trek, or are we winging it?"

"No Celeste suit." *Never again.* "I'm thinking something a little different."

"Oh?"

"I've not taken a break in the two years since my coronation. Not once."

"Really?" she said, looking him up and down. "But you seem so chill."

The glint in her eye had him moving in, watching as her chin lifted and her throat worked as the air between them disappeared. "I was thinking...we go south."

"We are about as south as we can go before landing in the Mediterranean."

"Not if we go to Garrison Downs."

Matilda's whole face changed. Shock, then joy, then a flicker of uncertainty, then back to joy. "Are you serious?"

"Deadly."

"But how? Why?"

He lifted a hand to sweep her hair from her cheek, and her bright blue eyes deepened. Darkened. The wish to kiss her again, to sweep her off her feet and into his bed, was potent.

"You've seen mine," he said, his voice rough as his gaze followed the sweep of pink warming her cheeks. "Only fair you show me yours."

Matilda blinked her way out of a haze, and shook her head. "Are you okay? Is there a chance you've come down with a sudden fever?"

He lifted his gaze back to hers. To that face. Open, trusting. Captivating. "You've come all this way in the hopes of protecting your home. And you're asking for my help to do so. I think it's only fair I see it in person."

Her smile was quick, but quickly chased by concern. For him, or on her own account he could not be sure. All he knew was that he had to do this. He had to know what he'd missed.

"Who will be in charge with you gone?" she asked.

"I will. It's called working remotely."

She looked to the door. "Is Andre okay with this?"

A muscle ticked in his jaw. "Do you want to show me Garrison Downs, or not? Because if I have to invite myself again—"

She shook her head, laughed, then threw herself into his arms. "I want you to come. Please."

As he held her, he thought how every step of his life, *including* what he'd thought had been that single summer of freedom, had been shaped, *reduced*, by some document or other.

A birth certificate, a royal decree, a political poll, a torn note, and now a looming marriage license, all of which decided the path his life would take.

He needed to do this. He needed to know what life might have been like if the choice had been his.

For whether he gave himself up to history, did what others deemed the right thing to do, or went his own way, in the end the choice had always been his.

CHAPTER SEVEN

Garrison Downs,
August

DESPITE THE COMFORT of a private plane, and diplomatic fast-tracking, after twenty-four hours in the air—including a light plane from Adelaide to a local airstrip—then a wild drive through miles of Mars-like Outback terrain that Matilda had *insisted* was part of the experience, Henri was relieved when Matilda slowed at a grand wooden archway, bull horns carved into the arch, heralding the entrance to Garrison Downs.

It was late afternoon, with patchy gum trees sending long shadows over the bumpy driveway, only to finally reveal a sprawling mansion, with wide front verandas, a high gabled roof, and stunning landscaping.

"So, what do you think?" Matilda asked.

"I admit I had pictured a few cattle grazing lazily in a paddock. A wraparound porch. Flies buzzing around a small dam."

Matilda grinned as she pulled the rented four-wheel drive up to the front of the house with a scrape of tyres. "We have all that. Just a million times better."

Henri alighted from the car and stretched his legs, red dust kicking up from the slide of his boot and coating the bottom of his chinos. For all the blinding sunshine, the cold was real. As if everything was bigger here, harder, tougher.

He liked it very much.

A collie jogged around the corner of the house, tongue lolling happily.

Matilda cried, "River! Here, boy!"

The dog bounded to her on old legs, stopping only as she dropped to her knees and pulled him into a tight embrace, her face nuzzling into his neck as she murmured sweet nothings.

When she scrambled back to her feet, the dog came to Henri. He held out a hand for a sniff. "River?"

"River. Was a working dog, now retired. Blossom, Rose's dog, and Lavender will be around somewhere. Come on, let's get your bag inside before the red dust makes havoc of the pretty leather."

"One moment," he said, pulling out his phone to tap out a message to Boris and Lars, who they had dropped at a motel in the nearest town, Marni, much to their protestations. He assured them he'd arrived safe and sound, as if they hadn't already secreted some kind of GPS tracker on his person.

Then, hooking his soft leather bag over his shoulder, he followed Matilda toward the house. Gum trees swished and sang overhead. The caw of a crow broke the heavy silence.

When his gaze dropped to Matilda, who had fallen into step beside him, it was to find her expression hopeful, vulnerable, as if it mattered to her what he thought.

There was also a glimmer of wariness. Which she soon explained, turning to walk backward toward the house, River jogging gently at her side.

"One small thing. My sister Rose, *still* doesn't know about you."

"In what capacity?"

"In any capacity. I rang to let her know we were coming, but Lindy—our housekeeper—answered saying Rose, Aaron—the head stockman—and a handful of the skeleton winter staff are at the Outstation for a few nights. Mobile coverage at the house is top-notch, but there's not much in the way of reception without a satellite phone out there."

She tilted her chin toward the beyond.

"So, she's in for a nice surprise upon her return?"

"Something like that," Matilda said, then turned and jogged up ahead to open the front door.

Once inside, she motioned for him to dump his bag in a mudroom hidden behind an elegant door, the space filled with gum boots, rain slickers, wide brimmed hats in lieu of woollen winter coats and scarves that would be found in such a room back home.

"Are you too tired for the grand tour?" she asked.

"No," he said, curious gaze taking in wide halls, cream walls, high ceilings, the polished wood floors, and antique furnishings.

But, eyes twinkling, she took his hand again and pulled him back outside. "Not there," she said. "There."

Then tipped her chin toward the acres of dry red landscape beyond.

It was midwinter in this part of the world and yet Henri could feel sweat dripping down his back.

Riding, to him, consisted of weekly lessons in a dressage ring. Polo tournaments in his teens. This was a completely different beast. The saddles were harder, the reins worn in for other hands. The terrain untended, all rocky pastures and tufty hillocks and boulder-filled streams.

Matilda, on the other hand, looked utterly at ease. Her hands loose, her shoulders relaxed, her body moving gracefully as the horse beneath her trotted briskly up unexpected rises and slowed to a lolloping walk any time they hit flat earth.

As if she could feel his eyes on her, she glanced back. Then with a quick smile, the kind that set off sunbursts behind his eyes, she made a clicking sound and set off at a canter toward a nearby hill.

Henri wished he had a moment to collect himself, lest his chances of ever producing a Raphael-Rossetti heir became moot, but soon his horse, a docile mount named Beryl, followed Matilda's mount with no help from him.

Atop the hill, low sunlight speared shards of pale gold wintry light through a canopy of trees, dappling the leaf-covered floor and creating a kind of dreamscape as Matilda slowly eased her way through, picking out a path.

Cocooned by the shuffle of hooves and soft nasal breaths of the horses, Henri could not have felt further away from the challenges of court. And soon his mind wandered.

An heir. It was a concept he'd refused to entertain, having been one himself and borne the scars of it his whole life. But wasn't that part of why he was here, in this wild, remote, upside-down place? To stretch the possibilities. To think new thoughts. To question everything that had brought him to this moment.

"All okay back there?" Matilda called. "You're terribly quiet."

That's because I'm having an epiphany.

"Just trying to stay upright."

She snorted. "I checked your seat. You're doing just fine."

He readjusted his grip and trotted so that he took a tree to the left while she took it to the right, and soon they were walking side by side.

"You've checked my seat?" he reiterated.

Her mouth twitched but she kept facing forward. "It's one of my favourite things about you."

With that, she was off again, a snicker and a trot and they burst from the copse to find themselves atop a ridge. Matilda pulled to a halt, and Henri—with Beryl's tacit help—pulled up beside her.

Henri wondered if she had any clue that she was humming; some song or other, or a tune that only she knew. It was something she did when she was feeling contented.

"We run the land as far as the eye can see. Saltbush and mallee scrub, rocky hills, sudden ravines, and shady canyons. Hectares of flat grazing lands marked by well-kept fences and neat cattle grids and dams filled with bore water or river water. We've all got the kind of water rights our neighbours would give up a kidney to get their hands on."

She resettled her hat with its wonky rim a little further back on her head. The glow of the setting sun painted a vibrant pink and orange haze on the horizon, making her blue eyes appear even brighter than usual.

"Pretty great, don't you think?" she asked, a smile tugging at the corners of her uptilted lips.

"I'm not sure I've seen anything more beautiful," he said.

A grin lit her face as she turned. It faltered when she saw his eyes were only on her.

"Henri," she chastised. But her eyes softened. Her gaze tracing the edges of his face.

With no need to be subtle here, or feel concern that some servant or citizen might notice his lingering gaze, Henri drank her in. Boldly. Blatantly. As if this place demanded it.

If the Matilda he'd known all those years ago had been a burst of joy, and the Matilda who'd popped up on the street in Côte de Lapis had been an extraordinary disruptor, Matilda Waverly on home soil was nothing short of transcendental.

"Rose can't give up this place, Henri," she said, her expression no longer sunshine and light. "It's her lifeblood."

"Could you?" he wondered, and then when her eyes widened he realised he'd said it out loud.

At least he hadn't said what he was really wondering, which was, *Could you give it up for me?*

Another reason why he'd had to come. So that he would be under no illusion as to all that he'd be asking her to leave behind if things worked out the way he was beginning to expect they might.

"Come on," she said, her voice soft as she turned her horse on the spot and nudged him back toward the Homestead.

Early the next morning, Matilda sat on the back porch of her childhood home, laptop open to the book she'd been working on, cupping a mug of cooling coffee, legs curled up on her favourite chair, a mohair blanket tucked around her legs, River snoring gently at her feet.

Ready for when Henri might stumble bleary-eyed from his room, the way she had after collapsing in a heap her first night in the château.

Till then, she soaked in the crisp wintry air. The earthy scents. The sky that went on forever.

If the front of the Homestead was a showpiece often featured in articles about the great homes of Australia, the veranda by the back door, with its older furniture, the view through gaps in the watery grey of the ghost gums to stockyards, sheds the size of airplane hangars, was the working heart of the Downs, where they truly lived.

And yet, despite how familiar it all was, how ruggedly beautiful, whether it was Rose's "vision board" text, or the amount of time she'd spent away, Matilda felt a kind of disconnect.

"You all right, Tilly?"

Matilda turned to find Lindy, their housekeeper, standing at the top of the back steps by the big, dented metal bell. It

harked back to generations gone when it had been used to
call in hungry workers with a holler of, "Grub's up!" The
girls had known the sound as their signal to cease whatever
mischief they were up to and come inside.

"Sorry, Lindy," Matilda said, "did I wake you?"

"Not at all. Plenty to do in a house this size, even if the
rooms are mostly empty these days. And now you're back,
there's more cooking and cleaning for sure."

Matilda went to laugh, to make some joke, falling into
her happy-happy joy-joy role as easily as sliding into old
slippers. But instead stopped herself and said, "Can I help?"

"I'm all good. Now, can I get *you* anything?"

Matilda held up her coffee. "I'm covered."

"And your…friend?" Lindy asked. "Does he need anything?"

Matilda had introduced Lindy and Henri when they'd
come in from their ride.

Once Lindy had herded him into the green guest room,
to "wash off the day," Lindy had asked Matilda if she was
absolutely sure there wasn't enough space in her *own* large
bedroom for such a dashing friend.

"As far as I know Henri is still gone to the world," said
Matilda. "If he rouses himself anytime soon, can you tell
him where I am?"

Lindy nodded. Then, with a glorious sigh, went back inside.

Leaving Matilda to watch the winter sun melting the frost
from the grass and the station stirring, and think about this
place. What it meant. And what they might all be willing
to do to protect it.

The way Eve had been acting since the reading of the
will, as if she'd somehow *known* about the affair… Would
she actually care if Garrison Downs was lost? Matilda was
certain that deep down she would.

Then there was Ana, who had no connection to the place at all. Yet she could. If they managed to pull this off, what an amazing opportunity it would be for them to cement their sisterhood.

And then there was wonderful, hardworking, caring Rose, for whom Garrison Downs was her life's dream.

Matilda looked toward the back door, thinking her way to where Henri slept. And she knew, even if this place wasn't what *she* wanted anymore, she'd still go a long way to protect it for those she loved.

"Tilly?"

Matilda coughed on her Vegemite toast, as she turned to find Rose moseying into the kitchen an hour later, covered in dirt from head to toe. She threw down her toast and ran to her sister, enveloping her in a hug.

"Hey!" said Rose, laughing, her arms out to the sides. "Are you sure you want to be doing that. I reek."

"You smell perfect."

Rose gave her a quick squeeze before peeling herself free, then heading to the fridge for a half bottle of orange juice, which she downed in one go.

"What are you doing back?" Rose asked.

It gave Matilda the perfect opening to say, "If Lindy hasn't spilled the beans as yet, I brought a visitor."

Rose stopped drinking.

"He's in the green guest room. Twenty bucks says he's still face down on the bed, snoring."

"He?"

"Yes, *he*."

"And he's a snorer?"

"Well, no, that was just a figure of—" Matilda snapped her mouth shut at Rose's quick smile.

Though it was quickly followed by a frown, brimming

with big sisterly concern. "And there I was thinking you've been spending your days staring down musty paintings and gorging on Nutella crepes."

"Sorry," said Matilda. "I wanted to wait for the right time to tell you. So as not to worry you."

Rose cocked a hip against the bench. "Ought I be worried now?"

"About Henri? On the contrary." Then, "But there's more."

Matilda told her. How they'd met, how they'd adventured, how they'd said "I do." Rose's face remained impassive until Matilda mentioned their mother, and a finger lifted to press against her lips.

"After Dad's will, I had to find out. In case our situation satisfies the condition."

"Oh, Tilly—"

"There's more still," Matilda said, holding out a staying hand. "You might want to sit down for this next bit."

Rose levelled her with a look. Before turning to click on the kettle.

"Fine. But I warned you. His name is Henri Gaultier Raphael-Rossetti. And he is a prince. But not just any prince, the Sovereign Prince of Chaleur."

After a few beats, Rose said, "Well, I'm glad he's not just *any* prince. If so, I'd have said to put him in the lilac guest room."

Matilda blinked. "You are being very blasé about this."

Rose popped a tea bag into a mug with the Marni Cup logo on the side. "That's because I know."

"*What* do you know?"

Rose pulled the band from her ponytail, then retied it, a sign she wasn't as cool about all this as she was making out to be. "Eve told me."

"*Eve?*"

"After you called her and left a cryptic message about—

let me see if I have this straight—*kissing a prince who might be your husband*, she called me to give me a right bollocking. How could I have let this happen?"

While it hurt that Eve hadn't called *her*, and while it must have been a tense phone call, Matilda was glad they'd at least spoken.

"My actions are not your fault. Or your concern."

"I think," said Rose, "it's the thought of our little sister out there, trying to save us all. That's what I was trying to say the other day. This is not your responsibility. We are not your responsibility. We will find another way."

"And if we don't?"

Rose looked at her then, not as a *little* sister, but as a sister in arms. "You do realise, even if by some miracle you end up with a marriage certificate in hand, Eve and I would have to magically find ourselves husbands as well."

"And Ana," said Matilda. "Don't forget Ana."

"How could I forget Ana!" Rose asked, hands flailing, before she regathered herself. "Sorry. That came out more harshly than I meant."

Rose blew out an exasperated breath before she put down the mug, came to Matilda, and wrapped her in her dusty, dirty, wonderful arms. "Tell me about him, so I can be forewarned."

"Henri?"

"Yes, Henri, unless you have a duke stashed here somewhere too."

"Ha-ha. Well, he's…he's lovely. Smart, and generous. Stubborn, determined, works too hard. Shy, I think, a little. Or introverted, maybe. He's well-read, loves Whitman. He's better at the wheel than he is in the saddle. He's openminded, but strong in his convictions. And he's working hard to make his country the best place it can be."

"And he's awake." That from Lindy, who'd appeared at

the kitchen door. "I heard the shower going in his room just now. Sorry, you asked if I could let you know."

"Thanks, Lindy," Matilda said, standing straight as her nerves switched on one by one at the thought of seeing him again.

"And you left out *gorgeous*," Lindy stage-whispered. Then to Rose, she said, "Just you wait and see."

Rose raised an eyebrow Matilda's way.

"Fine, yes, Henri is gorgeous. If you're into tall, dark, built, stupidly handsome royal types."

"Meh..." said Rose. Then, "That's a lot of nice things you had to say about the guy. Is it possible that you have feelings for him?"

"Rose," she said, feeling heat sweep into her cheeks.

"Is it?"

"I did love him, once upon a time."

Saying the words out loud, Matilda felt the rush of them. As if the feelings were freshly laundered. Clean, crisp, and bright.

Not that it mattered. It wasn't the point. Taking into consideration distance, duty, backgrounds, responsibilities, challenges they couldn't hope to foresee—love was complicated under *normal* circumstances. Add the situation in which her family had found itself, and who he was, and it would be a disaster.

"I'm going to shower," said Rose, checking her watch, "then head back out, so if I don't get to meet your prince among men in the hall now, I will see you at dinner. Okay?"

"Done."

Matilda found Henri in the hall.

He had showered, dark finger tracks ran through his hair, a Superman curl swishing across his brow. His cheeks had pinked in the cool air, contradicting the hard angles of his jaw. And rather than his usual smart suit, he wore jeans, a thick woollen jumper, and boots, his adorable attempt at farm chic.

"Morning, sunshine," she said, belying the thumpity-thump of her heart that had begun when Rose had asked if she loved him and was yet to subside. "Hungry?"

"Ravenous."

She handed him a piece of Vegemite toast and watched him muscle his way through it as if it wasn't offending every single one of his taste buds.

"I was going to take a walk," she said. "Want to join me?"

"So long as you never make me eat whatever that was ever again, I'll follow you anywhere."

It was a line, meaningless, and yet it lodged in her chest like an arrow.

Seriously, Tilly, get a grip.

"Warm enough?" she asked, when they stepped outside.

"This is balmy compared with winter back home. When we get snows, we get *snows*, the mountaintops covered, the aspens laden. You think Chaleur beautiful now, you should see it come Christmastime."

She opened her mouth to ask if that was an invitation, then remembered herself.

They spent a lazy morning ambling around the Homestead grounds, meandering past the Old House, staying clear of the Settlers Cottage due to its ghosts and mega snakes and all the things that had made it out-of-bounds when they were kids.

And Matilda tried her best *not* to think about the feelings she was feeling for Henri. Not when he stopped, breathed in deeply, and marvelled over the clarity of the air. Or when he reached out to take her hand to help her jump over a fallen tree.

Not even when he begged to spend the afternoon in his room, which had its own small lounge and desk with a view, like every guest room in the Homestead, to "check in." And didn't demur when she set herself up on an upholstered chair in the corner of his suite to work on her book while he worked at running a country. For it had become their ritual, that's all.

After one phone call that left him rubbing both hands over his face and into his hair, she said, "Tell me something you *like* about being prince."

He looked to her and laughed. A real laugh, loose and trusting and free. The sound moved through her like liquid heat.

"I was asked the same question recently by a second grader and I struggled to find an answer."

"It has to be the fervid adoration, though, right? Like that day on the street in Côte de Lapis? *'Henri, je t'aime!' 'So handsome, Henri!' 'You were always my favourite, Henri.'*"

He twisted in his chair so he was facing her. "So, I *am* your favourite. I did wonder."

"Pfft," she said, "you're like third, maybe fourth, on my list. There's Prince Charming. Prince Caspian. Flynn Rider becomes a prince when he marries Rapunzel, right? Straight to number one."

Henri smiled the smile of a man who knew better.

How? How did he know? Was it obvious that some switch had been flipped since coming home? That while her defences had been down, her sister had asked her a simple question and she'd turned to jelly.

"Your turn," he said. "What did you love most about growing up here?"

"Compared to what you've told me about your childhood, I might seem like I'm showing off."

"Try me," he said.

When Matilda realised what he was doing—asking the questions he knew he *should* have asked her back then— she capitulated.

"Fine," said Matilda, putting her laptop aside. "It was bliss. Surrounded by animals and trees to climb and staff who felt like family. Our father…" Her heart bucked. "He was built for running this place. Physically tough, financially savvy, quietly charismatic. While our mother was elegant, fiercely loving. She couldn't wait to see how we all turned out."

"She'd be very proud. I'd bet a kingdom."

Matilda lifted her eyes to his, to find a brimming intensity in his gaze. "If only you *had* a kingdom, not a mere principality."

"Alas." Henri smiled. His eyes midnight dark and so focused on her Matilda could barely breathe.

Why did you really make me bring you here? she wanted to ask.

If he said, *Because I adore you now as I adored you then, and it broke my heart to see you go, and if I'd only known how to find you I would have come on wings of fire*, while she sat in the house her father's guilt had built, she wasn't sure she could trust that it mattered.

And if he said anything other than those words, her poor reanimated heart might never recover.

Then the bell at the back door rang across the Downs.

"What on earth—" Henri said, flinching in his chair.

Matilda laughed, the tension releasing from her body a blessed relief.

"That'll be Rose calling us in for dinner. Ready to meet my sister?"

Henri stood and ran both hands down the sides of his jeans, as if he was nervous to meet Rose. And if that wasn't her favourite moment of the trip home so far, she couldn't say what was.

"Come on, Your Highness. Let's get this over with." She slid her hand into the crook of Henri's arm and led him unto the breach.

CHAPTER EIGHT

DINNER WAS…INTERESTING.

Lindy—having created a veritable feast in Henri's honour—nearly tripped over her tongue when Henri stood to help her carry the Waverly roast beef to the table.

While Rose made sure Henri knew the entirety of Chaleur could fit into Garrison Downs ten times over. Though Matilda watched her slowly become #TeamHenri when he asked salient questions about their stud stock and her favourite brand of tractor.

When Rose finally excused herself, claiming the need for an early night, she shot Matilda a glance to say, *Fine. He's lovely. But I'm just down the hall, and I know where to hide bodies.*

Matilda, too buzzed to go to bed, offered Henri a tour of the house proper. And Henri accepted.

"And this," said Matilda, as she stepped through a large doorway, "was my father's office."

The banker's lamp on the desk was on low, the lamp by her mother's chair in the back corner glowing softly. Both on a timer that switched them on every day at four in the afternoon.

It had never occurred to Matilda why that was, it had simply been. But now, with both her parents gone, and her version of their romantic history all muddled in her head, she realised *her father* must have kept it going after her mother had died. A reminder of his wife every single day.

"You okay?" Henri asked.

She blinked away the sheen in her eyes. "This room, it holds a lot of memories."

"Rooms can do that," he said, squeezing her arm gently as he swept by.

And she realised as she watched him move about the room, the warm light playing over his features, that he did understand. In fact, he might understand *her* in a way no one else ever would. Her sisters included.

Those crisp fresh feelings that had come over her in the kitchen that morning rose up again. She tried swallowing them down, but they would not be stopped.

She'd loved this man once, fiercely, with her entire being. And while he had changed, at his core he was the same kind, patient, inquisitive, warm, secure man.

Despite the fact her belief in forever love had been shaken, so much so that the book she had been working on so furiously of late was a collation of letters from *doomed* love affairs, was it possible that she—with time, with care, with courage—could really feel that way again?

He looked up. Caught her gaze. Raised an eyebrow in question.

"Look at this," she said, grabbing the remote from the coffee table in a panic. She moved to the centre of the room to show Henri how the artwork at the back of the room slid into a cavity in the ceiling to reveal a large screen her father had used for important video calls. "Pretty snazzy, huh?"

Henri's smile was warm. As if he knew exactly why she was babbling. And Matilda's heart twisted when it hit her how much she'd have loved to have introduced Henri to her dad. And her mother too. They'd have spoken fast French and debated politics. Her mother would have *loved* him.

Maybe, just maybe, that was the thing that hurt most of all. Not the secrets or the lies, but the fact her parents were gone. Gone before she'd had the chance to really know them. Before they had the chance to truly know her.

"This desk," said Henri, dragging Matilda back to the present. "It's Dutch?"

"A gift from the Royal House of the Netherlands in fact. Do you know them?"

"Rather well," Henri said with a smile.

"They're big fans of Dad's grain-fed beef."

"How old?" Henri asked, bending to take in the details.

"Two hundred years, give or take."

"Two hundred, you say?" He ran his finger along the edge of the desk. Then he dropped to a crouch to look more closely. Before his gaze lifted to hers. "Come here."

It took half a second for Matilda to realise what he'd found, and she was at his side in a heartbeat.

He took her hand, guiding it till she felt the catch. A hidden locked drawer. Right there, for anyone who knew where to look.

Matilda opened her mouth to call for Rose. Or for Lindy to go find Rose. Then stopped. She needed this. Needed answers. Needed some connection to her father that existed outside of the damn will.

Grabbing a letter opener, she jammed the thing in the hidden lock and jiggled till some part of the mechanism snapped.

Heart beating in her throat, she yanked the drawer open. And inside… It was the mother lode. In every way. For this drawer belonged to Rosamund.

Flicking through the pile of papers, she found her mother's will, including reference to the generous trust funds she had bestowed on her three daughters. Cards the girls had written to her—birthday, Christmas, Mother's Day.

And all the letters Matilda had sent. From boarding school, from university, from the summer she'd gone away.

The summer her mum had been unwell and not told a soul, knowing it would bring Matilda home.

Matilda's hand shook as it lifted to her mouth, to stop the sob gathering there.

"Matilda?" Henri said, his hand gentle at her back, his voice raw as if seeing her upset was cutting him to pieces. "Can I get someone? Can I do anything?"

"Stay." She reached back and held Henri's hand where it was. A lifeline. Essential. As she realised, like the lamp in the corner, her father had kept her mother's papers, near, right till the end. That *was* love. She was *certain* of it.

"Medical records," Matilda said as she pulled a thick folder with tattered corners and yellowed papers from the bottom of the drawer.

"From that summer?" Henri asked, moving in beside her. Cocooning her in his warmth. His support.

Matilda shook her head. "Several months after I was born."

Matilda's heart beat heavily as she skimmed terms such as self-harm, ideation, postpartum psychosis. And a long hospital stay.

"Oh," she said on an outshot of breath. Her mother had suffered terribly from postnatal depression after she had been born. For months, by the look of things, before a diagnosis came through. Around the time her father had had his affair.

Her fingers numb from shock, the pages spilled to the floor. She followed, dropping to her knees. Her hand landing on a notebook with a red leather cover, soft and aged. The edges of the pages were dusted in gold, her mother's initials embossed in the lower right corner.

Not a notebook. A *journal*.

Matilda turned and leaned against her father's desk. The solid wood keeping her upright.

She opened the book to find the first entry, written in her mother's long looping hand. Black ink, never blue.

*I write these words upon instruction from experts who
seem to believe it will help. I write these words so that
I might find my way back to my daughters, my life,
myself. I write these words to commit to my circumstances, and to bend them to suit my needs, the needs
of my girls, and the needs of my family. I write these
words as I choose to flourish, and no longer to fade.*

Tears running down her face before she got to the bottom of the page, Matilda read on. Immersed in her mother's
beautiful, painfully honest tales of her first few years at the
Downs. How stunning she'd found it, and how isolating.

She wrote of how unexpectedly raw and deep she found
her love for her daughters, and how bleak it had felt when
those feelings did not come. How she had worn her husband
to a nub as he had tried to "fix things." Wanting nothing of
him. Until he turned to another woman's arms.

Until one day she saw past her homesickness to know this
was deeper. The disconnection from her youngest, with her
sweet nature and her husband's bright eyes, was nonsensi-
cal. Once a diagnosis had been made, Holt had been there.
At her side the entire time. Promising that if she was back,
so was he. Promises that had saved their family. Their life.

Throat clogged, her face damp with tears, Matilda closed
the book and held it to her heart.

In trying to understand how her parents' love had been so
fractured, she'd been looking in the wrong place. Blaming
her father for making a wretched choice. This journal, this
unfurling of pain, pressed onto the pages like flowers between the pages of a heavy book, showed a different truth.
That circumstance had come at them, hard. And they'd beat
it back. Together.

Matilda looked up to find Henri crouched by her, his

hands over his mouth, his gaze on her. As if her pain was his pain.

She sobbed, choking on her breath, as the last vestiges of control she had over her feelings imploded. And she felt it all. Rage, sorrow, joy, love, hurt, disappointment, forgiveness.

Then Henri was beside her. Sitting on the floor of her father's office, running a hand over her hair, making soft cooing noises, and speaking in deep sonorous French, while she curled herself into his chest and cried.

After leaving Matilda with Rose—the sisters needing to deal with the revelations in their mother's journal together—Henri made his way to his room. And lay there, staring at the ceiling, his body aching with a kind of psychic pain, after seeing Matilda in such distress.

It was near three by the time his eyes finally drifted closed, only to jolt awake when he heard music.

He pushed back the covers, rubbed both hands over his face, then, still dressed in the jeans and woollen sweater he'd worn to dinner, followed the sound to find a room of plush white carpet, an elegant bar at one end, a piano in the centre.

Moonlight poured through the large French windows, sparking off a chandelier before dappling Matilda's hair and shoulders as she sat behind the instrument, her fingers trailing over the keys, playing something simple, slow, sweet, and haunting.

When he moved into the room, she looked up. Her eyes red, her expression raw.

"Did I wake you?"

"I couldn't sleep." Henri moved toward her, watching her fingers run silently over the keys. "What were you playing?"

"Nothing, really. Our mother wanted us to have lessons, culture being under her purview. I lasted about six months, got to the point that I could play 'The Entertainer,' and was done."

Henri noted the loose T-shirt draping off one shoulder, the striped flannel pyjama bottoms with a hole in the thigh, the fluffy socks on her feet. She looked so rumpled and warm he wanted to scoop her up and take her back to bed. His bed. Where he could take care of her, soothe her, make her feel better all night long.

The fact he'd been fighting the same desire for days, *weeks*, and had managed to not voice it so succinctly inside his own head, said something about the decision-making properties of three in the morning.

Instead, he looked to the pile of letters sitting haphazardly atop the piano. "What are they?"

"From my mother's drawer. The letters I wrote when I was traveling. I wanted to see if I had ever mentioned you."

His gaze lifted to hers, but she was ruffling through the papers before handing him one. And as he read, her voice leaped off the page. Pure joy and light as she told a tale of art and music, falling snow, and train rides through tunnels that went on forever. And at the bottom a PS.

I kind of met someone, Mum. It's been a bit of a whirlwind (sound familiar?) but I just know you'll love him too.

Henri read that final sentence a few times over, absorbing Matilda's certainty, after only a few days of knowing him, that she'd one day bring him home.

He folded the letter and handed it back to her. "Move over," he said, motioning with a nod for her to make room on the bench.

Her breath hitched, a shudder running through her, when his arm rubbed against hers. Her emotions erratic. But then she stayed, leaning there against him.

"Can you play?" she asked.

"Can I play," he scoffed gently. Then he lined up his fingers and banged out an enthusiastic version of chopsticks.

Matilda's fingers closed over his, drawing them to her chest. "Shush!" she said, laughing. "You'll wake Rose and Lindy!"

Henri looked toward the door, chagrined. "Are their rooms near?"

"Other side of the house. And my sister sleeps like the dead."

When he looked to her, her eyes were luminous in the moonlight. She shifted his hand so it nestled over her heart. And he knew he could have kissed her then. Taking up where they'd left off in the library. He knew he could touch her, hold her, taste her, lose himself in her as he'd once done. Back when losing himself had been his sole goal in life.

Only now the thought of losing himself felt like a forfeit.

He wanted to own his time. To do hard things and do them well. To consume life, to make a difference.

And despite the ache in his chest every time he looked at Matilda, for so much of this new focus he felt was because of her, he knew she was in a far more fragile place. And that he had to take care.

Not that she seemed to agree, for she lifted his hand, placed her lips on a knuckle. When he did not object, she kissed her way along them all. Her tongue swiping along the final dip, sending a shard of heat right to his core.

Then she uncurled his fingers and lifted his hand to cup her cheek. And she leaned into his touch, sighing, as if all the big feelings that had been flooding through her finally had somewhere to go.

Perhaps that's what he could be for her? The vessel into which she could pour her pain. He *could* take it. He could take it all.

Breathing out, he traced the dark smudge beneath her eye

with the pad of his thumb. Then the furrow above her nose. Then he leaned in and pressed a gentle kiss to her forehead. And closed his eyes so that he could absorb her warmth, her soft scent, the energy always coursing just below the surface.

"You should get some sleep," he murmured against her skin.

"I don't want sleep. I want to be right here. With you."

And his heart began to beat a steady tattoo. *Mine...mine... mine...mine.*

"Matilda," he said, his voice rough. "It's been a hell of a day."

"Henri," she returned, his name a breath. A *wish*. "It's been a hell of a few years. But having you here, finally, and knowing that you never saw my note, that you didn't cut me free as if I had meant nothing..."

His jaw tightened to the point of pain. "Matilda—"

She cut him off. "You know I've been tinkering with a book the past couple of weeks, right? I've actually been collating material for it for years. Letters. Hundreds of letters. The theme: doomed love affairs. *That's* how I've been choosing to expend my creative energy, trying to convince other people that love sucks."

She sniffed out a sorry laugh. "But that's not who I am. It's not who I want to be. I want—I want—"

Then, before she said another word, she grabbed him by the sweater, pulled him to her and kissed him. Hard. Her eyes closed tight, as if the *connection* was everything. As if she might expire without it.

After a long, loaded beat, Henri pulled away. A last chance to be rational. But the sound she made, the moan of displeasure at the lack of him, was like a siren call. And he knew he was done for.

His hand delved into her hair and when he kissed her again, a soft slow slide of mouths, everything deepened, softened. She mewled, moving against him, and he knew that if there was a single forfeit he could abide, it was to her.

Her arms slid around his neck and with one smooth move, she lifted off the stool and straddled him. Her back brushing the keys, creating a jangle of notes. The dissonance a hastening thing, a soundtrack to the feelings building quickly inside of him, cacophonous, unchecked.

The hand at her neck tugged her T-shirt over one shoulder to reveal the swell of her breast. The thin cotton catching on the uptilted sweep of her nipple, a shadow of colour. Pure temptation. He traced her collarbone with open-mouthed kisses and moved to the curve of her breast.

Matilda rolled into him. Then again. Both feeling too much and not enough.

If he had learned patience, it was in preparation for this very moment. The slow millimetres, eking out her pleasure, tasting her, relearning her tells. While Matilda, impatient as ever, chased connection, begged for relief in every shift of her body, every ragged breath expelled from her lungs.

And soon Henri was running the high wire between adrenaline and exhaustion, desire and care. Till she leaned back against the piano, draped over the thing. The growl he emitted at the sight of her, had her eyes blinking open, dreamy, only half there. And then she smiled, as if she knew exactly what she did to him. The control she could wield if she so chose.

And just like that, fear slipped into the cracks where regret had long lived. Fear that every day they spent together was a day closer to a time when they would have to part, and this dreamy expression would haunt his dreams for years to come.

Matilda curled herself back into his embrace. And she lifted her hand to trace his forehead. "You are thinking so hard right now."

He didn't deny it. Though when her hand disappeared

into the back of his hair, caressing, soothing, tugging, he couldn't remember why he'd been thinking anything at all.

He saw the cotton still snagged on her nipple and ran his thumb over the shadow. When he did it again, she followed his touch. He leaned her back again so that he could suck the cotton into his mouth, taking the skin beneath between his teeth, and a ragged sigh escaped her mouth.

When it became too much—the constriction of the hard seat and piano—he pressed the stool back. It resisted against the plush carpet, so he kicked it away, and it fell with a dull thud.

Then he lifted Matilda onto the piano proper, her feet landing gently on the keys in a tinkle of sound. Her hair fell over her shoulders in messy waves, catching on her tangled lashes.

His hands, full of the cotton of her shirt, pressed into her waist. Then lifted, slowly, dragging her T-shirt with them, until he finally found skin, warm and lush. Pinked with desire. He tilted her right back until her head landed gently on the piano lid, her back arched, her toes playing notes he'd never forget.

He shucked her shirt higher and pressed his face to her belly. Circling her navel with his tongue before lapping at the dip, again and again as her body began to tremble. His hand holding her in place, he kissed his way along the low rise of her soft pyjama bottoms. Scraped his teeth along the edge of her hip bone. Low enough to catch the scent of her.

As if she could feel the feral rising inside of him, she sat up just enough to whip her shirt over her head, reaching for him, saying, "Please, Henri." Before she began clawing at his sweater.

His gaze caught on hers, the universe therein. "I didn't stop to grab any protection when I followed the sound of your song."

She winced, then laughed. "I wasn't exactly planning

this either." Then she lay back, her head hitting the piano lid with another light thud.

Matilda. Naked to the waist. This was not a problem so far as he saw it. A world of ways he might pleasure her crashed over him, like waves on a stormy coastline.

He started by tracing a small scar beneath her left breast with his thumb, then followed it with a kiss. He caressed the lower incline of her breast, watching the way goose bumps sprang up in its wake. He followed the path of the flush that washed across her skin with the flat of his hand, then the rise of her ribs, the gentle mound of her belly.

When she gasped and bit down on her bottom lip, arching into his touch, he took advantage. Hooking his fingers into the soft elastic of her pants, he tugged them down her legs, over her feet, in one swoop, then tossed them over his shoulder.

An arm thrown over her eyes, her knees bobbed together and separated. Fretting. Teasing.

Till with a sweep of his thumb, he tugged her underwear aside and ran his nose up her centre, his tongue following with a long flat sweep. And she bucked against him, her breath leaving her in a gasp.

"More?" he asked, his voice rough.

"More," she begged, letting her knees go. And when her hands moved to his hair, tugging, directing, he took her legs, swinging them over his shoulders, and went to town.

The taste of her, the heat, the way she quivered under his ministrations—he could have lived in that place, holding her on the edge, savouring her pleasure for the rest of his natural life.

Her hands gripped his hair, her body restless, gasping, and open, until she lifted her hips to his mouth, her legs spilling outward, strained, a goddess in his arms. Before her breath caught, and time stopped for several long perfect seconds, before she shuddered around him.

Saying his name, sobbing it over and over again, till he felt her pleasure and her pain, her relief and her release. As if it had been inevitable.

When she whispered his name, just the once, on a long outward breath, he kissed her once more, saving his place, before he gently pressed her knees together and let her feet lower to the keys, where they scattered another low sweet tune. Then he circled his hand over her belly, chasing the quivers that kept going and going and going.

Eventually, she let her arms fall to the side, and she huffed out a laugh. Then another. Then laughed till she could scarce draw breath.

"That's not the reaction I was hoping for," he said.

She shot him a heart-stopping grin. "I was just thinking we were never even allowed to wear *shoes* in here." Then she laughed again.

With that, she rolled gracefully off the piano. Landing on legs that near gave way, thanks to him. Then she turned to him, all but naked, flushed, ruffled, and absolutely beautiful. Then held out her hand. "You coming?"

"You tell me," he rumbled.

"The Prince has a mouth on him," she said. Before a shiver racked through her. "Yes, he does."

He took her hand as she led him out of the room, finding it hard to walk, considering the hard-on pressed against the zipper of his jeans. His entire body was wound tight as drum.

She gathered up her clothes as they passed. Then over her shoulder said, "I'm really glad you're here, Henri."

No matter what happened from here on in, Henri was too.

Early the next day Matilda crept out of her bedroom, a blanket tossed over her T-shirt and pyjama pants, and padded into the kitchen.

With sunlight filtering gently through the skylight, angling shards of cream over the muted whites of the Hamptons style space, she made herself a quick piece of toast, then set her laptop up on the bench and opened a brand-new file.

The doomed love affair book was going on the backburner. She was filled with too many new ideas, lush ideas, of collections of letters with redemption themes or reunions, the kind that uplifted and gave people hope.

Rose walked into the kitchen and put her morning coffee cup in the sink.

Yawning, Matilda said, "Morning."

Rose looked to Matilda, her gaze still a little raw after the hours they'd spent going over the journal the night before. "Feeling better?"

Matilda put a hand under her chin. "Much. I promise. You?"

"Better," Rose agreed. "Your handsome prince still asleep?"

"I assume so," said Matilda around her toast. She'd left him face down, naked in her bed, his beautiful arms tucked under his pillow, the dark sweep of his hair falling across his cheek. If she wasn't so famished, she'd have climbed right back in.

Rose laughed into her coffee. "You have *the* worst poker face. If it was you trying to win Garrison Downs in that poker game, we'd have been screwed." Then, "But you really are feeling better?"

Matilda gave Rose the benefit of a beat of thought. "I really am. It's a lot—the journal, the medical records, learning Mum had had postnatal depressions after she had *me*. But it's also a relief to have some inkling as to why things went the way they went."

"Mmm," said Rose, something in her expression making Matilda sure *she* wasn't quite so ready to let things go. But she'd get there, Matilda was sure of it.

"Though there is one thing," said Matilda, "that is stuck

in my craw. Do you *remember* any of it? Remember them fighting when we were little? Because I honestly don't remember a harsh word. Unless Dad walked dirt through the house, but then he'd make Mum laugh or pull her in for a quick kiss and disarm her into forgiving him."

Rose, older than Matilda by a few years, said, "It was definitely different in the Old House. We were all crammed in, with Nanna and Pop, living on top of one another. Things improved once we moved in here." Then Rose's expression changed. "Why do you ask? Did you and Henri fight?"

Matilda *pffted*. "This has nothing to do with us."

Well, it did. A little. Okay a lot, actually. But not the way Rose imagined. More that she wondered if she was the way she was—leaping about, making sure everyone else was happy, avoiding conflict at all costs—because of how things had been when she was young.

"So there is an *us*," said Rose.

Matilda had to backtrack to get her meaning. "What? No."

"Tilly, the guy followed you here, from La Whoop-Whoop. I think *he* thinks there's an 'us.' So if you don't, then you might want to be careful."

Careful? After the night they'd spent together more than making up for lost time, it was a bit late for that. She'd never play the piano again without coming out in a sweat.

"It's *fine*," Matilda insisted. "We're on the same page. We both know the deal."

The reasons they were together, after all, had not changed. Despite the new intimacies, the long walks, the deep conversations. Despite a night so raw and tender and true, they were not *together* in any definable way.

As for the indefinable... It *was* different than before. Less whirlwind, more anchored. As if time, age, experience, heartache, and loss made them aware of the rarity and the fragility of what they'd once had.

As to what they had now—

"Tilly." Rose motioned to Matilda's mobile, buzzing at her elbow.

Saved by the phone, she said, "It's Ana."

After a beat, Matilda answered. "Hey, Ana Banana!"

Rose's eyes widened. Okay, so maybe that was a little much.

"Tilly?" said Ana after a long beat, her voice breathless. Then, "Sorry, I think I pocket-dialled you."

"All good. Where are you?"

"I'm at the dawn markets with my mother, picking out fresh fruit and vegetables for my grandparents' restaurant. At dawn."

"The things we do for family," she said, shooting Rose a look. Rose poked out her tongue.

"Any news regards the will?" Ana asked, her voice softer, as if she'd found an alcove somewhere.

"Rose would know. I'll put you on speaker." Rose waved a wild hand at Matilda, but it was too late.

"Hi, Rose," said Ana.

"Hi, Ana," said Rose. Then, her face scrunching, said, "Nothing new."

"Well, hopefully a plan will present itself."

Matilda pointed at her own chest and mouthed, *See.*

Rose shook her head slowly. Then she motioned that she was going to head off. Duty called. The station waited for no woman.

"Sorry," said Ana, "I have to go. My mother is a fast walker, and I'll lose her in the arugula section if I'm not careful."

Once they'd rung off, Matilda gave up on her book, made herself a coffee, then went to find somewhere to sit so she could call Eve. If voice messages got through to her, then that's what she was about to get. A barrage, starting with news of their mother's journal.

But when Matilda reached the back door, she saw Rose had only made her way as far as the tree swing in the back yard. Their dad had built it when they were younger—a plank of wood, hanging by chain from the branch of a big old gum tree, the seat just big enough to fit the three of them, even now.

The swing moved gently as if with the motion of the wind as Rose looked out over the gardens and beyond them to where the morning sun painted swathes of the most brilliant colours across the wispiest of clouds.

Then Rose lifted a hand and—

Had she just wiped a *tear*? Surely not.

Matilda watched, unblinking, and… There! Rose wiped the back of her hand across her cheek before tipping forward, her face landing in her hands as her shoulders moved in wracking sobs.

Oh, no. Oh, *Rose*. Matilda *knew*; it wasn't about their mum's journal. Rose had worked her way through that the night before. It was about Garrison Downs. About Ana. About the damn lawyer. About the gargantuan task ahead of them if they were to tie this up.

It was a much-needed reminder of why she was there—to show Henri what she was fighting for, so that when the time came to make a decision, it would take a harder man than he to deny her.

CHAPTER NINE

HENRI WOKE TO sunshine pouring through pale blue curtains. Book quotes framed in rustic frames on bright white walls. It took a beat to remember where he was, till he rolled over and caught Matilda's scent on the empty pillow beside his.

And the night came back to him. Every glorious moment.

Grinning like a fool, he sat up, his feet pressed into the carpet, and ruffled a hand through his messy hair. He grabbed his phone to find missed call after missed call from Andre.

He'd been letting his cousin sweat while also letting his cousin's words percolate. For while Andre's method of saving him from himself had been indefensible, he hadn't been altogether wrong.

Matilda's life till that point had been so cloistered, and Henri had not been in the mental space to make such a big life choice. Getting to know one another, as adults, these past weeks had been a slower, deeper, richer experience. One he could not bring himself to regret.

His phone buzzed. A message from Celeste. He opened it to read:

Celeste: Your Highness. Prince Andre has been in touch, querying if, and I quote, "there might be adequate enough internet service in the back of beyond so that he might engage you in a video conference call."

Henri laughed before he could stop himself, his cousin's tone clear as a bell. And he decided Andre had been in the doghouse long enough. Then Celeste's next message came through and the laughter turned to dust in his mouth.

Celeste: Your Highness. Prince Andre now says to let you know that he has a result on the mission you commanded him to undertake.

This was it.

Whatever Andre had uncovered, after this everything would change. A plan would be put in motion. Promises made and kept, so as to ensure the faith and happiness of his nation, which he had come to discover truly mattered to him.

For he had promised to be their prince. To work to uphold their values and needs. And that had to be his guiding light.

He showered quickly, dressed, then went looking for Matilda, finding her lying on a chair on the back porch, a blanket over her shoulders, her arm flung over her eyes. River panting happily on the floor beside her.

"Matilda," he said, quietly.

She lifted her arm and squinted. Then made to sit up. All flapping arms and messy hair, the mark from the cushion she'd been lying on pressed endearingly into her cheek.

"Henri," she said. "Sorry. I must have fallen asleep."

The reason why flickered through his mind like an old movie. Henri cleared his throat. "Last night, you showed me the screen in your father's office, the one he used for video calls."

"I did? I *did*. That feels like a hundred years ago."

"Andre has been in touch asking if we can conference in. He has news."

"News?" she asked, mid-stretch. Then she stilled. "*News* news?"

Henri nodded.

"Right. Then let's go." Matilda was on her feet so fast the old dog let out a bark, wagged his tail, and followed as she led them away.

Andre's face wavered onto the screen and Matilda tried to work out where he was in the château, which was mentally less fraught than finding herself back in her father's office, readying herself for *more* news that would irrevocably change her life.

"Are you done with your spat?" Andre asked, settling himself in. His eyes were unusually tight, sunken, no doubt due to the middle-of-the-night hour in Chaleur.

Henri slid an arm along the back of the couch that they'd turned to face the screen on the back wall. "A mental health break is not a spat. Welcome to the twenty-first century."

As if hearing a note in Henri's voice he'd not heard before, Andre stopped fidgeting and looked at his cousin. Then at Matilda. Then at River, who was curled up on the couch beside her, forcing her to snuggle into Henri. *Good dog.*

"Let's have it," Henri growled.

Matilda shot him a glance, looking for signs of the man who'd whispered sweet nothings to her all night long, spiralling her over the edge again and again. Only to find herself looking at a prince.

"Here goes." Andre leaned back, crossed his ankle over his knee. "For a marriage to be legal in Gibraltar, you have to have been in situ for twenty-four hours."

"Which we were, right?" Matilda asked of Henri, the note of hope in her voice telling. While Henri's cheek ticked, he did not look her way, and the first shiver of concern slithered through Matilda.

"You also had to be married by a registered officiant," Andre continued. "As it turns out a ship's captain having a legal right to officiate a wedding at sea is an urban myth. In the olden days when sea journeys lasted months, it was commonplace, but no longer."

Henri's head dipped. In disappointment? Or *relief*?

Before she could check...by smacking him on the shoulder or grabbing him by the chin and saying, *Hey, remember me?* Andre said, "It turns out *our* captain, bless him, was also a licensed marriage celebrant."

Henri's head snapped back up.

"So that's it then?" Matilda asked, no longer hopeful so much as wildly anxious.

And it hit her; she wanted this, not only because of what it might mean for the future of the station, but she *wanted* it. For herself. For the life she wanted. A life with Henri.

"Not quite," said Andre, holding up a hand.

And Matilda whimpered.

Henri looked her way. *Finally.* Only his gaze was dark, hard. If he too was struggling to marry his desires and his duties, he didn't show it.

"There is also a lodging of paperwork portion to the proceedings," Andre was saying. "Which has to occur *before* your nuptials, and it was not."

Gaze locked on Henri, begging him to give her a glimpse of the warmth beneath the facade, Matilda waited for the next twist.

She didn't have to wait long.

Andre breathed out hard, and said, "You, cousin, and Matilda, are not, and have never been, legally married."

Henri shot to his feet, leaving Matilda bereft for the lack of him beside her. She could hear her breath rushing behind her ears, could feel the blood moving under her skin. Her left hand came to her mouth as tears gathered in the corners of her eyes and panic swelled in her throat.

Her thumb began twirling the ring on her right hand the

way it did when she was stressed. Henri's ring. A treasure, a talisman that had kept her connected to him across time and space. One that had never truly belonged to her.

She knew her mind ought to have gone straight to Garrison Downs, to Rose and Eve and Ana and what it meant for them that she had fallen at the first hurdle, but her gaze followed Henri as he walked around the couch, his hands on his hips, his head down, as if he too was working his way through a thousand thoughts at once.

"Cousin?" Andre said. And Matilda flinched, for she'd forgotten he was still there.

Henri looked up at the screen, his face pale. Then he closed his eyes, nodded, and said, "Thank you, Andre. Get some sleep, you look like hell. I'll make plans to return to Chaleur as soon as possible."

What? No!

Yes, the entirety of the time they had spent together had been predicated on the marriage being valid, but this couldn't be *it*.

So much had happened, so much had changed. They'd come to know one another, truly, only for Matilda to discover that the man she'd fallen in love with was only a fraction of the man she knew now.

Yet Matilda could already feel Henri slipping away.

Andre lifted his hand in a half-hearted wave, his gaze raw, sorrowful, as if he too was disappointed in the outcome. Then the screen went black.

Matilda, her life swirling about her, plucked one thought from the air. Her mother's journal. How hard Rosamund had worked to have the life she wanted. Writing down every difficult word as if one day it might help her daughters do the same.

Matilda thought of Ana, quietly checking in. Eve quietly

checking out. And Rose quietly sobbing at the thought that they might lose all of this.

But Matilda had never been quiet, and she wasn't about to start now.

"So that is that," said Henri when he finally found his voice again.

And the certainty he'd felt in Matilda's bedroom only an hour before, that whatever happened his choice would reflect his commitment to Chaleur, had turned to ice in his bones. A dark fog had closed in around the edges of his vision, as if all the colour had been leached out of his life. Readying him, no doubt, for a life of challenging service, alone, to come.

"I am sorry," he said, still unable to look at Matilda, who was vibrating on the chair he'd abandoned, "that this puts you in a difficult position. That I was not able to help you with your requirements."

"Henri," she said on a soft huff of air that coiled inside him like woodsmoke. "You have nothing to apologise for."

When she uncurled herself from the couch, he moved further away. The last thing he needed was to catch her scent, feel her warmth, as if they weren't permanently imprinted upon him. "As I told Andre, I will make my way home as soon as possible."

"That's not necessary, Henri," Matilda said, reaching for him. Whatever she saw in his face had her whipping her hand back.

"No public announcement will be required," he said, making his way through a list of things that no longer needed to take up space inside his head, as if that might ease the pressure in his chest. "This is now a private matter. My people will not be affected."

As for him? He felt as if a future world he'd been imagining had been whipped out from under him to reveal that it had been built on a false floor all along.

He clasped his hands behind his back, rolled his shoulders, and looked between her eyes. Not trusting what he might do if he looked directly into all that bright blue.

"I hereby relieve you of any bond to the crown." With that he spun on his shoe and walked away.

"Wait!"

Henri flinched but kept on walking.

"Henri, come on," she said, her voice plaintive. "Stop with the imperious prince act for just a minute and talk to me."

When every survival instinct told him to walk away and never look back, to find a way to erase all memory of her, of even the possibility of her, his one chance of having something that was truly his own, Henry slowed. Then stopped.

"Matilda, please," he said. "This needs to be clear-cut this time. I beg you."

"I know. I get it. Just...hear me out. Please."

Henri turned, breathed deeply, and looked to her.

She stood by the chair, her hands outstretched, her expression not frantic as he'd imagined. Determined. "I know we said no promises, no plans, but you have to admit that neither of us have been following *those* rules. We have been living as if this news would go the other way. Planning for it even, if only in our heads."

He breathed in, breathed out—it was the best he could do.

"Apart from the lack of a single piece of paper, nothing has really changed. I still need to help my family, and now that you are locked in to the whole prince forever deal, you need a partner. And while I know I'm not classic princess material, I'm good with people, am a quick learner, and am not afraid of hard work. I'm offering to take on that role, right now, if you'll have me."

"Matilda," he said, barely able to make words. "Do you know what you are asking?"

"Yes," she said, her voice certain. Her bright gaze holding his. "A real marriage. Not for a year, for forever."

She took a step his way, her movements careful, as if approaching a wild horse that might yet startle and bolt.

"Just think it through. Last night proved, beyond any doubt, that we are both still attracted to one another. So that side of things will not be a hardship."

Henri shifted on his feet.

"And in the years since we parted, neither of us have found anyone more compatible. Or am I speaking out of turn—"

"No," said Henri, quietly. "You are not speaking out of turn."

"I can smile and wave. I've seen enough makeover movies to know that all it takes is a little keratin and teeth-whitening strips and boom, instant princess. I also adore your country—I mean, how could I not? The thought of delving into its history, perhaps even tracing more letters like the Louis XIII, is exhilarating to me. I think I can be of value to… To the crown."

Her hand moved into his vision then, her fingers slowly sliding against his as she took him by the hand. Her right hand, then the hand wearing his mother's ring. A ring he was now certain she had worn every day since he'd gifted it to her.

"You need me, Henri. As much as I need you. We can do this. Not some fanciful summer fling, but a partnership entered into with eyes wide-open."

The terms she was offering were carefully worded, clinical—companionship, compatibility, a partnership. The complete opposite of what he had proposed, telling her all the ways he adored her while holding her tight while on the bow of a super yacht, the soft air of the Mediterranean summer fluttering her hair across her delighted eyes.

Yet he found himself actually considering it.

The joining of two esteemed families, the parameters clear. What she was suggesting was a smart choice.

A royal choice.

She squeezed his hand and he looked up.

She smiled, but there was a flicker at the corners of her eyes. Showing him what it was costing her to lay herself on the line like this. And as if seeing into the future, generations beyond, he knew that she was it for him, and always had been.

Without Matilda, he would not marry. He would not bear an heir. And Chaleur would be worse off for not having her on their side.

But by accepting this offer, he would be tying her, intentionally, to a life that was no longer her own. Unless *he* could bear the brunt. Allowing her to choose where she spent her energy. Allowing her to be herself, completely. That he *might* just be able to do.

"Promise me," he said, his words like stone over gravel, "that you will not let anyone within ten feet of you with whatever the hell keratin might be. And that you will not smile unless you damn well feel like smiling."

She blinked, then laughed. "So that's a yes?"

"Stage one would be a gentle introduction to the people of Chaleur."

Matilda swallowed, hard, but her gaze held firm.

"Stage two, a press release proclaiming our engagement. We tell the truth—we enjoyed a romantic relationship some years ago and recently reunited. Stage three, Chaleurian law requires we enter into a binding contract, the Royal Marriage Decree, which is signed before parliament. Stage four, a royal wedding."

"And after that?" she asked, her gaze warming, then dropping to his mouth, bringing with it thoughts of the wedding night.

"And then we work hard. We live mindfully, with purpose. A life lived with a constant view to the future. Perhaps... Perhaps even an heir who, when grown, we will allow to decide for themselves, their relationship to the crown."

"A marriage," she said simply. "With plans *and* promises. I can do this. I want this."

"I want this," she'd said, not *I want you*. But he brushed it aside. Just as he had learned to brush aside his own needs, his own desires, his entire life.

Henri lifted her right hand, finding his mother's ring. When it wouldn't budge, he lifted the finger to his mouth, laved it with his tongue, then dragged the ring free with his teeth.

Two futures unfurled like ribbons before him. One in which he rose to the challenge of his position alone, and another doing so with Matilda at his side.

The decision, in the end, was no decision at all.

"Marry me, Matilda Waverly," he said, sliding the ring back onto her left hand, where it had always belonged. "Be my princess. Save your family farm."

From there it all happened fast, as fifteen thousand kilometres away in the middle of their night, the Chaleurian royal wedding machine cranked into gear.

Boris and Lars arrived at Garrison Downs within the hour, looking relieved to see both Henri *and* Matilda in one piece. Celeste—already in suit and heels as if she slept in them—was on near-permanent video call. A text to Matilda from Andre read Welcome to the family. Bonne chance!

After Henri promised Rose he would do everything in

his power to make sure Matilda remained Matilda, Rose hugged Matilda harder than she'd ever hugged her before.

And thirty-six hours later, they stepped off the royal plane in Chaleur to a shimmering tarmac and pale grey skies. A light summer rain bore down upon a brass band playing a rousing song Matilda didn't know.

Standing at Henri's side, but three inches apart, as was protocol, Matilda, in a cornflower blue dress she had found in Eve's cupboard, waved as if to a crowd, rather than a line of cameras and two rows of dignitaries huddled under matching black umbrellas.

Matilda murmured, "I guess I'm not in Kansas anymore."

Henri tilted his head to hers. "There is no right or wrong, not where you are concerned. Yes, there are traditions, and expectations, but I want us to shape this in a way that suits us. The last thing I want is for you to feel constricted."

Matilda nodded, fully aware that he was thinking of his own indoctrination into this life as a child. The way his uncle had made his life feel narrow and not his own. If *she* could help Henri not feel that way, take on some of load, it might go some way to thanking him for doing her this immense consideration. Because the balance was hugely in her favour.

Without thinking too hard about why, or whether it was the "right" thing to do, she lifted onto her toes and kissed Henri soundly on the mouth.

She felt his surprise. But then he made a sound, a soft growl that echoed inside of her, and when the stairs seemed to tip out from under her, she reached for him with her spare hand, gripping his arm.

When he pulled away his eyes were dark. Danger dark. His jaw a little tight, his smile raffish as he said, "Seems we have moved straight to Stage Two."

At the bottom of the stairs Celeste emerged as if from

thin air, collecting Matilda and Boris, while Henri—with Lars at his back—was taken to meet the waiting dignitaries.

Matilda, feeling the lack of Henri like a missing limb, looped her arm through Celeste's and held on tight. "I'm so glad you're here. I'm trusting you to get me through this without tripping over some heirloom or offending the national animal of Chaleur."

"The Cerulean Chaffinch."

"Who's that?"

"Our national animal."

Of course, it was.

Andre appeared on Matilda's other side. "So, you're back. Again."

"For good this time," she said, with a smile.

"Mmm. I'd ask if you were after his money, but I know what you're worth."

Matilda laughed, a loud, not so princessy bark. "Should I be concerned he's after mine?"

Andre smiled, despite himself. "I always did like you, Matilda."

"I know you did, Andre." And it was true. Despite what he'd done, she knew his heart was in the right place. He'd been Team Henri far longer than she had.

Together they reached the town car, and Boris moved out from behind her to open her door.

Andre moved in beside Celeste as Matilda slid into the back seat. "Keep an eye on this one for me, will you?"

Celeste gripped her folder a little tighter and said nothing.

"On Matilda's side already, I see. If not for the upcoming nuptials, I'd consider that insurrection." Andre leaned down, offering up a slow, meticulous, ever so slightly ironic bow, before he shut her door and swept away to reunite with Henri.

Celeste slid into the other side of the car and, before it

had even taken off, said, "I am in charge of your schedule if you would like an update?"

"Well, I was hoping to snatch a couple of hours to work on a letter I was sent just before we left. A truly gorgeous piece purporting to have been written by Elizabeth Barret Browning—"

"Non," said Celeste.

"Non?" Matilda parroted back.

Celeste waggled a finger. "There is much to do in preparation. You require staff. An updated, or at least an expanded wardrobe. As for—" Celeste leaned in, and stage-whispered "—the wedding dress... A designer must be chosen, measurements taken. Unless..."

Celeste glanced at Matilda's belly.

"No ho-ho," said Matilda, sucking in her tummy. "Henri and I are not in preparation of that."

Not yet. Though they had spoken, in their effort at being open and communicative, about the possibility in the future.

"D'accord," said Celeste. "We also require a new passport. And a speechwriter. And—"

Matilda held up a hand to stop Celeste's diatribe. "An hour. All I need is an hour."

"I'm sure you believe that," said Celeste, her face showing emotion for the first time ever, "but life from this moment on will not be the same. For you, Matilda, are to be Princess Consort of Chaleur. A position that brings with it import, history, privilege, esteem, power. You understand this? *Oui?"*

"Oui," said Matilda. For she had. At least she thought she did. She'd get there. She would.

She looked out the window to see the plane disappearing into the distance as the car swept her off the tarmac, while Henri, her touchstone in all this, was nowhere to be seen.

CHAPTER TEN

THE SUMMER FESTIVAL celebrations had begun with the summer solstice, then continued on for several weeks, with flower shows, baking contests, lake sports, fun fair rides, and the like. Upon returning from Garrison Downs, Henri agreed to take part in his fair share.

Meaning, despite his promise to himself to ease Matilda's load, he wasn't able to stop Celeste, who kept gleefully filling Matilda's calendar with meetings, lessons on the history of Chaleur, visits with stylists, and wedding planners. While anytime he saw Matilda yawn or droop, and insisted she ease back, she'd pat him on the chest, or tip onto her toes and kiss him, in an effort to distract him, before heading off to do more.

At the final event of the festival, the Annual Kinder Art Show, Henri listened with half an ear to a rather verbose patron, as a little girl with dark ringlets sidled up beside Matilda, tugged on her dress, then pointed to a painting of what looked like a tree.

Matilda's face lit up as she gathered her elegant blue velvet dress around her knees, and crouched to put herself on the girl's level.

After a short conversation, the little girl took the painting off the stand and handed it to Matilda.

Matilda's hand went to her heart. *"Pour moi?"* he heard her say. *"Merci."*

"Cinq euro," the little girl said, hand out at the end of a straight arm, chin raised, as if readying for the argument.

But Matilda had no intention of arguing. She coughed out a laugh, no doubt seeing a flicker of herself in the precocious girl. Then, glancing around, she plucked double the asking price in cash from a hidden pocket in her dress and handed it over.

The little girl's eyes widened, then she was gone, sprinting back to her parents.

Henri pressed a fist to his chest, to relieve the sudden tightness therein.

Matilda smiled at the painting, before tucking it under her arm, clearly chuffed with her purchase. She pulled herself to standing, wobbled a little on her high heels, then hid a long yawn behind the back her hand. Before she turned, breathed deep, plastered a smile on her pale face and went to find someone else to charm.

Which took half a second because the crowd enveloped her. Their impromptu kiss atop the plane stairs had hastened the timeline of their plan, and now everyone knew who Matilda Waverly was and who she would soon be.

Henri felt a moment of empathy for fairy-tale villains, for it took every ounce of royal training not to swoop in, sweep her up, take her home, lock her in their room, and force her to sleep for a week.

Andre sidled up to Henri, bowed to the patron, and carefully hustled Henri away. "Did Matilda just pay a four-year-old with cash out of her *own pocket*?"

"You must have imagined it."

"I give up."

Henri turned to his cousin. "Sorry?"

"I give up trying to protect you from yourself. I admit defeat. Your fiancée is stubborn, opinionated, uncontrollable. And now she gives from her own pocket… She's you, in a skirt."

Henri laughed, but he was so tired it came out as a sniff. "How do you think she is coping?"

"Brilliantly. Apart from the occasional rebellious flashes of ignoring protocol, or as the press are calling it, her 're-bellious Aussie flair.' She has them wrapped around her little finger. As for the rest of them—she is open, warm and they love her."

How could they not? thought Henri. And yet her capability had never been his concern.

The slow blinks. The crick of her neck. He could see her edges beginning to fray. He might have learned to forgive himself for the rocky path he'd taken to get to this point, but he would not be able to forgive himself for that.

"She's been walking the rose garden again," he said. "In circles. Like a caged cat."

Andre clamped a hand on his shoulder. "Good for her. Now I have to nab a fine painting of a dinosaur I spotted earlier before someone swoops in and buys it out from under me."

"I'm spent." Matilda kicked off her shoes, flinging them exhaustedly across the room.

The Art Show had been fun, mostly because they'd attended it together. A rarity—since she was trying to lessen Henri's workload as much as she could, it had made sense to work separately.

When Henri didn't answer her, she looked to find him standing by the bedroom window of what had been his suite. A blend of antique and modern, neutral colours, elegance, now with her clothes draped over the back of a chair, her laptop open on the coffee table, it was slowly becoming *theirs*.

She padded across the room, and he lifted an arm, curling her into his side.

"I was just saying," she said, "it was another big day, and it's nice to see a familiar face."

"That's what I am to you?" he asked, his voice tender, his face stern.

"My demands are crazy low."

His brow furrows grew furrows. "They shouldn't be."

"Meh." Then, when she realised how truly rigid he was, she said, "Did I do something wrong?"

"You don't hum anymore."

"Hmmm?" she said, humming and yawning at once, a true time saver.

"You hum beneath your breath when you are content. And I haven't heard you hum once since we returned to Chaleur."

"Sorry," she said, yawning again. "I'll try to do better."

"No!" He turned her in his arms and looked into her face as if trying to see inside her mind. *"Stop* trying. Stop putting your hand up for so much. Stop trying to do my job for me."

"Henri, I…" Matilda lifted a hand in query, for he was being unusually contrary, and cross. "Maybe now that the Summer Festival is over things will settle."

Henri's hands ran down her velvet sleeves and back up again, goose bumps scuttling over her skin. "They won't, Matilda. This job is a merry-go-round that does not end."

"I love merry-go-rounds. Must be the horses."

It had been a lame attempt to snap him out of his funk, but the longer he stood there looking so tormented, the shakier she felt. For an engagement was not a marriage. There was time for her to screw this all up still.

She breathed out hard. "I thought I was kind of nailing the pre-princess thing."

"You are," he said, his gaze wretched and beautiful and tragic and hot. "You are. *You* are perfect."

At which point he growled and gathered her in his arms, lifting her and carrying her to his bed. *Their bed.* He dropped her there with a soft bounce. On the cloud-soft mattress and baby seal eyelash blanket—or whatever unbelievably lush fibre it was made from.

Then he stood at the end of the bed, his hair a little mussed, his tie skew-whiff.

She tilted her head at his shirt. "You have a button undone." Because she'd undone it, when canoodling at the window.

And after a few fraught seconds, in which Matilda thought she might faint from desire, he undid the rest. Slowly.

By the time he peeled the shirt away, revealing sculpted shoulders and flat pecs covered in a smattering of dark hair, the kind that trailed away to a point below the button of his suit pants, she was at the edge of the bed on her knees.

"Pants," she said, fingers clicking, gaze glued to the need pressing against his zip.

He snapped the top button, yanked down his zip, then paused. The way his favoured black Y-fronts framed him, just so, deserved awards. All of them.

She looked up. "If you are waiting for me to say *Your Highness*, you've got a long wait coming."

Henri smiled, the furrows softening.

And Matilda was sure, despite any hiccups and speed bumps and the haste with which they had been forced to figure this all out, *this* part they had down pat. Meaning surely the rest would follow.

Then, as if he couldn't wait, he came to her, drawing her higher on her knees so he could slide his hands into her hair and tilt her face to his so that he could kiss her. Lush, deep, narcotic kisses that went on for days.

Then he pressed her back as he climbed over her, onto

the bed. Settling himself over her. Kissing her eyelids, her cheeks, her nose, as if making sure she was all there.

Please work out, she thought, with a soul deep ache that she understood all too well. *Please, please, please.*

For she loved this man. A love that was wild and gentle, consuming and thoughtful, eternal and new. All at once.

She'd loved him as long as she could remember and, if he'd let her, would keep on doing so for the rest of her life.

Then she gathered him to her and rolled so that he lay back on the bed, the Superman curl falling over one eye.

"I wasn't so sure about this dress," she said, straddling him and wriggling in a way that had him sucking in breath, the pale hazel of his eyes turning to pure smoke. "Till I realised it meant I could do this."

Reaching beneath one knee, then the other, she whipped off her underpants, twirled them over her head, and flung them to the other side of the room.

Then, sliding her hands over his hips, she shimmied his suit pants down just enough to set him free. Tracing the smooth length slowly, reverently, before she gathered up the layers of her blue velvet skirt and lifted to notch herself against him.

He took her hips in his hands, his nostrils flaring, his gaze adoring as she sank down, slowly, inch by inch, taking him, all of him. Till she felt full, rippling with beautiful certainty, that she was exactly where she was meant to be.

Henri sat up, and she gasped as he went deeper still.

Clutching him to her, she rocked, biting her lip to stop from crying out. So soon. Too soon.

He reached behind her, gathering her hair over one shoulder and sliding the zip from neck to the top of her buttocks. His fingers tracing her spine. And as he rolled the fabric down her arms, taking one breast into his warm mouth, then the other, the sounds he made, raw and primal, turned her to pure liquid.

The late evening sunshine poured into his room through the large windows creating a golden haven, as if even the season was blessing them.

And they made love. Delicate touches, eyes open, breaths shared. A slow, sensuous coming together that made Matilda feel as if her DNA had dissolved and been put back together differently.

When pleasure pooled inside of her, it was like a dark lagoon, bottomless and ancient. But she held on, feeling him build, and when she thought he might break, she pressed a hand to his hip and rocked back, and together they breached time and space, as she'd always known they would.

Later that night, after a long, leisurely joint shower, they curled into one another beneath the soft sheets. And Matilda saw a familiar book on Henri's bedside table. Blue leather. The collection of letters and poems she had bought him all those years ago. The one he'd claimed to have lost.

Only it seemed it had been found, after all.

Matilda tried to catch Henri's eye through the crowd of people who had crammed into the Royal Room of Parliament House, most speaking in Chaleurian-accented French so she could only pick up a phrase here and there.

Not that she minded, as it let her switch off for a few blessed moments.

Henri had been right about life not letting up after the festival, it had only become more frenetic. If this was the pace that she'd be expected to set, then she'd simply needed to make some changes. Exercise. Eat better. And sleep a whole lot more. Or the first two at least. For the nights in Henri's bed—their bed—made every hidden yawn worth it.

"Ms. Waverly." The Minister of State's hand hovered near an intricately carved chair. "Sit here, please."

Matilda took the proffered seat in front of the magnificent desk, one that gave her father's a run for its money. The room, in which every royal decree for the past two hundred years had been signed, was gilt-edged at every chance, the walls decked in marble columns, and the amount of red velvet hanging from the windows was almost suffocating.

Then there was the large piece of paper sitting benignly in front of her. A3, off-white, with a faint raised watermark and House of Raphael-Rossetti royal seal, and a short paragraph declaring her intention to wed Henri, and his to wed her, with spaces prepared for two signatures and a witness.

According to Celeste, once the contract was signed, their marriage was set in stone. The royal wedding, which had been in the planning since the day they'd left Garrison Downs, was for the people. This was for the law.

Matilda shook out her hands to get some blood to her fingers. Not that she was nervous. She was ready. For once the contract was signed, her part in satisfying the condition of bequeathment of her father's will was done.

After that, the rest of her life would be about her and Henri. Henri, who for all his attentiveness, his patience, had been slowly reverting back to the Henri he'd been when she'd met him on the street in Côte de Lapis.

Maybe it was nerves. Maybe he was having second thoughts. Maybe this was all a dream. She surreptitiously pinched herself on the wrist.

And reminded herself that she was here. That this was real.

And that she loved him. Had done before she'd known he was a prince. Before she'd even known his real name. And every day she spent with him, watching him work, learning his mind, holding him through the night, she loved him more.

Maybe she ought to have told him by now. So that he knew she wasn't doing this *only* to help her sisters. Told him that asking him to marry her was the single best choice she had ever made.

But the thing was, while she knew that he liked her, respected her, was attracted to her, and that he needed her, beyond that she wasn't *entirely* sure of the exact shape of his feelings for her.

But that was something she would think about tomorrow. Or after the wedding. Or when interest in their relationship cooled and they were both able to come up for air.

Matilda tugged at the neckline of her dress, where it had begun to itch. Chaleurian red, dainty lace, a high neck, fitted bodice and layers of tulle. A little fancy for her taste but it was a moment of historical import and she did not want to give Henri a moment's pause.

Henri, who was still nowhere to be seen.

Her heart was beating a little fast for comfort now. And she could feel sweat pooling in unmentionable places. If only she could see Henri, take a minute, maybe slip away into a room nearby to talk. To hold his hands and look him in the eye, feel the connection she felt sure of when it was just the two of them. Then maybe she *could* tell how she felt, before they signed this paper. Make a private promise to be his forevermore—

A bell rang, and Matilda flinched.

It was a light golden tinkle compared with the hearty rumble of the Homestead bell of Garrison Downs. Though this crowd understood its meaning, everyone quieting and finding their place around the edges of the room.

And then there he was. *Henri.*

No. In his midnight blue three-piece suit, his matinee hair

perfect, his cut-glass jaw tight and unsmiling, he was most certainly Prince Henri Gaultier Raphael-Rossetti, the Sovereign Prince of Chaleur.

She caught his eye and tried for a smile herself, but her mouth wobbled, as nerves now well and truly had her in their clutch.

His brow creased as he noted the trembling of her hands, and she quickly dropped them to her lap.

When he took the seat beside hers, a camera flash went off and Matilda blinked. Then the Minister of State began speaking in French, then again in English, but by then her heart was beating so hard his words were all muffled.

Matilda glanced at Henri to find him staring at the paper in front of them, his skin pale, none of that flush of lovely pink in his cheeks that she loved so much. Now even his brow furrows were smoothed away, as if he was running on backup power.

She opened her mouth to check if he was okay, when the bell rang again.

And the Minister called her name.

"Matilda Lavigne Waverly, do you consent to enter the state of matrimony with Prince Henri Gaultier Raphael-Rossetti, and in doing so agree to become a citizen of Chaleur and to dedicate your life to its people? If so, sign your name to the Royal Marriage Decree."

Matilda glanced back at Henri, to find him still staring ahead. The people watching, the stuffiness of the room began to make her feel as if the room was tipping. She reached for the pen, clicked the nib into place, and—

"Wait." Henri's voice cut though the quiet like a scythe.

Matilda's pen hovered over the contract as a collective gasp echoed through the room. "Henri, are you…?" Matilda swallowed. "Are you talking to me?"

His chin dropped, his hands clenching and unclenching on the table. And fear flashed inside her like a warning flare on a clear night at sea.

Then Henri declared, "Can we please have the room?"

And it was done within seconds. A hush of shuffling feet and muted whispers, then the snick of the door. And they were alone. Just as she'd wished only a moment before.

The marble and velvet and glints of gold made the room feel hot and cold all at once. Or maybe that was just her. Adrenaline and mortification a throbbing cocktail inside of her.

"Henri?"

Henri turned to her, *finally*, his expression now ravaged with emotion. "I should never have let it get this far."

Oh, God. Oh, no. "What? What do you mean?"

He who was so afraid of pitting a single foot wrong, he had worked himself to the bone. What he had just done would reverberate through the halls of this place in a nano-second.

Henri reached for her then, but she snapped her arm away, the pen clattering to the desk. Then she pushed her chair back, hard enough that it rocked before settling on an angle.

And she began to pace. Hands on hips, dragging in breath—not an easy feat considering the snug fit of the damned red lace dress. Tendrils dangled damply from her updo. Her knees hurt as her shoes were that smidge too high.

When Henri stood, all elegance and grace, he did not reach for her again.

"Matilda, I've had decades to prepare for this role, to truly understand the sacrifice. No matter how much I've fought it, I *was* born for this. And it's so clear to me now that forcing this life on you was the most selfish thing I have ever done. I cannot watch you walk barefoot circles in the rose garden, like a caged cat. I just can't."

The rose garden?

What was he talking about?

Matilda smacked a hand to her chest. "I made this deci-sion. I'm the one who practically *begged* you to marry me. If you didn't see the value in what I can offer, or couldn't imag-ine how we can make this work, long term, you might have said so before I came back here with you. Before I sat there."

Henri's jaw worked. "I will give you access to the best lawyers—"

"Don't. Do not. If you are really doing what I think you're doing, then I want nothing from you."

"But your situation—"

"I can count on both hands the number of nice local men, whose land isn't nearly as profitable as ours, who would jump at the chance of marrying into the Waverly family money."

Henri's cool evaporated from one blink to the next. His voice was dangerously low as he said, "Is that what you want?"

"Of course not!" She was merely trying to unhinge him as he'd unhinged her. "Henri, look at me. Look at where I am right now. If you can't see what I want, and the lengths I've been willing to go to get it…"

She wanted the whirlwind, and the settling afterward. The ache and the joy she'd read about in love letters. She wanted a partner who chose her the way she chose him. She wanted all that, with Henri.

"You forget," said Henri, his jaw taking on a stubborn set, "that I have now seen you on horseback, traipsing about in your gum boots, sassing your sister, snuggled up on the back porch with your lovely old dog. There you have space and air and time to do the work that inspires you."

Matilda swallowed back the tears that were threatening to spill, for she had to get through this. "And if I don't want that? What if I told you that I love exhausting myself and having to think on the fly and living by deadlines. Why are you the only one for whom that is allowed?"

"Because I have lived it, pushed it away, taken it back, and chosen it. As it has chosen me. But you…"

He held her gaze, his expression so intense he might as well have been holding her. For she could feel him with every part of her. "You can do anything, Matilda. Anywhere. Your life can be as vast as you want it to be. But not if you are here. Not with me."

Matilda opened her mouth to argue, but then it hit her.

It took two to make a marriage work. Two people who woke up every day and, despite the challenges life threw at them, said, *Yes. This. Together.* And Henri did not look in any place to be saying *yes.* In fact, he looked determined to go into battle. Against her.

She loved him. She would marry him in a heartbeat. On a yacht. In this ridiculously opulent room. In the ballroom back home. Up a tree. Down a well.

But he was trying to make it clear to her that he would not marry her.

And it didn't matter how he felt about her, or maybe it was because of how he felt about her, he had it in his head that it would be best for her if he let her go.

And she knew, in that moment, she could push him, she could twist him, she could convince him he was wrong. But unless he came to that conclusion on his own, he'd hate himself for it for the rest of his life.

She would sacrifice herself for her sisters, but she would not sacrifice him.

Heart beating in her throat, skin clammy, tears now streaming unimpeded down her face, Matilda asked, "Are you certain this is what you want?"

The look in his eyes—those beautiful soulful poetic eyes—told her all she needed to know.

So, Matilda did what Matilda did when faced with desperate situations—she hitched up her dress and fled.

CHAPTER ELEVEN

HENRI GRIPPED THE ancient stone rampart of the highest keep of Château de Chaleur, looking south over the dark, moon-kissed forest below.

After Matilda had fled the Royal Room of Parliament House, he'd had to stay back, asking for everyone's patience and assuring them that the country could go on in the knowledge that their prince was neither fickle nor a fool.

Now he had to convince himself. For while he knew that letting her go, giving her the chance to choose a different life, an easier life, a freer life, was the right thing to do, why did it feel so damnably wrong?

Andre's whistle heralded his arrival.

"Is she gone?" Henri asked.

"Boris drove her away an hour ago."

Henri's head dropped, his shoulders hunched, his fingers gripping hard enough to scrape.

"Want to talk about it?" Andre asked.

"So that you might smugly say *I told you so*?"

Andre reared back. "Do you think this is an outcome I approve of?"

Henri folded his arms as he turned to face his cousin, preferring to send all the ire that he felt with himself in that direction for a spell.

"Do you not remember me telling you that after you first set eyes on Matilda Waverly, right after scraping your molten heart off the floor, that I would make it my mission to find out who she was, where she came from, her net worth, and the…the name of the doctor who'd set her broken arm when she was seven."

"She broke her arm when she was seven?" How had he not known that? No, he couldn't start thinking about all the things they'd yet to learn about one another, or he'd go mad from missing her. And she'd only been gone an hour.

"My point, cousin, is—did you not wonder why it took me so long to find out that Henri Gaultier and Matilda Waverly did not have a Gibraltarian marriage license?"

Henri looked to Andre. Then looked harder. "Are you saying—"

"The moment you brought her through the château doors, it was clear that you still had feelings for her. While I stand by what I did all those years ago, it's sat inside me like a stone every day since… Matilda is good for you. She brings levity and balance and looks at you like you hang the blooming stars and moon. I considered giving you the time you needed to come to that conclusion on your own as my atonement."

When Henri had no comeback, Andre went on. "Which for you, dear cousin, took ten times longer than it ought, for you are a stubborn bastard with a martyr complex."

Andre droned on about Augustus "doing a number" on him and "classic transference," saying things Henri knew to be true, only didn't have the emotional vocabulary to verbalise.

Or *hadn't* for a long time. For he'd locked his feelings away in a place so deep he'd not recognised them when they had reemerged.

Feelings. Such an anaemic way to say that he loved her.

Because Henri loved Matilda. And had always loved her. It was that complex and that simple, all at once.

Henri blanched. "I've let that voice in the back of my

head, the one telling me that I am not allowed to enjoy being a prince, to make my decisions for me. Haven't I?"

Aw, hell.

"A *martyr* complex, you say?"

"Boom!" Andre held out both hands in revelation. "Just call me your fairy godfather."

"I'd rather not."

"Are you sure? Because I feel as if I have finally hit my straps—"

"I am sure. Now I need you to stop talking so I can figure out how the hell I can fix this."

"The plan, before you blew it up spectacularly, was to marry Matilda, make babies, live happily ever after. Why does that have to change?"

So much for not playing fairy godfather. And yet…the man was damnably good at it.

Henri strode to the stairs and hastened his pace as he made his way down, the cold of the ancient stone matching the cold in his limbs. The fear that he'd gone too far. That no matter what he might say to her, to explain himself, she'd finally hit her limit.

When he reached his suite—their suite—he found signs of the lack of her: the space where her laptop had charged, her messed-up side of the bed, the red lace dress she'd been wearing now draped over the back of a chair.

He'd told Matilda what he was feeling, but only to a point. For he'd not given her all the pertinent information. She deserved to know *why* he was so desperate for her to live the life she wanted.

Because he loved her. Deeply, desperately.

His job was not to fix things for her so that they were perfect. It was to trust her to make her own choices. And if they included him, he would wrap her up tight and love her so hard and be grateful every damn day.

He patted his pocket, looking for his phone to call Boris, to find out where they were, but having come directly from Parliament his phone was likely still in Celeste's care.

Dammit.

He searched for another way. Another means to get through to her…there. Beside the landline phone on his side of the bed sat a small, blue book, filled with letter and poems.

He grabbed the book, the tome fitting in his hand like it was made for that purpose, then crossed the room to sit at his desk. Where he pulled out a piece of paper, his personal stationery.

And he sat down and started to write.

It had taken a depressingly short time for Matilda to pack her bag. As if she'd been quietly concerned she'd not be there that long.

Only this time, rather than fleeing home and hiding within the safe cocoon of her family, she'd asked Boris to find her a hotel. Someplace close that she could hole up and think.

Because, despite her earlier certainty that giving Henri what he wanted was the most honourable thing that she could do, every minute that passed she felt more certain that what he *thought* he wanted was just plain wrong.

No questions asked, Boris had put her up in an apartment in Côte de Lapis owned by "the family," for it was secure, and the staff had been vetted and would know to keep her presence there private.

Matilda dumped her bags and trudged to the window seat, the Mediterranean dark, lights from the cafés and cars below creating a golden glow. And there she sat, curled up, licking her wounds. And trying to figure out where she'd gone so wrong.

The urge to call her sisters was there, as it likely always would be. Eve would tell it like it was. Ana would be sweet as hell. Rose would open her arms. But that's not what she needed. For this was on her.

She looked down at the ring she'd not thought to give back as she'd fled the Royal Room. The one Henri had given her several years ago. Had watched her toying with over the past weeks and never asked her to return.

Henri would never have done what he did lightly. Or without reason, deeply felt. Especially not to her. She'd seen the trauma in his eyes as he'd cut her free.

But he was also hyperaware of his place in history. And determined to never put himself ahead of the needs of others the way his forebears had. *To a fault.*

She sat forward, hugging her knees as puzzle pieces began to shift and move before settling into a new shape.

Was it possible that she made him *happy*, and he just didn't know what to do with it?

She coughed out a half sob, half laugh. For with a little distance and a little air, a little time away from his consuming presence, it *all* made such perfect sense.

Henri collated work with duty. Happiness with frivolity. And family with pain.

Marrying her, making her a part of his family, must have messed with his head, big-time. Especially since he cared for her. And, as he'd attested, wanted her to the live the best life she possibly could.

It had never occurred to him that her best life was with him.

Matilda uncurled herself from the window seat, her feet tingling with pins and needles as she tapped her toes to the floor, her legs jiggling as she tried to think her way through what it meant.

If only, rather than retreating, protecting *herself,* she'd been brave enough to tell him how she felt. That she loved him with every last bit of her soul. That she wanted to be with him wherever that might be. And that deep down, she had been sure enough of his feelings for her that she'd bet the station on it. Then she might be finally, legally, hitched to the guy by now.

Only now it was too late. Or was it? Weren't second chances, and third chances, part of the deal, if you loved someone enough?

There was only one way to find out. She switched on her phone screen, readying to call Andre, or Celeste, or Boris—

When a knock came to her door.

It was the porter, holding out a small package, wrapped in brown paper with a string tie.

"Are you sure this is for me?"

The porter nodded. *"Oui, mademoiselle."*

Only Boris knew where she was, meaning it had to be from him. Or someone he worked for.

Her knees a little wobbly, Matilda hurried back to the window seat, sat cross-legged, and opened the package to find a familiar, small, beaten-up, blue book of poetry.

Pulse fluttering in her wrists, behind her knees, in her belly, she opened the book and a piece of paper fell out.

A letter.

Written on stationery from the desk of Prince Henri Gaultier Raphael-Rossetti of the Royal House of Chaleur in Henri's own hand.

Matilda,
I offer you these words, even while knowing that you of all people, have read so many efforts at saying what I wish to say, from the pens of far better writers than I. And yet that will not stop me, for I trust that you will feel the truth in them. And at this point, after the mistakes that I have made, my truth is all I have left to offer you.
I asked you to wait, as I wanted you to be sure. Not stubbornly sacrificing your life for the sake of your sis-

ters, or generously stepping into a role that you knew would serve me. Sure, for you.

Sure, the way I am, and have been, for as long as I can remember, that being together is the thing you want most in the world.

Despite my struggles with the concept of fate—after being told my entire life that I was "meant to be" a prince—I walked into a club in Vienna and saw the woman I knew would change my life. Right in the moment I was ready for change.

Then, a few short weeks ago, while driving in Le Côte de Lapis, as I once again found myself in a moment of fractured time, of deep uncertainty, there you were again. A glance, a smile, a nod building the foundations beneath me that I had been missing.

How could I, a man unmanned by you, have hoped to offer a woman such as you the same foundations, the same certainty, the same protection and promises of forever? All of which you deserved.

Now, as I imagine you slipping further and further from my reach, all I can do is offer you what you have given me—care, faith, understanding, and as many chances as you need to be sure. Sure that a life with me, and all that that brings with it, including my heart and soul, is enough.

On my knees, I offer you my life, and the chance to share yours.

A life full of promises and plans.
Yours. In entirety. For eternity.
Henri

Matilda closed the piece of paper, folding it along the crease lines, carefully, before she brought it and the book to her chest. Holding it close as tears poured down her face.

This, from a man taught to be careful with his words. To behave and be proper and keep himself apart. Her pragmatic prince with the heart of a poet had finally, finally, stepped out of his head and into her heart.

And just like that, all the feelings she'd been holding inside released, hot and wild, like the blast of an explosion.

She'd loved Henri since the moment she'd set eyes on him. And feelings like that didn't just go away. They subsided like a flame starved of oxygen, and they waited. Waited until they were once again given air. Sunshine by a seaside town. A library filled with the dust and whispers of history. Boat rides on a crystalline lake. Tenderness, conversation, care.

And now they burned inside of her like a storm.

She uncurled herself from the window seat once more and spun in a circle. Looking for...what? Her phone. To call him?

Or call Boris to come and get her, so that she might storm the castle, literally.

Oh, did she want to call Rose—tell her everything truly *was* going to work out! Or Eve, to tell her to get the heck over herself, call Ana to tell her to make friends, go home, and stop being so isolated, because being brave and opening yourself up gave you the best chance at being happy.

Because she wanted them all to feel this good. Only it was not her job to pull the wheels and levers to make that happen. Not anymore.

It was her job to do whatever it took to make sure *she* was happy. And the good would flow from there.

Stage One—go get her man.

Henri paced the foyer of the château.

"Anything?" he barked, when Celeste dared to pop her head out into the hall.

She shook her head. Then shushed someone behind her before saying, "Though your cousin wishes for me to tell you that it is late, and you have a big day tomorrow what with that meeting with the Minister for Agriculture and the board of governors of the children's hospital we visited a few weeks ago and—"

"Tell your ventriloquist dummy to grab his keys, he's driving."

For since leaving to drop the book to Matilda, after refusing to give up where she was—the man's loyalties were seriously skewed, and yet, such that Henri wanted to give him a medal—Boris was not answering his phone. And Henri did not trust himself behind the wheel.

"Where exactly is he meant to be driving you? Your cousin wonders."

Anywhere. Everywhere. Till he found her and told her, in person, what he'd said in that damnable letter. Had it been a mistake? Too cryptic? Would she think it cowardly? Or would she understand that he wanted to connect with her in the ways that had meaning for her?

Then...

Was that a car door?

A few moments later Boris came through the door and, with a bow and a slight smile, said, "A delivery for you, Your Highness."

He stepped aside, and...

"Matilda."

In place of the red lace dress, she wore jeans and a T-shirt, flat shoes, her hair down, her face scrubbed of makeup. The kind of clean that came not only from soap and water, but from tears.

His heart ached at the knowledge he'd done that, his decision-making so poor.

After saying something to Boris that made him blush, Matilda's gaze lifted and found Henri's and everything else melted away.

He took a step, then another, then she ran to him, and she threw herself into his arms. Kissing his cheeks, his jaw, his mouth. Peppering him as if it might be her last chance.

The momentum rocked him back, before he gathered himself, and her, twirling her around and around and around.

When they slowed, the world slowed with them. Slowed, then settled. Like a tornado in reverse. The pieces sifting into perfect place.

Her tiptoes touched the ground, then with her arms still around his neck, she pulled back just enough to look into his eyes.

Henri didn't need to ask for the room, not this time. He could sense those who knew him best, his chosen family, who supported and care for him—not the crown, him—made themselves scarce.

"I'm so glad you didn't leave," he said.

"I'm so glad you wrote to me." She lifted one hand from his neck to show that she held the book, worn blue leather, the corner of his letter poking out the top.

He grimaced. "I'm more of a political writer—speeches, arguments and the like. Letters have never been my forte."

"Oh," she said, pressing herself against him, her eyes heavy, her teeth hooking against her lower lip, "I can assure you they are. And I'm an expert, you know."

"So I've heard." Henri drank her in. His Matilda, here, in his arms. Where—now that he'd seen the alternative—it was so clear that she was meant to be. "I meant every word I wrote."

"I know," she said, her fingers playing with his hair.

"Despite how it might have seemed in the Room of Royal Decree, there is nothing I want more than to have you in my life, Matilda."

"I know," she said again, this time her voice had a little burr.

"Not least of all, is because I am in love with you. And have been for a good portion of my life."

A dreamy smile flashed over her face before she said, "I know that too."

"You know a lot, as it turns out," he said, sliding a hand down her back.

"I do, in fact," she said, her voice getting that languorous edge that he loved so much. "Whereas you have some catching up to do. Such as that thing you said, about me walking barefoot circles in the rose garden—I do that not because I feel trapped, but because it reminds me so much of my mum's rose garden back home. That's all. I'm happy here, Henri. I want this. I want you."

Henri breathed out, relief flooding through him. That she knew him. Understood him. Had come back to him.

"And it would pay to remember that," she said, "so that next time you feel the urge to self-sacrifice for no good reason, you can look to me and I'll knock the thought right out of your head. In a loving way."

Henri's heart lurched in his chest. "In a loving way, you say."

Matilda nodded beatifically. Then a slow smile eased its way across her lovely face. "I love you, Henri. I loved you when you were a young man so desperate to find your direction. I loved you still when I saw how big your fairy-tale castle was."

He pulled her in a little tighter. "Is that so?"

"Mmm hmm. When I knew that it was inevitable, that the feelings you bring out in me, the way you conduct yourself, the man that you are had ruined me for all other men, was when we were ambling to the stables back home. You in what you thought was Outback chic, dust motes swishing past that face of yours in the hazy afternoon light, and then you accepted poor Beryl as your mount, without complaint...that was it for me, Henri. I was done."

Henri leaned down and pressed a featherlight kiss against her lips. Because he wanted to, and because he could. Then he lifted his hand to cup her face and kissed her properly.

The true sealing of their promise.

"That's it then," he murmured against her lips. "If I love you, and you love me, then we definitely make it official. Don't you think?"

She blinked up at him. "I've thought so for some time. But...do we have to sign that thing in that room?"

Henri understood her hesitation and was determined to do whatever it took to do it their way. "I believe we do but—"

"No," said Celeste popping her head out from the sitting room once more. For it seems they had not made themselves as scarce as he'd assumed.

"No?" said Matilda, peering around Henri's side.

"You do not."

Andre came out from behind Celeste, his hand sliding from around her waist. That was new. Or perhaps not, now that he thought about it.

"It is tradition, yes," said Andre, "but there is no law that says you must. Hey, Matilda."

"Hey, Andre. You been hiding in there the whole time?"

"Yes, I have."

"Then be of use, will you," said Henri.

And the way Matilda grinned, as if her heart bloomed at the sight of him being impertinent made him certain this was going to be a hell of a ride.

"Whatever Matilda wants, make it happen."

"We would like to sign the contract here," Matilda added, "an intimate affair, with witnesses of our choosing."

"D'accord," said Celeste, wincing a little at the move away from protocol as she took notes.

"Did she just curtsy?" Matilda whispered.

"I think she did."

"The wedding can still be a total blowout though."

Celeste looked up, her expression hovering close to true joy.

"I am so happy to hear that," she said, her fingers tapping madly over her phone.

"Only can we bring the timeline up?" Matilda added, her hand moving into the back of his hair. "As soon as humanly possible. Gotta lock this one down."

At that, Celeste grinned. "We can do anything."

"I like the sound of that," said Matilda, before leaning her ear against his chest and holding him.

Henri liked the sound of it too.

EPILOGUE

Chaleur,
late August

THE LEAD-IN to their wedding day was a beautiful blur.

When Henri explained to parliament that his hesitancy over signing the contract in such a formal space had been due to his intention to curate his sovereignty with a more contemporary bent, they had kindly taken him at his word.

The day itself boasted enough pomp to include crowns, sceptres, blessings from religious leaders and government officials, lots of papers to sign and promises made regards standing for the people of Chaleur.

Yet it was also heart-warmingly intimate.

With Chaleur being a country of artisans, Matilda could happily have chosen dresses by a dozen local designers, but in the end went with a floaty cream number Celeste had found her, with elbow-length sleeves and a cinched waist, the skirt falling in soft layers.

Henri had Andre as his best man. While, despite it being on the verge of spring on the station, and her sister working so hard to cement her position as the boss of Garrison Downs, Rose had moved heaven and earth to be there. To stand up beside Matilda as her witness, her maid of honour.

Eve, it turned out, *had* booked a flight home, back to Garrison Downs, for the first time in far too long, so couldn't be there, but in a rare and much appreciated message had sent her congratulations and promised Matilda she would "gorge" herself on what was sure to be an obscene number of photos as soon as she landed.

Since none of them wanted to swing any undue attention Ana's way, she stayed home. Though Matilda—already good to go on the ring side of things—had asked Ana if she could make Henri's wedding ring. Which she'd been tearily delighted to do.

Matilda did not have anyone give her away. She wanted it to be clear that this choice was very much her own.

They'd made their way, in horse and carriage no less, to the Cathédrale de Chaleur, in which the wedding was to take place. Then, once the dresser and hair and makeup people had finally swept out of the anteroom, leaving Matilda and Rose alone for the first time all day, the sisters looked at one another across the small room.

With tears in her eyes, Rose began to laugh as she took in the frescoes and antiques everywhere they looked. "Does this even feel real to you?"

"One gets used to it."

Rose's gaze dropped back to Matilda. "Does one?"

Matilda poked out her tongue.

"Well." Rose moved in and took Matilda by both hands, eyes roving over her beautiful boho dress, the Australian wildflowers in her hair. "You look so disgustingly happy I can't stand it."

"I am," Matilda said, squeezing Rose's hand only to find it cool and shaky, unlike her own. "Deeply, truly, revoltingly happy."

Matilda turned to look at herself in the mirror. Then she beckoned Rose to stand beside her; the colour of Rose's simple, sleek copper dress so reminiscent of the way Garrison Downs land looked when the sun hit just so, it was as if her sisters, her mum, and her dad, were a part of the day too.

"I will miss making life brighter, and easier for you all," said Matilda.

Rose snorted. "You, darling sister, were never easy."

Matilda grinned. "Yeah, you're probably right."

"If Mum and Dad could see you now, they would be so damn proud. Not that you've landed a prince, though Mum would have *loved* that. They'd be so chuffed that you figured out what you want, then went out and got it. That is the Waverly way."

Matilda reached back for Rose's hand and Rose rested her chin on Matilda's shoulder. "Despite their rocky road, they really did eat life up with a spoon, didn't they. A good example for us all."

And then it was time.

The grand organ stuck a familiar tone, Celeste swept into the room, made sure they had their bouquets—a mix of delicate native Chaleurian wildflowers, ivy from the stone walls outside the château, and imported Sturt's desert peas, fields of which could be found all around Garrison Downs—and hustled Rose, then Matilda, into place.

Henri, with Andre at his side, looked impossibly dashing. All broad shoulders, and brow furrows; so utterly Byronic it was a miracle her knees didn't give out from under her.

The hot hard gaze of his eyes making her certain that, like her, he could not wait for the official bit to be over so that they might truly start their lives together.

As husband and wife. Prince and princess. Henri and Tilly. Mad for each other and happy for the world to see it.

The ceremony itself went on as such ceremonies tended to do.

The moment Henri reoffered Matilda his mother's ring, this time it came with the knowledge of all of the history and the love and the burden that it entailed, which made it all the more special.

When she placed the ring Ana had made onto Henri's finger, she felt her fractured family click into place. As if rising from the ashes of the horrors of the past few months, it had been made anew.

They left the cathedral under a confetti of dried peony petals, before making it down the steps and out onto the beachside strip of le Côte de Lapis, where thousands of Chaleurians clapped and cheered. With Boris and Lars hovering not too far behind, Henri and Matilda shook hands, accepted flowers and wishes of *bonne chance* from people it was now her official duty to care for.

"They do love you," Matilda told Henri as she took him by the arm.

"It's you they love," he insisted, pressing a quick kiss to her hair. "Listen."

Voices called. *"Princess! Princess Matilda, over here! Je t'adore!"*

But while Matilda was honestly delighted, she was also only half listening, her focus on her husband and the expression on his face. How at ease he finally was.

She lifted to press a kiss to his cheek, then tucked herself into his side, which drew a huge cheer from the crowd.

True love, it turned out, wasn't all whirlwinds, and fluttering hearts, and high adventure. It was opening herself to someone, letting them see to the heart of her, and working hard to see to the heart of them. Flaws and all.

Then choosing that person again and again.

Every single day.

Every moment.

For ever after.

Which she knew she'd have no problem doing at all.

* * * * *

RELUCTANT BRIDE'S
BABY BOMBSHELL

RACHAEL STEWART

MILLS & BOON

For my writer sisters,

Ally, Kandy and Michelle.

Love you ladies!

xxx

PROLOGUE

London,
June

EVE STARED AT her laptop screen. The video-call countdown glared back at her, mocking her every attempt to remain composed.

She checked her bun. Not a blonde wisp out of place.

Smoothed down her royal-blue power suit. Not a crease.

Scanned her office backdrop. Not a thing out of place. The glass and monochrome oozed success and sophistication. Everything she wanted to portray.

You've got this, she mentally coached.

Only she hadn't and no amount of talking herself up would change that.

Her father had been dead a month. A *month*. And she hadn't shed a tear.

She hadn't attended his state funeral back in Australia. She hadn't stood by her sisters as they and the nation mourned him. She hadn't let herself think about him at all.

But now she had to.

She was being forced to dial in for the reading of his will.

A will she couldn't care two hoots about. She wanted nothing of his. Nothing to remind her of the life she'd left behind in Australia a decade ago. She had everything she needed here in London. A great life, a great apartment, and a great job as a PR exec with a reputation that people twice her age would covet.

Which is why you've got this!

She'd spent her entire adult life perfecting her appearance as well as that of others. This was just another chance to shine.

For appearances were everything.

They could hide a multitude of sins and take you far too.

The former she'd got from her parents. The latter from her grandparents, who'd taken her in when she'd discovered said sins and fled Australia for the UK.

It was her grandparents who'd taught her how to play society's game—how to talk, how to walk, how to command the room. How to lose the gangly awkwardness she'd grown up with, too. An awkwardness that had seen her own father nickname her Bambi. Bambi!

Was it any wonder Eve had spent her early teens permanently hunched over, trying to blend into the background while hoping one day she'd be as lucky as Cinders and Prince Charming would come along and sweep her off her feet.

Just as her father had her mother.

That was until Eve's eyes had been opened to the truth— their love, a *lie*—and she'd quit daydreaming. Thrown her romance books aside for business and finance. Success she could trust. Love not so much.

And success was hers. Listed in *Management Today*'s prestigious 'thirty-five under thirty-five' of the UK's highest-achieving young businesswomen at only twenty-eight, she'd truly made it.

And, in so doing, become someone her father would have been proud of…if she'd ever given him the chance to know her again.

Too late, now.

And too late to prepare.

The screen came alive, presenting a room so achingly familiar she feared she'd crack a tooth.

Dark wood, panelled walls, leather furnishings that she could feel beneath her fingertips if she were to put her mind to it…she balled her hands on the desk before her.

Dad's office at the heart of Garrison Downs. She should have known that was where they would be.

As one of Australia's largest cattle stations set deep in the Outback, it was famed throughout the country for its one and a half million hectares, tens of thousands of cattle, red dust and craggy vistas, ghostly gum trees and its own precious river. The room she was looking at now having featured in magazines and TV broadcasts, played host to world leaders and stars from agriculture, industry, and movies alike.

But when she was growing up, it had been Dad's office. Just Dad. Eve hadn't cared about the fame or the fortune. Only that he was her father and the station had been her home.

And what a messed-up joke that was.

She tightened her fists, forced herself to focus on the present rather than the past. The camera was set back, gifting her a decent view of the people in the room. Most were suited and booted, some were huddled in groups, others hovering aloof. More than she would have expected and only three that she recognised.

Dad's lawyer, George Harrington, sat behind her father's desk, his ageing form swamped by the solid dark wood.

Closest to her and easily identifiable by her blonde waves sat Matilda. Though sat didn't quite cover the curled-up, broken form her little sister represented on the velvet sofa and Eve's heart winced. Her lashes flickering as she fought the urge to reach out, wondering why Rose, their big sister, wasn't doing just that.

But Rose was sitting in the guest chair before their father's desk, stiff-backed and still. *Too* still.

Cut from the same cloth as their father but with the softness of their late mother, Rose had always been a beacon of strength. A tower of support. Only as Eve looked at her now, brown hair scraped back in a no-nonsense ponytail, workwear on, she'd clearly come straight from the land, no second spared. Still pushing on and giving Garrison Downs her all when life had thrown its biggest curve ball yet—the sudden death of a man she'd idolised because Rose, like most others, didn't know any better…

Was it possible that beneath her own front her big sister was crumbling, too?

'Ah, Evelyn!'

She stiffened as Harrington spoke, drawing the attention of the entire room her way.

'Can you hear me okay?'

She had the ridiculous urge to duck. A response that in no way reflected the woman she was now and, angry with herself for daring to think it, she straightened. 'I can hear you perfectly fine, Mr Harrington.'

Rose's shoulders twitched and Matilda started to turn.

'Please proceed.' Eve spoke before her sister could. She didn't want Matilda to address her, she didn't want *any* sisterly talk. Not in front of a room full of people she didn't know, and not when she was feeling at her most vulnerable.

A sense she hadn't experienced in too long and had no idea how to handle.

'Very well…' Harrington cleared his throat '…we'll get straight to business.'

And so it began, the reading of the will, an outline of their father's wealth and its distribution…words, just words, and Eve was numb to it all. The figures, the properties, the stocks and the shares. None of it a surprise. All of it vast. She might not respect Holt as a father or as a husband, but she couldn't fault his savvy handling of all things financial.

And then Harrington shifted gears, from the business to the personal, and Matilda shifted in her seat, her pain increasingly evident.

Move, Rose, she silently urged.

But it wasn't Rose who obeyed. It was River. Their father's old lilac border collie. He appeared in the lower half of the screen and joined Tilly on the sofa. Eve eased back, grateful to the dog for giving her sister the comfort she so dearly wished to give but hadn't been able to face a homecoming for…

Coward.

Harrington gave a rumbling cough, drawing Eve out of her self-reproach.

'To my daughters,' he was saying, 'I leave all of the above, and all my worldly possessions not listed hereupon, including, but not limited to, the entirety of Garrison Downs.'

As expected. As it should be.

And Eve would swiftly hand over her share to her sisters at the earliest opportunity.

'Let it be known,' Harrington went on, 'that it is my wish that my eldest daughter, Rose Lavigne Waverly, take over full control of management of Garrison Downs. If that is her wish. If not, I bow to her choice.'

Again, just as it should be. So why did Rose flinch?

Did her sister not anticipate this? Who else could possibly take it on? No one knew the land and the job as she did...

'At this point,' Harrington said, eyes sweeping over the guests, 'could we please clear the room of everyone bar family?'

Slowly, the room emptied out, every delayed second playing on Eve's nerves. When, finally, it was just them, Harrington gave a warm, sympathetic smile. 'Now that was quite the ask, I know. But necessary to cover all the intricacies of your father's will, with those who will best help you manage the ongoing running and reputation of the station...'

Eve couldn't care, she only wished she'd been gifted the chance to leave with the others.

'...there is just one more thing.'

He paused to rub a hand across his brow and Eve got the distinct impression he was delaying...but why?

Something was up. Something big. And bad.

Eve braced herself, ears straining.

'There is a condition placed over the bequest. One that has been attached to the property since its transfer to your family years ago.'

The lawyer removed his glasses and laid them on top of the papers in front of him.

'As I'm sure you know, the history of Garrison Downs is complicated, what with your great-great grandmother having won the land from the Garrison family in a poker match in 1904.'

Complicated? More like stupid.

To Eve's mind, if the Garrisons had been willing to risk their lands in a game, they deserved to lose them. And it wasn't as if they'd suffered too greatly. They still owned and ran Kalku Hills, a huge station in the south.

But the locals loved to big it up. The legend that was the poker match, the rivalry between the two families, the hatred...

'Any time the land has been passed down since,' Harrington continued, 'certain conditions had to be met.'

Conditions? Eve's gaze narrowed as the lawyer donned his glasses once more, hands unsteady as he lifted the papers to read directly from them.

'Any male Waverly heir, currently living, naturally inherits the estate,' he said, giving Rose a fleeting look when she murmured something Eve couldn't catch. 'But if the situation arises where there is no direct male heir, any and all daughters, of marrying age, must be wed within a year of the reading of the will, in order to inherit as a whole.'

Eve tucked her chin, blinked and blinked again. Had she *heard* the man correctly?

Their birthright would be *lost* if they weren't married before the year was out?

Married!

She laughed. The sound abrupt and startling the room, startling herself too.

'You think this is *funny*?' Rose fired as all eyes turned to the camera, to her.

'I think it's hilarious, Rose! I mean, come on, what century do you think we're in, Harrington?'

Rose lifted her hands. 'What am I missing?'

Did her sister *really* not get it?

'The land,' Matilda said quietly, 'is entailed to sons. If there is no son, the Waverly women can inherit—you, Eve and I— but only if all of us are married.'

Rose shot to her feet, pacing like a caged animal. 'That can't possibly be legal! Not in this day and age, surely!'

'Too right, it can't be,' Eve said, grateful that she wasn't the only one seeing this for what it was. Utterly farcical.

'It is…arcane,' Harrington said, 'but it has been a part of the lore of this land for several generations. So far as I see it, and so far as your father must have wanted, it stands.'

'How has this never come up before?' Rose said.

'Sons,' Matilda replied as Eve stared dumbfounded at the surreal scene playing out before her as if it were some movie and not reality. *Her* reality. 'Dad was an only child. Pop only had brothers, though one died of measles and the other drowned, meaning the farm passed straight to him. Waverlys have always been most excellent at having at least one strap- ping farm-loving son. Until us.'

Eve's stomach twisted. The idea that her mother could have been deemed a failure for this too was an unwanted but very real thought.

'And what happens if we refuse to…marry,' Rose asked, staring Harrington down.

'If the condition is not met, the land goes back to the cur- rent head of the Garrison family. Clay Garrison.'

Rose scoffed. 'That double-dealing, underhand, two-faced old goat can't tell the back end of a bull from the front.'

'The son seems a reasonable sort—'

'*Lincoln…?* If he stopped partying long enough to even no- tice the level of responsibility coming his way…' Rose pressed her palms to her eyes. 'If our land, our home, the business that we've built fell into their hands, I—I can't even *think* it.'

'Don't waste your time worrying about it, Rose,' Eve said,

finding her voice at last. 'Because it isn't going to happen. Not now. Not ever.'

Harrington cleared his throat. 'As it stands, unless all four of Holt Waverly's daughters are married within twelve months of the reading of this document—'

'Twelve months?' Rose shot back. 'But I can't... I'm not... I mean, none of us are even *seeing* anyone right now. Are we? Eve? Tilly?'

Never mind the months!

Eve's nose was right up against the screen. She *must* have misheard him this time. He said four, *four* daughters...

'Wait!' Matilda sat bolt upright, startling a dozing River. 'Back up a second. You said *four* daughters. There are only three of us.'

Then her sister's gaze drifted to the far corner of the room... a spot Eve couldn't see.

'Who are you?' Matilda said softly.

Who is who?

Everyone else was supposed to have left...

'Who are you talking to, Tilly? I can't see,' Eve said, desperate to turn the camera.

'Ana,' came a disembodied voice. Unsure. Hesitant. *Young.*

Harrington stood and stepped around the desk. 'Come forward, girl.'

Ana, who on earth was *Ana*?

Slowly, a dark-haired woman appeared in the bottom half of the screen and Eve felt the remaining blood drain from her face as her brain raced ahead for an answer.

Please let her be a distant cousin, an unexpected discovery on the depleted family tree, anything but...

'Anastasia,' Harrington said, 'this is Matilda Waverly. That there is Rose. And up on the screen is Evelyn. Girls, this is Anastasia Horvath.'

The stranger made the smallest sound, lifted her hand in what Eve took to be a wave. Matilda gestured back. Rose simply stared. And Eve... Eve didn't react because her insides were doing all the reacting for her, telling her before Harrington could who this girl was and why she was present…

'Ana here, is your father's daughter. Your half-sister. And therefore, according to your father's will, due an equal share in the estate. And equally beholden to the condition.'

Silence. No one moved. No one spoke. Eve couldn't. She was drowning in a sea of pain. All that hurt of old, the reason she'd left, the reason she never wanted to set foot on Garrison Downs again, the lie… She was staring at the product of that lie and she couldn't breathe.

'Impossible,' Matilda suddenly blurted.

Only Eve knew it wasn't.

It was entirely possible. Probable. True.

She fought for control, for something that wasn't the raging torrent within. Sense told her it wasn't this girl's fault that she existed. It wasn't this girl's fault that their father had been unfaithful. It wasn't this girl's fault that Eve had been forced to secrecy by her parents. That she'd been caught up in the lie, messed up by it, too.

But to learn that it wasn't just a fleeting affair, a thing of the past, a moment in time.

To learn that the consequences were as far-reaching as a child! A secret sister!

She couldn't bring herself to look at her. Harrington was still talking but Eve had heard enough. Too much!

She was going to vomit, she was sure of it. Right here, in her pristine glass-walled office for all her employees to witness.

'Rose?' Matilda started.

'Hang on.' Gripping the back of her chair, Rose lifted her head to seek out Eve on the video screen and Eve knew she was piecing it all together. 'Evie…'

Not now, Rose, she silently pleaded, head shaking. *Not now.*

'Did you *know*? Is this why—'

'I have to go.'

She cut the call and the lid of her laptop in one, pressed her trembling palms into the top. Beyond the glass, her assistant Kim's eyes met hers.

You okay? she mouthed.

Eve could only stare and Kim was on her feet, inside her office and closing the shutters before anyone knew any different. 'I'll clear your schedule. You get yourself home.'

'No,' Eve whispered. 'I'm better off here.'

'You'll be better off at home.'

Home. London. Her apartment. Not Garrison Downs where her sisters were now coming to terms with this news. Her father's legacy as contentious and destructive as the man himself—a secret half-sister and a conditional bequest that sought to control them from the grave. To force them all into marriage, a bond he himself hadn't been able to honour.

The hypocrisy wasn't lost on her.

Well, you can forget it, dear old Dad.

She'd promised herself long ago that she would never tie herself to another, not in marriage and not in love, and she wasn't about to change that stance now. Not for anyone or anything, and least of all her liar of a father.

But she wouldn't see her sisters lose their birthright either.

The condition had to go, and she would see it gone.

Woe betide *anyone* who stood in her way.

CHAPTER ONE

A few miles out from Marni,
South Australian Outback,
September

IF SOMEONE HAD told Eve three months ago, she'd be taking a three-month sabbatical and returning to Garrison Downs, she'd have laughed in their face. On both counts.

Work was her life.

And the Downs was her living hell.

Yet here she was in the back of a cab heading into Marni, the nearest Outback town to the godforsaken place.

Far enough away from the station to hide a little longer, but close enough to feel its proximity like an invisible noose around her neck.

She rubbed at her nape. Her hand coming away damp. Didn't matter that the car's air con was dialled up, her stress levels had her overheating from the inside out. She checked the temperature display—a cool sixteen degrees—she could hardly ask her driver to lower it again. The look he'd sent her as he'd tugged his sweater on the last time she'd asked told her she was mad enough.

Instead, she pulled out her laptop, aiming for distraction. What she got was a streak of goosebumps to accompany the clammy sheen, because staring back at her was the image that had triggered this mad dash across the world.

Matilda. Her little sister. A bride!

And not just any bride, a blushing bona fide *princess* bride!

Eve wasn't sure what shocked her more, the fact that she'd married royalty or the fact she was married at all!

Oh, Matilda *claimed* she was in love. Claimed she was happy. Swore it had nothing to do with the blasted will and everything to do with her heart.

But Tilly, dear sweet adventurous Tilly…?

She stared at the photograph. A feature of the official royal press release showing Matilda with her husband in all their wedding finery, but it was their smiles and the look in their eyes that caught at Eve most.

Was it possible? Had her sister really found true love? A real-life fairy-tale castle for a home too?

She choked on a laugh. It was surreal. As surreal as the situation it left her and the rest of her sisters in…

She couldn't help Tilly now, she'd made her bed and, as her sister had pointed out on their latest call, she was very happy rolling around in it. *Not* the image Eve had wanted but she'd smiled despite herself. Her sister's joy too infectious to resist.

But if that joy were to expire, then Eve would be there to help pick up the pieces. For it didn't matter how happy Tilly looked right now, how happy a couple they seemed…how would they be a year or two or ten down the line when life tested them? What then?

And as for her other sisters, the pressure…

Three months she'd spent trying to find a way out of the condition. Three long months of speaking to lawyers in the states, going around in circles and getting nowhere. Refusing to admit defeat and feeling it all the same…

She scrolled down the article until the small headshot of her father came into view. As if the world needed a reminder of who their father was and who they were by association…

Eve swallowed the rising sickness and slammed the laptop shut.

How could he do this to them when his own marriage had been such a sham?

To think her parents' love affair had been lauded across Australia, their famed whirlwind romance leading to a lasting Happy Ever After with three daughters and a glorious happy home, a tale to be celebrated.

And it had all been a lie...

At least her sisters now knew the truth, she wasn't alone in shouldering it any more, but the clock was ticking. They had nine months to wed or get out of this mess. And get out of it she would. For Rose's sake.

Garrison Downs might be a distant memory for Eve, but for her big sister, it was her home, her livelihood, her everything. Eve had no desire to return, let alone own any part of it. And Matilda now had a whole kingdom of her own to go at.

As for Anastasia, heaven knew what she made of it all and Eve didn't want to care. Ana was a reminder of the affair Eve wanted to forget. So, no, what mattered was Rose and securing it for Rose.

But *marriage*?

The idea made her shudder, fear setting in. Because if Matilda was already married, what was to stop Rose doing the same? Throwing away her life, her happiness, because she couldn't see another way out.

Or Ana for that matter. She might not know the girl but no woman deserved to be chained to a man because of their father's screwed-up legacy.

One of them had to keep a clear head and she feared she was the only one with a heart detached enough to do it.

Home of the Harringtons, Marni,
South Australian Outback,
September

'You'll need to keep a close eye on those Waverly girls.'

'Women, Dad. They're women.' Nate turned from the study window where he'd been watching his mother tend to her vegetable patch, preferring the sight of her presence out there over the company this side of the glass. 'Last I checked, they're all in their twenties now.'

His father gave a rattling cough, one frail hand trembling in his direction as he shifted in his seat behind the desk. 'Don't be so pedantic.'

Nate held his tongue. He didn't have the taste for a fight. Not when he was still coming to terms with the sight of his father like this. Broken. Weak.

His thick dark hair streaked with grey and thinning on top. Skin an unhealthy shade of pale and hazel eyes, dim and yellow, obscured by small round spectacles. Spectacles he'd never needed before. Just as he hadn't needed the walking stick…or for his son to hurry home and take on the family firm.

He stifled a derisive laugh. *Needed*. By his father of all people.

There'd been a time when Nate would have cherished that call. Cherished the moment his father acknowledged that he was good enough for Harrington Law, good enough for him.

But that call hadn't come because George Harrington finally thought his son was good enough, it had come because he was desperate. Forced into retirement on the grounds of ill health, a move considered long overdue by everyone else but the man himself, and he had no one else to ask.

'They'll always be Holt's girls to me,' his father said, garnering strength from somewhere. Grief for his oldest client? Concern for the women now without their father? 'And they need looking out for.'

And where was this concern for Nate growing up?

If only his father had shown a fraction of it, how different things could've been. Maybe he wouldn't have left for Sydney and set up on his own. Maybe they would've had a relationship, something that wasn't this…

'Looking out for them would be seeing this arcane stipulation thrown out.'

'That arcane stipulation is there for a reason.'

'So you say…'

'It's for their benefit as much as the land.'

He widened his gaze, his nod slow as he drawled, 'Right.'

'Don't mock me, son.'

'I'm not mocking you. I'm mocking the condition.'

'The condition, as executor of the will, you're now responsible for overseeing.'

'Whatever you say, Dad.'

Nate went back to the window, buried his hands in his jeans as he watched his mother fill her basket with fresh pickings. Her floral dress as bright and summery as her smile had been when he'd arrived. Her relief to have him home as obvious as her joy. It twisted him up inside. Guilt for not coming home more. Guilt for not wanting to be here now.

'You're not filling me with confidence.'

Nate's bitterness rolled with his laugh. 'When did I ever, Dad?'

He kept his eyes on his mother, seeking her out as he had as a child, when he'd needed the calm, the warmth, some affection…often finding her doing the same, tending to the garden or cooking up something delicious in the kitchen. Carving out her own space within the home that had always felt broken to Nate.

No wonder he'd migrated towards her. He was his mother through and through. Blond hair, blue eyes, an easy smile and ready zest for life…something his father had done his best to stifle growing up. More work, less play. A hard word spoken worth a thousand soft. How his mother coped, Nate hadn't a clue.

'This is important, son. You need—'

'What I *need* is for you to let me do my job,' Nate interjected. 'I said I'd come home. I said I'd take on the firm. I said I'd see this job done and I will. I don't have to like it.'

His father muttered something incoherent, but Nate was done with the discussion. He was done with the entire visit. He didn't want to be here. For as much as he loved his mother, he couldn't bear being in the same room as his father. The man's presence enough to see the inferiority complex Nate grew up with creep back in. Weaving like a vine through everything he'd achieved, suffocating and smothering until it no longer existed.

Didn't matter that he'd made youngest equity partner his global law firm had ever seen, his penthouse overlooking Sydney harbour as sought after as his legal clout, his father still had the ability to make him weak.

'Just tell me one thing,' he said, 'how did it get to this point? Holt must have realised the implication of having no sons...'

'He never raised it with me.'

'And you, *you* didn't think to raise it with him?' His frown was sharp...whatever he thought of his father, he'd never doubted the lawyer in him. 'Or does the idea of four women being forced into marriage sit well with you?'

Another cough racked his body and Nate bit back a curse. Hating that he cared.

It was time to go. He'd done what he set out to, collected the keys for his father's office in town—now his—and arranged for the boxes of paperwork he had squirrelled away here to be shipped back. He could leave.

So why were his feet still rooted?

The answer walked past the window, her eyes lighting on his and her smile worth every chilling second in his father's company. He waved.

'He will have had his reasons.'

'Reasons he never shared because you failed to raise it?'

'Holt knew that document inside out, to raise it would be to question his judgement.'

'But as his lawyer...?'

'As his lawyer—' He broke off, coughing harder, unrelenting. He beat his chest, struggling to catch his breath and Nate stepped forward, panic rising.

'Dad—'

'Don't!' His father urged him back. 'Don't you dare pander to me.'

Pander? Nate shook his head. Frustrated by his father's re-action, frustrated even more by the concern he couldn't quash. 'I wouldn't dream of it.'

'As his lawyer and his friend, I respected his wishes.'

'And you honestly think he wished for this?'

'I think he wished for his daughters to have someone to share the vast responsibility of Garrison Downs with, just as he had Rosamund. She was his rock.'

'How can you say that when you know of the affair?'

Nate had been thrown by the discovery. Up until recently, he, like everyone else, had believed the idyllic fairy tale that was the great romance of Aussie tycoon Holt Waverly and English socialite Rosamund Lavigne. Nate had believed the man to have everything he wanted for himself one day. A ca-reer, a wife, children, a happy home perfectly in balance. Not like his childhood. Not like this home.

But then it hadn't been quite so perfect, after all. Anasta-sia's existence proved that.

'Granted, they had their challenges in the early days, when the girls were young and Rosamund was unwell, and neither knew what was wrong.'

'And what was wrong?'

His father gave him a peculiar look. 'It's not my place to say. Just take my word for it, the affair was short-lived. Their marriage survived and their love was stronger for it.'

Nate shook his head. 'If you say so...'

'I do. Though...' His father hesitated, his gaze drifting to the window and giving Nate the impression he was losing him to his thoughts. Eventually, he said, 'Truth be told, I think Holt hoped the bequest would unite them.'

'Unite them?'

'The sisters.' He met Nate's confused frown. 'Aside from Rose and Matilda, they live very separate lives and I think he feared that would never change. He saw Rose as too married to the land. Evelyn never coming home. Matilda never leav-ing. And as for Anastasia, he may have regretted the affair, but he loved her and what better way to ingratiate her into the family she's never known than to permit this?'

Nate was reluctant to admit it, but there was something in that…not a lot, but something.

'It may not be fair and could be deemed sexist and anti-quated but—'

'There's no may or could about it, Dad.'

His father gave a heavy sigh, removed his glasses and rubbed a weary hand across his brow. 'But it's how Holt left things and I need you to do this for me. After that, you can do whatever you wish. Go back to Sydney and your fancy city life, forget all about Marni and what it means to be a part of this community…'

Nate would contradict him if he thought his father would hear him. Experience told him he wouldn't.

'Hell, maybe you'll decide to stay and make something of my legacy as I'm sure Holt's daughters will do with his…your mother would certainly like that.'

He scoffed and his father's gaze collided with his.

'Please…' he clenched his fist upon the desk '…do this one thing for me and make me proud?'

'Proud?' Nate choked out.

'Is that too much to ask?'

After thirty-five years of trying, it was.

'Son?'

Nate shook his head. He could fight back, but what was the point? His father wouldn't change and he wasn't the boy desperate for his father's affection any more.

'I'll do my job. No more, no less. Now, if that's everything I'll be off…'

He headed for the door and his father shot up faster than he would have thought possible. 'You're leaving?'

'I think I've served my purpose by being here, don't you?'

He paused to give his father his full attention and the man studied him back, his gaze making Nate's skin prickle and his ears burn. 'Your mother was hoping you'd stay for dinner.'

His mother... There he went again, putting it all on her.

'And you?' he dared to press. 'Were you hoping the same?'

'I'm sure we can put our differences aside for one meal.'

He shook his head, huffed out, 'Not today.'

He tugged open the door with more force than it required and fought the urge to slam it shut behind him. He took a breath, waited for his pulse to ease before heading off in search of his mother.

He didn't want to upset her with his mood, and yet upsetting her was par for the course whenever he and his hypercritical father were in the same room.

'Sweetheart!'

As if sensing his distress, she appeared in the hallway, hope alive in her sparkling blue eyes. He forced a smile.

'Mum...'

'I was coming to see if you'll be stopping for dinner. I've just picked the most glorious-looking carrots and—'

'Sunday, Mum. I'll come on Sunday.' He gave her a kiss to the cheek to soften the blow. He needed to get over this initial visit, then he could stomach food in his father's company. 'You know how much I love your roast.'

'But you can come Sunday, too. Really, darling, I don't know why you're not staying here...' Though the hesitation in her gaze told him she knew well enough. 'We haven't seen you in so long and your room is all ready for you.'

'Another time...'

'Let the boy go, Sue-Ellen,' came his father's stern command, and his mother's eyes widened, still pleading.

'I'll see you Sunday, Mum. I'm back for good, remember.'

And ignoring his father, he gave her another peck to the cheek and strode out.

Plucking his helmet off the back off his Harley, he shoved it on and mounted the bike. Started the engine. Gave it a hearty, head-clearing rev and rode off. Blasting his father out as he headed deeper into town.

Perched on the edge of a desert, Marni had the essentials—

a shop, a school, a tiny cinema and pubs. Lots of pubs and one with rooms. His home until he could find somewhere to rent. And he was sure he'd find the company far more to his liking there. Company that he hadn't enjoyed in too long.

Sydney had its perks but the people…no one could beat the laid-back scene of the Outback. Give him jeans over a suit any day, preferably with a coldie and his evening was made.

And that was just what he needed to see off the remnants of his father.

The pub, the chilled beer and the…the *company*?

He slowed the bike as he neared the quirky century-old pub, its single-storey sandstone walls, corrugated-iron roof and wide shady veranda, a rustic welcome sight. The country music and cheer spilling out of the open windows and doors inviting too. But amongst the trucks and the motorcycles lined up outside sat a sleek black town car.

At least it would have been sleek before the red dust of the Outback had given it an extra layer. As for the woman step-ping out of it…

She had the grace of a swan and dressed the part too. White flowing skirt, sleeveless white blouse, white heels that threat-ened to touch the sky and hair as gold as the sun starting to dip behind the horizon.

No one wore white in the Outback. Not if they wanted it to stay white.

He chuckled. So much for leaving the city behind…

CHAPTER TWO

EVE STEPPED OUT of the cab, stretched her travel-weary limbs and almost recoiled back into the air-conditioned cabin.

It wasn't as though she'd forgotten how oppressive the heat of the Outback could be, but it was spring. *Not* the height of summer. And the sun was already low in the sky, its amber glow casting shadows over the shack-cum-pub that was to be her home for the night.

As a child, Eve had strolled past The Royal Oak many times but never once had she ventured through the double swing doors. She couldn't say the music and raucous laughter spilling through the shuttered windows were encouraging her to do so now either but, as it was the only place in town with rooms to rent, she had no choice.

Pushing her sunglasses into her hair, she wrinkled her nose. It would be an experience. An experience that beat flying straight to the station where Rose and the pain of old were waiting for her.

Eight years it had been.

Eight years since she'd last visited as an outsider at her own mother's funeral…she pressed a hand to her chest, suppressed the rising shiver.

'That's everything,' her driver said, setting her luggage down. 'You want me to take them in, ma'am?'

Her mouth twitched. Ma'am? Really?

'No. Thank you.' She hitched her handbag under her arm. 'I can take it from here.'

'Fair enough.' The chap frowned at the building and scratched the back of his head. Probably wondering what a woman like her was doing in a place like this. Not that she could blame him. She looked like the outsider she was and that suited her fine. She didn't want to belong. Marni was her past and the sooner she could put it in the rear-view mirror again, the better.

He dipped his cap and drove off, a cloud of red dust kicking up in his wake, and she flapped a hand. Coughed. Whether it was really in her lungs or not, the pesky red stuff was everywhere, clinging to every surface and now her white linen culottes too.

She grimaced and flicked at her thigh, creating streaks out of the tiny specks and making it so much worse.

And why did that feel like some omen?

Ignoring the foolish thought, she threw her travel bag over her shoulder and grabbed the recessed suitcase handle, pressed the button to extend it and strode forth—promptly falling back again.

What in the...?

She eyed the unmoving handle, the stubborn suitcase with it. Rocked the entire thing side to side and tried again, her cool rapidly depleting in the cloying heat. There was no breeze, no reprieve. And that wasn't all the years in London talking, this smacked of a heatwave. Just what she needed when she was so far out of her comfort zone already.

'Come! On!'

She yanked at her case, her outburst drowned out by the roar of an approaching motorcycle. Its pace slowed and her neck prickled. The last thing she needed was some biker coming to her aid or, worse, sitting back as an amused audience to her plight.

The engine cut and she kept her gaze averted. Tried every angle, every move, her other bags threatening to hit the dirt.

'Need a hand, miss?'

Ma'am. Miss. What she wouldn't give to have a good old British luv thrown at her!

The bike creaked as he dismounted, boots hitting earth.

'I'm fine!' she hurried out, staring at the unresponsive case as if she could murder it with her mind. 'Thank you!'

'Suit yourself,' came the deep burr, though she sensed his eyes still on her. Probably as bemused and bewildered as the cab driver.

She ignored the prickling awareness running down her spine. Awareness and perspiration—*ew*!

Lifting one foot and bracing it against the case, she gave the handle a hefty tug, so hefty it almost sent her toppling back as, finally, it came loose. With a triumphant harrumph, she moved before she could appear any more inept and pushed her way through the doors into…into…

Oh, dear God.

The country music vibrated through the floorboards into her dainty stilettos as she breathed in the stench of beer and… *cowboy*—the only suitable descriptor for the masculine tinge in the air.

All around her, Outback paraphernalia cluttered every wall. Beer bottles and mats, cans, street signs, local notices, trophies, awards. You couldn't see the ceiling for Akubras, well-worn and well-stained. Her nose wrinkled further…if it kept on going it would disappear inside her head.

And that was when she felt it, every eye in the room on her.

Locals who hadn't so much as turned her way, but she sensed their gazes shift beneath the rims of their hats as they assessed the stranger in their midst. Because no one would know who she was. No matter the fame of her family, she bore no resemblance to the girl who'd left all those years ago. The alias she'd used to book the room ensuring she flew under the radar of the Marni gossip train and local media for as long as possible.

She straightened and teetered forward, careful not to lose a heel in the craggy floor, and cleared her dust-filled throat.

A drink. She'd have a cool drink and then she'd... She peered over the counter at the line of fridges and fell at the first hurdle.

Did this place not serve *wine*? They were in South Australia, for goodness' sake!

'G'day, darl.' The bartender approached, his age impossible to decipher with a bushy beard hiding half his face and an impressive hat-shaped wedge in his hatless hair. 'What can I do you for?'

She checked out the other patrons beneath her lashes. Everyone clutched a beer.

'Do you have... Prosecco?'

He arched a brow. 'Prosecco?'

She nodded—*You're the customer, stick to your guns.*

'Right, you are. Ey, Betty, love! Get this one a glass of that bubbly stuff you like.'

A woman appeared from the back, brown hair swinging in a ponytail, shirt tied in a knot across her midriff, bootcut jeans and a wide smile.

'Grab yourself a seat, darl, I'll bring it over.'

She hesitated, looking around. She didn't fancy taking up one of the huge barrels acting as tables in the centre of the room, so she headed to the end of the bar. Out of the way. Set herself down beside an Akubra-wearing longhorn skull, a companion long past judgement, and propped her handbag on the bar just as her phone buzzed from within. She slotted her sunglasses away and pulled out her phone to find a message from Rose.

Landed yet?

She flinched. There was no softness, no kiss, which Eve was sure she'd add for Tilly. Not that she could blame Rose. Her sister had taken it hard when she'd left for the UK with no explanation, taken it ever harder when she'd stood by their grandparents for Mum's funeral and then failed to return for

Dad's. And though Eve knew Rose had pieced some of it together, they had yet to have *that* conversation…

She kept her response equally brief.

Here. Safe and Sound. I'll be with you tomorrow.

Sure you don't want me to come get you?

Eve clenched her teeth. And spend a full hour's car journey in confined quarters suffering in awkward silence, or, worse, battling it out?

No, thanks. You have the station to run. I'll find my own way.

She then texted Gran to let her know she'd arrived safe. Since her grandfather had died six years ago, Granny Lavigne had transferred all her concern Eve's way and Eve often wondered how much of it was regret over the past and a wish for a better future, one in which she could embrace all her granddaughters again.

Another good reason for Eve to be here and help bridge that gap.

Another huge feat.

'Here you go, darl.' Betty set her drink down with a bowl of crackling and a wink. 'You look like you could do with it, honey.'

Do with it? Do with what?

'I wouldn't take offence.'

She started—that voice, the biker…oh, dear God.

She lifted her drink, an *actual* flute, and gulped down a mouthful without tasting. Then, because social etiquette dictated, she forced a smile and turned to face…to face…

Chris Flipping Hemsworth!

Okay, so not really Chris, but maybe his secret brother. She had a secret Ana after all.

'Hi. The name's Nate.'

He offered out a hand—a strong, super-capable hand. Attached to a strong, super-capable forearm, well honed and well inked. Not that she could make out enough of the design before it disappeared beneath the rolled-back cuff to his black shirt.

Eve swallowed air. Ignored the hand and the arm.

'Hi.'

If her body wasn't already cooking in the Aussie heat, her neglected libido would have it stoked to a flurry of flames. No bushy beard here. He sported the very definition of designer stubble cut to enhance a masculine jaw, cheekbones even she would kill for and lips so full and captivating, they made one think of kissing.

Kissing and hot summer nights.

And, jeez, Louise, give it up.

She went back to her drink, took a gulp.

'No name?'

She flicked him a look. His brows were drawn together over eyes that were as bright and as deep as the azure blue sea, though that breath-stealing grin remained wide. She took another swig and told her ovaries to douse the fuse.

'I don't make a habit of giving my name to strangers.'

He chuckled, the sound low and rumbling its way through her. 'Mind if I sit?'

She managed a shrug, crossing her legs and angling away as he slid onto the stool beside her. If only her eyes could be as easily diverted. Instead they drifted his way. Still attractive, still making her blood zing. Windswept hair, overlong, somewhere between blond and brown and streaked with sun-kissed gold.

He leaned into the bar, those ink-adorned forearms flexing with the move, his denim jeans stretching over thick, strong thighs…

He gestured to Betty behind the bar and she came over with a bottle of beer and the obligatory wink.

Either he came here often enough for Betty to know his order, or she'd taken a wild guess. But then Eve was the only one without a beer, it was hardly a leap. She went to take another sip and realised she was out already.

'If you're hoping that'll quench your thirst, you'll be disappointed.'

She sent him a well-rehearsed, unimpressed glance. 'Is that so?'

'Only a coldie can hit that spot…'

His eyes flitted to her chest, where she knew a trickle of perspiration had disappeared down the V of her blouse…and why did it feel as if he'd touched her there too?

She squeezed her legs against the sudden pang.

'Unless…' His eyes sparked with challenge, his mouth lifting to one side.

'Unless what?'

She wet her lips, eyed the condensation on his bottle as he raised it to his lips and her disloyal mouth salivated, her eyes drinking in the motion. His mouth against the bottle, the broadness of his neck, the bob to his Adam's apple, all the way down to the hint of another tattoo where his shirt fell open at the collar…

'Unless you're too fancy for a good old-fashioned beer?'

She shimmied in her seat, righted her shoulders in indignation. 'Not in the slightest.'

His hypnotic blue gaze danced. 'No?'

'I just don't think alcohol is the right drink to quench one's thirst.'

Oh, how prim and proper you sound—Granny Lavigne would be so proud.

'Hence the…' He gestured to her empty glass.

'I was about to order a water.'

'Right,' he drawled, 'course you were.'

She bit back a stubborn retort. Why was she letting him get to her?

He isn't getting to you, he's exciting you! Giving you a buzz you haven't felt outside work in far too long and it's freaking you out.

Hardly surprising when he was so different from the men she dated in London. All designer suits, clean-shaven and careful with every word. Always the gentleman too. Not that he wasn't but…

'Someone say water?'

Betty popped a bottle in front of her and Eve gave a surprised, 'Thank you.'

More grateful that she'd saved her from her rambling thoughts than the drink itself.

'Not a problem, darl. Can I get you another fizz?'

'Please.'

Biker smirked and before she could stop herself, Eve called her back. 'Actually, I'll get…' she grasped for the name of a beer, *any* beer, her jet-lagged brain drawing a blank '…same as what he's having.'

Another ovary-rousing chuckle. 'Don't change your order on my account.'

'Don't flatter yourself, buddy.' A defiant tilt of the chin, her gaze on the barmaid. 'I don't do anything I don't want to.'

'And you want a beer?'

His deep Australian drawl was too damned appealing, as was the pull of his tease and scepticism…

She turned to face him, all fired up. 'Too right I do.'

Said drink appeared beside her and, without looking, she picked it up, arched her head back and drank. Every…last… drop.

Take that, buddy.

Nate watched her neck the beer. Head thrown back, golden hair almost touching the bar, glossy lips wrapped around the bottle as her elegant throat bobbed with every swallow… *Holy mother of…*

With a satisfied 'Ah', she righted the bottle and herself. Eyes sparkling, lips damp, she checked the empty contents. 'You're right, that did touch the spot.'

'You've done that before.'

'Might have.'

Her eyes widened and she tucked in her chin, pressed the backs of her fingers to her lips as she contained a definite burp.

'Excuse me,' and then she laughed. Surprised, horrified, amused. Likely all the above. 'I don't normally do that.'

'Laugh or belch?'

She laughed some more, blushed too. The flush of colour making her blue eyes shine and softening every hard edge she'd been projecting until now. She uncrossed her legs, eased a little closer and he realised he was wrong earlier; it wasn't a skirt but wide-leg pants. The fabric as delicate as she'd first appeared.

But this woman was far from delicate. She was a force of nature, and he was loving every second of their interaction, rebukes and all.

'Actually, come to think of it…' she sobered, as though re-membering what she was about '…both.'

'And that's a mighty shame.'

She gave him the side eye, a look he was coming to enjoy more than he should. Part flirtation, part rack off. 'You want more belching?'

He grinned. 'I want more laughing but if it takes some belching first, it's a price I'm willing to pay.'

Her mouth twitched at the corners. 'How very accommo-dating.'

'Not something I'm used to hearing, but I'll take it.'

She looked at him properly now, twisting in her chair. Her knee brushed against his thigh and his skin came alive, a tan-talising warmth pulsing its way straight to his groin. He took up his beer. Made it appear all causal when he desperately needed the cool distraction…especially when he could sense her cogs working overtime.

'What?'

'You're right, you don't *look* the accommodating type.'

'No?' He narrowed his gaze, lowered his beer. 'How *do* I look?'

She nipped her lip. 'You really want to know?'

Was she *flirting* with him now? Or was that just wishful thinking on his part?

'I wouldn't ask if I didn't.' Though maybe he should reconsider because that look in her eye was taking this somewhere he hadn't expected…somewhere he doubted she had either.

'You look the exact opposite.'

'Which would be?'

'Unmoving. Unobliging.' She leaned closer with each descriptor, and he supped his beer again, finding safety in the distraction. 'Inflexible. Stubborn.'

Definitely flirting, and he was definitely liking it.

'Hard.'

He nearly spat his beer.

'Well, you did ask,' she said, throwing back some water.

'And do you always say what you think?'

She shrugged. 'When it suits me or the task at hand.'

'And is that what I am, some task at hand?'

Her blue eyes pinned him. 'Would you *like* to be my task at hand?'

Woah, this was going too far, too fast, yet he had no desire to make it stop. And clearly, neither did she.

'You're not from around here, are you?'

And just like that, he'd stamped on the brake. He might as well have thrown ice over her for the sudden chill in the air. He was torn between changing topic and asking what was wrong.

The former was the least contentious, especially when they were nothing more than strangers. But the latter was what he really wanted so he opted for something in between.

'Sorry, but those shoes gave you away. Reckon they'll do you some mischief in these parts…'

She pursed her lips, her eyes coming alive again.

'Then there's your accent… English if I'm not mistaken.'

'Very perceptive.'

'Perceptive,' he drawled, raising his brows. 'I'll add that to accommodating. My positive traits are growing.'

She was smiling now. Enough for him to bite the bullet

and say, 'So tell me, just what is a woman like you doing in a place like this?'

'Would you believe me if I said I was on holiday?'

'Alone?'

'Who says I'm alone?'

'The luggage at your feet and no companion to be seen.'

'Who says I'm not meeting someone?'

'Are you?'

'Might be.'

'Lucky someone.'

She laughed, her eyes sparkling like Sydney Harbour on a bright summer's day. 'Are you always so smooth?'

'Smooth, perceptive, *and* accommodating. I'm winning today.'

She shook her head. 'Winning indeed. And no.' She pulled a strand of hair from her lip, its glossy fullness holding his eye a second longer than was wise. 'I'm not meeting anyone. I'm here because…'

She blew out a breath, giving herself cheeks like a hamster—not something she'd appreciate hearing, he was sure, but adorable all the same.

'Because?' he pressed when she didn't continue, her gaze falling to the empty beer bottle as she rocked it against the bar.

'Because I have a family issue to take care of and…' she cast her gaze over the room '…it's complicated.'

'In my experience, families always are.'

'You too?'

He took a swig of beer and sucked the air through his teeth. 'Let's just say my father and I don't get along.'

'Now there's a tale I understand…' She clinked her bottle against his, warming to him again. 'What is it with yours?'

'Aside from me being invisible to him growing up?' He doused the bitterness with another sip. 'Nothing I ever did was good enough.'

'Let me guess…' her eyes were soft with understanding,

the kind that came from experience '…another sibling steal the limelight?'

'No. No siblings. Just me. I guess you did though.'

She nodded.

'How many siblings stole your stage?'

Her mouth twisted. 'Too many.'

'Sisters, brothers?'

'All sisters.'

He winced. 'So what are you? The eldest, the youngest, middle…'

'Second eldest.'

'Forever in your older sister's shadow?' he surmised. 'Or overlooked for the younger, the needier?'

'You really are quite astute…'

'So you've said. Perceptive, remember.'

'For a man, it's quite refreshing.'

'And I'm sure I should be accusing you of sexism now.'

'So why aren't you?'

'Because I'm too interested in what makes you tick.'

She shook her head, her laugh more strained now. 'Are we really doing this?'

'Doing what?'

'Having a dose of family therapy at the bar?'

'Better some therapy than none.'

She stared at him. 'Are you always like this with people you've just met?'

'When they interest me.'

She gave a soft chuckle, held his eye as she took a swig of water, then, 'If you really must know, my older sister is my father in female form, she could do no wrong. My younger sister is all sunshine and light, and again…'

'She could do no wrong,' he said with her. 'And your other?'

Her jaw pulsed, her eyes evading him as she muttered something that sounded much like, 'Damned if I know.'

'I'm sorry?'

'Nothing.'

'Let me guess…' he smiled softly '…it's complicated.'

'Got it in one. So what was your father's excuse?'

'He was married to his work.'

'Something else that sounds familiar…'

'You too? What does he do?'

'Did.' She swallowed, her jaw pulsing again. 'He's dead.'

He stilled, his hand reaching between them. 'I'm sorry, I didn't—'

'I'm not.' Though it came out forced, too quick, too learned.

'In that case, I'm even more sorry.'

'Don't be, I lost my father long before he left this world.'

Her eyes blazed but beneath the fire there was pain. Unresolved. Potent.

'Want to talk about it?'

She cocked a brow at him, scoffed, 'No.'

'Okay, "want" is the wrong word to use, how about "need"? Because I'm willing to listen. No judgment. All ears.'

'Nice try, but I'm not all mouth so…' She sipped her water, her mouth very much drawing him in as she dismissed the turn in conservation as readily as they'd hit on it.

What was it about this woman that made him want to go deeper, to dig beneath the cool facade to the woman beneath?

When was the last time he'd felt such a pull…?

Had he ever?

He forced himself to relax back on his stool, to ease up. If she didn't want to talk about it, it wasn't right for him to push it. 'I rarely talk about my father either.'

'And your mother?' she asked, coming back to him a little.

'She's an entirely different breed from him.' He smiled. Thoughts of his mum making the gesture easy. 'Soft, loving, always willing to listen. Always nagging me to come home too.'

She blinked, her gaze falling away but not before he swore he caught a tear. 'That's nice.'

'It has its moments,' he said, carefully. 'What about yours?'

Though he sensed her answer in the melancholic air, whatever had tainted her relationship with her father, it didn't seem to extend to her mother because there was no bitterness now, only sadness. 'Also, dead.'

He reached out again but this time he covered her hand, warm and soft beneath his own. 'I'm sorry.'

She took a shallow breath, gave the tiniest of shrugs. 'It was a long time ago now. I don't know why it hurts so much.'

'She was your mother. It's always going to hurt.'

'She was my mother but…'

She slipped her hand from his, gripped it in her lap.

'But?'

She gave a rapid shake of her head, rolled her shoulders back, parking whatever it was some place deep and not to be examined. 'It's…'

'Complicated?' he finished for her.

'And you know…' she murmured, her eyes lifting to his, their sudden spark catching him unawares, 'I'd much rather talk about these.'

She reached out to lightly trace the tattoo on one arm, her touch firing up the nerve-endings beneath and making the muscle twitch, his entire body tense.

She snatched her hand back, making a fist. 'I'm sorry. I shouldn't have—'

He shook his head. 'Not at all. I just wasn't expecting it.'

Not the delicate touch or the way it powered through him, coiling through his core. Making him want more. So much more.

'How about I trade you background on my tattoos for whatever has that frown forming just there?' He gestured to the crease between her brows, resisting the urge to reach out and smooth it away with his thumb.

'It's an interesting proposition,' she murmured, tilting her head to the side.

'An agreeable one?'

'I'm not so sure…how do I know if it's a fair trade?'

'You don't.'

'You're not selling it very well.'

'On the contrary, I'm rousing your curiosity.'

She laughed, shook her head. 'Is that so?'

'And you seem like a woman who thrives off taking the odd risk.'

She laughed harder. 'At work perhaps, but in my personal life…'

'In your personal life they reap the biggest reward.'

Her lashes fluttered. 'Now I know you're talking nonsense.'

'And you're a woman who avoids talking about anything deep and meaningful so…?'

'You think you have me sussed.'

'I think I have a fair idea of the woman you are and we haven't even exchanged names.'

'Oh, we did… You're Nate.'

'And you are?'

She gave him a cocky grin. 'Doesn't my lack of identity make this connection all the more thrilling?'

'Thrilling for you, yes.' And he had to admit, he liked her putting words to it. A connection. It meant she felt it too. This intense attraction that had his body so attuned to hers while their verbal sparring had his head firing too. 'But it puts me at a disadvantage.'

Her smile widened. 'Just where I like you.'

'Beautiful *and* power-hungry. That's quite the combination.'

She leaned a little closer. 'In my line of work, it pays to be both.'

'And what line is that?' he pressed, sensing he was close to learning something real.

'Public relations, advertising, marketing people's wares…'

It certainly fit the image.

'Any hobbies on the side?'

'Just work.'

'No husband, no partner…'

'No time for a man.'

He cocked a brow. 'Don't you ever get lonely?'

'I don't have time to get lonely.'

'Yet here you are, in a bar…'

'I'm on a three-month sabbatical.'

And she didn't sound happy about it.

'Already missing it?'

'Quite.'

'Now you remind me of my father.'

'Ouch.'

She was teasing, he wasn't. The similarity should have been enough to see him giving his goodbyes…instead his butt was rooted, his body leaning closer.

'So, do I get a name?'

She pursed her lips, narrowed her gaze…

'What name would you give me?'

'Oh, no, you don't.' He eased back. 'I'm not playing this game.'

'Why not?'

'Too much at stake.'

'How so?'

'I give you a name you don't like and you wrinkle your nose like you did when you stepped out of that cab back there. Or the opposite happens, I give you a name that implies I find you attractive and send you running. There's no right answer and, thus, I cannot win.'

She laughed softly. 'You're probably right.'

'So?'

'It's Eve.'

'Eve?'

Her gaze flicked over the room. 'Just Eve.'

'Well, *just* Eve, you have improved my day a hundred times over and for that, I thank you.'

'No thank you necessary, you've done the same for me. I've dreaded this trip and I was counting down the seconds until I can escape again. Meeting you has put a temporary pause on that ticking clock.'

He frowned at the depth of feeling behind her words, at how much she hated it here… Or hated what had brought her here?

'What's with the frown?' she purred.

'I'm disappointed you're in such a hurry to leave.'

'Why? Are you sticking around because, pardon me for being so blunt, you don't look like you're from around here either?'

'I don't?'

'You're a little rough around the edges, granted, but your beard is too groomed, your accent too city-like…'

'Very perceptive,' he said, throwing her own compliment back at her and coaxing out another smile.

'Something else we have in common. So…' She tilted her head once more. 'You didn't answer my question—are you sticking around?'

'If things work out how I plan, yes.'

'Things with your family or…'

'Family and work.'

'And what plans are those?'

'I thought you didn't want to sweat the serious stuff, right now?'

She gave him a slow smile. 'Okay. Tattoos it is…'

And then her hands were back on him, her fingers tracing the black ink, and it was all he could do to keep his cool and concentrate on the words passing through her lips rather than what he wanted to do with them.

'Tell me about this one…'

He shifted in his seat, told his body to behave. 'You like him?'

'Him?' She raised both brows. 'I don't know, I can't see *him* properly.'

'Is that you asking for a better look?'

'Maybe.'

He chuckled low in his throat, placed his beer down and rolled back his cuff. She lowered her gaze, eyes distinctly hungry, their heat working its way through him too as she reached out to lift his arm closer and gave a breathy, 'Oh!'

She might as well have had an orgasm and been blissful in

its aftermath for the image that simple sound evoked. Did she have any idea what she was doing to him? Her appreciation. Her extended touch. Her blazing blue eyes.

'That's impressive.' She stroked her fingers over his skin, tracing the intricate sketch of a wolf emerging from a forest, one paw reaching down his arm.

'Not what my father thought,' he said, recalling the showdown with a grim smile. 'Nor my mother, though she came around eventually.'

'How old were you when you had it done?'

'Eighteen. A rebellious move born of a rebellious teen.'

'Your father's words?'

'Words of that ilk, yes.'

Her eyes lifted to his. 'And what was it for you?'

'He wasn't entirely wrong. The wolf represents what family should be about, the pack instinct. Loyalty, communication, protection, shared wisdom…everything my father isn't.'

'Oh…' no bliss now, just sadness '…hence the rebellion?'

He nodded, holding her gaze—the sense that she got him, that they got each other overwhelming, overpowering even. A connection that ran far deeper than such a brief encounter would ordinarily permit.

And then she smiled, her lashes lowering, one hand lifting to his neck.

'What about this one…?' She touched her fingers to his clavicle, the pads soft and tantalising as she stroked them lower.

'That's the tip of a wedge-tailed eagle in flight.'

'An eagle?' Her eyes didn't leave his chest. 'How big is it?'

He took hold of her hand. 'It goes from here…' he traced her finger along his collarbone '…to here…' around his shoulder '…and all the way along the back, to right about…here.'

With her hand now hooked over his shoulder, he leaned closer, his gaze falling to her softly parted lips. 'He represents strength, courage, and freedom.'

'Freedom from your father?'

Yes, she got him, all right.

'Are there more?'

'More?' He was struggling to focus. This close he could see the inner ring of fire around her pupils, could see the light dusting of freckles beneath her make-up, along her cheeks and the bridge of her nose, all the more prominent with the lustful flush to her skin. And her lips, hell, she kept wetting them, leaving a glossy trail that was driving him crazy.

He tried to breathe but all he got was her scent…sun and sex, tangled up in the beer they had drunk. A surprising and enticing aphrodisiac.

'More animals,' she said, 'more ink?'

Right, they were still on the tattoos…

'Yes.'

'I'd like to see.'

'You would?'

This wasn't the norm. He didn't just meet a girl, share a few drinks and… He swallowed the sudden tightness in his chest. A sudden burst of nerves that he didn't understand.

She nodded. 'If you'd like to show me…?'

'Are you sure?'

She blinked, the fire in her eyes dimming. 'Not if you're not.' She started to turn away. 'I'm sorry, this really isn't like me. I don't know what I was thinking—'

'I think you were thinking exactly what I was thinking.'

She gave a choked laugh. 'You don't know what you're saying.'

'Don't I?' He took her hand, angled her back towards him, waiting for those blue eyes to reach his before assuring her, 'I don't do this either. But this connection between us is something else and if you're sure you want to explore it, I will take you to my room right now. *Every* tattoo yours to read.'

She pressed her lips together, her nostrils flaring with her breath, her eyes alight once more. 'I'd like that.'

CHAPTER THREE

EVE HUFFED OUT a breath and tucked her head beneath the pillow, hiding from the dawning light threatening to penetrate her eyelids before she was ready.

What had she been thinking?

Thinking? Her self-conscious laughed. *There had been* no *thinking.*

She'd been too busy losing herself in the company of a man who made her feel more than she had in years, revelling in his attention, his flirtation, his genuine interest in everything about her.

Not her skills as a PR specialist, not her standing in society, not her sisterly wisdom as the emotionally detached outsider of the family.

Just her. Eve.

And it had been thrilling and intoxicating and everything she'd needed from the moment she'd stepped off the plane onto Australian soil.

And now she was in his bed. Not her hotel room. His.

And though she hated to admit it, reality beckoned, aka Garrison Downs and her sisters, and it was time to move. But first…she wasn't so crass as to kiss and run.

Though 'kiss' was an understatement of epic proportions.

A night of wild, intense lovemaking with a sprinkling of therapy more like. A connection that she hadn't been looking for, hadn't needed, but it had found her anyway.

The kind of connection life had taught her to run from—

not indulge in. Because intense passion was for fools. It didn't last. It didn't equate to the perfect life, happy wife. Life lesson learned, courtesy of Ma and Pa.

So exit stage left…if she could just find it…or him.

Because now she thought on it, she couldn't hear him. She wasn't aware of him close by. No heavy breathing. No movement. Just the gentle hum of the air-conditioning unit.

Reaching out, she tentatively probed the sheets. Cold. Vacant. She peeled open one eye, wincing against the light leaking through the pale curtains.

White walls, wooden floor, a bedside table, wardrobe, her carelessly tossed clothing on a chair and two doors. One to the bathroom, one to the outdoors.

But no man.

Had he left before she could? Something deep within her squirmed and it wasn't the relief her head told her to feel.

She groaned and hid back under the pillow. Night one of her homecoming and she'd already lost her head. It didn't bode well for the rest of her trip, didn't bode well at—

The door clicked open then closed. Her pulse tripped out, rapping as loud as his boots against the floor. She peered out from beneath her fluff-filled haven and…*oh my*, he was even better looking the morning after.

'Hey…' She scraped her hair out of her face, tried to moisten her mouth that felt as dry as sandpaper.

'Morning, gorgeous.'

Gorgeous? Hardly!

'Took a punt you were a coffee drinker.'

He lifted his hands. Two takeaway cups, paper bags too— he'd been out fetching her breakfast! Her heart gave another wild beat and she pushed herself up, tugging the sheet with her.

'I can't believe you brought me coffee.'

'I did, but if you'd rather something else I can nip back out.'

'No. Coffee's perfect.' She tried for a smile. 'Thank you.'

Coffee was more than perfect. He was more than perfect. How did he look so good so early? Smell so good too. All fresh and masculine. Citrus and oak. He must have showered while she'd slept and the idea of him naked in the next room, under the jets, was enough to slice through the morning fog and have a heat coiling down low.

He passed her a cup. 'You're sure?'

'Absolutely.' She strengthened her smile, lifted the lid off the coffee and breathed in the aroma with a sigh. 'Caffeine. The nectar of the gods.'

'You'll hear no argument from me.' He settled back beside her. The scene too cosy by far. She peeked his way. Watched as he took a sip of his own, marvelled at his profile in the fresh light of day and decided. He was the best-looking man she had ever met. And last night... Her cheeks and belly warmed. Scenes flashing before her mind.

'About last night...' She wet her lips. 'I'm sorry if I was... I hope I wasn't...too much.'

His mouth twitched, his eyes flashed. 'Define what you mean by too much.'

She swallowed her rising blush. 'I know I can be quite forceful.'

'You were that.'

'And demanding.'

'You were that too.'

'And I like to take control.'

'You definitely do.'

There was no swallowing *this* blush. But he was grinning, the heat in his eyes nursing the salacious ache low in her abdomen.

And then she remembered how she must look, how she must...*smell*.

'You okay?'

'Yeah.' *No.*

'You're doing that nose thing...'

'I'm fine.' She forced her nose to behave, tried to smooth back her morning bush of a hairdo and sipped at her coffee, praying it would reinstate her sense of calm.

'I'll pretend I believe you.'

His response tickled her, provoking a smile she wouldn't have thought possible.

'Breakfast?' He offered her one of the bags. 'Now, in the interests of full disclosure, I figured you were an avocado on sourdough kind of a girl, but this is what you really need.'

She eyed him, eyed the bag that already had signs of grease seeping through, and her nose wrinkled further. 'Which is?'

'One of Jenna's infamous brekky burgers.'

'Jenna of Roarke's Cafe?'

'You know it?'

She looked inside the bag. Greasy and very much *not* her thing. 'I didn't think Jenna would still be there.'

'So long as Jenna walks the earth, she'll be there.'

She smiled, the bittersweet memory of Mum taking her and her sisters there after school for the occasional treat coming back to her. The stacked pancakes, lashings of syrup and bacon. Even a dollop of cream too.

'Now, that smile's more like it.'

The approval in his tone caught at her chest. Coupled with his kindness and compassion, he was teasing at a part of her she kept locked away. A part she *needed* to keep locked away.

'Ever tried one?'

'Huh?'

'A brekky burger?' He gave her a bemused smile. 'It's not as bad as it looks, I promise.'

Grateful he'd misread her reaction, she placed her coffee down and rolled back the paper. 'If you say so.'

'You'll thank me for it later.' He took a bite of his own with an unrestrained groan. 'And they're as good as ever.'

Unconvinced, she gave it a tentative sniff. 'And what's in it? Exactly.'

'Best just try it first… Dare you.'

A laugh bubbled up. 'You *dare* me?'

'Uh-huh.'

She shook her head, her smile growing. What was it about

this guy? Knowing just what to say to make her smile, laugh, to do just as he asked…

She scooped out the overstuffed bread roll, met his gaze and took a hefty bite and… *Oh, my!*

She chewed as her taste buds sang, confused but elated. So much going on, so much deliciousness and naughtiness and all in one mouthful. Bacon. Egg. Cheese. Potato. Onion. And…oh, that sauce!

She took another bite, and closed her eyes on a blissful sigh. She felt better already. Okay, so it seemed coffee, a brekky burger, and Nate were the perfect wake-up call. She opened her eyes to admit he was right and found him watching her, the heat in his gaze working with the heat still simmering within her.

'Jenna should get you to advertise, she'd make millions if not billions.'

'I really don't think any company would want me as their frontman right now.'

'How can you say that?'

'Because I haven't bathed, haven't done my make-up and my hair looks like I've been zapped by lightning. I'm hardly the vision of health.'

'You couldn't be more wrong.' It was gruff, sincere, the intensity of his gaze stealing her breath away. 'Your cheeks are glowing, your eyes are bright, your hair is wild for sure, but it suits you. And it's taking my all not to throw breakfast aside and devour you instead.'

'You need glasses…' but it came out breathless, heated, the riot of butterflies within her impossible to ignore.

'There's nothing wrong with my sight.'

'You sure about that?'

'Never more.'

She swallowed the wedge in her throat, wet her lips and he tracked the move, hungry but not for food. 'Your burger will get cold.'

'A price I'm willing to pay.'

'Nate, I...'

You what? You want him to stop saying all the sweet things? You want him to stop making you feel *all the sweet things? Just get out of bed, get dressed and take your breakfast with you. Thank him for a great night and leave it at that.*

It was the sensible thing to do.

The right thing to do.

Only her body wasn't obeying.

He was leaning closer, the sheet covering her modesty slowly slipping away, caressing her sensitised skin...

'Nate,' she breathed.

'Eve,' he breathed back.

They came together, fierce and desperate. Breakfast shoved aside for their lips, their bodies...

She tugged his T-shirt up and over his head as he joined her beneath the sheets, his fingers biting into her behind as she hooked her leg around him, moaning as the hard ridge of his jeans came up against the sensitised heart of her.

She arched back as he deepened their kiss, heat rushing through her middle, filling her breasts as her nipples hardened against the tantalising wall of his chest. The rough friction of his body driving her to the precipice.

He pressed his forehead to hers, sucked in a breath. 'How can you not see what a temptress you are?'

She laughed, the sound tight in her chest, her throat, his words too much like something out of a romance novel. Books she had once loved and devoured, then dismissed as fantastical nonsense the day she'd learnt the truth about her parents.

About the fickleness of love.

'Anyone ever tell you you talk too much?' she murmured, beating back the chill trying to work its way in as she pushed him onto his back and fenced him in with her thighs.

He gave a throaty chuckle. 'And there she is, the lioness coming out to play.'

She nipped his lip. 'Are you complaining?'

'Not for a second.'

She held his fiery gaze as she undid his jeans. 'Good, because I don't need you whispering sweet nothings, Nate.'

'Even when they're not nothing?'

'Ooh, a double negative,' she teased, though her throat contracted, her heart too.

'I'll give you a double...'

He palmed her neck and brought her swiftly down to meet his kiss. Hard and unrelenting. As though he sensed her need to block out all else but this.

They kissed until her panic subsided and need took over. Kissed until it was him on top of her and he finished the job she'd started, shucking the rest of his clothing. He reached into his jeans for his wallet and protection, sheathed himself in a heartbeat and then he was rising over her. His mouth feverish against hers, his hands stroking and teasing and making her plead.

'Please, Nate, I want you.'

He nudged her thighs around him. 'I want you too.'

He pushed inside her with a groan that had her body trembling and tightening in one. He pressed a kiss to her ear, defiantly whispered sweet nothings—delicious things about the way she felt, the things he wanted to do, all things that her body revelled in and she was helpless to deny. Driving her higher as she rocked with him, savouring it all.

Life forgotten in a moment of bliss that had her crying out his name, over and over.

She clung to the high, wanting to keep it, extend it, rejoice in it for ever...

Though for ever was an impossibility. She knew it even as she fought for it. And as he cried out her name, she reciprocated, her muscles contracting as pleasure took over, shattering within her, a thousand tiny eruptions making her shudder and shake.

She rode the wave with him, moved with him, breathed with him. Perfect unison.

Until he sank down beside her, his arm heavy across her

middle, kissed her shoulder and held her close. Held her as though she were his to hold. And she stared at the ceiling. Stared so hard she could blame the dampness in her eyes on her failure to blink because, hell, she wanted to cry. Again.

And why?

It was silly. Stupid. They'd had a great night. A great morning.

She should be happy, elated. Ready to leave on a high.

'Coffee, a brekky burger and sex for breakfast,' Nate murmured, his breath hot on her neck. 'I'd say we're the vision of domestic bliss, wouldn't you?'

Hell, no. Because domestic bliss suggested something more. Something serious. Something with the impossible: longevity.

'I should go.'

His body pulled taut, his head lifting. 'Now?'

'Yes.'

He was trying to catch her eye, but she was inching away, slipping free of his grasp.

'But you haven't finished your breakfast.'

'I'll take it with me.'

She was already on her feet, gathering up her clothes and her suitcase as she hurried into the bathroom. She closed the door and fought the urge to sink against it, refusing to succumb to her racing thoughts as she focused on what she had to do, as a robot would a routine. Freshened up. Tied her hair back. Forwent the usual make-up. Threw on the first clothes that came to hand—silk cami and floaty pants—and donned her ballet pumps for a quick exit.

She needed to get out of there.

When she emerged, he was clothed and sitting up against the headboard, one leg crossed over the other. Everything about him relaxed save for his eyes as they met her own.

'Better?'

She cleared her throat, gripped the handle of her suitcase as though it were the only thing holding her up. And it probably was. Her body still weak with the echo of her orgasm, the rebellious desire to lose her head and slip back beneath the sheets, too.

'Much. Thank you for breakfast…and for last night.'

'No need to thank me.' His voice was rich, thick with whatever thoughts he'd been entertaining in her absence. 'I think we both got something out of it.'

'We did.'

She headed for the door, kept her focus on it and the sensible decision to be free of whatever this was between them.

'You really are going, then?'

She missed her footing. Thank heaven she was wearing flats. 'I think that's for the best.'

'Can I see you again?'

She swallowed. Didn't turn. 'I don't think that's a good idea.'

She heard his feet hit the floor, the bed groan as he stood. 'Correct me if I'm wrong but everything we've shared so far has felt pretty good.'

'It has,' she conceded, her voice husky with the lustful remnants of the night, the morning, the way he made her feel, not just with his body, but his gentle words too. He paused behind her, his proximity warm against her skin, and she made herself turn and face him. 'Let's not ruin it by trying to make it into something more.'

'Who says it'll ruin it?'

'I do. I'm only in town for a few months and then I'm getting out of here. And I don't intend to look back.'

Not on you, or this place, her head added for emphasis, trying to drown out her heart, which wanted more, so much more.

'Months in which we can have more fun and get to know one another.'

Months in which he could learn that there was nothing more worth loving beneath the surface. Months in which she would be forced to watch the fire in his eyes die out and his interest wane. Months when she should be concentrating on the mess she and her sisters were in, and not the messed-up state her parents' marriage had left her in.

'Nate, there's no future here. I have no interest in getting serious, not now, not ever.'

'That's quite the statement.'

His brows drew together, a lock of hair teasing over one and making her fingers itch to stroke it back. She curled them into her palm.

'What it is, is the truth. I told you, work is my life. I don't have time for a relationship. I don't want a relationship.'

His mouth tugged to one side as he cocked his head, his gaze intense, searching… What was he looking for? A sign that she was lying? A chance to change her mind?

'I have to go,' she whispered.

'Scared you'll change your mind?'

'No. I formed this opinion long ago and one night isn't going to change it. No matter how much fun we had.'

'Fun we were still having up until twenty minutes ago.'

And don't think on it, Eve, not right now.

She turned away before he could lure her in.

'I'm not asking you to marry me, Eve, I'm asking you to date me.'

Now she laughed, his choice of words as amusing as they were triggering. If only he knew the real reason she was here, the 'M' clause, what would he say then?

'Eve?' Gently he turned her to face him. The look in his sexy come-to-bed eyes made her heart sigh. Would it be so bad? A little bit of fun to offset the misery of returning home.

Fun that had the capacity to turn into something else. Something more. Something dangerous. She only had to think on her parents to know that giving such passion any real airtime was asking for a lifetime of regret. Only…

She pressed her lips together, her eyes falling to his. One last kiss in exchange for a lifetime of denial couldn't hurt, could it? She reached up, breathed in his scent, pressed a palm to his warm chest and swept her lips against his, savouring every bit of it, of him.

Then…

He blinked down at her as she fell back, a thousand unspoken questions in his depths and, for one senseless second, she yearned for him to tug her back. Then she remembered her mother's pain, her father's guilt, and her grandmother's cautioning words, 'If you lose your head to your heart, what can you expect?'

Heartache. That was what.

'Goodbye, Nate.'

CHAPTER FOUR

THIS WASN'T HOW Eve had planned her return to Garrison Downs to go.

She'd planned to use the taxi ride to clear her head, her emotions…to see to it that she strode in as the woman she was now. Always composed. Always in control. And determined to get the answers she needed to put an end to this insanity.

Instead, her head was as messed up as her heart.

And she missed London. She missed the hustle and the bustle and the ability to think straight in a sea of people she didn't know.

They'd been driving for almost an hour, red dirt and blue sky for as far as the eye could see. The only verdant relief coming from the sporadic pockets of mallee scrub and saltbush, not a building or a human in sight.

So very isolating and…*ha*, she wanted to say cold, but the chill only existed within her. Courtesy of the past rather than her surroundings. And the closer they got to her childhood home, the more her gut shifted from brekky-burger splendour to roller-coaster turmoil. Because she couldn't be here without feeling it, every memory trying to work its way to the surface. The good, the bad…the ugly.

There was a part of her—a worryingly large part—that wanted to race back to Nate's hotel room and seek out the oblivion he effortlessly provided. Because by his side she hadn't cared about any of this.

No, that wasn't quite true. She'd *cared*, but she'd felt invincible, untouchable, able to deal with anything and everything because he'd been there. Helping her rise above it.

'Here, miss?'

The taxi driver sent her a look over his shoulder and she nodded, her gaze drifting to the gates looming tall on the horizon. The wooden arch with its giant bull horns and the name Garrison Downs burnt deep into the vertical posts. Posts that bore another man's name...a man who now had a chance to take it all back.

She cursed. 'Over my dead body.'

'What was that?' The taxi driver caught her eye in the rear-view mirror and she nipped her lip.

'Nothing. Just thinking aloud...'

Only it wasn't 'nothing', it was everything. For Rose at least. And she had to see the future secure for them all, her sisters, her family...even if that word had lost some of its meaning over the years.

The car slowed as they rolled through the gates, the noise within changing as the road smoothed, the winding driveway almost as long as the town of Marni itself, though the house ahead was more Parisian paradise than Outback grandeur. The luscious gardens surrounding it, too.

An architectural masterpiece, two years in the making and built when Eve had been a child. Dad's project. For Mum. He'd wanted to create the ultimate home from home, a home that was hers rather than the one they'd shared with his parents. Both long gone now but, back then, Grandma's austere and judgemental presence had been enough to make anyone want their own space. Pop included. And though the old home-stead still existed, it was tucked off to the left and hidden by the countless trees Dad had seen planted—the perfect finishing touch to what had been a romantic gesture of gargantuan proportions.

Or so her father claimed.

Now Eve thought about it, Ana's age meant it had to have been built around the time she was born. And didn't that make it the ultimate act of guilt, rather than a gift born of love and thought, care and devotion?

Her stomach rolled anew, and she tugged her gaze from the incriminating structure to take in the distant hills to the east. Hills that housed steep ravines and shady canyons. Dams fed by the many water sources Garrison Downs was blessed enough to have access and the rights to use. Hectares of land for the station's cattle to graze.

She imagined Rose out there now, working hard with her jillaroos and jackaroos. September was their second muster season, she'd be busy from sun-up till sundown, likely too busy to see Eve until she rolled home that night.

Too late and too exhausted to talk…one could hope.

The car came to a stop and Eve lowered her sunglasses.

You've got this.

Pulling her handbag over her shoulder, she reached for the door handle just as movement from the nearest paddock caught her eye. A bay horse and its rider were galloping towards her, a dog hot on their tail.

Rose. She didn't need to see a defining feature to know it in her blood. She took a breath…*here goes*…and pushed open the door.

At least Rose wanted to welcome her back…that was a good sign at least…or not.

Rose drew to a halt at the edge of the field, dismounted and secured her horse's reins to the fence before turning to face Eve. Eve whose heart was in her throat as she stood, ballet pumps rooted to the hard-packed dirt, head racing with how this would play out.

Did she hug, kiss, stand back…shake a hand even?

The derisive slant to Rose's mouth didn't help, not when it was all she could see of her sister's face beneath the rim of her hat as she strode towards her. The dog in step beside her.

'I'll be off then, miss,' the cabbie said, depositing her luggage at her feet.

She thanked him and he sped off, likely keen to get back

to civilisation and she fought the urge to run after him, her attention back on Rose. *Forbidding*, Rose.

In this moment, they appeared as different as night and day.

Rose in her well-worn boots, equally worn Akubra, functional brown ponytail, dust-covered jeans and long-sleeved shirt. All designed to protect as much of her from the sun as possible. While Eve had no such concern.

Her cami was too skimpy, her floaty pants too thin, and she hadn't donned a hat of any kind in so long…unless it was ladies' day at the races, for which she'd wear the most elaborate hair accessory. All for show. None of it practical.

'You remembered where we live, then?' Rose paused a few strides away, her familiar lilt making Eve's heart warm even as she held herself back. The invisible gulf between them ever more pronounced now that they were face to face, her sister's taunt making clear she wasn't ready to cross it.

But then, neither was Eve.

She cocked her head. 'Morning to you too, sis.'

Rose pressed her lips together, her eyes drifting to the luggage at her feet.

'I thought you were staying for a few months…?'

'I am.' Eve lifted her chin. 'I can travel light, you know.'

Travel light and with clothes that wouldn't last two seconds in this part of the world…*nice one, Eve!*

A blatant sign that her brain had quit firing as it should days, if not weeks, ago.

Rose's eyes returned to Eve's, her Waverly blue depths flashing with something…defiance, anger, hurt…but Eve was too caught up in the realisation that they all had those eyes. Dad's eyes. Ana, too. And it was a punch to the gut.

'Well, come on, then,' Rose blustered, flicking the dust out of her ponytail and waving at the house. 'You want a hand with that?' She gave a clipped nod at the case.

'No.' Did her sister really think her *that* incapable? 'I can do it myself.'

Just as she had with all the other, metaphorical baggage she'd carried around all these years…

She threw her travel bag over her shoulder and yanked the case into motion, grateful that it behaved this time, and followed her sister to the house, grimacing as her ballet pumps collected red dust like static on a balloon.

'Thinking about leaving already?'

She looked up to find Rose staring at her from the deck of the porch, her eyes bright with the accusation. Her dog made its own noise too as it sank down next to a bowl filled with water.

'Good girl, Blossom,' her sister murmured, without looking. And Eve realised it was staying put. As a working dog, she wouldn't be allowed inside the house. A rule their mother had laid down…

Hats off, boots off, leave the work at the door!

Save for Father's study, of course. That was his domain. His rules.

And, of course, Rose would be the same.

'Eve?'

'Of course not,' she said, dragging herself out of the memories and up the steps.

But it was no use. As she crossed the threshold, the past assaulted her from every direction. The family heirlooms from their father's side, the exquisite furnishings carefully chosen by their mother, paintings and artefacts inspired by Mum's love of travel…travel that she'd rarely got to enjoy after her marriage because Dad had been married to the land first.

And it didn't matter that it was a vast open space, light and tranquil. High ceilings, white walls, dark-wood accents and polished parquet floor. She might as well have been buried six feet under for all she was suffocated by it.

'You look like you've seen a ghost…'

Barely aware of Rose's remark, Eve gave the smallest shake of her head.

'Why don't you leave your bags there?' Rose tossed her hat

and boots into the mudroom and Eve followed suit with her pumps. 'I've had Lindy arrange us breakfast out by the pool.'

'It's okay, I've already...'

Rose sent her a look that had her refusal dying on her tongue, the uncertain teen she'd once been creeping to the surface...

But you're not that teen any more. You're a successful businesswoman with your own mind, your own will.

'I've already eaten,' she said, releasing her suitcase and dumping her travel bag on top.

'I haven't.'

Eve's mouth twisted to the side. Her sister's message clear. You're coming with me, whether you're eating or not.

And looking at the shadows beneath Rose's eyes, the worry creasing up her brow, Eve realised she owed her big sister this. A conversation that was long overdue.

'Okay,' she acquiesced. 'Breakfast it is.'

They walked through the house, Eve's gaze fixed on her sister and not the memory prompts clamouring for attention. Finally able to breathe when they entered the colonial-inspired pool room with its many French doors thrown open to the gardens beyond. It was a secluded oasis, a place where one could readily forget where they were in the world...where *she* was.

'Thank you, Lindy,' Rose said as a dark-haired woman, buxom and petite, hurried in with a heavily laden tray. 'Eve, this is our housekeeper, Lindy.' Rose pulled out a chair at the table and sat. 'Lindy, meet Eve, my sister.'

Lindy gave Eve a shy smile, her cheeks flushing as she set the tray down with barely a clatter. 'It's a pleasure to meet you.'

'And you,' Eve said, taking a seat beside her sister as Lindy laid out all the items. Water, coffee, juice, toast, fruit, eggs, meats...

Rose surveyed the outdoors as Eve surveyed her. The shadows beneath her sister's eyes were ever more prominent in the bright light of the room, the lines of worry in her face, too... but it was the hollowness to her cheeks that concerned Eve most. Was her sister not eating properly? Was it the exhaustion? The grief? The threat to the station?

'You knew, didn't you?' Rose said quietly, after Lindy had left. 'All this time you knew about Dad's affair and you said nothing.'

'What *could* I say?' Eve said, just as soft. 'You were Dad's shadow, you idolised him.'

'So?' Rose came alive, her head flicking around, her ponytail with it. 'You shouldn't have shouldered that on your own, Evie. I'm your sister! Your *big* sister. It was my responsibility to bear that burden, not yours!'

Eve choked on a laugh. 'You think being the oldest means you deserve that burden?'

'No one deserves that kind of burden…but you could've shared it.'

'I shared it with Mum. I shared it with Dad. And believe me, that only made it worse.'

Rose's eyes blazed. 'They both knew that you knew?'

'About the affair, yes. But I didn't know about Ana. I don't think even Mum knew about her…'

Rose took an unsteady breath, shook her head.

'It's why Dad let me go to England without a fight.'

'He was scared you'd tell us?'

'No, I think he knew his sordid secret was safe with me. It was bad enough to have my own illusion shattered. The idea of you and Tilly suffering the same… I couldn't do it. And Mum didn't want me to. She'd already gone through enough.'

'So why let you go?'

Eve gave a twisted smile. 'I don't think he could bear the look in my eye, it wasn't love that he saw any more, but judgement, hatred even.'

'And did you? *Hate* him?'

No words would come. No rebuttal. No affirmation. Eve… Eve couldn't answer.

Instead, she leaned forward and poured them both some

iced water. Took a sip of her own, wishing it could get rid of the bitter taste in her throat.

But only an end to this conversation had that power.

'How did you find out?'

Eve's breath shuddered through her, the ice rattling in her glass as she placed it down before she dropped it. Now she wished she'd said something—*anything* to stop her sister asking that!

'I'm sorry, Evie, I don't want to cause you any more pain but—'

'I was fifteen,' she said over her, forcing the words through clenched teeth, knowing she had to get it over with and hating it all the same. 'It was the night of the Marni Cup ball...'

An event that was considered the highlight of the year at Garrison Downs. People travelled from all over to attend the two-day racing carnival hosted by her parents. Everyone who was anyone in attendance. It took weeks to prepare for and was the talk of the social elite long after it was over. But for Eve, that night had been memorable for all the wrong reasons.

'I was smitten with the new station hand Dad had employed. Rip, remember him?'

Rose frowned. 'Cook's cousin's kid? He was a right 'un...'

Eve gave a gruff laugh. 'He was a little rough round the edges, I admit, but I had this fantastical notion that I could change him.'

'Just like all those books you loved to read.'

'Just like all those books...' Eve echoed. 'I was so busy mooning over him as he played valet outside that I was barely aware of the ball and the company within. I'd managed to lose myself in the curtain when Mum passed by, Clay Garrison hot on her tail.'

'Clay? I swear that man's name is cropping up far too often these days.'

'Yeah, well, he was talking to her, his voice too low to hear but I could tell Mum was trying to get away. She was pale and jittery. And the more Clay smiled, the more Mum wilted.

I forgot all about Rip and became Mum's shadow after that. She wasn't the same. She was polite with everyone, you know Mum, for ever the hostess, but she was distant. She wasn't so quick with the smiles, or the conversation, and I was worried. I thought about asking her outright, but I didn't want to make it worse, so after the party was over, I went to Dad's study. I wanted to tell him something was wrong. He was Mum's greatest protector, right? I trusted him to get to the bottom of it and fix it. But Mum was already there. They were arguing.'

'Oh, Evie…' Rose pressed a hand to her chest, clearly sensing where this was heading, and Eve nodded, swallowing down the sickness rising with the memory.

'Clay had seen Dad with someone in Melbourne, claimed they looked *close*.'

'Why, that piece of…'

'Dad swore it wasn't how it looked. Swore he'd ended things with Lili years ago. Lili! Like, who the hell was Lili? And what did he mean, *ended* it?'

Eve shook her head, remembering the moment she'd heard her own father confirm the unthinkable. Her father. Her hero. The man she had so desperately wanted to please, to be seen by…to finally step out of Rose's shadow and be noticed by… had been no better than a scoundrel, a cheat…unworthy of her love, or any love for that matter.

'I was so angry, Rose. I stormed in, tore a strip off him and he…' Eve choked on unshed tears '…he cowered. I'd never seen Dad cower, but he did. He sank behind that massive desk of his, head in his hands, and I carried on, consumed by this… this *anger*.' She fisted her chest, the visceral strength of it vibrating through her. 'Mum tried to calm me down, pleaded with me to stop, that I didn't understand… I mean, what was there to understand? He'd had an affair, betrayed her, betrayed us all. I couldn't bear it. There he was hiding behind his desk and Mum was *defending* him! *Actually* defending him! Telling me it wasn't as simple as all of that…that one day I'd understand. Like somehow, I was too young to get it.'

'You were fifteen...' Rose whispered.

'Plenty old enough to understand what Dad had done.'

'But not the reason.'

Eve's frown was sharp. 'Don't *you* start defending him!'

'I'm not. I'm...' Rose took a breath. 'I'm angry that he kept Ana from us. I'm angry that any of it had to happen at all...'

'Why do I feel like there's a but coming, Rose?'

Her sister was quiet for a long moment. Too long.

'Rose!'

'You should read Mum's journal,' her sister said, soft but sure.

'The one that Matilda found in Dad's study?'

She nodded.

'I don't want to read it.'

'It will help you to understand.'

'By reliving Mum's pain, no, thank you.'

'Dad was hurting too.'

Eve snorted, pulling her knees up to her chest and hugging them tight. A defensive move she hadn't needed in so long.

'They both played their part in the breakdown of their marriage, Evie, but they came back from it. Stronger and more in love than ever. You'd know that if you read the journal.'

'They lied to us, Rose, they lied to the world. Playing at happy families. What a joke.'

'It wasn't a joke, it was real. Their love for each other and us.'

'How can you say that after Ana?'

Rose picked at some invisible speck on her thigh. 'Because I remember before, I remember when things weren't right, and I'd catch them arguing...'

This was news to Eve but then Rose was older, she would have seen more, been more aware.

'...times when things weren't so good, and Mum would withdraw. She'd sit in that chair in Dad's study and lose herself in the view.'

'I used to think she did that because she longed for him to

come back,' Eve said, remembering the same. 'Now I think she did it because she longed for home. For England. For her life from before. Like a prisoner looking out from her cell.'

Rose's wounded blue eyes flicked to her. 'That's a bit extreme.'

'Is it?' Eve blurted back. 'You just told me it's where she would retreat to.'

'When times were bad, yes. Not helped by her parents cutting her off like they did—'

'They were hurt, Rose. Devastated when she left.'

'And I'm in no mood to argue about *them* right now.'

And neither was Eve. The time to try and heal her sister's relationship with Granny Lavigne would come…she just had to stick around long enough.

'Yes, Mum may have missed home, but she was happy, Evie. She got better, and she was happy—she *was*,' Rose stressed as Eve arched her brows. 'And she took to that chair and counted down the seconds until Dad returned from the paddocks. She also sat there, longing for our return too. From school, from days out without her. She'd sit there and wait for you and Tilly to come back from boarding school in the holidays, heartbroken when you stopped coming.'

'Don't twist this onto me.'

'I'm not. I'm trying to make you see that there's more than one side to a story and until you take them all into account you won't see the full picture.'

Rose watched her, waiting for her to accept it rather than reject it. And Eve stared at the pool, mocking her sister's patience because as much as Eve's heart wanted to listen, her head was saying no. It would be a cold day in hell before Eve picked up that journal.

'At least go and see Ana. She's our sister, Evie.'

'*Half*-sister,' she corrected, heart fluttering inside her chest.

'Still our sister, and, from all I can gather, her mother did right by ours. Lili loved Dad, too. And she didn't want to tear our family apart. There's something to admire and respect in that.

She isn't the enemy, and neither is Ana…and neither is Dad. He wasn't perfect, no man is, but he loved us. He loved *you*.'

Eve said nothing because she couldn't. Inside, her heart was shattering into a thousand tiny pieces and she didn't know how to piece it back together. It was *too late* to piece it back together.

'Please, Evie, you need to find closure before it ruins you and your life.'

'Me and my life are doing pretty darn well, thank you.'

'So, you think it's okay that you fled from your home, from us, and you've carried on fleeing.'

'I'm hardly fleeing, Rose,' she threw back at her. 'I'm here now, aren't I?'

'You didn't come to Tilly's wedding.'

'I was tying up loose ends at work so I could be here now.' Rose raised both brows.

'Okay. Okay, so I didn't want to come and put a damper on the whole affair.'

'You should have been there. If you'd only seen for yourself how happy they are.'

'I know they're happy, Rose, I don't doubt it. But for how long?'

'I'm not saying they won't face their challenges, everyone does, but so long as they have their love, they'll get through it.'

'Just like Mum and Dad…'

'*Yes.*'

Eve was being sarcastic. Rose wasn't. And after a long delay where her sister was probably hoping for some miraculous change on Eve's part, Rose sighed.

'I wish you'd said something. All these years, I could've been there for you, we could've faced it together.'

'What difference would it have made?'

'It could've made all the difference. We could've confronted them together. Mum might have opened up. She might have told us about her postnatal depression. Given us both the chance to understand and for you to make amends before…'

Rose swallowed, blinked away the tears that threatened and Eve did the same, silently finishing her sister's sentence for her…*before it was too late.*

Before they'd lost them both and Eve had lost all those years too.

'What ifs don't help anyone, Rose.' Eve had realised that a long time ago. 'And learning about Mum's depression from her journal…' she shuddered '…and the doctor's notes Tilly found. It just feels wrong.'

'I don't know. I think if you read them, you'd feel differently. It feels like Mum wanted us to—'

'Leave it, Rose. *Please.*'

Her sister dragged in a breath, her blue eyes swirling with sorrow, and it pained Eve that she'd put that look there. No, not entirely her, it was their father too.

And it was his legacy that had them stewing in this crisis now.

'You know what gets me,' Eve said, clinging to the anger. 'That Dad did nothing. That a man who couldn't even stand by his own vows, was happy to see us forced into giving our own.'

Rose huffed. 'I'm not sure he knew about the condition.'

'Oh, he knew, Rose. Dad knew everything there was to know about this place. He wouldn't have missed that clause.'

'You think?'

'You don't?'

Rose considered it a while then, 'If that were the case, why didn't he do something about it?'

'Damned if I know, but I'm going to get us out of it.'

Rose gave a weak smile. 'I appreciate your optimism but, until we have a plan, I fail to share it.'

'Look, I know we said we'd keep it a secret, the condition, Ana's existence…but maybe it's time we went to the press with it all, or at least consider leaking it.'

'Hell, no!'

'Think about it, Rose, they'd have a field day. The very idea that an inheritance would be denied because we're the—' Eve made air quotes '—*weaker* sex? Can you imagine?'

'I am imagining, and it would be hell.'

'Worse than marriage to some guy we barely know, because I'm not seeing anyone and I'm pretty sure you're not.'

Nate flashed before her mind's eye and she promptly put him back in the box.

'Yes, worse! They'd be camped out on the doorstep. Ana and her family wouldn't be able to breathe for the speculation, the gossip, the cameras and the interrogation. And then there's that cad, Clay, he'd be straight on us trying to make sure we don't comply just to see the land return to him and that can't happen, Evie.'

Their gazes drifted to the garden, to the land that they could lose, the air weighing heavy in their silence as the wind rustled through the trees.

'I'll pay Harrington a visit first thing Monday,' Eve said eventually. 'Apply some pressure, see what's what.'

'Okay.' Rose nodded. 'That sounds like a plan. You can take the truck, but tread carefully, won't you? I don't think George is all that well.'

Eve's ears pricked up. 'Really?'

'The last few times I've seen him, he's not been right.'

'In what sense? Poorly or…?'

'Yes, poorly, what else did you think I meant?'

'I was wondering whether his ability to do his job had come into question.'

'I don't think there's any suggestion of that.'

'I'll suggest it if it means we can find a way out of this mess.'

'Play nice, Evie.'

'He's a man, I don't need to play nice.'

'Not all men are bad.'

'Not all men are good either.'

And just like that they were back to Dad.

'The affair was a moment, a blip. They chose to move on

from it together and they made it work. They *loved* one another.'

Eve said nothing, answer enough, and Rose blew out a breath. 'Right, I should get back.'

'You don't need to tell me twice,' Eve murmured, looking up as her sister stood. 'It's muster season, it's all hands on paddock.'

Their father had said it so many times over, Eve could hear him now.

'It's good to know you still have the Outback in you somewhere.'

And Dad, her sister meant, and Eve shook her head with a choked laugh. 'Buried *very* deep. Now go, get yourself out of here, before Aaron has to come find you.'

Rose grimaced. 'Don't even joke about it.'

'Problems in paradise?' Aaron was her second in command…could there be tensions between them now Dad was gone?

'Nothing I can't handle.'

Eve didn't doubt it. Rose would handle it as she handled *everything* in life. With care and stoic determination. She hadn't run at the first sign of adversity. She'd stuck it out. Built her life around it.

Unlike Eve, who, as Rose had rightly pointed out, ran.

Just as she'd run from Nate that morning. Nate and his sweet breakfast offering and sexy grin. Her heart gave a squeeze.

'Make sure you take some food with you,' she said, doing her best to ignore it and focus on her sister. Her sister and her worryingly slender finger. 'You have a long day ahead.'

Rose scrunched up her face as she redid her ponytail. 'I may have bent the truth when I said I hadn't eaten…'

'Oh, right, sneaky.'

'I had to get you to talk to me.'

'I know,' Eve said softly, 'and it feels good to have talked.'

'It does.'

They shared a smile, so much passing between them as they blinked away fresh tears.

'I'll see you later, Evie.'

'I'll be right here when you get back.'

You can count on that, sis, she silently added, watching her walk away, knowing she had so many years to make up for.

River, Dad's old dog, appeared from the shadows and trotted up to her. She smiled and gave him a stroke. Stayed there, petting him long after Lindy had cleared away the untouched food. The courage to walk the halls of the house non-existent. Which was ridiculous. It wasn't a living and breathing threat. And yet it felt like one.

She looked down at River. 'What's wrong with me, hey?'

River cocked his head with a whine.

'You're right, I should get it over with.'

Together they headed back inside. The hallway was deserted, her bags too had gone, and she felt the chilling emptiness of the house to her very bones.

She couldn't remember a time when it had been so quiet. She couldn't even hear Lindy. Just the patter of River's paws on the wood, the pad of her own bare feet. She wandered through the rooms, the kitchen, the dining room, the lounge, the family room, refusing to pause until she came upon the piano room. And there she froze.

She clutched a hand to her throat. Eyed the luxurious white carpet, the opulent chandelier that cast light around the room even when it wasn't on, and the magnificent bar that was worthy of the finest hotel. She could almost see her father there now mixing a drink, while Mum played a classical sonata at the piano, and she and her sisters sneaked down the hall to the cinema room and the popcorn machine. Loading up on sugar while Mum and Dad had their time...

Their time. Something they'd always carved out and something Eve had forgotten about until now...

Didn't mean it was love though. Real and true.

She squeezed her eyes shut and turned away. Opened them

again to see her father's study door glaring back at her. Heavy, dark and taunting. She dragged in a breath. She had no desire to cross that threshold.

'Come on, River, it's time to find my own space in this hellhole.'

She headed to the other end of the house, to the bedrooms and her own. Expecting it to remain unchanged like the rest of the house but unable to stop the way her skin prickled as she stepped inside and saw she was right.

The same white and gold baroque-style furnishings, pale pink walls, white cotton bedspread, fluffy pink throw and matching pillows, so OTT but everything she'd wanted as a child.

And then she saw it. The bundle of neatly folded clothing at the bottom of the bed, an old Akubra resting on top...

She crossed the room, reached out with fingers that quivered like her heart. Mum's Akubra? She could see her now, smiling out from beneath its rim. Eyes warm and loving and... *Oh, Mum!*

She clutched it to her chest and a note fell to the floor. She dipped to pick it up...

Ride Jade.
She's perfect for you.
Rose x
PS Mum's hat is yours.
Take care of it, as it takes care of you!

She smiled, eyes welling, words blurring as she read it again, hovering over the 'x'.

'Oh, Rose.'

A kiss. Rose had given her a kiss. Not just that, she'd come in from the paddocks to welcome her home. She'd chosen the pool room to give her breathing space. She'd sorted out clothing without Eve having to ask for it. And they'd talked, properly talked.

Maybe they weren't so broken after all…

She pressed a kiss to the note, her resolve building with her love for her sister. They might not agree on the past, or her father, but they did agree on the future.

And Eve would fix it.

She would.

Come Monday she'd stride into Harrington Law and have it out with George. See to it that the man saw this whole situation as the nonsense it was.

Until then—she scooped up jeans and a shirt off the pile—there was a horse with her name on it…

CHAPTER FIVE

NATE DIDN'T HATE MONDAYS.

He was one of a rare breed that relished the start of a new week, fresh with possibility and the gains that could be made.

This Monday, however, he would gladly give it up as a bad job.

He'd got up, done his morning run, grabbed a shower, a coffee, and a breakfast bagel and hit the office for eight. Just as he would in Sydney. Only here, it was his father's office, he was sitting in his father's chair, and he might as well have had his father sitting over him for the suffocating tension in the air.

He twisted in his leather seat, rolled his head on his shoulders, and tried to ignore his surroundings that were stuck somewhere in the eighties. Wood panelled walls, retro colour scheme, even an avocado-coloured phone that had a cord, of all things…

None of which should impact his ability to do the job. And still he struggled. He was supposed to be looking into Holt Waverly's daughters, making a note of their contact details so that he could get in touch and introduce himself. Instead, his mind kept circling back to the family dinner he'd endured the night before.

Perhaps if he called his mother and apologised, he could put it to bed and get some work done. But apologising meant he was in the wrong. Not his father.

And he wasn't willing to go there.

Not when it was Dad who'd picked the fight. Who'd accused

him of being distracted and caring more for the swanky city than his hometown. For thinking himself above Marni and its people. For staying away so long because he saw himself as better than his own family.

And how wrong could one man be?

Perhaps he should have fought back, told his father the truth. That the reason he was so distracted came down to a woman he'd met on Friday night in the very town he criticised him for hating.

And that the reason he'd stayed away all this time wasn't down to Marni, or its people, but his father himself.

That would've wiped the smug look of judgement off his face. An outright attack, laying the blame where it truly belonged. But the argument that would've ensued with his mother as a witness…after all the effort she'd put into making the evening special. No. Just no.

Far better to walk away and see to it that he saw his mother alone next time… He'd send her flowers. That would help. Flowers and a promise to take her to lunch later in the week. Better.

As for the striking city swan who'd wandered into his life, stirred it up and walked straight back out again, she'd made her thoughts clear and he should be grateful. She wasn't the woman for him, no matter the crazy connection. They were on opposite ends of the spectrum when it came to their lives and what they wanted from them.

Didn't stop him thinking about her though. Wondering. Wanting. Wishing…

When what you should be doing is focusing on the job!

He had four sisters in three different countries to speak to. One was recently wed—to royalty no less. That left the other three to comply and, as ridiculous as it sounded, their love lives or lack thereof far outweighed his own…

He was picking up the phone to dial Rose, Holt's eldest daughter, when his office door flew open and in strode…

'Eve!'

* * *

'Nate!'

Eve froze to the spot. She must be seeing things.

Her lurid dreams of the weekend making her conjure up the man who had filled them because it wasn't possible. It couldn't be. *He* couldn't be.

Yet she knew him. Her body *knew* him. Every inked stretch beneath the dark suit trousers, crisp white shirt and skinny black tie…

'I'm so sorry, Mr Harrington, she just barged right on in!' The disgruntled receptionist hurried up alongside her, her tiny form a blot in Eve's rapidly blurring vision. Of all the men in the world she had to walk in on, she had to—

Her brain halted, rewound. The receptionist had said, 'Mr Harrington'. *He* was Mr Harrington.

'It's okay, Penny. You can stand down. Eve and I are good friends.'

Good friends—*really?*

And if he was a Harrington, where was the other one? The older, less distracting one. The one she needed. And exactly what relation were they if he was a Harrington too? Surely not his…she swallowed…*son*?

'Oh. I see.' Penny gave her the once over, her heavily wing-tipped eyes narrowed with suspicion, her pillar-box-red pixie cut adding to her don't-mess-with-me air. 'In that case, can I bring you both some coffee?'

Nate smiled at Eve. 'Would you like some?'

'Some what?'

His eyes sparkled. 'Some coffee?'

'Would I—? No, I don't want coffee.' Coffee reminded Eve of Saturday morning, of being all cosy in his bed, an image that wasn't helping her come back down to earth. And why wasn't he as freaked out as she was by this unexpected encounter?

'We're good, thank you, Penny.'

He waited for the other woman to leave before stepping

around the desk. 'I wasn't expecting to see you again quite so soon.'

'I wasn't expecting to see you again ever.'

The corners of his mouth twitched. Did he find this *funny*?

'That's brutal.'

'It's the truth.'

'The brutal truth. And yet, here you are…' he swept a casual hand around him '…in my office of all places, tracking me down?'

'What—? No! I thought this was George Harrington's office. I'm here to *see* George.'

He frowned. 'Sorry to disappoint but my father is now retired. As of last week, I'm the new face of Harrington Law.'

'You're not!'

His frown twitched.

'I assure you I am.' He offered out his hand. 'Nate Harrington at your service.'

'You're a *lawyer*?'

She was deflecting from the hand he still held out, deflecting from the entire awkward, discombobulating, unbelievable situation! Instead she sounded as if she was questioning his ability to do the job altogether.

'Is that so hard to believe?'

'No, I just…' Words failed her.

'I was an equity partner at Spectre Cowan based in Sydney. This is now my firm. You can look up my credentials if you so wish.'

She shook her head—equity partner. Spectre Cowan. Huge business. Impressive. She'd tell him as much if she weren't still reeling….

She eyed his hand and felt her fingers twitch, knowing what the contact would do to her, and forced herself to comply. They needed to get on a professional footing asap. The undercurrent had to be dismissed as an inconvenient rush. Friday night, Saturday morning, ever more so!

Though knowing him like she did…perhaps it was a good thing. An aid to her cause, so to speak.

'Eve.' She shook his hand, ignored the way the contact zipped along her veins, the way his gaze seared her. Warm and enticing. 'Though your father knows me as Evelyn. Evelyn Waverly.'

His hand pulsed around hers, eyes widening. 'Eve—Evelyn! How could I not have—? *You're* Holt's daughter.'

'Eve, please. Evelyn makes me think of my father. And yes, second eldest, for my sins.'

They were still bonded together, palm to palm, gazes locked.

She remembered what she'd told him in the bar. What he'd told her in return, about family and work bringing him back. Of his intention to stay if things worked out how he intended. Why hadn't she dug deeper? Realised who he was sooner? Done anything but slept with the one man who held her life in his hands.

'I thought you were in England.'

'Most people think I am and that's the way I'd like it to stay for as long as possible.'

'You look nothing like I expected.'

She balked. 'And what did you expect?'

'I'm not sure I should answer that.'

'Why?'

'For fear it could incriminate me.'

The tension eased a fraction. 'Like the "guess my name" game.'

'Pretty much.'

She laughed against her will and brought herself up sharp. She had a job to do and getting carried away on the connection wasn't getting it done. She released his hand and stepped away, clearing her throat. 'I never knew George had a son.'

'Doesn't surprise me.' He gave her a wry smile and settled back against the edge of his desk. 'My father never was one to talk about his family.'

'But you didn't come to any functions at the station?'

'When I was younger, my father didn't want the distraction, and when I was older, he didn't want the embarrassment.'

He stated it matter-of-fact. No emotion. No pain. But she felt the ache of his words deep within her chest. Knew how it felt. The station always came first at Garrison Downs, less home, more work HQ. So much so she'd feared being in the way as a kid, always falling over her own feet and causing unintentional trouble for Dad. And then she'd been a horrid reminder of the past, distracting her father from his perfect life …someone to be shushed, kept out of sight, out of mind and she'd cultivated that, *wanting* to hurt him.

'Now *that* I can understand…'

He tilted his head, eyes sweeping over her. 'I got the impression that Holt doted on his daughters—you were his pride and joy?'

'No. Rose was his pride and Matilda was his joy. There wasn't a lot left for me.' She lifted her chin. 'Not that I cared in the end. I fared much better without him in my life.'

A shadow chased across his face. 'And it seems our conversation Friday night has come full circle.'

'You remember all of that.'

'I remember everything, Eve.'

His eyes torched her from within, the urge to close the distance between them and lose herself in that look hard to resist.

'Now it seems we're in messy territory.'

'Messy?' she said.

'As Holt's daughter, you're effectively my client and I don't make a habit of sleeping with the people I represent.'

She swallowed. Good. No sex. No confusion. No muddying the waters. 'You'll hear no argument from me.'

'I don't know whether to be offended or relieved.'

'How about both?' Fighting talk. Better. Much better.

He chuckled. 'Disappointed, too.'

She gave an edgy laugh, ignored the way his honesty cut effortlessly through her armour.

'If I told you I have nine months to get married, might that help take the edge off?'

She expected him to laugh with her, give some indication that the idea was as ludicrous as it felt, question it even. Instead, he fell silent.

'You know about it, don't you…? I mean, of course you do. Your father would have filled you in.'

'He did.' His nod was grave, all sign of humour gone. 'As his most important client and closest friend, my father ensured I was up to speed on all matters Holt Waverly related the second I returned. My first job today was to reach out to each of you, offer my condolences and introduce myself.'

'Right. Well, as you've probably surmised, I don't need the condolences and, as I'm acting on behalf of us all, let me save you some calls too and we'll get straight down to business.'

His eyes narrowed. 'Which is?'

'How you help us get out of it.'

'Out of it?'

'Yes. Surely you of all people can see why a condition requiring that any heiress marry to inherit is absurd and has no place in today's world.'

'It has a place,' he said, without hesitation, 'because it's in your father's will.'

Was he for real?

He looked genuine. Leaning back against his desk, arms now crossed, face as serious as one could be. But surely not?

'And we can just as easily write it out again,' she tried, 'yes?'

'No.'

Eve folded her arms, spine tightening. 'What do you mean, *no*?'

He returned to his seat behind the desk and gestured to the chair opposite. 'Why don't you take a seat?'

'I'd rather stand.'

Because confronting Harrington Senior about the marriage

clause had been one thing. Confronting the man she'd slept with as recently as Saturday morning was something else…

'I don't know what you want me to say, Eve. Your father's last will and testament states quite clear that all women of marrying age must be wed within twelve months of the will reading. There's no debate.'

'*I'm* debating it. Right here. Right now.'

She couldn't keep the panic out of her voice, the anger too. Whether it was the ticking time clock, hearing him say it, hearing him say it without any understanding or compassion for what she and her sisters were going through, or the way he still made her feel…she didn't like it. Not one bit.

'How can you say it like it's okay?'

'My father has entrusted me with his work and that includes watching over you and your sisters and seeing to it that the clause is met.'

'Even if it's unjust, sexist, *insane*…?'

He leaned back in his seat, steepled his fingers together. Cool. Calm. Collected.

Everything she wanted to be…

'Tell me something, Eve. There's clearly no love lost between you and your late father. And as I remember it, you're counting down the days until you can escape…'

'I am.'

'So why are you so het up about the inheritance? Financially you're already taken care of by your mother's trust and—'

'This isn't about me. This is about my sisters and what's fair. The station is Rose's life, she was born to take it on, and she should be the one to pass it on to her children, and her children's children. Not have it ripped out from under her because she isn't of the right *sex*.'

'Okay, so what do you want from me?'

She bit back her rising temper. 'Isn't it obvious?'

'Enlighten me…'

'I want you to find a loophole. I want you to help us out of it. I want you to give us legal advice and stop being so irritatingly cool about it.'

'Have you considered just doing it?'

'Doing *what*?'

'Finding yourself a man, drawing up a prenup, something I can help with and—'

'Are you *serious*?'

'Quite.'

She gawked at him. This was crazy, as crazy as…

'Hang on…' She thrust out a hand, her gut twisting with the sickening conclusion she was rapidly coming to. 'Did you know all along?'

'Know what?'

'Who I was? Is this all an act? Did you *sleep* with me because you knew and wanted *in*?'

He shot forward in his seat. 'You can't be serious.'

Finally, a reaction!

'Can't I? You're the one telling me to put a ring on it like it's the easiest thing in the world.'

'And you think I engineered our night together in the hope it would put me in the running. That I would withhold my identity and pretend I didn't *know* you, share the night with you, bring you breakfast…'

'Be all sweet—yes!'

'Because I want your inheritance?'

'Yes! You wouldn't be the first man to swindle his way into money and you wouldn't be the last.'

'Person.'

'What?'

'The first *person*. Or are you truly as sexist as you sound?'

'In my experience, men are the weaker sex, far more likely to be led around by their…' She twirled a finger at his desk, her target clear, and swallowed the inconvenient rush making a return. 'That and their greed.'

'Wow, your father really did do a number on you.'

The fire within her promptly died and the blood seeped from her cheeks.

'No, Eve,' he said coolly. 'I can assure you, had I known who you were when I met you, I would have steered well clear.'

Her heart winced and she straightened against it, clung to the common sense telling her she was right to fight. 'Scared of the gossip, the speculation that you lured me in?'

'No.'

'Then why?'

'Because as you said yourself...' he was back on his feet, walking towards her, blue eyes raging a storm '...you have no intention of getting serious. Not now. Not ever.'

He was repeating her words back at her, only they felt colder, harsher from his lips.

'You have no desire for love, and I have *all* the desire for it.'

'You couldn't know that before speaking to me,' she whispered, breathless with his increasing proximity, his reasoning too.

'No. That's true enough. But I do know, and so you should know this in return.' He paused a stride away. 'When I marry, Eve, it will be because I cannot bear to live without that woman by my side, because I love her and I want to spend the rest of my life with her.'

She gave a chilling laugh. 'How very noble of you.'

'It's not noble. It's natural. As natural as breathing. Craving love and giving it in return is what we were born to do.'

Emotions clogged up her throat, words difficult to form. 'How can you say that after the way your father treated you?'

'Because my father taught me how not to love and my mother gave it in abundance. She never tires of dishing it out and I won't either.'

His words snaked through her, making her want and making her want to recoil. Contrary and dizzying with it.

'If you're truly up to speed on my father and the inheritance, you must know my father was unfaithful to my mother and that I have a sister we never knew existed. He kept her from us. What kind of a man cheats on his wife, fathers a child and then refuses to bring that child into the family?'

'A man who's trying to protect that family.'

'We didn't *need* his protection. We needed his honesty.'

'And now you have it.'

'Too much too late. What good is it now? When all those years have been lost?'

'What's done is done, Eve.'

She gave a choked laugh, shook her head. 'You don't understand.'

'I understand more than you know and I'm telling you, don't let the past destroy your future.'

Now he sounded like Rose. 'My future would be just fine if you could hand me a way out of this.'

'Your future isn't fine, not while you think it's okay to project your father's behaviour onto others, onto me...'

'I'm not projecting.'

'No?'

She took an unsteady breath, the fight dying within her. 'Look, I didn't come here to fight...well, I did, but not about this. I wanted help, a way out for me and my sisters.'

She held his gaze, pleading with him to understand.

'Surely you can see it from our position, from mine. I don't want to be forced to take vows I cannot keep.'

'Who says you can't keep them?'

'I do. I won't marry for convenience and I won't marry for love. The former is a lie and the latter is too fickle.'

'If that's truly how you feel, then you need to accept that Garrison Downs will return to its original owner. It was your ancestor's wish.'

'But it's a part of us now, it's a part of Rose. She can't lose it.'

'Then as far as I see it, you have only one option, Eve.'

'Which is?'

'Find yourself a husband.'

* * *

Have you heard yourself? came Nate's inner conscience. *She may have made some nasty assumptions about you and lashed out, but she's cornered and asking you for help.*

And she was right. It was archaic and sexist…but no more sexist than she was being.

And if he was honest with himself. There had been a moment. A split second of inexplicable madness where he'd felt her desperation deep within his gut and thought, why not him?

Plenty of people married for a lot less.

But he wasn't in the plenty.

He wanted love.

And she wanted her life in London back, her job that by her own words was her life. She was his father through and through.

'I don't believe this.' She threw her hands in the air and paced away. 'You know, for a man who talked so much sense on Friday night, you aren't making any now.'

'I'm making perfect sense.'

'Really?' she threw over her shoulder.

'If you're not bothered about love, then why not get married to someone, a friend, an acquaintance, someone who understands your situation. I can ensure you're protected with a prenup, the other party too, because as far as I'm aware, but I'd need to double-check, there's no time constraint on that marriage. Nothing that demands you *stay* married. You could be a free heiress within another year.'

She paused before the window. Quiet.

'Eve?'

'I'm… I'm thinking.'

'What is there to think about? You secure your part in the inheritance and go back to your life in London. It's a win-win.'

He'd be one step closer to satisfying his promise to his father too.

And yet he felt cold at the prospect.

'It's a lie, is what it is.'

'Newsflash, Eve, people lie all the time.'

'Some do it easier than others.'

And he knew she was speaking of her father, her shoulders hunched as she hugged her middle.

'I'm sorry for what your father put you through.' He walked up behind her, careful to maintain a safe distance, one from which he could resist the need to touch her. 'And I'm sorry you struggle to trust. But I promise you, I didn't lie on Friday and I'm not lying to you now.'

She turned into him, her perfume lifting with the movement and transporting him back to that night when they'd been as close as any couple could be. When they'd been on the same side of the fence, waging war against their fathers. United by that bond.

'I had no idea who you were,' he said into her eyes that swirled with so much emotion he could feel his resolve crumbling. 'All I knew is that from the moment I saw you step out of that cab, I wanted to get to know you and the more I learned, the more I wanted you.'

And he felt it now, the power of it, the desire…an innate lure that he was struggling to smother.

'Then tell me something else…' she whispered.

'What?'

'Do you want me now?'

He cursed. The lie impossible to give. The truth impossible to act on.

'Because I want you, Nate.' She wound the end of his tie around her fist, eased him closer and he could scarce believe the change in her, let alone the thrilling heat streaking through his body. 'And that terrifies me as much as it energises me. I've never met anyone who can empty my head with a simple look…but you do.'

'And you, me.' The words were out before he could stop them, her coy smile worth every weakened second of his confession.

'Then please…' she wet her lips '…help me out of it.'

Ice flooded his veins. *Legal assistance.* That was what she truly wanted. Not him. Not this. Just a way out.

'Clever, Eve.' He grabbed her wrist. 'Very clever.'

And he was a fool.

She frowned. 'I don't know what you—'

'I will help you *through* this, Eve. But I can't get you out of it. I swore to my father I would take care of you and your sisters and see the terms of the will met. And that is what I'll do.'

Her eyes shot daggers, her cheeks flushed deep. 'Why play the dutiful son to a father who doesn't deserve it?'

'Because I can, and I think deep down you wish you could too.'

Her lashes fluttered, her mouth falling open. It was a low blow but he feared her bitterness, her inability to make amends with the past. There was so much anger in her, so much hurt. It was high time she faced it head-on. The loss and what it meant for her, for the relationship she would never get to repair.

'You think I care that he's gone?' It came out tight, her eyes burning bright, their sheen telling him more than she ever would.

'I think you care more than you want to admit, and the sooner you accept it, the better for all those around you.'

'I didn't hear you complaining about my company Friday night.'

'Friday night you held your cards close to your chest, but it was still there, eating away at you beneath the careful veneer.'

She fought against his words, his hold, his gaze. Locked in a fierce battle, blue eyes piercing blue, her glossy lips parted but nothing coming out.

He wanted to kiss her. Kiss her until lust took out the pain. Kiss her until she could admit her grief. Kiss her until she let the tears fall and she could be reborn. That bit brighter, that bit freer.

And what a weird fantasy that was…

'Now I suggest you leave before we end up where you almost had us.'

'What makes you think…?'

He lowered his gaze to where the delicate fabric of her blouse betrayed her body's desire and she snatched her hand out of his grasp, gripped it before her chest.

'Why, you…'

He gave a tight chuckle because, for all he was teasing her for feeling it, he felt it too. A hundred times over.

'You said it yourself, Eve, and, like me, you're no liar.'

She stared back at him hard. 'Fine! You won't help us. I'll find someone who will.'

'You do that. And when you find him, I'll be right here waiting with a prenup.'

'That's not what I meant.'

'So you say…'

She opened her mouth, closed it again, made a noise akin to a growl and spun away. She yanked open his door, giving him one last murderous glance…

Hell, she was hot when she was angry. Something else she'd hate hearing and he would take too much delight in saying.

And then she was gone and he was no better off than he had been Saturday morning, only then they'd parted on polite terms, and it had been wishful thinking that he'd see her again. Now he *knew* he'd see her again.

See her again and see her married off too. But the idea of Eve getting married to someone else…

Nate had never thought of himself as the jealous kind.

It seemed his gut thought otherwise.

'Why, of all the pig-headed, egotistical, arrogant…'

Eve stormed through the station, doors slamming in her wake as she headed straight for the bar. She paused outside the piano room just long enough to slip off her shoes before crossing Mum's precious white carpet and resuming her stomping.

'Hey, what's all the racket?'

She didn't turn at Rose's question. Though she was surprised her sister was around. 'What are you doing here? Shouldn't you be out there still…?'

She waved a careless hand to the outdoors as she spied her drink of choice and plucked both bottle and glass off the shelf, setting them down with a satisfying clink against the marble.

'Are you trying to break everything?'

'I'm trying to work my frustration out of my system. Is that okay, Boss?'

Rose gave a tired laugh.

'What's so funny?'

'It's been a long time since I've heard you call me that.'

Eve harrumphed as she plonked some ice into her glass and poured herself a decent measure. 'Clearly this place is getting to me.'

'In a good way, I hope.'

'So long as you don't start calling me Bambi, I'd say we're okay.'

Rose leaned into the door frame, careful to keep her body angled outwards and her dust-covered workwear away from the carpet. 'I never understood why you took such issue with being called it. We always thought it was endearing.'

'Button was endearing. And Boss was to be admired,' Eve said, referring to their father's pet names for Matilda and Rose, respectfully. 'But *Bambi*?'

'You just saw the bad in it.' Her sister's expression turned wistful. 'You didn't see that it was because you were adorable, with your big doe eyes and sweet smile.'

'You forgot my spindly legs,' Eve said, taking a nerve-quenching swig, 'and my habitual ability to fall over my own feet.'

'All cute.'

Eve shook her head, her laugh unsteady with the past, the sentiment, the sentiment in Rose, too. Maybe there was something in what her sister said, but the man wasn't here to ask. Just as Nate had so kindly reminded her…

'So…' she said, ignoring the wound doing its best to open up and focusing on her sister, who looked increasingly beat. 'You want one of these too? Because you look like you could do with it.'

'You're kidding, right? The day's going to be long enough as it is. Alcohol isn't going to help.'

'It dulls the pain though.' Eve took another ice-clinking swig and joined her sister on the threshold. 'So why are you here instead of out there?'

Rose rubbed her brow. 'I had some calls I needed to make. I have three jackaroos down with a bug at the worst possible time and I need to lean on our neighbours for help…'

'Isn't everyone busy this time of year?'

'They are, hence the personal calls. If we don't get the yards processed asap we'll be up the proverbial creek without a paddle.'

'Is it that bad?'

'It is when we've more pregnant heifers than we've had in years due to the recent rains, now a heatwave to boot, and I want them out the yards as soon as possible. We've yet to ear-tag the calves and the trucking company is demanding I grade two roads at the southern boundary before they'll drive in. Like I said, the proverbial creek.'

With every word, Eve felt her guilt swell. Her sense of uselessness too. Something she hadn't felt in years. Not since she'd left this place.

Less than a week in and Garrison Downs had her regressing.

Calling Rose 'Boss'. Feeling inferior, useless, a spare part… and getting nowhere with the one task she had been assigned.

'Can I do anything?'

'You are doing something.' Rose smiled. 'You're getting us out of this marriage clause.'

Of all the things her sister could've said…

'I meant with the station, with the mustering?'

Rose's mouth quirked. 'Are you offering to saddle up?'

Eve gave a cautious shrug. 'Why not? My roping skills might be rusty but I'm sure I'll get the hang of it again.'

Rose's gaze drifted over Eve's silk blouse, pencil skirt, daintily painted toenails before returning to rest on Eve's hand around her glass.

'That manicure won't last a second.'

'There are more manicures to be had…' She waggled the fingers of her free hand and Rose chuckled.

'You're serious?'

'I wouldn't offer if I wasn't. Just put me to work, Boss.'

And if she was working, hopefully Rose wouldn't ask how her other task was going because right now she didn't have an answer. Other than Nate's.

Find yourself a husband.

How the man had the audacity to even stand there and *suggest* it…

Rose gave a sudden frown. 'You're sure?'

'Huh?'

'You just turned the air blue.'

'I did what?'

Rose cocked a brow. 'You swore…'

'It's all the excitement.'

'If you say so…' Rose's eyes danced, clearly torn between laughing and biting her hand off. 'Okay then, you'd best go get yourself changed. We're heading through the ravine to the east and, thanks to the rains, it's extra boggy.'

She gave a mock shudder. 'Wet *and* dirty—my favourite.'

'You'll do just fine, Bambi.'

'Don't! Please!' But Eve didn't feel the customary prick of bitterness with the name. All she felt was the warmth of Rose's love. 'You know, I think I preferred it when we weren't really speaking.'

'And I think I preferred it when you were a shy and retiring bookworm, but we can't all have what we want, can we?' Rose grinned. 'Now, get yourself off, we're setting off in ten.'

Eve was already moving.

'Oh, wait a sec!' Rose called after her. 'How did the meeting go?'

So much for escaping it...

Slowly, she turned, took in Rose's hopeful gaze and forced a smile.

'It went. George Harrington has retired. Seems you were right about his health. We're dealing with his son now.'

'His *son*? I didn't know George had a son.'

'Neither did I.'

'How was he?'

'*He* was a pig-headed, egotistical, arrogant arse.' The truth flowed from her lips with surprising force and she realised she couldn't lie to Rose about their situation. She was done keeping stuff from her sisters when it affected them as much as her...though she'd keep the sex to herself. *No one* needed to know about that.

'You do have a lovely way with words, Evie.'

'It's my job.' She downed the rest of her drink. 'As for his job...you'd think his age would make him more sympathetic to our cause, instead he's quite the opposite. Committed to seeing us abide by the ancient nonsense our ancestors have dished out.'

'Hence the tantrum when I came in?'

'I wasn't having a tantrum. I was venting.'

Rose surprised her with a grin. 'He really got to you, didn't he?'

'I wouldn't be grinning about it, Rose.'

'I'm grinning because he doesn't know what he's in for, having you as enemy. I'm just glad you're on my side.'

Now Eve smiled, the sisterly camaraderie boosting her when she'd feared her news would set Rose back further.

'Always. Now let me go so I can get out of my finest and plough my frustration into something useful...'

And forget about the way a certain pair of blue eyes and inked skin made her feel.

Especially when they belonged to the man so determined

to see her and her sisters marched up the aisle, she was surprised he hadn't got the shotgun out.

Then again, shotgun weddings implied something else entirely.

And that thought was about as unhelpful and disturbing as the man himself.

CHAPTER SIX

WORKING FOR ROSE, with Rose, did work to an extent.

While the bug did its rounds within the bunkhouse, Eve filled the role of a jillaroo with as much effort and determination as she did her PR role in London. Though nothing about this job was glamorous or image focused, it didn't exhaust her creative brain to the point that she struggled some days to tell the lie she'd spun from the truth.

And it was liberating.

It had even been kind of fun, getting stuck back into station life…a life she hadn't wanted to be a part of any more, but it seemed without the destructive secret, that life wasn't quite done with her.

If her colleagues back in London could see her now, they wouldn't recognise her. Hair loosely tied back, dust motes making a home in her costly honeyed strands, her make-up-free cheeks flushed with colour from the outdoors. Kitted out, rough and ready. But as she looked out over the land, the sun setting behind the mountains and casting an orange glow over the dirt that didn't look quite so dirty any more…she found she didn't care.

'What's that smile about?' Rose asked, stepping onto the deck with two coldies in hand and offering one out.

'Thanks. I was just wondering what my colleagues in London would make of me now.'

Rose gave a soft laugh as Eve took a swig from the bottle and almost brought it straight back up. Odd, the bitterness was hitting her all wrong. She checked the date on the bottle as Rose joined her on the swing seat.

'In my opinion, you look good for it, Evie.'

Did she? Or was Rose just being kind? Probably, a bit of both but she was happy enough to take it.

They settled back into the cushions, Rose gently rocking the seat with her heel as Eve let the warmth of the setting sun soothe every aching limb. There was something to be said for a hard day's labour and being able to bask in the rest. Something blissful and satisfying.

'Have you heard any more from Harrington Junior?'

And just like that she stiffened. 'No.'

Because although she'd managed to push Nate out by day, rejecting every attempt he'd made to contact her, her nights were filled with him. Dreams she couldn't control. Thoughts that would wander when she lay awake, work unable to distract her.

'How did you leave it when you saw him in Marni?'

Eve huffed into her beer and promptly lowered it. Its scent made her stomach roll. Or was it Nate and the way he'd managed to get under her skin?

'Honest answer—he said we should get ourselves husbands with an expiry date.'

She expected Rose to laugh or at least be as cross as she was.

But she was quiet. Contemplative.

'You're not seriously considering it?'

'I won't lie, Evie, the thought has occurred to me, too.'

'You are joking!'

'Would it really be so bad if it got us what we want?'

'Please tell me you're joking…'

But of course her sister wasn't joking…this was precisely the reason Eve had come home. To ensure her sister didn't do something so drastic to keep it.

But hearing her *say* it.

'I don't know.' Rose shrugged. 'Marriage for a set period

and then being able to move on with our lives without this hanging over us, I can't deny the appeal.'

'*Appeal?* Have you heard yourself?'

'I know, but I'm tired, Evie. Physically. Mentally. And what am I without this place?'

'You're a wonderful woman who deserves so much more than a forced marriage of convenience that wasn't of your choosing.'

'I *choose* this place, though.'

'I know.' And Eve did know, it was what worried her so much.

'Have you come up with a better idea in the month you've been here?'

Eve's heart launched into her throat. A *month*.

'Has it really been a month?'

'Time flies when you're having fun, right?'

'Yeah...' Though Eve wasn't really listening. She was doing the maths. A month equated to four weeks. Twenty-eight days and she hadn't had a period.

And she was as regular as clockwork.

And... She raised the bottle to her lips, got the same whiff that sent her stomach churning.

No. *No*, she couldn't be.

'You want a Pinot Grigio instead?' Rose said, spying her distaste. 'We have plenty of Mum's old favourite.'

'No—no, I'm not in the mood.'

'Really?' Rose frowned, scrutinising Eve's face. 'Are you okay?'

'I'm fine.'

'You really don't look so fine any more.'

'Can you manage without me in the morning?'

'Of course,' her sister said, frown deepening. 'How come?'

'I need to pop into town.'

'You're going to try again with Harrington Junior?'

Eve gulped—sickness, unease, panic all rising up. 'You never know.'

'So long as you remember this isn't all on you, Evie. We each have a role to play, whether it's getting out of it or not. But I'm glad of it for one thing. It brought you back home, and for that I'm grateful.'

Eve's smile quivered, her sister's love battling against the inner panic.

'Me too, Rose,' she whispered, taking her sister's hand and giving it a squeeze. Because she was. She had her sister back. Had found a place within the station again. But a baby. Pregnant. *Her.*

Tomorrow, she would buy a test, many tests…and then she would know for sure.

Though she suspected she already knew.

'This is incredibly sweet of you, Mrs Cooper, but it's really not necessary.'

'Nonsense!' the old woman said, shoving the Victoria sponge at him and giving Nate no choice but to take it. 'With all the help your father gave us over the years, it's the least I can do. You know, if it hadn't been for him after my Charlie had fallen off that ladder and his company refused to pay out, I don't know where we'd be now.'

'So you've said.'

Several times over now. And Mrs Cooper wasn't the only 'client' to swing by and tell him stories of his father's generosity, and bring gifts, mainly of the richly unhealthy variety. No wonder his father's health had taken a severe turn for the worse if he ate like this on a regular basis.

'But, you see, it was your father who insisted he represent us. We couldn't afford it. He took all the risk, did all the work and only took a fraction of what he was due. He was a godsend.'

A godsend. He'd heard his father called that many times over too. Or words to that effect. All of them effusive, all of them bearing no resemblance to the man he'd been brought up by.

And he wasn't surprised their views differed because his father's focus had always been on work, work and his clients, but these people weren't *paying* clients. Not in the way Holt and his peers were.

This was pro bono.

The time it would have taken. Time when he'd resented his father for caring more about money and business than his own family.

Had he been wrong to judge his father so harshly?

But then how could he judge him any different—*know* any different—when his father had never been around?

With a tight smile, he acknowledged Mrs Cooper's praise. 'I'll be sure to pass on your regards.'

'You see that you do.'

'Now, is there anything I can help you with?'

'Oh, no, not at all.' She gave him an eye-crinkling grin and reached out to pat his hand. 'I was just passing and wanted to introduce myself. It's good to know you're here filling his extra-big shoes. We're sure to be safe in Harrington hands.'

'That you are, Mrs Cooper. Now I really must get back to work.'

Actual work because the past few weeks had been dominated by Mrs Coopers wanting to feed him up while waxing lyrical about his father. Probing mothers assessing him as husband material for their daughters, and husbands sent in by their wives for the same. And don't get him started on the single ladies.

He ushered her towards the open door. 'Penny, can you see this cake is stored somewhere safe?' He slid it onto his receptionist's desk and they shared a look that said, *If this doesn't stop, gym membership will need to be added to the employee benefit scheme.*

'I'll pop some around to my father later,' he assured them both.

'Oh, that's a lovely idea.' Mrs Cooper beamed as he escorted her onto the street. 'He really is such a wonderful man, so kind and generous and thoughtful.'

'Goodbye, Mrs Cooper.'

He watched her amble away and scratched the back of his head. He was struggling to marry together the two versions of the man that was his father. Would have carried on debating it too if his senses hadn't prickled as a blonde woman stepped out of the pharmacy across the way.

Head down, face mostly hidden by a dusty Akubra. He couldn't see her features enough to identify her but there was something about her. Something that had him inexplicably drawn.

Maybe it was the hair. The way the golden hue caught the light as it fell in a loose ponytail at her nape. Or the way her tall and slender figure moved with the grace and confidence of a...*swan*.

Eve? But it couldn't be. Dressed as she was. Bootcut jeans, a flannel shirt tucked in at the waist, dusty work boots, the hat...and yet—

'Eve!'

Her name was out before he could think better of it. They'd hardly left things on good terms, and she'd ignored every call he'd made since. But as her lawyer, he needed to fix things. As her ex-lover, if you could call it that, he owed her much more.

Only, she wasn't slowing. She was speeding up, the paper bag she was carrying clutched to her chest.

No doubt in his mind now, he leaned inside the office. 'I'll be back shortly, Penny.'

And legged it after her, narrowly missing a battered Jeep that honked its horn. He waved an apology, tried again. 'Eve!'

He picked up his pace, caught up to her as she rounded a parked truck.

'Eve, wait, please!'

She yanked the door open, tossed the bag inside and he stepped forward, fearing she was about to follow it in when she slammed it closed again and leaned back against the metal.

Silently, she lifted her head, blue eyes blazing out from beneath the rim of her Akubra.

'Look, I'm sorry for how we left things. I've been trying to get hold of you but—'

'I've been busy.'

'So I gather… Helping Rose with the station I take it?'

Because why else would she be dressed like so…

'And we're coping just fine, thank you.'

'I didn't doubt it. I'm just…' he swallowed, chose his words carefully '…surprised to see you looking so different.'

She cocked her head. 'You ran over here to comment on how I look?'

'No—no, of course not. I ran over here to apologise. I didn't want to hurt you, Eve. It was never my intention. I'd never have let things go so far if I'd known.'

'That makes two of us.'

'So if we agree on that, can we also agree to put it behind us and work together to move forward?'

'Are you ready to forgo your father's favour to help us?'

'It's not as easy as that.'

'No?'

'You don't understand.'

'What don't I understand? Because last I checked you didn't owe him anything.'

'It seems…' His eyes drifted to the front of Harrington Law, his head and heart at war with all that he had learned of late. 'You know how you think you've known someone all your life, like really known them, and then…' His eyes came back to hers that were spearing him, daring him to finish that thought. 'Of course, you do, I'm sorry.'

'And there I was thinking you were trying to dig a deeper hole… So your father's not the man you thought either. This is my surprised face.'

He gave her a meek smile. 'I didn't mean to poke at an old wound.'

'Don't worry, this old wound has been opening up again ever since I returned.'

'Yeah, well, mine doesn't know whether it's opening or closing or taking on a whole new shape.'

Her nose wrinkled. 'This conversation has taken an icky turn.'

He gave a soft laugh, grateful for the slight thaw in her demeanour. 'Fathers and their hidden lives.'

'Mine had a whole other family, what was yours hiding from you?'

His mouth twisted up. 'When I came here, I thought I was taking on a shrinking business. Dad's big clients were going the way of your father and he wasn't replacing them.'

'Death becomes us all,' she said smoothly, though she wasn't as unaffected as she wanted him to believe. The flicker to her lashes giving her away, the defensive stance too as she crossed her arms.

'True.'

'I'm assuming this was your father's wind-down plan though. He wouldn't want to leave anyone in the lurch when he retired?'

'Again true, though he thought he had a few more years in him.'

'But life had other ideas…'

'Yes.'

'Hence your secondment.'

'It's more than a secondment.'

'So you say, though I find it hard to believe you can give up somewhere like Sydney for the backwaters of Marni.' She had the decency to look a little sheepish as she checked she hadn't been overheard. 'It's not like it doesn't have a *certain* appeal, but compared to the hustle and bustle of the city, the life…?'

'I always intended to return one day, Eve, make a life here. I don't want a family in a place where I can't let my kids roam free for traffic and people. My—'

Her sudden pallor had him frowning, silencing his spiel.

'You were saying,' she said, her voice muted, her arms hugging her middle tighter.

What was wrong with her?

'Nate?'

He pressed on, still distracted by her reaction but determined to make her understand his life's ambition. 'My intention was to make Harrington Law into something deserving of my name over the door. I wasn't doing it to make my father proud. Work was everything to him and I set out to prove it didn't have to be. That I could have a successful business and, eventually, a family. The whole package. And I'd do it better than him, because I'd never neglect those that I love to achieve it.'

'It's a lovely ideal,' she whispered.

'It's more than an ideal, it's my future. One I'll see happen, but I never envisaged my father playing any role in it. He was always so distant.'

'And now?'

'Now it seems my father isn't the man I thought, or he is, but there's another side to him, one I never saw…'

'And one that changes how you feel?'

'I don't know. All I know is that high-paying clients like Holt gave him the income to support those who couldn't afford his services. When he wasn't working for your father et al, he was working for the locals. Sometimes free of charge, sometimes to cover costs alone, sometimes in exchange for *cake*, but always working.'

Eve's mouth quirked up. 'Cake?'

'It would appear that way.'

'So your father was a modern-day Robin Hood minus the stealing?'

Nate pressed his lips together. 'Unless you count the hours he robbed from his own wife and son to be able to do all that. Yes, he was.'

Her eyes flitted over his face. 'I'm sorry. I know how much you resented his work growing up, but maybe this can help you understand why he did what he did. At least his motives were pure, altruistic even. No one can say that about mine.'

'I don't know. I'm fast learning that things aren't always as black and white as they seem. My father believed Holt to be an honourable man, a man who wasn't proud of what he did, but he did his best to make amends and look after all concerned.'

'By keeping Ana a secret?'

'Think about it, Eve. Your family was fragile back then. My father hasn't gone into much detail, but I do know that keeping Anastasia a secret was as much about keeping your family together as it was about doing the right thing by her and Lili.'

'Your father seems to know an awful lot about it.'

She lowered her head, hiding beneath her Akubra as she scuffed at the ground with her boot.

'You could talk to him if you think it would help.'

'Your father?' Her head shot up, her eyes clashing with his. 'It's not me who needs to talk to George, but you.'

'You wouldn't say that if you saw us in a room together.'

'Don't you think it would help to get it off your chest, to tell him how you felt growing up? Give him the chance to fix things while you still can?'

'Just because you regret not having it out with your father, it—'

'That's not what I regret.'

'It isn't?'

'No. I had it out with him. I had it out with him in front of my mother, too, but I never had the courage to stay and deal with the fallout, I didn't *want* to give him the opportunity to make amends, to explain away what he did. What I regret is all those years I could have had with my mother, my sisters… I don't know whether things could have been different with my father and I don't get to find out, but maybe you can tell me something?'

'What's that?'

'In all those conversations with your father, has there ever been any hint as to *why* they didn't do something about it?'

'The condition?'

'Yes.'

'I asked my father the same.'

'You *did* question it?'

He looked away. He couldn't lie to her but neither did he want to give her false hope.

'I was surprised to see the condition, yes. Surprised even more that my father and Holt hadn't tried to see it changed. Especially when it risks the land going back to the Garrisons.'

She cursed the name, reaffirming what he already knew about the mutual hatred between the two families.

'And what did he say, when you questioned it?'

'He said that the station was a huge responsibility and that he believed Holt didn't want his daughters shouldering it alone. My father believed your mother was your father's rock, that they were stronger together—'

'And look how he repaid her.'

'Eve, he was unfaithful, I know, but my father truly believes they came through that period stronger. Your mother was unwell and—'

'Don't. Don't go there.'

He hesitated but knew it wasn't his place. Talking hearsay on something so personal.

'That wasn't all my father had to say…'

'No?' She was wary now, he could sense it in her held breath, her stiffened shoulders.

'But these are my father's words, not Holt's.'

'Understood.'

Nate took a breath and recalled the conversation he'd had that very first day back in Marni. And now he knew more, especially where Eve was concerned, he realised there wasn't just 'something' in it, there was a lot.

'According to my father, Holt feared you sisters would never come together again.'

He paused, thinking she may say something—reject it, accept it. Nothing. Not even a blink of the eye.

'He was scared that Rose was too married to the land to ever find a husband to share the load with. Matilda would never leave. You would never come home. And as for Anastasia, she needed a reason to be brought into the fold, a reason that would bind you all together, something that requires you as sisters to come together for a single goal.'

Still, she said nothing. One second. Two. And then she laughed. Outright laughed.

'My God, your father is a soppy old fool.'

Nate frowned. 'Not the reaction I was expecting.'

'It's crazy. Fanciful. As fanciful as the clause itself!'

'But you've come back, haven't you? Not only that but you're changing. You're not the same woman who landed here a month ago. Visually. Physically. Mentally. Even I can see that. And you're glowing, Eve.'

She also sounded less English, more Australian, but she already looked horrified enough by everything he'd said so he kept that to himself.

'You don't know what you're talking about.'

'Don't I?'

'No, you don't, and neither does your father. Or mine. If he truly felt that way. Rose doesn't need a man to run that land with her. I don't need a man to tie me to it. Tilly—well, it's just a fortunate mishap that she fell in love with a prince and has left for pastures new. And Ana…well, I don't know much about Ana yet, but I will, just as soon as I can get myself over to Melbourne to see her.'

'Which is when?'

'I don't know.'

'But you will see her?'

'Of course. She's my sister.'

He was smiling, he couldn't help it. Could she not see how much his father's supposition was ringing true?

'I hate to tell you, Eve, but this is hardly a convincing argument.'

Her cheeks coloured, her eyes flashed. 'You can say what

you like, but you don't know us. You don't know Rose and how capable she is. If you spent one day at the station, you'd realise what a nonsense this all is.'

'Is that an offer?'

'Is what an offer?'

'Are you inviting me to spend a day at the station?'

She lifted her chin higher, her blue eyes shimmering in their intensity. 'It's a busy time of year and we're short-handed, I'm not sure now is the ideal time.'

'Surely the challenging circumstances *make* it the ideal time to prove what you say.'

Her throat bobbed.

'What are you so afraid of?'

'I'm not afraid.'

'You could have fooled me.'

'I'm *not* afraid.'

'Tomorrow, then. I'll see you and Rose tomorrow.'

'But I haven't checked with Rose.'

'Then check with Rose and let me know. Because I'm coming to visit, Eve, whether you like it or not.'

CHAPTER SEVEN

EVE PLACED THE stick down beside the steadily growing line of tests on her en suite sink.

Different brands, all with the same result.

Was it possible that they could all be wrong?

That the sticks and her body could *all* be wrong?

She pressed her fist to her mouth and knew the answer well enough. She really was pregnant and she hadn't a clue what to do about it. Which seemed to be the story of her life lately.

'Evie, you coming?' Rose hollered from down the hall. 'If we don't get out there now, we're going to be chasing our tails for the rest of the day.'

She hurried to scoop up the tests, fearing her sister was about to walk in, and tossed them in the pedal bin, pushing the sluggish lid closed.

She was supposed to be here to help. Supposed to be here chipping in with the work and seeing to it that Rose kept the station for evermore. Not making matters worse.

Before she'd at least had the *option* of finding herself a husband...

Now the only man she could even consider marrying was the baby's father. And, yes, she'd teased him, accused him even, of wanting exactly that, she hadn't *meant* it.

But then she hadn't meant to get pregnant either.

'Eve!'

'Coming!'

She raced from the room to find her sister pacing at the rear porch, gaze intent on a document in her hand. She glanced up as soon as she saw her. 'About time.'

'Sorry, Boss.' Eve dodged her eye as she tied her hair back. 'What's that?'

'Another report that needs filing.'

'Need a hand with it?' Eve took her Akubra off the rack, hiding her face beneath it as she shoved her feet into her boots.

'Nah.' Rose tossed the report aside, giving Eve her full attention as she tried to hurry past her. 'Hey, you feeling okay?'

Perspiration broke out over Eve's skin.

'I'm fine,' she said, without slowing, grateful for the fresh air that hit her as she stepped outside. She sucked in a lung full and kept on going.

'Have you had breakfast?' Rose called after her.

'Not hungry.'

'Evie, you need to eat.'

She threw her sister a look. 'Pot and kettle springs to mind.'

Rose plucked a paper bag off the boot bench and tossed it at her.

'What's this?'

'Breakfast.' Rose strode ahead of her and Eve peeked in the bag, grateful her sister couldn't see her face that was sure to look as green as she felt. The grease enough to have her tossing it into the nearby hedge.

She apologised to Mum's golden grevilleas, something wild would sure enjoy it later, paper and all, and continued after Rose. The horses were already saddled in the yard, the station hands well enough to work were gathered and the quad-bike engines purred.

'You ate that quick,' Rose remarked as she checked the girth on Opal's saddle and Eve did the same with Jade. 'Are you sure you're—?'

'Rose!' Aaron hollered, unwittingly coming to Eve's aid. 'We've got a problem.'

'What now...?' Rose said under her breath as the guy jogged

up to them, his tall and burly frame a silhouette against the sunrise.

'We have a bore pump down to the east and Jacko ain't fit to see to it.'

Rose cursed, pinched her nose.

'You go. Take Kylie with you.'

'But what about—?'

'It's fine, we'll manage.'

'How? You won't—'

'I said we'll manage.' Rose stared the big bloke down until he dipped his hat and left.

'Rose,' Eve said, 'don't we need Kylie on—?'

The roar of an approaching motorbike broke through the bustle in the yard and Rose turned in its direction. 'Who on earth…?'

But Eve knew. Without looking she knew. Felt his presence like a sixth sense.

'Stay here.' Rose swung herself up into the saddle. 'I'm going to check who this is.'

And she was off before Eve could stop her. Stop her and explain. Because though she'd told Nate she would check and report back, she hadn't done either.

Call it denial, distraction, or whatever, she hadn't mentioned anything to Rose and now that he was upon them, she realised what a bad move that had been.

Eve mounted Jade, clicked her tongue and spurred her horse into following. She caught up with Rose just as her sister reached their unexpected visitor and she watched, helpless, as Nate cut the engine and tugged his helmet from his head, stealing Eve's breath in the process.

Didn't matter that she was well versed in how he looked, Nate in leathers with the soft glow of the dawning sun setting off his blue eyes, the bronze of his skin, his easy smile…he was something else.

He was also the father of the child within her…

Jade shimmied to the left as her hold on the reins slackened and she straightened, tightened her grip…wishing she could get a hold of her feelings as readily.

'Who are you?' Rose demanded, edgy at having an uninvited guest on her land.

Nate looked to Eve, his sparkling blues narrowing. 'I take it your sister didn't tell you I was coming.'

Eve's hackles rose with her chin. 'I told you I'd check and get back to you.'

'And when you didn't, I figured no news, no objection.'

Rose looked between them, Opal tossing her head as though sensing her rider's confusion. 'Would one of you care to explain?'

'Rose, this is Nate.'

'Nate Harrington,' the man himself said. Dismounting and offering a hand up to Rose.

'George's son?'

'The very same.'

Rose shook his hand with continued reservation. 'And you're here because…?'

'Your sister suggested that it might benefit your cause if I were to see you in action, spend a day in your shadow, so to speak.'

Rose snapped back upright. 'Eve suggested *what*?'

She looked to her and Eve could do nothing but shrug. Her throat was too tight, her stomach rolled like a revolving door, and she feared if she opened her mouth anything could come out.

'Hell, I don't have time for this. If you're shadowing us, you can make yourself useful. You ever mustered before?'

'I got involved with my fair share of competitions in my teens.'

Rose's lips quirked. 'Still ride?' She eyed his bike. 'A horse, that is.'

'It's been a while but—'

'Good. Get a horse. Get a hat.' She turned to Eve. 'And *you* can explain later. Make sure he has all he needs. You can catch us up in the paddocks.'

She urged Opal into a canter and Nate watched her go, a slant to his smile. 'Is your sister always so…welcoming?'

'If you'd *been* welcome, yes.'

He gave her the side eye and her belly danced. 'Are you saying I'm not welcome, Eve?'

'I'm saying you should have waited.'

'I waited plenty. And I had a sneaking suspicion I'd be six feet under if I carried on wating for you to come to me.' He faced her fully now, those blazing blue eyes sending her weak at the knees—thank heaven for Jade beneath her. 'It may surprise you to know but I'm not one for sitting back and letting someone else take the lead. Not even when that someone is as sexy as you.'

Her heart gave a betraying little leap, Jade gave a whinny, and she pulled on the reins, dismissing his words as swiftly as she dismissed the way he made her feel. 'This way.'

She urged Jade into a canter, uncaring that he couldn't keep pace. She needed the space, a moment to recover. A moment to get over the shock of having him here when she was still reeling from the shock she had yet to share.

News she didn't know how to deliver.

Though she had to.

Secrets had crippled her family and she wasn't about to let this secret do the same. Not that they were family, but then…

Her stomach lurched and she pulled back on the reins, slowing Jade as she touched a hand to the invisible life growing inside her. *We're family.*

She'd never envisaged this in her future, but she wouldn't fail her child. And she wouldn't keep their presence from their father either. She'd tell him as soon as the day was done. As soon as Rose had received the help she needed.

And then she might start coming to terms with it herself.

* * *

No sooner had Nate entered the stables than Eve was shoving an Akubra at his chest.

'This isn't some joke, you know.'

'I didn't say it was.'

'Then quit with the grinning and stick this on. I'd lose the jacket else you'll cook. You got a decent shirt on under that?'

She waved a hand over him, but not once did her eyes reach his.

'I'll be fine.'

'And don't expect Rose to go easy on you. *Every*one pulls their weight on the muster.'

'I wouldn't have it any other way.'

'Good.'

She gave an abrupt nod and started to move away. He caught at her arm, forcing her to pause and the pulse in her throat gave a betraying leap. He was getting to her. He just wasn't sure why…unless…

'I'm sorry if I overstepped.' It was the only reason he could think to explain her behaviour. The way she couldn't even look at him. 'The sexy remark, I mean.'

Not for the turning up unannounced, because she'd had her warning there.

She wet her lips, her eyes slowly lifting to his. 'It would help if you—'

'Here you go, Eve. Mercury was saddled for Aaron, but he's taking the Jeep so…' A tall brunette woman led an *extremely* tall black horse towards them. Glossy coat. Warm eyes. But how tall!

Nate had a flash of sanity. The last time he'd got on a horse had been…well, too many years ago to recall. Still, it had to be like riding a bike. Surely. He hoped.

'Thanks, Sally.'

Eve took the reins and handed them over, mouth twitching. 'I'm sure you'll be very happy together.'

She knew he was nervous!

Standing taller, he perfected his grin. 'Jealous?'

Her eyes flashed. There was something she wanted to say but she was biting her lip, and he knew better than to ask with an audience.

'Shall we get to work?' he said, tossing his jacket on a nearby barrel.

Her brow puckered, tease shifting into genuine concern. 'Are you sure about this?'

So she did care…or was it more that she didn't want an injured lawyer on her hands? On Rose's hands?

'Mustering? I wouldn't do it if I wasn't.' He turned to Mercury, gave the fine animal an affectionate stroke, which he returned with a nuzzle to his shirt. 'See, already one. Now lead the way before your sister accuses me of keeping you too long.'

That got her moving.

And watching Eve launch herself into the saddle and ride with effortless ease was as captivating as watching her walk. He followed suit, slightly less graceful but he had Mercury trotting and that was a start. Though he was more than aware of the barely constrained power between his thighs and was careful to respect it. Riding was as much about the mental and emotional awareness as it was the physical. He remembered that well enough.

They joined Rose and the stable hands in the field. Rose gave him a brief nod and the others followed suit. No one looked surprised so she must have filled them in.

'You okay?' Eve called over. Skin and hair golden with the rising sun, she made quite the sight and he almost lost his seat.

'Never better,' he called back, giving Mercury an apologetic pat for his ineptness while covering up his slip.

She gave a laugh. 'I'll ask you again in a few hours when that bum of yours is protesting the saddle.'

She clicked her horse and moved off, reintroducing the distance she'd created when he'd first arrived and this time, he let her go. There would be time for them to talk later.

Right now, he'd enjoy the view. The mountains in the distance and nature all around—this was what he'd come back for. Sydney was still beautiful in its own way, but nothing could beat this.

Especially when a certain blonde woman and her bay took centre stage.

'Who'd have thought it?'

Rose came up alongside her, her eyes on Nate in the distance as he rounded up two escapees.

'Thought what?' Eve said, doing her best *not* to look his way. He was too much of a distraction. Had been all morning. Not because he wasn't capable. Because he was the exact opposite.

'The pretty boy can muster.'

Eve gave a choked laugh. 'I guess he can.'

'Works hard too.'

'He was a top lawyer in Sydney. I think he knows how to work hard.'

'With those tattoos?'

He'd rolled his cuffs back just enough to give them away...

'I don't think his tattoos affect his ability to work, Rose.'

'That's not what I meant, more the being a lawyer with all that ink...'

'Uh-huh.' Maybe that was why Eve had never guessed at his identity that first night, prejudiced from the outset...

'But this kind of graft is a different beast entirely.'

'Uh-huh,' she repeated, trying to dull her body's innate response to him that was increasing with every passing remark. Even though her sister was only saying everything she'd already thought. Her admiration increasing with every passing muster minute.

Rose gave her an odd look, which Eve promptly ignored.

'Right, we're going to stop for lunch,' her sister said, nodding to the river ahead. 'Let the cattle get some water. I need to catch up with Aaron on the satellite phone. You okay taking care of...?'

Rose's eyes were back on Nate and Eve swallowed. 'No problem.'

Only of course it was, because the secret was pressing between them, as was the incessant chemistry.

She urged Jade into a trot and, as though sensing her approach, Nate turned in his saddle, eyes bright beneath the rim of his Akubra, and her heart fluttered. Would there ever come a time he wouldn't do that to her?

'We're going to stop for lunch,' she said once he was within earshot. 'There's a shaded spot at the edge of the ravine. We can keep an eye on the cattle from there.'

'Right you are, Boss.'

His voice too, it got to her in all the ways she shouldn't let it but couldn't prevent.

And his unwitting use of Rose's nickname almost had her rejecting it out of hand. But it felt good. Earning that respectful title in the paddocks. Something she'd craved for so long. Even if he hadn't meant it in the same way they all did when they spoke to Rose.

She found a spot to secure the horses and threw a blanket over a nearby rock. Taking the food and water from the cooler pack, she set it all out. Ignored the sense that this was far too cosy and focused on the sticky heat and sweat of hard labour. Nothing sexy about that.

She plonked herself down and he lowered himself beside her.

'Here.'

Blindly, she offered him a sandwich, which he took with a gruff, 'Thank you.'

She heard him chug down some water, felt the heat of him relax back beside her as she took in the view. The craggy ravine to one side with the river running through it and the open red land to the other, the sparse pockets of green and the sun beating down. The cattle and the horses happily making the most of the water. The station hands finding a spot to settle for a spell…though she felt anything but settled.

She picked up her drink, took a swig, wishing it could chill her out too…

'You've impressed Rose,' she said, needing to say something to break the silence that was loaded with so much—the pull, the secret…

'Not you though?'

She could hear the tease in his voice and felt her lips curve. 'All right, don't get a big head about it. You've impressed us both.'

'I must be doing something right if you're back to dishing out compliments.'

She shook her head as she recalled that first night. It felt so long ago and yet it was only a month. So much had changed. She had changed. *Everything* had changed.

'To be honest,' he said, 'it's good to do something physical for a change.'

Physical. Not the evocative word she needed right now. 'Well, you're good at it.'

'So are you.' He took a bite of his sandwich as her body bloomed with his praise. 'Seems us office types can still pull it out of the bag when required.'

She gave a huffed laugh. 'I guess we can.'

And did that mean he'd been in awe of her all morning, as she had been in awe him? She'd sensed his eyes on her often enough but each time she'd checked him out his attention had been on the cattle…busy doing the job she was supposed to be doing.

'It is beautiful here,' he murmured while she picked at the sandwich she'd taken up.

'It is.'

He gave a chuckle that jarred her into looking at him. A foolish move. With him this close and laid back, propped up on one elbow, legs outstretched, the hat, those tattoos, the sheen of hard work…*why* was that sexy?

She tugged her gaze away. 'What's so funny?'

'After your whole speech in the bar I expected you to tell me how horrid it all was.'

'I never said it was horrid.'

Though all those weeks ago he was right…but now…

'No.' He took another bite of his sandwich, swallowed it with relish. 'You only gave that impression with the whole dreading-it thing and wishing for escape.'

She drank more water. Waited for her pulse to calm. Her nausea to ease.

'I love London. I love my life there.' All things she was trying to convince herself of as she said them because how could that change within a month? Because of Nate, Rose, her family…or the baby? Sure, it blurred things, shifted her priorities, but she still loved what she had back home. Didn't she? 'It gave me everything I needed when I left Australia.'

'Which was?'

'The aforementioned escape.'

'From?'

Like he didn't already know…but then she hadn't told him the full story. She shoved her sandwich aside and brought her knees to her chest.

'I found out about the affair when I was fifteen and it broke me. It broke my life. I couldn't bear being under the same roof as my father…or my mother. I also couldn't bear being around my sisters knowing what I knew.'

'You never told them?'

'How could I? It was bad enough that I knew. I couldn't destroy their happy bubble too. They found out the day your father read Holt's will.'

He cursed under his breath.

'Precisely. I stopped coming home from boarding school in the holidays and left for England as soon as I was able. My grandparents took me in. Gave me all the love I could have wished for. I guess I filled the hole my mother left when she married my father and, though I never told them what my father did, their resentment towards him was enough to reaffirm how I felt. That I was better off out of it.'

'Did they really not speak to your mother after she married him…? Sorry, I'm not one to listen to gossip but it's hard to avoid that story.'

She picked at some muck on her boot. 'I know the stories, but my grandparents were good people. They loved Mum and they missed her terribly. They resented Holt for taking her away. They didn't trust him to do right by her and they didn't trust the intense passion they shared. Time proved them right.'

'Did it?'

'He had the affair, didn't he?'

'But then they had all those years…?'

'Doesn't change the heartache in between.'

'But if they hadn't cut her off, maybe your mother wouldn't have felt so isolated and—'

'And there you go again, sounding just like Rose.'

'She thinks the same?'

Eve nodded.

'But not you?'

'I don't know what to think. But I do know they regret it. My grandfather died a few years back and he told my grandmother to fix it.'

'Fix it?'

'To heal the rift. I love my grandmother and I love my sisters. To see them come together after all this time would be…'

'Would be wonderful, for sure.' He finished for her. 'But if your grandmother deserves a second chance, don't you think your father…?'

She glared at him.

'Seriously, Eve, think about it… How do your sisters feel now they know the truth?'

She went back to the muck on her boot. 'They loved my father, still love him, but it's different for them.'

'How is it different?'

They'd read her mother's journal, for a start.

'Eve?'

'They're convinced there is another side to all of this and one that I'd get if I just—'

She broke off as she thought of the aged leather book on her bedside table. It had turned up when she'd been in the shower one day courtesy of Rose and her unwavering hope that she would one day have the courage…

'Just?'

She swallowed. 'If I read my mother's journal.'

'Your mother kept a journal?'

'Her doctor recommended she keep one, when she was sick… She had PND—postnatal depression—after having Tilly. She was to use it as a way of pouring her feelings onto paper, a kind of therapy, I suppose.'

'And your sisters have read it, but you haven't?'

'No.' She shivered and clutched her knees tight. 'It feels like an invasion of privacy. Too personal and too wretched.'

'But she was your Mum.'

'I know, and Rose and Tilly think she meant for us to read it one day… A way of her explaining the past in a way that we as adults would understand, but…'

'That sounds reasonable.'

'I'm glad you all think so because it gives me the willies.'

He chuckled softly. 'Not a phrase I've heard in a long time.'

She managed a smile.

'Willies aside, it could be a way for you to get some closure on the past. Answers to all those questions you still have?'

She looked at him. 'You really do sound like Rose, you know?'

'Having witnessed your sister in action this morning, I'm going to take that as another compliment.'

'You would.'

'I'm also going to say that, for someone who professes to love London, you do look rather at home here.'

'It seems it's in my blood more than I thought, but I struggle to understand how you can give up your life, your work in Sydney, to come back for good.'

'Like you, I left as soon as I could. I didn't want to stew in my own anger and resentment and make things worse for Mum. I figured getting away made it easier. My father couldn't overlook me any more, because I wasn't here to be overlooked.'

She lowered her knees and twisted to face him. 'Have you spoken to him yet?'

'No.'

'But now that you know more about the past, about him, don't you think you owe it to you both to clear the air? He's not a bad man. He's made mistakes. And I know I sound like a hypocrite...'

'You do.'

'But what if he doesn't realise that's how you felt growing up? What if—?'

'Doesn't change the fact that it happened.'

'And yet, you want to make a life for yourself here now.'

'I told you, it's where I want to settle, where I've always intended to settle. Sydney gave me the career to build up a nest egg that, with the right investment, I don't need to work the hours that I did in the city. I'm in a place where I can take time out. I can even help the people of Marni like my father did before and still have a life, marry, make a home.'

Marry. Make a home. *Children.*

She covered her stomach with her palm, the truth rising within her. 'Nate, I—'

A whistle pierced the air. They both turned to see Rose gesturing.

'Lunch over already?' he asked.

She nodded. As was the time to talk. Not that now had been the time or the place for it...

'We need to keep moving if we're to make it back before nightfall.'

Then she could talk to him. Alone. No distractions.

No more secrets.

* * *

To say Nate struggled to focus for the remainder of the day was an understatement.

Eve was a distraction like none other.

Majestic on her bay, forthright with the cattle, the rhythmic sounds coming out of her throat enough to make him want to dance to her tune.

Regardless of what he'd told her that morning…

'I'm not one for sitting back and letting someone else take the lead. Not even when that someone is as sexy as you.'

He'd hardly been playing it cool. The words coming out of his mouth before he could wind them back in. And she'd fled from him. No sooner had the spark come alive in her blue eyes, than it had been snuffed out and she'd ridden off. He was beginning to spy a pattern. Any time he evoked anything close to the passion they'd shared that first night, she ran.

And he got it.

She feared it because she didn't trust it. She didn't trust it to last and not bite you on the arse when it was done.

But it existed. Between them. And damned if he could snuff it out.

The attraction, the chemistry, the inability to get her out of his head. The admiration that ran far deeper than attraction. The last few weeks she'd dedicated herself to Garrison Downs and her sisters' cause, whether it was pulling apart the will or physically working herself to the bone to keep the station ticking over. It all pointed to her huge heart that she refused to give to anyone else. And what a crime that was.

He'd tell her as much if he didn't think it would send her even faster in the other direction. His eyes drifted back to her, prepared for more of the same—appreciation, admiration, desire…instead his senses came alive with concern. Her pace had slowed, her head lolling with the movement of her horse, her posture slackening…

He looked to Rose, alert in her seat, no sign of tiredness. But then, Rose lived and breathed this life. Eve was like him.

Unaccustomed to such labour. He'd been at it a day and he was dog tired, but he knew Eve had been at it for days, weeks even, and something wasn't right.

She wasn't right.

He stiffened and Mercury whinnied in response, the horse jerking towards Eve as his body instinctually did the same.

'Sorry, boy.'

He adjusted his seat, patted the horse's neck, all the while keeping his gaze trained on her. He wanted to get to her. Wanted to check on her. It was far enough to fall when you came off a horse, but with the driving cattle, too…it didn't bear thinking about.

He scanned the area, the station hands all spread out. They were thin enough on the ground as it was, he couldn't break formation. To get to Rose and warn her. Or get himself to Eve's side.

He cursed, wishing their pace to quicken even as he wished her off that horse and in his arms. Safe. He edged as close as he could without confusing the cattle and gritted his teeth. Held steady. Denying the impulse to speed up when the homestead appeared on the horizon, a tiny speck but a welcome sight.

Sweat trickled down his rigid spine, the tension nothing to do with the muster and everything to do with Eve. Though she seemed to perk up as they neared the house. Her posture returning, the odd smile too.

Maybe he'd been projecting his weariness onto her, worrying unnecessarily…

'And that's a wrap!' Rose called out as the gate was swung shut on the last of the cattle. 'Great job, guys. Rest up, catch your beauty sleep. It's going to be a big day tomorrow.'

Then she turned to Nate. 'Toss your reins to Kylie and she'll see Mercury back to the stables. Thanks for your help today.'

'My pleasure.'

He sought out Eve, surprised to find her still mounted on Jade and walking steadily away. Then he took in her hands slack on the reins, her head starting to droop…

'*Eve!*'

He dropped Mercury's reins and ran, catching the attention of the entire yard. Rose's head and horse snapped around. But his every sense was on Eve. Desperate, unable to breathe, praying her horse wouldn't startle as he came up alongside her. He reached a hand up to steady her as he slowed Jade to a stop and Eve slumped towards him, silent, unmoving.

His heart lurched. 'Eve…?'

He eased her into his arms, stroked the hair away from her face. Took in the pulse working in her throat—reassuring. The paleness to her skin—less so.

He cursed and her head lifted, her lashes fluttering open for the briefest spell. 'You kiss your momma with that mouth?'

Hell, he wanted to kiss her just for saying it. For giving him some fire.

'Evie!' Opal skidded to a halt in a cloud of dust and Rose swung herself down.

'It's okay. I've got her. I've got her.' His words were for Rose but his tone, soft and soothing, was all for Eve.

'How did you…?' Whatever Rose saw in his face stopped her from finishing. 'I should have noticed.' She cursed, snatching Eve's fallen Akubra off the ground. 'Aaron!' she yelled towards the bunkhouse as a guy appeared in the doorway. 'Get these horses back to the stables. Eve's taken ill.'

The chap jogged up to take the reins and Rose led Nate to the house. The second they crossed the threshold, she was hollering, 'Lindy! Lindy!'

A short brunette woman came running up, an old border collie trailing behind. 'What is it?' Her eyes widened on Eve in Nate's arms. 'Oh, my!'

'Get me a bowl of fresh water and a cloth,' Rose commanded. 'Iced water to drink and some food. Some soup. Eve's unwell.'

'I'm fine,' Eve murmured, her body still slack against him, her voice otherworldly.

'Like hell you are.' Rose spun to face them. Blue eyes, so

like her sister's, ablaze. 'I *knew* there was something wrong with you this morning, I never should've let you work.' She tugged off her hat, ran a hand over her hair. 'You've likely caught what they've all had.'

'This isn't on you.' Eve shifted against him, tried to lift her head. 'It's not your fault.'

'Like hell it isn't.'

He could see the anger in Rose, anger that she lay wholly at her own feet.

'It really isn't, Rose,' he said softly, trying to reassure her, for her own sake as well as Eve's. Rose's self-loathing was only going to exacerbate Eve's condition. 'You have a station to run and you were doing it.'

She blew out a shallow breath, muttered something that sounded an awful lot like *'But at what cost?'* and turned away. 'Follow me.'

He did as she asked, barely aware of the grand surroundings and the dirt they were traipsing through as she led him down the hallway to a door towards the end. She pushed it open and strode on in, switching on a bedside lamp and throwing back the duvet. The dog came too, alert to something amiss as it took up position at the foot of the bed.

Everything was pink—the walls, the bed, the chair before the window… Was this Eve's bedroom? Was this how she'd had it as a child? All sweet and romantic and soft?

He set her down gently and Rose tugged off her sister's boots, still tutting and muttering. Nate set his hat down on the bedside table and stroked her cheeks, felt her forehead for a temperature. They were inches apart, so close he could catch her unique scent, feel her breath upon his skin. Her blue eyes blinked up at him, her gaze far off and smile meek. 'My hero.'

Unadulterated pleasure morphed into white-hot panic as her lashes fluttered closed again and she sank back into the pillow. He lurched forward, tapped her cheek. *'Eve?* Eve, stay with me.'

'I'm fine.' She tried to bat his hands away. 'I'm just—just tired.'

Lindy came in with a bowl, her frown deep. 'Aaron needs to see you, Rose. He says it's urgent.'

'Right now? I can't—'

'Don't worry, Rose,' Nate said, taking the bowl from Lindy. 'I'll take care of your sister. You do what you need to.'

A small crease formed between her brows. A moment where she studied him intently, then gave a sharp nod. He had the oddest sense that he'd just been read, tested, and given some kind of approval.

'I'll be right back.'

'You don't need to do this,' Eve mumbled as Rose left and he shushed her as he eased himself down beside her, wringing the cloth in the water.

'I want to.'

Gently, he mopped her brow, her cheeks, her neck, cleaning her skin while cooling her down. Always careful, always aware of her every reaction. The flicker of her lashes, the reassuring rise and fall of her chest, the way she turned into his touch...

Lindy came in and placed a jug of water and a glass beside the bed. He nodded his gratitude, and she hurried off again.

'You can go now,' she whispered.

'Always so keen to get rid of me, Eve.'

Her lips quivered into a small smile. 'You've served your purpose.'

'Thought you said I was your hero.'

'For saving me from a nasty fall...'

He dabbed at her temple. 'I think a hero would stick around, don't you?'

She gave a soft laugh. 'Don't be getting a big head.'

He recalled her saying the same at the ravine, when she'd told him how impressed she'd been, and he smiled. 'I wouldn't dare.'

'Though I wish mine would stop banging.'

'You have a headache?'

She nodded and winced in one.

He scanned the room, spied the door to her en suite. 'Don't go anywhere…'

'Fat chance,' she said softly.

He headed into the bathroom—just as pink, just as girly—pulled open the bathroom cabinet and found a blister pack of paracetamol.

'I have tablets,' he said, returning to her side. 'Do you feel up to taking them?'

She scooted herself up the bed in answer and he poured a glass of water.

'I've really made a fool of myself,' she grumbled, eyeing him from beneath her lashes, the colour in her cheeks deepening.

'What you've done is worked too hard and your body needs a break.'

He popped out the last two tablets in the pack and offered them out with the glass.

She threw them back with a sip of water and screwed up her face. 'So much for proving we can run this place.'

He took the glass from her as she sagged back into the pillow.

'Really messed that up, didn't I?'

'You didn't mess it up at all. Seeing you Waverly sisters in action was quite something.'

'Quite something…in a *good* way?'

'Yes, Eve, in a very good way.'

Her eyes lifted to his. Surprise, doubt, gratitude, a swirling mist within the blue and he had to look away. Look away before the connection brewing got the better of him. He placed her glass back on the bedside table and saw the leather-bound book resting there. Aged and initialled with RW. 'Is that…?'

She followed his gaze. 'Yes.' She swallowed. 'Rose is ever hopeful I'll pick it up.'

'Does she not know how stubborn you are?'

She gave a soft laugh that was music to his still-worry-spiked pulse. 'Jokes aside, maybe it's time, Eve. Maybe it's time we both dealt with our parents head-on. You with your mother's written word and me with my father.'

'Are you offering some sort of a deal?'

'Perhaps.' He let his gaze drift back to hers, saw the hair that had fallen across one eye and tucked it back behind her ear. 'But maybe not tonight, hey? Tonight, you need to rest.'

She raised her hand to cover his, held his palm against her cheek. 'Thank you.'

'What for?'

Her blue eyes glistened and she wet her lips…

'Eve?'

But no words came. The room was so quiet save for their gentle breaths, the light so soft it felt as intimate as any embrace. He had the strangest sense of being where he belonged, of being beside the woman he belonged to…

It didn't matter that she wasn't the woman for him, that under any normal circumstances she was married to her job just as his father had always been, that she had no interest in marriage, kids, a family of her own.

He wanted her to be the right woman because she was everything he wanted.

'How's the patient?'

His head flicked around as Rose stepped into the room.

'Sorry, I didn't mean to startle you.'

'You didn't, I was…' What were you doing? Fantasising about a future that wasn't possible, with a woman who wouldn't want it in a million years. Because this wasn't *Eve* Eve. This was Eve on sabbatical, exhausted and strung out.

'I've asked Lindy to make up one of the guest rooms for you,' Rose said, rescuing him from his runaway thoughts as she checked Eve over. 'It's too late to be travelling back now and it's the least we can do for all your help today. Not to mention rescuing Bambi here.'

He cocked a brow. 'Bambi?'

'Rose,' Eve moaned. 'Do you have to?'

'Sorry, little sis,' she said softly, 'couldn't resist.'

'You don't need to know,' Eve mumbled, reaching for his hand and squeezing it.

'Need, no.' He covered her hand around his. 'But *want*? Definitely.'

She growled.

'Eve can explain it to you tomorrow,' Rose said. 'For now, I can take it from here.'

He wanted to argue. Say he was happy to stay. But Rose was her sister, and he…well, he was nobody by comparison.

Reluctantly, he stood.

'There's nothing to take, Rose,' Eve said. 'I'm fine.'

'You will be when you get some soup in you and a decent night's sleep.'

'All things I can do by myself.'

Snatching up the empty strip of pills, Nate headed to the bathroom, listening to Rose fuss and Eve deflect, warmed by the sisterly to and fro. All signs that Eve would be okay.

He flicked up the lid of the pedal bin and tossed the strip in. A good night's sleep and she'd be—

He froze. Eyes on the contents of the bin as the world spun around him. There, lay the empty blister pack. And beneath it, a tiny mountain of tests—*Pregnancy* tests.

All with their own version of the same result:

Pregnant
Positive
+

Eve was…*pregnant*?

Dazed and confused, his eyes drifted to her on the bed. Rose, in the position he'd vacated…

This room was Eve's. This bathroom was Eve's. Those tests *had* to be Eve's.

She chose that moment to look in his direction, their eyes

connecting, hers falling to his foot still on the pedal bin before launching back to his face, panicked and wide.

He knew in that moment. The baby was his.

She started to push herself up.

'Oh, no, you don't.' Rose pressed her back.

'But, Rose…'

Nate moved before all hell broke loose, heading for the door as everything within him went into full-on turmoil. Every emotion at war. 'Thank you for the offer of a bed, Rose. I'll see you both in the morning. We'll talk then, Eve.'

When she was rested and he was dealing with her at full strength. Because there could be no confusion where their baby was concerned. Where the future was concerned.

The idea that she would simply return to London and take their child with her…that he would become worse than his father, a true absentee dad, access restricted by the miles and granted as and when life permitted. *Hell*, no.

Eve might have proven that Holt Waverly's daughters didn't need husbands to run these lands, but, as the mother of his child, she *would* marry him.

CHAPTER EIGHT

'*NATE!*'

Eve woke with a start, Nate's face as he'd connected the dots the night before injecting her with adrenaline and sending her bolt upright in bed. Hand clutched to her chest, she sucked in a breath and another, her heart beating so hard she was sure she'd break a rib.

'Good. You're awake…'

She turned at the sound of his voice, her heart struggling to return to its normal rhythm. Immaculate in the clothes from yesterday—dark shirt open at the collar, blue jeans, buckle belt and blond hair styled to perfection—he was everything her panicked heart wanted to see and not.

'You look…fresh.' She'd hoped to coax out a smile as he crossed the room, instead she got a cool aloofness that had the hairs prickling along her bare arms. She hugged the quilt to her chest, lowered her gaze from his eyes that seemed to look right past her. 'I take it Lindy managed to clean your clothes.'

'Rose insisted.' He paused beside the bed, pressed a gentle hand to her brow. His touch warm but his voice… 'How are you feeling?'

'Better.' But it came out gruff, fearful, choked with the mood in the room. She glanced up. Took in the shadows under his eyes, his mouth…*that* mouth, normally so quick to smile, drawn into a pensive line.

She'd done that to him. Worried him. Shocked him. Made him into this cool replica of himself…

'Where's Rose?' Was that really her voice? So quiet and unsure.

'You've been asleep a while. She left shortly after the doctor arrived.'

'Doctor? What doctor?'

'He helicoptered in from Marni this morning. His assurances that you weren't in any immediate danger are the only reason Rose isn't here now watching over you.'

'Oh, my God, does she know?'

He backed away, his 'No' short. 'I surmised she had no idea about—about the situation.'

Situation. That was one word for it.

And the feeling of guilt welled with the panic.

Guilt that she was adding to her sister's burden. Guilt that Nate knew but not from her lips. And panic that she'd lost any grip on the situation as the man before her pulled away. Emotionally as well as physically.

Where was the connection they'd shared not twenty-four hours ago? The man who had nursed her, cared for her…made her feel safe and invincible?

He paused before the window, his back to her, rigid and unmoving. Did he even breathe?

'I'm sorry.'

He didn't flinch, there was no sign he'd even heard her.

'I hate that you found out like that.'

She wrapped her arms around her knees and her rapidly chilling middle. Watched as he turned his head, just enough for her to see his profile, the grim set of his mouth, his eyes downcast. 'How long have you known?'

She clenched her teeth and swallowed. This wasn't how she wanted this to go, wasn't how she'd expected it to go. But then, she hadn't really known *what* to expect. She knew what she craved though. Some of his usual warmth, his charisma, his care…

'I suspected a couple of days ago.'

Slowly he turned to face her. 'Why didn't you say anything when I saw you in town?'

'Because I didn't know. Not for certain. That's why I was there.'

'The pharmacy—that's what you were doing?'

'Buying them out of every brand of test, yes. I took them yesterday morning. They say it's best, more accurate, if you do it then.'

She threw back the covers, making to rise, and he was before her in a heartbeat. 'Oh, no, you don't, you're staying there.'

'I'm pregnant, Nate! Not debilitated.' They both froze at her declaration, and it was Nate who recovered first. Taking a step back.

'I'd appreciate you staying there until the doctor has spoken to you. There are tests he needs to carry out.'

'I don't need a doctor.'

'You fainted, Eve, multiple times.'

'I just needed sleep and some food. I feel fine.'

She didn't but she wasn't about to tell him that. She didn't want his pity. She *did* want him to wrap his arms around her and show her that he still cared though.

He surprised her with a curse. 'You should've said something sooner! If I'd known I'd never have let you...'

'What, ride? Help Rose? You really think you could have stopped me?'

'But it's not just you you need to think of now, Eve! There's our baby to consider.'

'And don't you think I know *that*? I may not have planned to be a mother, I may not have experienced the whole ticking of the biological clock, but I tell you now, I'll be a good one. I'll make sure of it.'

'I don't doubt it, but we need to talk about what we do now.'

'What we do?' She frowned. 'There'll be appointments, for sure. I haven't sorted anything as yet, but I guess with the doctor here...' Her voice trailed off at the look in his eye. 'That's not what you meant, is it?'

'No. Though we do need to talk about your prenatal care. You won't want for anything, you or my child. I can promise you that.'

And it should have warmed her, the passion in that statement, only...

'So if you didn't mean that, what did you mean?'

'I want to talk about us.'

'Us?'

'Yes.'

She frowned, shook her head. 'I'm not sure I follow...'

'You've made it clear that love is an emotion you will never fall foul of...that you don't want it in return and have no desire for it in your future.'

'Yes,' she whispered, even as her heart called her out for a fool and a liar. 'Though I'll love our child, Nate, don't doubt that.'

'I don't.'

'So what are you—?'

'Marry me, Eve.'

Her breath caught in her lungs, her eyes burning as she stared at him. He couldn't have just said... *'What?'*

'Hear me out, okay?'

'Hear you out,' she repeated numbly, shock fixing her in place.

'I refuse to be like my father. You already know this about me. I won't bring a child up wondering when they'll next see me, when the next scrap of affection will be tossed their way. I wanted for nothing financially growing up, but emotionally...' He swallowed. 'I won't do it. I can't.'

'But *marriage*?'

'I want to be there every day, not just at weekends or when our schedules permit it. I want a home, with a wife and our child.'

'But, Nate...' She was shaking, from her toes to the tips of her fingers. 'You can't mean it.'

'I do. You need a husband to satisfy the conditions of the

will and I refuse to let another man bring up my child, Eve. I want you to marry me. I'm *asking* you to marry me.'

'You don't know what you're saying.'

'I know exactly what I'm saying.'

'But you want love, Nate, you *deserve* love.'

'What I want is your hand in marriage. What I deserve is a home where I see my child every day.'

Her ears rang, her heart raced.

'I know you don't want love, Eve, and I'll respect that, if you will respect my wishes in return.'

She studied his face, searched for the man she had come to care for so deeply…

'But where will we live? Have you thought about that? My life is in London, my job, Gran…the idea that I would leave her like Mum once left her…'

'You won't have to.'

'But—?'

'We'll move to London.'

'You're going to come to London? With *me*?'

'I'll move anywhere to be there for my child, so long as it's a place that can give them what they need.'

She swallowed. 'But London?'

He nodded.

'I can't believe you're serious.'

'Why can't you? It works for you too. This way, you secure your part in the inheritance and can return to London with a free conscience. Go back to your job, your life.'

Ha. Her life was unrecognisable now. Couldn't he see that?

'And you, what will you do there?'

'I can be a lawyer anywhere.'

'But what about continuing your father's good work in Marni?'

'I'm sure London has its fair share of people in need of legal aid.'

'But what about your love of the land here, the home and the life you wanted for your child?'

'We can do all that in London.'

'In the city? That is as busy and as bustling as Sydney?'

'I'm sure there'll be quieter suburbs, somewhere we can both be happy.'

Happy. It didn't sound happy to Eve. It sounded cold and lonely and…and…she couldn't bear it.

'What about when I'm working and my job takes over once more? When I'm no better than your father for the time I'll have spare?'

He shifted on his feet, not quite so quick. 'I'll deal with it. I'm not a teen craving attention any more, Eve.'

No, he was a man craving love. The kind she didn't trust and sure as hell didn't know how to give.

'You don't need to decide this second. I've told Rose I'll stay on for a few days and help with the muster.'

'*I* should be out there helping.'

'You're going nowhere.'

'But, Nate, it's the busiest time of the year. She needs me.'

'What she needs is her sister and the niece or nephew she doesn't know exists healthy. The doctor will decide if and when you're ready to help again.'

She blinked at him, speechless. How had it come to this? How had she become such an epic burden to her sister who she'd come here to help? And this man who deserved so much more than she felt capable of giving?

'In the meantime, I'm here to take your place so you needn't worry about Rose and the station.'

'And what about your work?'

'You and my child come first, Eve.'

Something else she'd always known about him…so why did it still leave her cold?

'I'm going to let the doctor know you're awake.'

He moved and she shot up. 'Nate, wait—'

He paused, looked back, but she couldn't find the words. None that made sense anyhow. Because all she really wanted was for him to hold her. Hold her and make her feel as though everything would be okay. Just like he had that first night.

But she wasn't so sure that was possible…or if it ever would be again.

As for the offer he'd put to her…marriage, the inheritance, their child.

Was there really any other answer she could give?

'Eve?'

'Yes,' she said over him.

He took a sharp breath. 'Yes?'

'I'll marry you.'

CHAPTER NINE

I T WAS F RIDAY EVENING.

Five days since she'd said yes. Six days with Nate under the
same roof, helping Rose and the station. Helping her.

And still no one knew. Not about the engagement or her
pregnancy.

Well, save for Nate and the doctor.

She hadn't wanted to distract Rose. Or so she'd told Nate.
But really, she hadn't wanted to put words to it. It all felt too
surreal.

Her. Pregnant and engaged.

She felt railroaded. Not by Nate. Never, Nate. But by the
situation. The situation brought about by her father and the
inheritance. And then the baby, the baby that she wanted to
ensure would be brought up encased in love, from both their
parents, and would never doubt that love. Not for a second.

It was like some parallel universe where she was doing the
very opposite of every plan she'd made since hitting adult-
hood. Every dream.

She watched from the front deck as Rose and Nate rolled
home with the troops. Signalling the end of a very long week
and the start of a new life for Eve, because tonight was the
night. Nate wanted to visit his folks, share the 'good' news,
and she wanted to break it to Rose before they left.

Taking some nausea-easing breaths, she eased the swing
seat beneath her back and forth. Waiting as they dismounted
in the yard. Waiting as they crossed the ground towards her,

laughing and joking as if Nate had always belonged here. Waiting until...his eyes met hers, her heart did its little dance, and she gave the half-smile she'd perfected in Rose's company of late.

'You look nice,' Rose said as she stepped up onto the deck, stripping her hat and sweeping a hand through her hair. 'It's good to see you looking more like yourself.'

'Thanks.' She only wished she felt like it. Her eyes flitted to Nate, seeking his approval too. She hadn't known what to wear and had settled on a blue button-up midi dress, covered in tiny roses, feminine and sweet. A light dusting of make-up, hair loose in styled waves, she'd even misted on some perfume...

Perfect fiancée material.

'You do,' he said with a hint of warmth, of appreciation, but it was quickly masked. Hidden by the cool facade. Something she was getting far too accustomed to seeing. So much so she questioned whether the glimpses were all in her hormonal imagination. 'My parents will love you.'

Love...?

'Your parents?' Rose frowned at Nate.

'Nate's taking me for dinner with them tonight.'

Rose cocked a brow. 'Is he now?'

Eve swallowed. 'Yes.'

He gave her a discreet nod. 'Which means I need to get moving if I'm to freshen up before we leave.'

Rose watched him go, her mouth quirking to one side. 'First, he rescues you from a fall he saw happening long before I did. Second, he helps nurse you back to health. Third, he has his receptionist bring clothes so that he can stick around to help our station get through the week. And *now* he's taking you to see his parents?'

Her gaze returned to Eve, blue eyes curious and questioning. 'Come and sit with me?'

She frowned, sensing something amiss, but did as Eve asked.

'Though I'm not coming any closer with this layer of muck. I'll ruin your dress.'

Eve managed a smile.

'So…you going to tell me what's going on between you both?'

Eve pressed her palms into her knees and took a breath. 'We're getting married.'

'You're *what*?'

Eve winced. 'Do you want all the dingoes to come running?'

'But you…you only met a month ago. How can you possibly be…? Is this the will? Because when I said I'd consider marrying, you were…'

Eve was shaking her head.

'Wow.' Rose tugged on her ponytail, looked to the sun setting over the land. 'I can't believe this. I knew there was more going on. I knew he cared for you. But *marriage*? So quick?'

'We've spent a lot of time together.'

Her sister gave her a disbelieving look.

'More than you know.'

The look stayed.

'So much time, we're actually… I'm…we're…'

Rose leaned closer. 'You're…'

Eve swallowed the rolling sickness within her. 'I'm pregnant.'

'Pregnant!'

Again, Eve winced and this time Rose apologised, leaned closer to give a hushed, '*Pregnant?* And it's…?'

Eve cursed. 'Yes, it's his!'

'Sorry.' Rose pinched her nose. 'I'm just…surprised. It's a lot to take in.'

'Tell me about it.'

'But when you first met, you were steaming angry.'

Eve coloured. 'That wasn't the first time we met…'

Rose's head lifted a nudge. 'It wasn't?'

Eve shook her head, wet her lips. 'We met in Marni the night I arrived... We hit it off.'

'Some hitting it off!'

The flicker of a smile touched Eve's lips. 'Bonded over Daddy issues, would you believe?'

'That old chestnut?'

Eve nodded. 'I can't explain it, Rose. There was just this *connection*. This intense, out-of-this-world connection. We didn't know who the other was, but we learned plenty, and we had this chemistry, and it was enough. We slept together. A lot.'

Rose gave an awkward laugh, held up a hand. 'Okay. TMI.'

'Sorry, but it was crazy,' she stressed. 'I've never known anything like it.'

'Me neither,' Rose said. 'But I'll tell you who has...'

'Don't go there. Please. That connection destroyed, Mum.'

'I was going to say Tilly but, yes, Mum too. And it didn't destroy her, Eve, you're wrong.'

'Am I?' she threw back, fired by her panic and confusion over Nate. 'Dad felt it too and look what he did to Mum when she needed him the most.'

She saw the pain in Rose's eyes, felt it as fresh and as real as her own.

'People aren't perfect, Evie. Not you, not me, not anyone. And if you carry on placing everyone on that same infallible pedestal you did Dad, you'll be disappointed for ever. If you accepted that we all make mistakes and learn from them, your life would be so much easier.'

But if she did that, if she accepted that her father did indeed love her mother, that they did indeed love one another, then she'd also have to accept that she'd cut them out of her life for nothing. She'd lost them for nothing. Sacrificed all those years when she could have been with them, with her sisters, all that time with her family that she could never get back.

'Please, sweetheart.' Rose pulled her in for a hug and Eve went willingly, uncaring of the dirt, needing her sister's love and warmth more. 'Read Mum's journal. Give yourself the opportunity to make peace with them.'

Eve eased out of her sister's hold, eyed her hands as she twisted them together in her lap and thought of the little leather book beside her bed.

'I'm a firm believer that everything happens for a reason.' Rose covered Eve's hands with one of her own. 'What happened with Mum. Dad. Now you... I've watched that man as he's watched over you, Evie, and there isn't anyone else in this world that I would trust more with your future happiness. Well, save for me, but I don't really count.'

She met her sister's earnest gaze, wishing with all her heart she could believe it.

A week ago, she might have. Before the news of the baby and everything had changed between them. When they'd had the chemistry, the connection, when he'd smiled at her in that way, teased her, endearingly tried to tackle her past with her, then she would have believed it.

But now he was so detached, so aloof. Aside from his concern for her well-being, but then she carried his child. He had a vested interest in her health.

'Are you ready, Eve?'

They both turned to see the man himself standing in the doorway. Hair damp from the shower, white shirt rolled back at the cuffs, jeans, boots, and a smile so reserved Eve thought she might cry on the spot. Something that was happening an awful lot lately.

Hormones. Just hormones.

She stood with a nod.

Rose clutched her hand, gave it a squeeze, her eyes sharp as she looked to Nate. 'Take care of my sister.'

'Always.'

'How did she take it?' Nate asked when he couldn't handle the silence in the truck any longer.

'She was shocked. Even more when I told her about the baby.'

No surprise there. *He* was still in shock.

'But I think...'

She fell silent and he glanced her way. This past week he'd witnessed a change in her, and it wasn't for the better. She was quiet. Reserved. Wary. The confident city swan was no more and he didn't know how to get her back. It was taking everything to keep his cool around her, to keep his feelings tightly locked away.

Maybe he should have given her longer, given her more time to adjust...

And the chance to change her mind?

His hands pulsed around the wheel, his voice tight with his thoughts. 'You think?'

She gave him a wry smile.

'She says that she believes everything happens for a reason.'

He frowned, trying to read between the lines. 'So she's *okay* about it?'

'If she wasn't, you'd know.'

'Now that I believe.' He gave a strained laugh. 'That woman is fierce when protecting her own.'

'She is...' Her voice trailed off, her gaze too. 'Not that I deserve such protection.'

He balked at her whispered remark. 'Why would you say that?'

'Why would you question it?'

He fought the urge to reach for her. 'Eve...'

'What, Nate?' she threw back at him, twisting in her seat. 'I abandoned her when I left all those years ago. I wasn't around when Mum died. I wasn't around when Dad died. She went through all that hell and I didn't come running to help her.'

'Because you shouldered a secret you thought would destroy her. You can't condemn yourself for that.'

'I can, because I should have told her.'

'But you didn't, and you can't change that. Your motives were pure even if you regret it now.' He flexed his grip around the wheel. 'Is that what all this has been? Weeks of hard labour, of sacrificing your life in London to come back and fight their corner…some kind of penance?'

She didn't respond but he knew he was right.

He should pull over. He should make her listen to him.

But where would that end? On a deserted road with the tensions running high between them, the undeniable chemistry he'd been suppressing for days, too.

He took a steadying breath. 'You abandoned your life in London to come back for her. You chose to face your past and the pain it so evidently brought you, to be here for your family now. You deserve all the care and the love in return.'

His voice grew husky, his feelings creeping too close to the surface…feelings that would help to convince his mother their engagement was real but freak Eve out. And for that he had to warn her…

'Look, Eve, I don't know how much you know about my parents.'

'Right now, I love them for getting you off the topic of me.'

And he couldn't agree more. They both needed the change up.

'I didn't spend any real time with your father when I was younger,' she said, sincerely now. 'The will reading was via video call and I've never met your mother. All I have to go on is what you've told me.'

He rolled his head on his shoulders, trying to ease the budding tension along his spine.

'They're quite…traditional. Especially when it comes to marriage. More so my mother. And with me being an only child, I think those values are magnified.'

'By values, what you're really saying is she wants you to marry for love?'

'Yes.' His mother most definitely. As for his father, heaven knew what George wanted but the fact that Eve was a Waverly would outshine all else.

'And you're telling me this because…?'

'Because I'd appreciate it if we could at least pretend.'

She didn't blanch, didn't flinch. She seemed calmer than he thought possible.

'Of course.' She stroked her stomach, a gesture he'd caught her doing numerous times and he wondered whether she was aware of it. Or if it was some innate response. He certainly wanted to do it. *All* the time. Hold her, hold *them*. 'What have you told them?'

'Not a lot.'

'What's not a lot?'

'That we've been dating and that I'm bringing you for dinner.'

'That's it?'

'That's it.'

'Okay,' she drawled as he pulled into his parents' drive and then she gasped.

'What is it?' His eyes shot to her, his pulse skipping over with worry for her and the baby.

But she was smiling, eyes wide as she took in his childhood home. The white picket fence that bordered his mother's flourishing garden, the love seat beneath the desert oak tree that had been there long before he'd been born. The potted plants that lined the steps up to the veranda where his mother's favourite swing seat had pride of place.

'It's like something out of a fairy tale, a gingerbread cottage… You grew up here?'

He nodded. 'My mother is an old romantic and my father had it built for her.' He turned to look at her, surprised to see the returning sadness in her eyes. 'What's wrong?'

'What is it about men building homes for their wives?'

He shrugged. 'Beats me.'

'And yet, you're offering the same. Offering to uproot your life here to build a home for us in London.'

'Your job is your first love.' No bitterness, just fact. 'You adore your grandmother. You adore your life in London. And you're desperate to get back to it. Have I missed anything?'

She stared at him, quiet and pale, and he feared he'd gone

too far closing himself off. He softened his voice, held her gaze. 'Look, Eve, I know how you feel about your mother uprooting her life in London to move here for your father. I know you think that fed into her misery.' He reached out to cup her cheek, wishing he could absorb her sadness through his palm and bring back the joy. Joy that he was witnessing less and less since his proposal. 'Knowing all this, I could never, in all good conscience, expect you to go through the same. To risk the same. I won't. You came back to help your sisters and once you've done that, we can leave.'

'But, Nate—'

Movement from the house caught their attention, his mother appearing on the doorstep. She waved, her eyes bright and smile wide. He took a moment to wave then turned back to Eve, who'd shrunk into her seat. Hiding from his mother or hiding from the reality of their situation, he wasn't sure.

'All that I ask is that we visit. Often.'

'But are you sure?' she whispered. 'Maybe we should take more time to think—'

'We're about to make my mother's dreams come true, Eve. There really is nothing more to think about...'

Because thinking about it meant questioning everything.

And questioning everything would bring answers.

And those potential answers terrified him.

Eve was ushered into the Harrington abode with all the care and affection one would expect to receive as a long-lost family member. Not a virtual stranger.

However, George had made it clear that, despite her absence, her father had spoken of her so often, he felt as though he already knew her. And Sue-Ellen hadn't stopped smiling. Her gaze darting between Eve and Nate as if she couldn't believe her eyes but adored what she saw.

And there'd been no fall out between the two men. Yet.

They talked about her sisters, the station, Rose and the mustering. There'd been the unmissable pride in his father's voice when he'd praised his son for stepping in and helping with the staffing. She wondered if Nate had noticed it too.

She looked at him now, sitting beside her at the cosy dining room table, and took his hand in hers. 'I really don't know what we would have done without Nate this past week.'

His eyes darted to hers, a momentary flare and then he caught her cue. Smiled softly.

'Yes, well…' George cleared his throat as his mother beamed on. 'It was very good of you, son, very good indeed.'

Nate gave her the smallest of nods—*Are you ready for us to tell them?*

A nervous smile—*Yes.*

Nerves ran riot in her gut. The news had been a shock to Rose and she'd had time to see them together, was convinced of their feelings too. His parents had witnessed one meal.

He grinned and the butterflies within her took off.

'It was nothing…especially for my soon-to-be wife.'

Woah. Had he really just thrown it out there like that?

His mother gasped. His father choked on his wine.

Yes, he had.

'Are you saying…?' His mother clasped her hands beneath her chin, eyes glistening.

'I've asked Eve to marry me…' he met Eve's gaze and she held it, for strength, for the confidence to see this through '…and she's said yes.'

George was back to clearing his throat. 'But—I don't understand. You've only known each other a month. How can you know each other enough to—?'

Nate's hand tensed beneath hers as his eyes snapped to his father's. 'I can assure you I know her very well.'

'Is this about the will?' his father said, eyes sharp behind his glasses.

'What are you talking about, George? Our son has just told you he's getting married and you're—'

'I thought you would be happy,' Nate interjected. 'Holt was, after all, one of your dearest clients, closest friends.'

'That doesn't answer my question.'

'I know more about Eve after a month than I knew about you my whole life. Making a home with her will be a joy by comparison.'

His father paled, his mother made the strangest noise, and the very air stilled. The pain in that one statement… He was defending their engagement, he was protecting his mother, and hating his father for daring to expose the truth in front of her.

And Eve couldn't bear it.

'Nate…' his mother started. 'I don't—'

'Leave it, Sue-Ellen. The boy clearly has something to get off his chest, so have at it.'

Nate turned to Eve, his tormented blues making her shiver inside. She squeezed his hand again. 'Why don't I help your mother clear away the dishes, and you two can clear the air?'

'I have a better idea.' Sue-Ellen got to her feet. 'Come with me, Evelyn. I have some champagne I've been saving for such a special occasion. We can enjoy it in the garden room.'

Eve looked to Nate and he gave a slight nod, releasing her hand.

'That's sounds lovely, but a sparkling water will suit me just fine,' she said, following the other woman out and wishing with all her might that Nate was okay. That he *and* his father would be okay.

To say Nate had sat on his resentment for decades, it all came spilling out with surprising ease. Everything he had told Eve, right down to his tattoos and his belief that his father had no pack mentality.

And George took it. Leaning back in his seat, he kept his lips sealed. He didn't interrupt or try to argue back. Just listened.

When finally he was done, his father leaned forward. 'That was quite the list of misdemeanours—'

Nate opened his mouth to object.

'I'm sorry, son, I don't mean that in a derogatory sense,

what I mean to say is… Hell…' He raked a weary hand down his face, hazel eyes grave. 'I brought you up like my father did me. And his father before him. We were the breadwinners. We threw ourselves into our work, proved ourselves through it. I didn't question it. I didn't think… I guess I didn't know how to be a different father. I didn't know that's what you needed… I took your rebellion as a sign of your nature, of boredom with this town and its limitations. I saw it as you acting out against it…'

'I *was* acting out, but not because of where we lived. I'd played the moral student, the moral son, got the grades, and you never looked my way for long enough.'

'And you figured bad behaviour would be different?'

Nate swallowed. 'I have regrets, believe me. My intention was always to come back and show you I could have it all—a legal career to be proud of, a wife and a family I actually spend time with. I wanted to show you how it should be done.'

'And you think marrying a Waverly will do that and more?'

'No, Dad. Who her father is doesn't factor into it. I'm marrying Eve because I want to.'

He nodded, the silence stretching between them.

'The thing is, Dad,' Nate said, realising there was more to say, to admit. 'Had I known what you were doing, all those people you were helping, it might have changed things. At least it would have made me see you in a different light.'

'And if you'd told me how you felt long ago, I would have made strides to be a better father to you, to come home more…'

'I remember Mum asking you to come home, it rarely worked.'

'She did, but then she also knew the good I was doing. And I love that she loved me for that.'

'You'd rather she loved you for the good work you were doing in your absence rather than your presence?' Nate shook his head. 'Dad, really?'

'I know, son, but I'm trying to make up for it now. With your mother. And with you, if it's not too late?'

'Too late?'

'To have that relationship?'

Nate raked a hand through his hair, his father's sincerity choking up his chest.

'So long as we're both living and breathing it's never too late.'

His father smiled, the hint of tears brimming. 'And this marriage, it truly is what you want?'

'More than anything, Dad.'

'How would you feel about an engagement party?'

Ears straining for sounds further inside the house, Eve took a second to register Sue-Ellen's question, then…

'A party?' she blurted.

'Yes, darling. For all George and I have been married for years, we rarely attended functions together. It was partly my fault. I always found it a little nerve-racking being on show like that. Everyone knew him and flocked to his side and I was always a little worried I'd embarrass him.'

Eve recalled Nate saying something similar… Was it possible he'd picked up on his mother's insecurities over the years too?

'Of course, it was all in my head,' she was saying, 'and it's high time I got over it and what better way to do that than to have a wonderful party celebrating your fabulous engagement?'

'What's that I hear?' George's voice was suddenly upon them as both men appeared in the doorway. 'A party?'

Eve shot up, eyes searching Nate's.

How did it go? You okay? Do we need to run, stay…make hay?

She rushed forward, took his hand and he smiled—a *real* all-is-okay smile.

'Don't worry, Evelyn. Me and my boy are fine.' His father hooked his arm around his approaching wife's waist. 'Or we will be. Won't we, son?'

'We will,' Nate confirmed, squeezing Eve's hand.

Sue-Ellen covered her mouth, her eyes welling up. 'And to think, this is what it took…'

'So what was it you were saying about a party?' Nate asked, his voice less certain.

'Your mum suggested we have one to celebrate our engagement.'

'An excellent idea,' George said.

'But I'd rather we didn't have the press getting wind just yet,' Nate said. 'Eve will want to put a statement out at some point and—'

'It's okay, Nate.' She pressed her hand to his chest, sensing he was more concerned about her reaction to it than anything else. And if the party was such a huge step for his mother, it made it all the more important to Eve. 'It makes sense to do something. We have to announce it at some point anyway. We could do something at the station, an intimate gathering of our nearest and dearest. I'm sure Rose would approve.'

'And I would help,' his mother chipped in.

'How about Friday evening?' his dad suggested.

'*Next* Friday?' Eve said.

'You really think you're up to a celebration so soon, Dad?'

'Oh, don't you start, son. It's bad enough with your mother on at me.'

'And your father's been feeling so much better,' the woman herself said.

'Still…' Nate cautioned. 'People will have plans. Friday is only a week away.'

'As soon as people see the invitation from Garrison Downs,' his father said, 'they'll drop everything to be there. You mark my words.'

'They're in full-on muster season, Dad. This is the last thing Rose needs on her plate.'

'If we wait for muster season to be over, it'll be December.'

December. It felt so far away and yet not. She'd be in her second trimester and likely showing.

'Your parents are right, Nate. It makes sense to have the celebration now. Especially with us wanting to get married so soon.'

Nate looked down at her in his arms. 'Are you sure? Maybe you should speak to Rose first, love?'

Love. She tried to reply and failed, nodding instead.

'That's settled, then,' his father said.

'Oh, how exciting!' His mother's voice cracked, the tears now escaping as she pulled them both into a hug. 'I couldn't be happier for you.'

'I could,' his father murmured. 'I believe a dessert was mentioned?'

'Not for you, there isn't.'

'Come on, Sue-Ellen, a tiny sliver isn't going to hurt.'

She rolled her eyes. 'Caramel slice, anyone?'

It was late when they said their goodbyes, Nate insisting he drive Eve back to the station when his mother offered up his old bedroom. She didn't know whether it was the idea of sharing a room with her that had him rushing her out of the door, or concern for how she felt about it.

But she knew which one she hoped it to be.

The glimpse of old Nate while performing in the presence of his parents had her craving more. Whether it was wise with the way her emotions were spiralling, she didn't care, she just didn't want their loved-up cover to end. So when he saw her into the truck and climbed in beside her, she said, 'Kiss me.'

His head snapped around. 'What?'

'Your mother's looking out the window,' she said, as calm as she could manage, and she wasn't lying. Sue-Ellen was there, keen as any loving mother would be, waving them off.

'She is?'

She nodded and reached into his hair, pulled him close. 'Yes.'

He didn't resist, he didn't initiate it either, and slowly she closed her eyes and kissed him. She kissed him with all the affection she'd been forcing down inside. Telling him with her actions what she couldn't tell him with her words.

He wrapped his arm around her, pulled her in close. So close she swore she could feel his heart beating through his chest, as fast and as unsteady as hers. The cabin became hot, humid, stifling. She wanted to strip him of his clothing, of his blasted mask too. She wanted him as exposed as she felt. As vulnerable, too.

And then he stopped, sucked in a breath as he fell back in his seat. 'Thank God she's already gone.'

She flicked him a look beneath her lashes. 'Sorry.'

'It's okay.' And just like that he was back to cool and composed Nate. His streaked cheeks the only sign of what they'd shared as he started the engine and slammed the truck into reverse. 'If there'd been any doubt in her mind, your kiss would have seen it off.'

'My thoughts exactly.'

Only they weren't. Because her thoughts had been racing with so much more. Her heart was racing with so much more.

You want *so much more if you'd only admit it to yourself.*

She settled back into her seat, left Nate to his thoughts as she lost herself in her own. She didn't intend to fall asleep, but something about her father's truck and having Nate at the helm made her feel cocooned in some way, content almost… the gentle rumble of the dirt beneath the wheels, the deserted moonlit road lulling her into a comfortable slumber. One that she was loath to leave and when the engine cut some time later and Nate reached over to touch her shoulder, she batted his hand away.

'We're home, Eve,' he murmured.

Home? Me and Nate. Home.

She squinted up at the well-lit porch. Rose must have kept the light on for her.

'I'll call you in the morning.'

'You'll…' Her heart plummeted. 'You're not staying?'

'I think I've put Rose out enough already.'

'As if. Without you she never would've kept on top of everything this week.'

'Wait until you tell her you've a party to organise.'

'Your mother and I will take care of that. Rose only has to turn up and look pretty, which she does on a daily basis anyway. No trouble.'

His chuckle was low and slow, his eyes dark as they continued to connect with hers. 'I don't think it's a good idea.'

'What? The party, or you staying?'

He didn't answer.

'Nate?'

He leaned back into his seat, eyed the porch rather than her. 'It makes sense for me to be in Marni tonight. I have a long day of catch-up meetings tomorrow.'

'On a Saturday?'

'A weekend doesn't get in the way of clients that need me. And Dad wants us to go for a drink… I think he's trying to make up for lost time as quickly as possible.'

She straightened against the disappointment that swamped her. 'That's good, Nate. Really good.'

So good it almost took the edge off her disappointment. Almost.

'It's a start.'

'When will I see you again?'

He gave her a surprising smile. 'We have a party on Friday, remember.'

'But that's a week away.'

'Afraid you're going to miss me…?'

Yes, she wanted to scream, *yes*!

Only he was teasing, and she wasn't.

'You wish.' She unclipped her belt and shoved open the truck door, then paused as she caught sight of his motorbike. 'Take the truck though, won't you? It can't be safe on two wheels this time of night.'

He gave her a lopsided grin. 'So you do care…'

More than you know and I want to admit, she thought as she closed the door and headed up the steps to the house.

She didn't look back. Not once. Fear that he would see her for the fraud she was propelling her forth.

Rose was in the hallway with River as she entered, and her sister's tired smile was the last thing Eve needed to see. 'Hey, honey, did you have a nice—? Evie, what's wrong?'

Eve waved her sister down, tried to tell her she was fine and failed at the whole darn lot. Rose opened her arms and pulled her in close and Eve sagged and let it all out. Let Rose hush her and soothe her. See her to bed. She didn't press her for answers, didn't press her for anything.

She was just there, as sisters should be.

CHAPTER TEN

'YOUR FATHER AND I are so proud of you.'

Between tears and smiles, his mother patted his tie into place. A move she had done a hundred times over. He'd thought about stopping her but decided it was far better to let her preen. Especially as he had yet to break the news that they would be moving to London at the end of the year.

'Okay, Sue-Ellen, let the boy go. You'll wear that tie away.'

His father entered the hallway, dressed like Nate in a dark suit, they *looked* like father and son, and Nate felt the fresh bond between them grow. His father kissed his mother's cheek before turning to Nate.

'Can I borrow you a moment?'

'Sure.'

He sent a questioning look his mother's way, but she only shrugged and, pocketing his hands, he followed his father into his study. Watched as he pulled open the drawer behind his desk and took out a small black box.

'I have something for you…or rather, I have something for you to give to Evelyn.'

Nate buried his hands deeper into his pockets. 'You do?'

'It's been in the family for generations, passed down to the eldest son.'

'Another one of those…' Nate tried to tease.

'Another one of those…' his father agreed. 'Though it went to at least one daughter, your grandmother, and since she was still alive when I proposed to your mother, I refused to take it from her. I told her that one day, God willing, I'd have my own child to give it to. And that time has finally come.'

Nate eyed the velvet box in his father's outstretched palm as though it would suddenly grow eight legs and fangs.

'I couldn't help noticing that Evelyn didn't wear a ring and as my mother called this a promise ring it seems perfect, don't you think…? If Evelyn likes it, of course.'

Slowly, Nate took it, opened it up. An oval diamond sparkled back at him, dazzling in its intensity, its meaning too.

'What do you say, son? Will she like it?'

'She'll—' He cleared his throat. 'It's perfect.'

Because it was.

It was Eve in every way. Beautiful. Elegant. Bright.

'And as the woman who's claimed your heart, it's all hers.'

Claimed his heart…

The blood drained from his face. Hot and cold all at once.

'Don't look so worried, son.' His father chuckled. 'The hard part's over already. She's said yes, remember.'

And then he pulled him into a hug, something he hadn't done since Nate was a child.

'I know I haven't told you enough, but I *do* love you, son, and I'm proud of you.'

'I love you too, Dad.' Because he did. It was why it had hurt so much over the years, why it hurt now too.

His mother appeared in the doorway and his father backed up, coughed away the emotion.

'Our car is here,' she said, her own voice laden with emotion.

'Good to go, son?'

Nate nodded and they shared one more look. A look that had Nate wondering, if this was his impassive, workaholic father after all these years, was there a chance that Eve could change too? That one day she'd be ready for such sentiment, such love? Could she trust him with it?

The box pinched into his tightly clenched hand—*don't be a fool.*

Because for all tonight was about their engagement, it wasn't about love.

This was Eve. Eve who refused to love, to trust, to risk it all. Eve who'd run from the very suggestion that it meant more.

Engage head.

Disengage heart.

Simple.

Or so he told himself.

Eve was ready. Physically at least.

Her hair had been styled by Lindy, who it turned out, could turn her hand to anything.

Her make-up was bold and dramatic—red lips, smoky eyes, slight blush—just how she liked it.

Only it felt all wrong.

She felt too made up. Too fake.

'You look beautiful, Bambi.'

She turned to see Rose in the doorway, a glass of bubbles in hand, work gear still on.

'For you…' She lifted the glass and stepped inside. 'It's a non-alcoholic variety, that way no one will be any the wiser when we toast your engagement tonight. Thought you might like to sample it.'

She smiled up at her sister. 'Thanks, Rose.'

'How are you feeling?'

'Nervous.'

That was honest at least.

'Don't be. All will be wonderful, I'm sure.' Rose pressed a kiss to her head. 'Now I need to shower else I'll be greeting our guests in this.'

Eve's smile lifted to one side. 'You still look stunning.'

Rose laughed. 'Now I know you're lying.'

She turned to leave and spied the blue gown Eve had pulled out. About the only thing she'd brought from London that she'd get to wear. Aside from the dress she'd worn to Nate's parents'.

'Is that what you're wearing?'

'Yes.'

Rose turned back to her, the slightest quiver in her lips.

'Rose, what are you…? You're not…'

She wafted a hand at her face. 'I'm sorry, Evie, I just wish they were…'

Her voice trailed off, and Eve knew where she was heading but didn't dare.

'I know,' she whispered.

Rose smiled as she swept from the room, though Eve thought she caught a hiccup-cum-sob, the absence of their parents weighing heavier than ever.

Her gaze drifted to the journal still beside her bed and, without thinking, she crossed the room, picked it up with a trembling hand, willing her mother's presence into being. Her love. Her bond.

Nate had faced his demons and spoken to his father, it was high time she faced hers…

Running her thumb down the gilded gold edge, she let the book fall open. Her mother's handwriting, elegant in its long, looping style, filled the page. Word upon word blurring as tears welled.

The first entry was over twenty-five years old…

I write these words upon instruction from experts who seem to believe it will help. I write these words so that I might find my way back to my daughters, my life, myself. I write these words to commit to my circumstances, and to bend them to suit my needs, the needs of my girls, and the needs of my family. I write these words as I choose to flourish, and no longer to fade.

Eve's breath shuddered through her. 'Oh, Mum.'

She wanted to stop but made herself continue. To straighten out her head, she had to straighten out her heart. She knew that now more than ever.

In the pages, her mother's version of events was laid bare.

How she'd felt alone, trapped in her own head. She hadn't been able to love Holt. Hadn't been able to love her children. Hadn't been able to love herself. Cold and detached. Disconnected and scared. Until finally she'd been diagnosed. Diagnosed and treated. And when the affair had come to light, her mother's world had crumbled. Their love had been tested and found wanting. It had taken time and understanding on both sides to find their way back to one another. Time in which her father had to move on from Lili and her mother had to forgive. In her beautiful, evocative way, her mother wrote of her hope that one day Holt, too, would forgive himself. For they loved one another and always would. And that was the greatest gift of life—to love and be loved.

Eve sobbed into her fist, clutched the book to her chest. Understanding rocking her to the core. All those years Eve had hated her father, hated the lie she felt they'd *both* portrayed… when it had been no lie at all.

She was the liar. Marrying for all the wrong reasons when, inside, the truth was desperate to break out.

She looked to the window, imagined the spot in the hills where her parents were laid to rest and knew what she had to do—where she had to be.

Throwing on some clothes, she hurried to the stables and mounted Jade. She clicked her into a gallop as soon as she was able and didn't slow until she saw the ancient flame tree. Its branches sprawling out at the peak of Prospect Hill, its orange-red flowers vibrant in the setting sun. Its base littered with wildflowers—yellow, reds, purples, pinks—a cacophony of colour that she'd never paused to appreciate before. The sign of life when life was no more…

She dismounted and took the journal from the saddlebag, led Jade to the tree and the two gravestones resting there. She sank to her knees, her 'Sorry' taken away by the breeze.

She swept her hair out of her face, clutched the journal to her chest. 'I love you and I miss you. And I wish with all my heart that you were both here to guide me now.'

The wind whipped up around her, her hair stinging at her eyes, catching in her mouth.

You know in your heart what's right. Trust it.

Where the words came from, she didn't know...but she was finally ready to listen.

'Evie, what are you doing?'

Rose accosted her as Eve kicked off her boots, tossing them into the mudroom.

'I had to go and see Mum and Dad.'

'You *did*?' Then she saw the journal in Eve's hand. 'Jeez, you really do pick your moments, sis.'

'I know, I know.' Eve rushed towards the bedroom, Rose hot on her tail. 'But I'm glad I did it.'

'In that case, I'm glad too but your absence has been noted and your future husband isn't looking too happy. I think he's worried you're about to run.'

Eve faltered in her stride.

'I'm not planning on it.' In fact, she was planning on doing the opposite. Whatever the outcome of tonight, she was staying indefinitely. Because the more she thought on it, the more she didn't want to go back to her life in London, not the way it was, and certainly not to the job that hinged on the image of others. Selling falsehoods, bending the truth to suit...

And Garrison Downs finally felt like home again. She wasn't ready to give that up.

She had ideas forming, ideas that involved making the old homestead her home—if they kept the station and her sisters were happy for her to take it on...

'I'll leave you to get ready.'

She nodded and changed quickly, freshening up her make-up, checking her hair. She left the room, following the sound of music and chatter all the way to the ballroom, where she was immediately set upon by every guest. All congratulating her on the news, most genuine, but others...their restraint bordered on hostile. The reason for the latter became apparent when Betty from the pub teetered up to her.

'Don't worry too much, darl, they'll recover.'

'Recover?' Eve said, still getting over the last strained greeting. 'From what?'

'From your Nate being off the market.'

'Oh…*oh*!'

'You really are oblivious, ain't ya, darl? All those loved-up pheromones doing their thing!'

'Uh-huh,' Eve said weakly.

'His return has been the talk of the town, right up there with yours. All the mothers, the fathers too, were hoping their daughter would be the one to snap him up. As for the daughters, well, you can see their tiny broken hearts for yourself.'

She forced a smile. 'Good to know the Marni grapevine is still functioning.'

Betty laughed. 'Always, darl.'

The crowd chose that moment to shift and Nate came into view, his gaze clashing with hers and locking on. Deliciously sexy in a dark suit and skinny tie, hair immaculate, designer stubble too. She felt starved of him, her body aching with it. A week without sight and she wanted to feast on him for evermore.

He leaned to mutter something to his companion, though his gaze didn't leave hers. Then he was striding forwards. Eyes ablaze with what, she didn't know. Eve gulped. The epitome of Bambi caught in the headlights. Unable to move from the danger fast approaching.

He paused a step away. 'Good to see you, Betty.' Though his eyes remained fixed on Eve.

'And you… And I'll just leave you to—' a wave of her finger '—*this*.'

Eve fought the urge to yank her back, wrinkled her nose. 'I'm sorry I'm late.'

His jaw pulsed. 'You're sorry you're late?'

'That's what I said.'

'Not for the riding like a madwoman?'

'You saw that?'

'I saw that.'

Anger reverberated through his words. Anger that she didn't understand.

'You're angry?'

'Of course I'm angry, Eve,' he said between his teeth.

She eyed the crowd around them, noticed the discrete looks being cast their way and stepped closer. Lowered her voice. 'I was late. I didn't plan on it. I went to my parents' grave and I lost track of time.'

'You did what?'

'I wanted to make amends. I *did* make amends.'

His eyes flickered, softened, though the tension remained. 'I'm glad you've made your peace with them, but, *Eve*, the way you were riding. I thought we'd gone through this. You can't just do what you want, when you want, how you want. You need to think about the risks. You're a *mother* now.'

His words slammed into her, his accusation too.

'I can ride, Nate. When I was a kid, I could ride better than I could walk.'

'And what if Jade had got spooked? What if she'd thrown you? Then what?'

A memory from her childhood flashed across her mind, a time when a snake had startled her horse and she'd ended up with a broken her arm. She cursed. He was right. How could she be so foolish? What kind of a mother would put her child at risk like that?

But she hadn't been thinking. All she'd wanted was to get back. To him. To this. To find a way through it all that led to happiness, not more pain and regret.

'I'm sorry, I—'

The chime of metal on glass rang through the room, the music stopped and the chatter died away. Eve's heart fading with it.

George Harrington stepped up to the microphone as a glass

appeared beside her. Rose. She mustered up a smile, for her sister and the room, and took the drink.

Nate placed his palm against her lower back and the contact pulsed through her. She glanced up at him. Wishing to see the same reaction in him and getting nothing. His smile, his possessive touch, all an act, a performance to project the happy couple. A lie.

His father's toast was a blur, Rose's too. The cheers and the congratulations landing on Eve's deaf ears because all she could hear was Nate's words. *'You can't just do what you want, when you want, how you want... You're a mother now.'*

And what did she know of being a good mother? What did she know of being a good wife too?

She was one of many women in Marni who'd set their sights on Nate, but she was the only one who had done it against her will. And hell, he could do better. He deserved better.

She forced herself to sip at her glass when the room toasted their engagement. Forced herself to smile and play nice when all she wanted to do was run. Run as she had all those years ago.

'I think that makes it my turn to say something...'

Her eyes shot to his, heart in her throat.

Please, no. God, no. No more lies.

'The moment I saw you, Eve, I knew there was something about you...'

He held her gaze as he directed the words at her but spoke to the room. And she was pleading with him. Pleading with him to stop. But his eyes...they were sincere...or was that an act? Was he putting that look there for everyone else but her?

'A connection that caught me in its grasp and wouldn't let me go. Your beauty, your intelligence, your wit, and your fire. Not necessarily in that order...'

The room chuckled and he smiled, taking her hand in his as he raised it up between them and dug into his pocket with his other.

'I should've done this sooner, but it feels appropriate to do it now in front of our nearest and dearest—'

'Wait, wait!' Rose hurried out. 'I need to video this for Tilly and A— everyone who couldn't make it!'

Ana, she was going to say Ana. Eve gave her sister a smile, her gaze swiftly returning to Nate's pocket, where his hand still rested, and she swallowed the wedge in her throat. Why hadn't she anticipated this? They were engaged. There was bound to be a ring of some sort...

Rose held her phone out. 'Go!'

And Nate chuckled, lowering himself to one knee, all charismatic and perfect, and Eve could almost believe this was real. Not a lie that was eating her up inside.

He pulled the box from his pocket, opened it up. An oval diamond shone out, dazzlingly exquisite but glaring in its meaning. She clutched her throat, eyes watering. Tears, more *blasted* tears.

'Eve, I believe we were destined to meet that night in Marni, our lives taking a simultaneous twist that brought us back to our families at the same time. Our bond was instant and unbreakable.'

The bond was their child. Eve knew it. Nate knew it.

As for destiny, it was right up there with love. The kind of sentiment she would have denied, laughed off even, but not any more. It danced around her heart, teased her, goaded her. Broke her that bit more as more tears came.

'This promise ring has been in my family for generations, an outward sign of that inner bond. Of love and its infinite longevity.'

'But what if it doesn't fit?' she whispered and the people near enough to overhear chuckled. Not realising she meant it in the figurative sense. A ring representing love... Eve and love. She tried to force the two puzzle pieces together, and no side would fit.

Nate took the ring from the box, held her hand in his and said softly, surely, 'We'll make it fit.'

And with that, he slid it over her finger as smooth and as easy as breathing…

Breathing when she wasn't in front of a crowd of people, her emotions rolling wild within her.

'It's perfect,' she choked out and the crowd whooped. Nate swept her up into his arms and she knew what came next, anticipated it even. But nothing could prepare her for the brush of his lips against hers as he stole her breath and her heart in one.

'Thank you,' he murmured, so quiet no one else could hear.

Her lashes fluttered open, gratitude shining down on her.

Gratitude, for what? Continuing the performance? Not running?

The music started up again, the sound jarring her out of her stupor.

'We should dance,' he said.

'Dance?'

It was the last thing she wanted to do. Too jolly. Too free. Too easy. But she let him sweep her onto the dance floor, let him guide their every move. So very aware of every place their bodies touched, so very aware of how fleeting every connection was, as if he couldn't bear it, too.

Remember why you're doing this, Eve.

Remember why he's doing it, too.

For your family. For your child.

And still, she couldn't shift the chill.

While the sham of a marriage ate away at her, the ring on her finger too, she should have been safe in the knowledge that this marriage couldn't hurt her.

But that was before she'd understood her past. Before she'd realised that, for all it could bring pain and hurt, the only bond that truly tied people together for ever was love.

Without it, they had nothing. No joy. No future. No bond.

And she was already hurting. Deeply and unequivocally.

CHAPTER ELEVEN

'GOODNIGHT, SON.'

'Night, Dad. Sleep well.'

Nate closed the door on the guest room his parents were using for the night and made his way back to Eve's.

He'd say he was relieved that the night was over, but his biggest challenge was yet to come.

A night in Eve's bedroom. Alone. Nothing to keep this heat or emotion at bay.

They hadn't slept together since Marni, hadn't even kissed properly…save for the show of carried-away affection outside his parents' house.

Not what he needed to be thinking of right this second.

He tugged his tie undone, unbuttoned his collar. He'd been so angry this evening, angry and fired up on something else entirely.

Stunning in blue satin, she'd taken him over the second she'd appeared. Everything about her accentuated by that dress—her hair, her eyes, her body—but there'd also been a vulnerability about her. A vulnerability that had fed his fears and compounded his alpha instinct—to protect, to possess, to toss her over his shoulder, take her home and never let her out of his sight again.

And it was laughable, not laudable, because she wanted none of that.

And now he had to suppress it all while they slept in the same room together.

What was he? A monk!

Cursing the impossible, he shoved open the door and strode in. There was always the bathtub… 'Eve, I think—'

He froze, his head emptying out as the door clicked shut on its own momentum.

Eve blinked back at him from across the room, just as frozen, just as stunned. 'Did you ever hear of knocking?'

'Did you ever think to shout?'

'Shout what?' She thrust her hands up, a move he *really* didn't need with all that skin on show.

'I don't know! Some warning!'

'Like what?'

'Like, hey, I'm naked!'

And naked she was, unless you counted the scanty piece of blue lace doing a very poor job of concealing anything below the waist.

She folded her arms, which only lured his eyes down. 'You're daring to take issue with my nakedness?'

Her bare breasts shifted with her defiant breath, her small rose-tipped nipples hardening beneath his stare.

'I'm not taking issue with your…'

He cursed. Could the woman not see what she was doing to him?

'You could have fooled me.'

He forced his gaze back to hers—blue eyes blazing, wide and wounded. Her lips, still stained from her lipstick, pouting. Lips he didn't dare get any closer to, and yet he took one step forward.

'I'm not, Eve.'

One brow lifted. 'No?'

Another step. 'I'm taking issue with myself.'

'For what, exactly?'

'For wanting to do this…'

And he quit thinking, quit questioning and tugged her to his chest, claimed her gasp with his kiss and kept on striding until she was up against the wall.

'Tell me to stop and I'll stop,' he rasped out.

'No.' She hooked her leg around his waist, tugged at the lapels of his jacket to drag him closer. 'Don't stop.'

He was in heaven and hell at once. Wanting. Craving. And knowing it was wrong. They needed to talk, they needed to clear the air. 'We should be talking.'

'This first, Nate.'

He cupped her breast, rolled his thumb over its pleading centre, felt it pucker beneath his touch and lowered his head to suck it into his mouth. She cried out, her fingers forking through his hair, gripping him to her. All the while his brain screamed at him to quit. But he was done listening to anything but her.

'I want you,' she whispered, hitching her leg higher, undulating against him. 'I only want you.'

Mouth rough, he grazed kisses back up her body, kissed her deeply as he lifted her legs around him and carried her to the bed. He set her down, shucked his jacket, his tie, his shirt. She rose and stripped his belt, unbuttoned his trousers. Fingers trembling, breath uneven. Desperate. Hungry.

She reached inside his pants, gripped his length and he bucked inside her hold.

'Steady, sweetheart.' He grabbed her wrist, his thighs trembling as he fought the inevitable. 'It's been a while.'

He eased her hand away as he stripped the rest of his clothing and lowered himself to the bed. Encouraging her to lie back as he trailed kisses from her mouth to her breasts, to her stomach, where the wonder of their baby lay…then lower still.

She rocked up as he flicked his tongue over her swollen nub, gripped his head as he circled her, rolling and flicking, letting her every reaction drive his tempo. Letting it feed his own desire too.

'Please, Nate,' she panted, 'I want you.'

He looked up into her eyes, saw the need, the desperation and something else—was it the fear, the vulnerability he'd spied earlier or something else?

He pressed a kiss between her legs and she shifted. 'Please?'

Helpless to deny her, he moved up her body, swallowed her plea with his kiss as he guided her back into the sheets. He searched her lustful gaze as he eased himself inside her. Fighting for control as her heat surrounded him and her eyes seared him, branded him, made him hers. Not that she could know...

She bit her lip, her whimper making him groan. She was taking him to the brink and there was nothing he could do.

The more she moved, the more he moved with her. Faster, harder, deeper.

He was losing it. Every last remnant of control. His body vibrating and tensing in one.

'Eve!' My God, she was beautiful. Stunning. Everything he could ever...

'Nate, I can't... Nate...'

'Let go for me, baby. Let go and I'll catch you.'

I'll always catch you.

His own release came with hers, dizzying and thought-obliterating. His guttural growl so loud he feared there'd be questions from the neighbouring residents come morning.

Morning. He didn't want to think of that now. He didn't want to think of anything but this moment that had felt so perfect in every way.

His body sagged and he rolled onto his back, gazed up at the ceiling. 'That was...'

'Unexpected.' She finished for him.

'I was going to say needed, but unexpected works too.'

She touched her left hand to her stomach, the Harrington ring glinting in the lamplight. An outward sign that she was his, but inside...

Eve would only ever belong to herself.

The chemistry between them didn't change that.

No matter how intense, or perfect, or all-consuming.

It chewed him up inside, a genuine sickness rising that made him want to wretch. He pushed himself to sitting, took a breath so that he could trust his voice. 'I'm going to freshen up.'

He tugged on his pants and headed to the bathroom, felt her confused gaze on him the whole way. He washed his face twice over, brushed his teeth, and still didn't know what to do with himself. The sensation was still there, rolling inside him. He gripped the edge of the sink, stared at the face looking back at him. He'd aged a decade in four weeks, the lines in his brow, the shadows beneath his eyes...

It was getting harder and harder to understand what this was between them. Where the line of convenience ended and it all became real.

'Sorry.'

He spun around. There she was, resting against the door frame. Her hair wild about her shoulders, her eyes soft, smile small. A pale slip thrown over her that ended mid-thigh. And his heart ached for her even as he told it not to.

'What for?'

'For embroiling you in this mess.'

He shook his head, stepped towards her but she moved away. She dropped into the chair before the window, brought her knees to her chest.

The sight tore at his heart. She looked so lost.

'I chose this path, Eve.'

'But you can't want it.'

'The marriage?'

She nodded.

'You're wrong, I want it all. The child. A wife. A family. It's what I've always wanted.'

'I know. You've made that clear from the moment I met you, but you can't want it with me. And you can't want it in London, not when you came back to make a home here.'

'I can and I do. And if we have to do that in London...'

'But your father, your relationship, you're finally getting what you've always wanted.'

'And I can still have that in London. There's video calls, we can visit...'

She was shaking her head, refusing to listen. 'You say that now but...'

'But what?'

'You'll resent me for it eventually.'

'How can you say that?'

'How can you not say that? How can you not see it? You deserve a woman who can love you and give you the life you deserve. Not someone like me.'

'Someone like you?'

'I'm broken, Nate. You know that. I don't know how to love. I don't know how to trust. I don't know what to trust.'

This woman—so unsure, so lost—was so different from the woman he'd met that first night. She *was* changing, she *was* questioning—was there a chance her heart was shifting with the tide?

'Why don't you start with trusting your heart, Eve?'

She huffed into her knees. 'I did that once and trusted my parents unconditionally. What I saw as their deceit broke me.'

'I thought you'd made peace with the past.'

'I have,' she said quietly. 'But it doesn't change what it did to me. It doesn't change the fact that I don't know how to be a good wife, a good mother...'

'You just have to be you.'

'Are you forgetting the riding incident?'

'No, but you're not either.'

'And what if I'm not enough? If I can't give enough?'

'The fact you're even asking that tells me you will.' He stepped towards her, wanting to pull her into his arms and re-assure her. 'You'll be the best mother our child could wish for.'

She looked up at him, searched his gaze. 'I meant for you, Nate. What if I'm not enough for you? My mother and father, they loved one another but she wasn't enough. In her darkest days, she wasn't enough and he went elsewhere and I couldn't bear it if you, if we...'

'Eve!' He dropped to his knees, touched his palm to her cheek. 'I would *never* betray you.'

The very idea had his gut twisted in knots.

'It's easy to say that now when we've not been tested.'

Tested? She was testing him right now!

'I'm not naive, Eve. I know what we're agreeing to.'

'Do you, Nate? Truly? A marriage without love…'

'People marry for a lot less than what we have.'

'Not you.'

'And you never wanted marriage in the first place,' he said, purposely cold, his hand falling to his side. Overly aware that if he said the wrong thing, *did* the wrong thing, it would all be over.

'No, I didn't. But then I didn't want a lot of things that have found me in life.'

She was withdrawing from him, her eyes turning distant.

'What do you want me to say, Eve? How can I make this right?'

'You can be honest with me.'

'I've always been honest with you, and I will *always be* honest with you.'

'Do you love me?'

His chest contracted around his screaming heart, squeezing tight. Her direct question thwarting his every attempt to stay calm. 'How can I say I love you when it's the one emotion you openly run from?'

'That's not an answer.'

'It's a good enough answer for me.'

'I wanted a yes or no.'

'Then no, Eve. I don't love you.'

Because when it came down to it, how could he love a woman who, as soon as her sabbatical ended, would be too wrapped up in work to notice him? How could he love a woman who by her own lips could never love him back?

She stared back at him, so quiet, so calm, the silence deafening as his heart continued to blare. Then she blew out a breath, looked to the dark outdoors and the moonlight dancing in the gum trees.

'And I won't be a hypocrite, Nate.'

'A *what*?'

'I resented my parents for what I saw as the lie they presented to the world, to us… What I saw as their *fake* love. When all the while, it was nothing of the sort.'

'What's that got to do with—?'

Her eyes flashed to his. 'We're doing *exactly* what I accused them of, hated them for. Don't you see? Presenting a fake front, a fake marriage, a fake love, and I won't do it.'

'Even for the sake of our child.'

'I'm *doing this* for the sake of our child. I won't turn our child into me! Have them grow up resenting us for being together for all the wrong reasons, or, worse, perceive us as lying to them. I won't.'

'But it doesn't have to be like that.'

'Doesn't it? What about when the distance between us grows because I can't give you what you need?'

He shook his head, defeat heavy on his shoulders. 'So that's it, it's over and you're going to move back to London and take my child with you?'

'No, I'm done selling images, fake or otherwise. I want to make a home here. A new life for myself and our child, one that keeps you in it, whether we get to keep the station or not.'

'But it's not the same, it could never be the same. You know that.'

'I know our child will be happier knowing their parents are living the lives they chose for themselves.'

He stared at her, unwilling to believe this was happening when not minutes before they'd been as close as two people can be.

At least be happy that she's saying in Australia…

But it wasn't enough. He wanted her.

'One day you'll meet the woman that you were destined to love and you'll thank me for it.'

'Thank *you*?' he choked out.

'A child isn't a reason to marry. And neither is some an-

cient marriage clause. I release you from your promise, Nate.'
She eased the ring from her finger and placed it in his palm.
'Find someone who deserves this, someone who loves you as
you do them. Find your happiness.'

'We can be happy together.'

'Without love?' She closed his hand around the ring, pressed
a kiss to his forehead and rose up, her eyes so sad they crushed
him whole. 'You can't be happy…and I'm not sure I can either.'

She climbed into bed, pulled the blanket over her, and rolled
away. The room far too quiet with the roar inside his head,
his heart… He opened his hand, looked down at the ring and
sagged into the chair.

What did he do? What did he say? His dreams were slipping through his fingers like grains of sand and he couldn't
catch them. Because he realised in that moment, with absolute
certainty, that he was the only liar in this room.

He loved her and he couldn't tell her.

Damned if he did and damned if he didn't.

And what kind of cruel twist of fate was that?

CHAPTER TWELVE

EVE DIDN'T SLEEP.

She *pretended* to sleep, right up until the point that Nate left the room, and then she packed. Sneaking out at the crack of dawn to hitch a ride on the mail plane before anyone could wake up and confront her.

Despite her desire to be strong and accepting of the future she had now chosen, she wasn't ready to tell anyone that it was over.

It hurt too much. The idea of not marrying Nate, of not being bound together...

So she'd left Rose a note:

Gone to Melbourne to see Ana. I'll call you later.
Eve x

And fled.

Though this was different from all those years ago when she'd run with no intention of returning. This time she was coming back and she would face it all.

But first, she needed to face the last piece of her painful past—Ana.

A meeting that was long overdue and the only thing that she could think to do that would heal rather than hurt. She should've spoken to her half-sister months ago. Done as her sisters had and welcomed her in.

Not pushed her from her mind to tackle what she saw as the more pressing issue of the two—

Issue?

Ana wasn't an issue. She was her sister. Her blood. Another unbreakable bond.

So here she was, standing on the streets of St Kilda, staring at the front of the sweetest little Hungarian restaurant owned by Ana's grandparents. She'd tried her home and a neighbour had told her she'd find Ana and her 'lovely family' here.

She'd smiled her thanks, asked for directions, and hurried away before a tear could escape. *Lovely family.* Rose and Tilly had been lovely too. But Eve?

Heaven knew how Ana saw her and she only had herself to blame.

She stepped towards the door and paused. The scent of food had her taste buds tingling, and she could hear the muffled sound of voices and laughter, but the restaurant was closed. They must be preparing for service.

She peered through the glass. Wooden floors, bentwood chairs, crystal chandeliers and prints of an ancient city filled the walls. An eclectic delight—warm and inviting—but what really caught Eve's attention were the four people sitting around a table in the middle of the room. Four people with love in their eyes and cheer in their voices. Ana and her family.

Eve smiled, the sight warming her even as it labelled her the outsider once more.

At that moment Ana turned, her eyes narrowing and widening just as quick as her chair scraped back and Eve jerked away. She'd intruded on their moment. She should've knocked, should've messaged, should've…

The door swung open. 'Eve!'

She lifted a weak hand. 'Hi, Ana.'

'What are you—why are you—?' Ana shook her head as her mother came up behind her. Same dark hair, same slight frame, though her eyes were a rich brown. Kind, too.

'Ana, who is it?'

'Mum, it's—this is Eve. Holt's daughter.'

Now they were both staring at her and she knew she needed to speak up, say something before they thought she was as deranged as she felt. There was so much she wanted to say and she was struggling to latch onto any one thing. The past, the present, the future that was so uncertain. But nothing would come except tears. They streamed down her face and Ana leapt forward, pulling her into her chest.

'It's okay, Eve,' she soothed. 'It'll be okay.'

Eve shook her head, wanted to apologise, instead she let them usher her inside. Ana's mother and grandparents set about bringing her food, water, and some drink they said was good for the nerves. Though Eve couldn't really taste it. All she was aware of was the love in the room. The love and the care. And she felt relieved.

Relieved to know that all those years where their father had kept Ana out of their lives, her life had been no less rich, because she'd had this.

'I'm sorry, Ana,' she managed at last. 'I should've come sooner.'

Ana gave her a shy smile. 'I'm just relieved that you're here now…and if it's not too bad to say, I'm also a little relieved that you can cry. I had my doubts.'

Eve winced and Ana gave her a nudge. 'I am kidding… well, maybe just a little.'

She gave a choked laugh and Ana wrapped her into another hug. 'So do you want to tell me why you're here when you've only just got engaged to that sexy hunk of a lawyer?'

And just like that Eve was crying again. Uncaring that she had an audience of four. Six if you counted the two chefs prepping in the open kitchen behind, their curious gazes suggesting they heard more than they ought.

But what did it matter anyway? The story of her failed engagement would hit the press at some stage so she might as well get used to it.

* * *

'Rose! Rose!'

Nate chased the woman across the yard, gave no thought to the fact he was wearing the same clothes from the night before. His only thought was Eve and the fact she had disappeared into thin air.

He'd spent the night in her father's study, seeking a way to release the sisters from the marriage clause. Ploughing his fitful energy into something that could help rather than hinder the woman that he loved.

Rose stopped, her shoulders sagging, her head dropping forward.

'Rose?'

He came up behind her and she turned to face him. 'What is it?'

His nerves pricked at her tone, the look in her eye...

'Where is she?'

'So, you care where she is, but you don't care enough to love her?'

His frown was sharp, the spear through his heart sharper still. 'What?'

'I rang her this morning, after I found her note.'

'Her note? What note?'

'Telling me where she'd gone. I rang her and she told me how you couldn't love her.'

'That's not—it's not—' God, it sounded so awful, so cold and callous. 'I had no choice, Rose. You know Eve. You know what she's like. I feared she'd run.'

'And in your fear, you what? *Lied* to her?'

'I was lying to myself, too. Please, Rose. I've spent the night trying to find a way out of this marriage clause. Determined to give her something, a thread of hope, anything! I didn't mean to fall asleep. I didn't mean to let her slip away. I can't...' He thrust both hands into his hair. 'Please, Rose, I need to get to her. I need to make this right.'

'You mean tell her the truth?'

'Yes!'

'Because you do love her, don't you?'

'Yes! With all my heart, I love her. And I know she doesn't want to hear it, but I can't go another day without her knowing it.'

Like the sun coming out from behind a cloud, Rose grinned. 'In that case I'll do more than tell you, I'll fly you. To Adelaide at least, then you're on your own.'

'Why? Where is she?'

'Melbourne. Visiting Ana.'

His heart eased just a little. She was continuing her journey, making amends with her family... He was glad of it. Even if he'd rather have her in his arms right now.

'Are you coming?' Rose said, when he didn't move.

'Absolutely!' He fell into step beside her.

'But, Nate...' She paused, tilting her Akubra up so that she could pin him with her eyes. 'Break her heart again and I'll break you, is that clear?'

'Break her heart...?'

How could he break her heart if she refused to give it to him...?

'I mean it, Harrington.'

So did he...

'I'd rather die than hurt her again.'

Eve was so full.

Emotionally and physically.

Ana's grandparents, Dori and Zoltan, were firm believers that a full stomach made for a happy heart, and she did her best to oblige. Though she knew, without Nate, her heart would never be so again.

'Now, you should try our apple strudel, it's delicious,' Dori was saying, her wise old eyes bright and encouraging.

'I don't think I could eat another bite.'

'I think we've fed her enough,' said Lili, coming to her rescue. The other woman's continued kindness moving Eve to tears when she thought of how she'd once hated the faceless woman. Dad's mistress.

But reading Mum's journal, then hearing it from Lili herself. The way she had genuinely loved her father. How their relationship had been born of circumstance and misunderstanding. A belief that his marriage had been over and there had been nothing left to ruin, nothing left to save either.

How wrong they had all been.

But the biggest thing was Lili's lack of regret. Because meeting Holt had given her Ana and she wouldn't change that for all the world.

'Thank you,' Eve blurted. 'All of you. For taking me in, for letting me talk and explain and fix things.'

Lili took her hand and gave it a squeeze.

'We're family,' Ana said, scooting into her side. 'Family always has time to listen and be there for one another. And I'm so happy to have sisters. *Three* sisters!'

Eve touched her head to Ana's. 'Me too.'

'Who on earth…?' Dori frowned at the window. 'Zoltan, there's a man peering through the glass. Go tell him we're not open for another hour.'

Zoltan stood up with a grumble. 'I don't know why we bother putting signs up in the window when people just—'

'Wait!' Ana's head lifted. 'Eve, isn't that—?'

'Nate!' Eve shot to her feet, her heart soaring with her, scarce able to believe it was him, but her heart would know those eyes, that hair, that mouth anywhere. He looked harrowed, desperate…was it all for her?

He's here, isn't he? Tracking you down?

'As in Nate the lawyer you were engaged to?' Lili asked, but Eve was already moving, numb to anything but him.

'Yes, Mum,' Ana said for her. 'And I think we should give them some privacy.'

Chairs scraped back as Eve pulled open the door.

'Eve!' He launched forward, his tortured gaze lighting a fire beneath her feet that had her backing up.

'Nate?' So soft, so confused. 'What are you doing here?'

'I had to see you.' He hesitated. 'But I can leave and talk to you later. Once you've done what you came to. I don't want to intrude. I just—I had to see you.'

Eve looked to the back, to the swinging door that marked the mass exodus of Ana and her family. Though she had the oddest sense that there were four sets of ears straining to listen on the other side.

'If you're worried about me, you needn't be,' she said, eyes coming back to him, shoulders righting as she found strength in the presence of her extended family. 'I'm grateful that you told me the truth and—'

'That's just it, Eve, I didn't tell you the truth and it's been killing me ever since. Even more because I know you struggle to trust, but I was lying to myself too. I was scared. So scared you were going to run, and I was this close to having everything. You, the baby, a family of my own. I couldn't risk it.'

'Risk what, Nate? I don't understand.'

He closed the gap between them, his hands gentle on her cheeks as he tilted her face to his. 'Then let me be clear. No lie. No twisting of the truth to suit some ancient clause, or duty to our baby... I love you, Eve. I loved you the moment we met and I will continue loving you whether you want me to or not. Because love isn't something that we get to choose or get to control, it just is.'

Her lips parted as her breath left her. Both head and heart struggling to catch up with all he had said, to *believe* all he had said.

'It just is?' she repeated dumbly.

'I'm sure there's a better way to put it, but right now...'

She shook her head to try and clear it. He loved her. He truly loved her.

'You can refute it all you like, Eve! Refuse it, reject it, all the r's, but it doesn't change the fact that I love you!'

She covered his hands on her cheeks, found her voice. 'Can I *return* it?'

His brow furrowed, his hands slipping away. 'As you would an item from a store…?'

'No, silly…' She choked on a laugh—disbelief, happiness, love filling her chest to the brim. She looped her arms around his neck, breathed in his glorious scent. 'Maybe I should have used the word reciprocate, that's an "r".'

'Reciprocate?' he rasped, eyes widening. 'You mean…'

She nodded and smiled and cried. 'I mean, I love you, Nate. I think my heart has known for a while but my head took a while to catch up.'

'Why didn't you tell me?'

'Because I was confused and I was scared. Scared of trusting my heart and having you break it. Scared I wouldn't be enough for you and I would trap you into a marriage that you'd one day regret and resent me for.'

'Never, Eve. I swear it.'

She smiled softly. 'I'll remind you of this conversation again in ten years' time…'

His mouth twitched and she leaned that bit closer, wanting so much to kiss him. 'You can remind me of it every decade here on in and I'll tell you the same.'

She toyed with the hair at his nape. 'Is that so?'

'Yes.' He hooked his hands around the base of her spine. 'But what about you? Will you regret it, resent me for it?'

'Never, Nate.' She pressed her body into his, purposely using his words. 'I swear it.'

'In which case, Evelyn Waverly, would you do me the honour of becoming my wife?'

He'd used her full name intentionally, she knew it, bringing something of her father into the moment, and her heart bloomed—no regret, no pain. 'Yes, I'll marry you.'

And then she kissed him, long and deep, right up until the point that the rear door swung open, and Ana and her family fell through it.

'I'm so sorry, Eve!' Ana exclaimed. 'Nagypapa, I told you not to lean on the handle!'

Nagypapa blushed and Eve laughed. Her adoration swelling for them all. She glanced up at Nate, who was blushing almost as much as the rest of them.

'Everyone, this is Nate. Nate, this is Ana and her wonderful family.'

'Hi, everyone,' he said as Ana came forward and did the introductions properly, keeping Eve tucked into his side as if he'd never let her go again.

And that suited her just fine. She was exactly where she belonged.

She touched a hand to her stomach...

We both are.

EPILOGUE

Garrison Downs,
South Australian Outback,
late November

'EVIE, ARE YOU ever coming out of there?' Rose called through the dressing room door. 'Nate's going to think you've fled on the mail plane again if we don't hit the aisle soon.'

'I'm coming! I'm coming!' Eve looked over her shoulder at Lindy, who was still fussing over some detail at the rear. 'Am I ready?'

Lindy backed away and gave a nod. 'You *look* ready, but only you can decide if you're truly ready. Marriage is a huge step.'

Not the effusive answer Eve wanted to hear, but then Lindy was right. This was a huge step. Massive!

And it wasn't helping her nerves…or her jelly-like legs. If she wasn't careful, Bambi was going to make a return and that was the last thing she needed.

Taking a breath, she tugged open the door. 'Rose, you're going to have to hold onto me tight because these legs aren't feeling so hot right now and—what's wrong?'

Her sister was doing a fine rendition of Munch's, The Scream.

'*Rose*?'

She gave the smallest shake of her head, her glossy brown hair quivering with the move.

'Oh, no, what is it? What have I done?'

Eve teetered up to the full-length mirror and froze, finding herself doing the exact same. Munch would be proud.

'I look like…'

'Mum,' Rose said, joining her before the mirror, the satin of her blush pantsuit barely rustling.

It had been Rose's idea for her to wear their mum's wedding dress. They were similar in so many ways—tall, slim, blonde, blue-eyed. But it was more than that, it was a sense of feeling. A bond. A bond Eve had so desperately wanted to regain and she finally felt as though she had.

'It's perfect on you.'

The strapless mermaid dress had been inspired by Mum's love of Old Hollywood, the ivory satin handstitched by her favourite designer in Paris, too. With the pointed sweetheart neckline, ruched bodice, and flowing skirt, it was everything her mum had been—cultured, elegant and beautiful beyond words.

And now Eve was wearing it.

'She'd be so proud.' Rose swept a loose curl over Eve's shoulder. '*I'm* so proud.'

Her voice cracked and Eve balked. 'Don't be starting with the waterworks, Rose! You'll—'

'Is she ready yet?' Tilly burst into the room, surprisingly swift considering the floor-length satin blue dress she wore. Her gaze lighted on Eve and she came to an abrupt halt, rocking on her heels as Ana followed suit, her dress identical in style to Tilly's but mint green.

Now they were both staring at her, tears welling.

'Not you guys as well!'

'I'm sorry, I can't help it.' Tilly flapped a hand over her face. 'Seeing you in Mum's dress… I always thought you looked like her but this…this is so poignant and I'm… I'm…'

Ana stepped forward, taking Tilly's hand in hers.

'You do look beautiful, Eve.'

And they looked like sisters. Ana's brown hair flowing as

free as Tilly's blonde waves, their obvious love as uniting as their Waverly blue eyes.

'I want to hug you!' Tilly said. 'But I'm scared I'll crease you!'

'I can take some creasing.' Eve held out her arms. 'Especially if it'll stop you all crying.'

They hugged and, darn it, Eve felt a tear escape. 'My make-up is never going to survive the day.'

'Something tells me your groom won't care,' Ana said as they all broke apart. 'Not if that display in Nagymama and Nagypapa's restaurant was anything to go by.'

'Ooh, do tell us more,' Tilly said and Eve blushed.

'Let's *not* do that.'

Rose laughed. 'Oh, we're definitely doing that, but later. First we need to get you married.'

'And before we do that, I have something for you!' Tilly reached into the front of her gown and pulled out a blue pocket square. 'It was Dad's…' Tears fresh in her eyes, she handed it to Eve. 'I figured it could be your something blue.'

'Oh, Tilly!' Eve fed it through her shaky fingers, raised it to her lips and closed her eyes. 'Now I have them both with me…'

'You have us all,' Tilly said, wrapping her arm around Ana to make sure she knew they included her too. 'Now you have your something blue from Dad, your something old from Mum—what's your something new?'

'My—my underwear…?'

They all laughed, and Ana offered out her hand. In it was a small velvet pouch with the logo of Ana's handmade jewellery store. Something Eve had learned all about after her and Nate's extreme PDA in Melbourne.

'I was going to save this as a leaving gift for your honeymoon, but…'

Eve took it from her, marvelling at her sister's generosity, her talent too.

'You already made our wedding rings, Ana, you really

shouldn't have—*oh, my*!' In her palm fell a silver chain with a white diamond-embellished swan. 'It's— It's…'

'It was something Nate said to me when he came to Melbs and I thought—well, I hope you like it.'

'Like it? I *love* it!' She tugged her sister in for a hug. 'And I love you!'

'I love you, too.'

'And I love you all, but we really need to get moving.' Rose took the necklace from Eve and looped it around her neck.

'Best stick that hanky where I had it, sis,' Tilly said. 'You're gonna need it.'

Eve eyed the front of her gown and shrugged—if it was good enough for Princess Tilly…

'And don't forget your flowers,' Rose instructed.

Plucking their rose bouquets off the bed, Eve's the largest of them all, they left the room. Ana and Tilly first, then Eve and Rose. All quiet with their thoughts.

It wasn't far to the ballroom, but it felt like an eternity as Eve took in the hallway and the memories of old, a smile touching her lips as she focused on the good. The echoes of happy chatter, her mother tinkling on the piano, her father's deep and rumbling laugh…

Family. Memories. Love. And hope. She'd let them all in and she'd found happiness.

The only person not here to witness it was Granny, but Eve and Nate would see her very soon. The first stop on their honeymoon across Europe was London. And they'd fill her in on every glorious detail…

'Here we go, sis,' Rose murmured as they reached the entrance to the ballroom.

The double doors swung open as if by magic, and though the grand room with its ivory panelled walls, subtle gilt detailing and twin chandeliers was decorated as she'd planned, it still took her breath away. Blush and cream flowers adorned every surface, every chair, every set of French doors that showcased a glorious end to spring outdoors.

The music changed tempo, the officiant signalled the room and row upon row of guests stood and turned, but all Eve saw was Nate. Waiting for her.

He looked over his shoulder and caught her eye, his mouth lifting to the side—a look she had come to know well. He liked what he saw. And so did she.

I love you, she mouthed.

I love you, too.

And then Tilly and Ana stepped between them…

'Patience, Bambi.' Rose eased her back as she tried to follow. Too eager. Too quick. 'You know you get to spend the rest of your life with him, right?'

'I know. I just can't wait.'

And she couldn't.

I get it, Mum, she mentally whispered. *Love and all its many peculiar facets. I finally get it.*

* * * * *

MILLS & BOON MODERN IS
HAVING A MAKEOVER!

The same great stories you love,
a stylish new look!

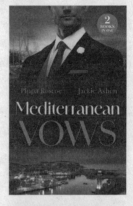

Look out for our brand new look
COMING JUNE 2024

MILLS & BOON

COMING SOON!

We really hope you enjoyed reading this book.
If you're looking for more romance
be sure to head to the shops when
new books are available on

Thursday 9th
May

To see which titles are coming soon, please visit
millsandboon.co.uk/nextmonth

MILLS & BOON

MILLS & BOON®

Coming next month

THEIR ACCIDENTAL MARRIAGE DEAL
Nina Singh

Where had she thrown her dress? Or maybe Alden had taken it off her. That thought had heat rushing to her cheeks. She had woken up in his suite, on his mattress, curled up against his side.

All that alluded to a possibility she'd been avoiding speculating on. Had they...?

Hannah gave her head a brisk shake. She couldn't deal with that question just now.

'I have to find my dress.'

He finished throwing on a pair of gray sweatpants and glanced around the room. 'It's gotta be here somewhere.'

Hannah had to resist the urge to ask him to put a shirt on.

Luckily, Alden distracted her from that train of thought by locating her dress. It had been hiding in plain sight below the glass coffee table.

She thanked him and quickly threw it on.

'You're welcome,' he answered.

Hannah rammed a hand through her curls, her heart hammering in her chest. Between her physical discomfort and the shock flooding her system, she was sorely tempted to just crawl back into bed and forget any of this was even happening. To be oblivious again to reality, as she'd been just a few minutes earlier. When she'd been snuggled close and warm in Alden's arms.

She bit out a curse under her breath.

'What's that?' Alden asked.

Hannah gave her head a shake. 'Nothing. I was just thinking that we absolutely can't mention any of this to Max and Mandy. Or to anyone else, for that matter.'

Alden nodded once. 'Agreed. This weekend should be all about the two of them.'

'Agreed,' she repeated.

Several moments passed in awkward silence. Finally, Alden cleared his throat. 'As far as getting ready goes, I don't have to do much. I'll help you. Whatever you need.'

'I might need to take you up on that. Thank you,' she said. He could probably start with helping her uncover the mystery of exactly where her room was and how she might be able to get into it, considering there was no room key in sight.

He shrugged and smiled at her with a playful wink. For a split second, the sheer beauty that was Alden Hamid served to take her breath away and she could easily see why in an altered, uninhibited state of mind she would have pledged to marry him with eager enthusiasm.

'You're welcome. It's what any decent husband would do.'

Continue reading
THEIR ACCIDENTAL MARRIAGE DEAL
Nina Singh

Available next month
millsandboon.co.uk

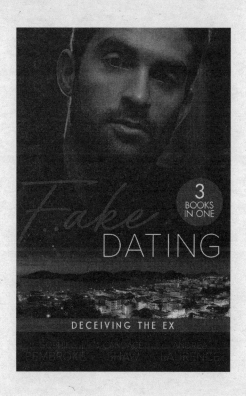

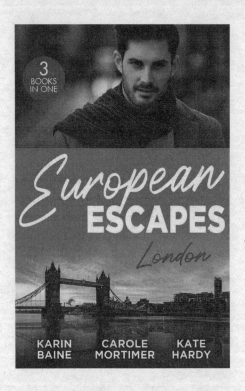

LET'S TALK
Romance

For exclusive extracts, competitions
and special offers, find us online:

- **f** MillsandBoon
- **X** @MillsandBoon
- **⊙** @MillsandBoonUK
- **♪** @MillsandBoonUK

Get in touch on 01413 063 232

MILLS & BOON

THE HEART OF ROMANCE

A ROMANCE FOR EVERY READER

MODERN
Prepare to be swept off your feet by sophisticated, sexy and seductive heroes, in some of the world's most glamourous and romantic locations, where power and passion collide.

HISTORICAL
Escape with historical heroes from time gone by. Whether your passion is for wicked Regency Rakes, muscled Vikings or rugged Highlanders, awaken the romance of the past.

MEDICAL
Set your pulse racing with dedicated, delectable doctors in the high-pressure world of medicine, where emotions run high and passion, comfort and love are the best medicine.

True Love
Celebrate true love with tender stories of heartfelt romance, from the rush of falling in love to the joy a new baby can bring, and a focus on the emotional heart of a relationship.

HEROES
The excitement of a gripping thriller, with intense romance at its heart. Resourceful, true-to-life women and strong, fearless men face danger and desire - a killer combination!

From showing up to glowing up, these characters are on the path to leading their best lives and finding romance along the way – with plenty of sizzling spice!

To see which titles are coming soon, please visit

millsandboon.co.uk/nextmonth